What people are saying about …

DANGEROUS MERCY

"Kathy Herman's latest, *Dangerous Mercy,* brings up a question many Christians face—how to help without taking unnecessary risks. More importantly to readers, it's a riveting suspense ride, set in the Louisiana bayou country. A can't-miss!"

Lyn Cote, author of *Her Abundant Joy*

"This book gripped my attention from the very first paragraph and never let go. Kathy Herman's writing shines in *Dangerous Mercy.* This is a powerful and thought-provoking story about loving the unlovely and following God, no matter what the cost."

Carol Cox, author of *Dog Days, Who's That Girl?,* and *Tea and Sympathy*

"A well-drawn mystery with characters who leap off the page and into your heart. It's a story of redemption and hope, forgiveness and unconditional love—and the reminder that we are *all* redeemable through Christ. If you're looking for a good book to snuggle with in front of the fire, this is it."

Lynette Eason, best-selling, award-winning author of the Women of Justice series

Praise for ...

FALSE PRETENSES

"Kathy Herman has cooked up a spicy Cajun mystery featuring a likable cast of small town characters. This intriguing yarn is sure to satisfy the appetites of murder-mystery lovers."

Creston Mapes, author of *Nobody*

"With its perfectly-paced suspense, Cajun flair, and riveting look at the high price of deceit, Kathy Herman's *False Pretenses* is a true page-turner. Highly recommended!"

Marlo Schalesky, author of the Christy–Award-winning novel *Beyond the Night*

"Kathy Herman has raised her own bar for an action-packed novel with rich conflict and realistic romance. *False Pretenses* is deep and soul-searching with nonstop excitement. It will lead to nonstop reading."

Hannah Alexander, author of *A Killing Frost* and the Hideaway series

"Mysteries abound in Kathy Herman's latest foray into suspense. Though we know some of the characters well, new ones will intrigue readers. The story entwines the secrets of the past with the secrets of today. You'll enjoy this trip to Cajun country. A solid read!"

Lyn Cote, author of *Her Abundant Joy*

"In *False Pretenses,* Kathy Herman has begun a wonderfully intriguing new series set in Louisiana's bayou country—Secrets of Roux River Bayou. *False Pretenses* gets the series off to a fast-paced start filled with suspense, tension, and mystery that will grip readers from the first page."

Marta Perry, author of *Murder in Plain Sight*

"Kathy Herman has written a powerful story of tension, mystery, and danger. Anonymous messages point to a secret from the past that can destroy the future. But there's also a tender love story to challenge that secret."

Lorena McCourtney, author of the Ivy Malone Mysteries and the Andi McConnell Mysteries

DANGEROUS MERCY

SECRETS OF ROUX RIVER BAYOU

BOOK 2

KATHY HERMAN

DANGEROUS MERCY
Published by David C Cook
4050 Lee Vance View
Colorado Springs, CO 80918 U.S.A.

David C Cook Distribution Canada
55 Woodslee Avenue, Paris, Ontario, Canada N3L 3E5

David C Cook U.K., Kingsway Communications
Eastbourne, East Sussex BN23 6NT, England

David C Cook and the graphic circle C logo
are registered trademarks of Cook Communications Ministries.

LCCN 2011934294
ISBN 978-0-7814-0341-2
eISBN 978-1-4347-0470-2

Published in association with the literary agency of Alive Communications, Inc, 7680 Goddard St., Suite 200, Colorado Springs, CO 80920

The Team: Don Pape, Diane Noble, Amy Konyndyk, Caitlyn York, Karen Athen
Cover Design: DogEared Design, Kirk DouPonce

Printed in the United States of America
First Edition 2011

1 2 3 4 5 6 7 8 9 10

073111

To Him who is both the Giver and the Gift

ACKNOWLEDGMENTS

The amazing bayou country of south Louisiana provides the backdrop for this new series and many of the images I describe in the story. But Saint Catherine Parish, the town of Les Barbes, and the Roux River Bayou exist only in my imagination.

During the writing of this second book, I drew from several resource people, each of whom shared generously from his or her storehouse of knowledge and experience. I did my best to integrate the facts, as I understood them. If accuracy was compromised in any way, it was unintentional and strictly of my own doing. I also made good use of numerous Internet sites relating to idiosyncrasies and customs of the Cajun culture and language.

I owe a debt of gratitude to Retired Commander Carl H. Deeley of the Los Angeles County Sheriff's Department for a wealth of information he's shared over the past several books. Carl, it's been fun creating Sheriff Jude Prejean, and I hope I've made him to your liking. I prefer showing the human side of my law enforcement characters—glimpses into the person beyond the professional demeanor. You added so much to my understanding.

I want to thank my friend Paul David Houston, former assistant district attorney, for explaining the pitfalls of withholding evidence and helping me understand the crime of moral turpitude. Paul, you're such a great resource guy! Your thorough, concise, and speedy replies to my questions are so appreciated.

I'd like to express my gratitude to my cousin Mark Phillips and his wife, Kim, former owners of Sedalia House Bed and Breakfast in Sedalia, Missouri, for explaining to me the fundamentals of B and B operations. I hope you enjoy Langley Manor on the pages of this story. This one is for Aunt Carol! Something tells me our two moms are smiling down on us.

I am so thankful to my faithful prayer warriors: my sister Pat Phillips, friends Mark and Donna Skorheim and Susan Mouser; my online prayer team—Chuck Allenbrand, Pearl and Don Anderson, Judith Depontes, Jackie Jeffries, Susie Killough, Joanne Lambert, Adrienne McCabe, Deidre Pool, Kim Prothro, Kelly Smith, Leslie Strader, Carolyn Walker, Sondra Watson, and Judi Wieghat; my friends at LifeWay Christian Store in Tyler, Texas, and LifeWay Christian Resources in Nashville, Tennessee; and my church family at Bethel Bible Church. I cannot possibly express to you how much I value your prayers.

To the retailers and suppliers who sell my books, the church and public libraries that make them available, and the many readers who have encouraged me with personal testimonies about how God has used my words to challenge and inspire you: He uses *you* to fuel the passion that keeps me creative.

To my agent, Joel Kneedler at Alive Communications. Thanks for all the times you've called just to encourage me. And for all the ways you look out for my best interests. Nothing you do goes unnoticed or unappreciated.

To Cris Doornbos, Dan Rich, Don Pape, and the amazing staff at David C Cook Publishers for believing in me and for getting my books into the marketplace. It's a good partnership. I'm increasingly proud to be part of the Cook "family."

To my editor, Diane Noble, for graciously granting me extension upon extension so I would have the time to do my best work. Thanks for your insightful and challenging editorial suggestions. I'm always amazed at the ways you see to strengthen the story that never even occur to me. You're such a joy to work with.

And to my husband, Paul, the other half of my heart, who kept pace with me as I ran this eighteenth race to the finish line. Thanks for cheering me on and pushing me until I got a second wind. We made it—again!

And to my heavenly Father, for pouring out Your lavish mercy on me. May everyone who reads this book see a picture of Your goodness and mercy through the characters I brought to life. Let my words glorify Your name.

CAJUN FRENCH GLOSSARY

Andouille— A coarse-grained smoked meat made using pork, pepper, onions, wine, and seasonings; spicy Cajun sausage.

Beignet— A pastry made from deep-fried dough and sprinkled with powdered sugar—a kind of French doughnut.

Bon rien— Lazy, good-for-nothing man.

Boudin— Sausage made from a pork rice dressing (much like dirty rice), which is stuffed into pork casings.

Breaux's— Cajun restaurant on *rue Madeline* that features live music.

Canaille— Sly; sneaky.

Capon— Coward.

Ça viens? — How's it coming?

Cher— Dear.

Co faire— Why?

Comment ça va— How are you? How are you doing?

Down the bayou— Cajun way of saying south.

Étouffée— A Cajun dish, similar to gumbo, that is typically served with shellfish or chicken over rice. It is most popular in New Orleans and in the bayou country of the southernmost half of Louisiana.

Fais do do— Go to sleep. Also a Cajun dance party.

Fuh shore— For sure.

Honeychile— Honey child.

Hot hot— Very hot. This kind of double adjective is used for emphasis (e.g., It was cold cold outside last night). Some African cultures speak this way. It may have come from the slaves in the region.

Lâche pas la patate— Don't let go of the potato or don't give up.

Lagniappe— 1. Chiefly southern Louisiana and southeast Texas: a small gift given with a purchase to a customer, by way of compliment or for good measure; bonus. 2. A gratuity or tip. 3. An unexpected or indirect benefit.

Make a babine— Pout.

Mère— Mother.

Mes amis— My friends.

Mon ami— My friend: masculine.

Mon amie— My friend: feminine.

Moitié fou— Half crazy.

My eye— Cajun expression meaning "No way!"

Pain perdu— French toast fried in butter and served with powdered sugar sprinkled on top.

Papère— Grandfather.

Piquant— Thorn.

Petite fille— Little girl.

***Rue Madeline*—** Madeline Street.

Skinny mullet— Skinny person.

Slow the TV— Turn down the TV.

Un jour à la fois— One day at a time.

Up the bayou— Cajun way of saying north.

PROLOGUE

"Blessed are the merciful, for they will be shown mercy." Matthew 5:7

The intruder dragged Girard Darveau's limp body to the huge oval bathtub and hoisted him over the side, faceup in the water, his graying hair undulating as he lay completely submerged. All signs of arrogance disappeared from the man's fearful eyes, which seemed to beg for mercy despite his drug-induced paralysis. How long would it take the high-and-mighty Darveau to drown?

Five minutes should be enough. He set the heat timer, then dropped a thirsty towel onto the blue-and-yellow tile floor of the lavish bathroom suite. With his shoe he pushed it over the wet surface around the tub, then tossed the soggy towel into the corner.

He folded his arms across his chest and stared down at the man in the water. Could it be any more appropriate that Darveau was wearing an Italian silk suit and Gucci leather oxfords? Wouldn't this narcissist want Monsignor Robidoux to be impressed when he came to administer the last rites?

Surely people would stand up and cheer when word got out that this heartless bank CEO was dead. How many home and business foreclosures had he sanctioned in the past few years? How many people on Roux River Bayou had lost everything while Girard Darveau lived in this opulent mansion, cavorting with gold-digging women half his age and feasting on rich food and twenty-year-old Scotch? No one would mourn Darveau's passing, least of all his bitter ex-wife, or his son and daughter, who would inherit his fortune.

It's still murder. It's wrong. He lifted his gaze to the waterfall that rained down a ten-foot wall of imported marble.

No. What was wrong was allowing this ruthless control freak to steal the future of longtime patrons who helped to make him rich. Taking Darveau's life was a community service.

He ambled around the spacious bathroom, running his gloved hand over the gold fixtures and polished marble made even more beautiful by the glow of natural light coming through the glass bricks and circular skylight.

"This is quite a showplace, Darveau. You've got more money tied up in this bathroom suite than my parents owed on their entire mortgage. Was it really necessary to call their note? That house was all they had. Couldn't you have at least agreed to work with them until Dad found another job? Didn't their loyalty to your bank all those years mean anything to you?"

The timer dinged. He walked past the dolphin fountain in the center of the room to the bathtub. Darveau's haunting stare seemed vacant now. No air bubbles.

"That was easy." He reached into the pocket of the leather satchel that contained the ten thousand dollars Darveau had given him from the safe and pulled out a can of spray paint. He shook it, then carefully wrote *#1* on the tiled wall behind the Jacuzzi.

"You're the first. But I'm just getting started."

He put the spray paint back in the satchel, hung the strap on his shoulder, then walked out of the bathroom and down the back staircase to the kitchen. Who was that singing?

He crept over to the window and peeked out the curtains. A middle-aged Hispanic woman was coming up the back walk. The housekeeper! Why was she here so soon? Would she notice the lock was broken?

He slipped around the corner into the dining room, his ear to the wall, his pulse racing.

The woman stopped singing. The door creaked. "Señor Darveau?"

The room was pin-drop still.

"Señor Darveau, it is Carmela. Are you here?"

Not a sound. Then the soles of her shoes squeaked across the wood floor.

"Hello?" Her voice went up a few decibels. "It is Carmela. Can you hear me? Say something, please. Señor Darveau?" Her voice was suddenly muffled. Was she headed up the stairs? "It is Carmela. Can you hear me?"

He waited several seconds—and then darted across the kitchen and out the back door, running into the shadows of the massive live oaks toward the fence at the far end of Darveau's estate.

A scream came from the house just as he stumbled over a raised tree root and fell forward, landing on his elbows. He picked himself up and ran about half the distance of a football field, finally spotting the large hole in the fence where he had sawed off the bars. He squeezed through the opening and kept running—in the direction of his truck, which was parked on a dirt road, just off Marchand Highway.

He laughed out loud. He did it! He had pulled it off! Ten grand was pocket change to a wealthy man like Girard Darveau. But it would go a long way to help the people the guy had ruined.

He yanked the satchel higher on his shoulder, the thrill of victory pulsating through every fiber of his being. Would he feel this great after he scratched off #2 on his list? If everything went according to plan, he wouldn't have long to find out.

CHAPTER 1

Adele Woodmore steadied herself with the hand-carved Black Forest cane she had bought in Germany and hurried across the living room and into the coat closet. She left the door cracked and dabbed the perspiration on her cheeks and nose with her monogrammed handkerchief.

"O-kaaay," she sang out. "Come and find me."

"Where are you, Addie?" the little voice replied.

"I'm over heeeere." Adele smiled, wondering how she had survived all those years without knowing the joy of loving a child.

She heard the sound of little feet racing straight for the closet. The door slowly opened, and Grace Broussard, looking like a Hummel figurine with her rosy cheeks and blonde pigtails, peered inside.

"Peekaboo. I find you!" The two-year-old squealed and clapped her hands with delight.

"Goodness! You found me again." Adele came out of the closet and straightened Grace's pink-and-white sundress. "Addie needs to cool off. This July humidity gets to me. Why don't we sit down and have our ginger cookies and milk?"

"I want this many cookies."

Adele met the child's pleading gaze and kissed the three fingers she held up. "Why don't we start with two and see if you're still hungry? We don't want to spoil your lunch."

"I wuv cookies!"

Adele chuckled. "Me, too. If I didn't know better, I'd swear we were related."

She held Grace's tiny hand and walked out to the kitchen and pushed the button on the intercom.

"Yes, Mrs. Woodmore?" Isabel Morand's voice filled the room.

"We're ready for that snack now, hon."

"Yes, ma'am. I'll be right there."

Grace's topaz eyes grew wide and animated. "Where Izzybell?"

"She's in the laundry room, darlin'. When I talk into that silver gadget on the wall, Isabel can hear me, and I can hear her. It saves Addie from having to shout or go looking for her."

Grace cocked her head, a smile dimpling her cheeks.

"Clear as mud, eh?" Adele brushed the little wisps of curls that framed the child's face. "After we have our cookies, I'll *show* you how it works."

Isabel breezed through the door, her thick, dark hair falling over her shoulders and down to the middle of her back. "Ready to try those gingersnaps we made?"

Grace gave a nod. "I wuv cookies."

"Let me get you some milk to go with it."

Adele got Grace situated in her booster chair while Isabel set the plate of cookies, a glass of milk, and a sippy cup on the table.

The doorbell rang.

"Gee"—Isabel winked at Grace—"I wonder who *that* could be on a Monday morning?"

"It's probably Murray," Adele said. "Would you let him in, hon? I asked him to come paint that back bedroom a nice shade of pale blue. I'm not fond of lilac.... Why are you smiling?"

"I was just wondering what you're going to do when you run out of things for Murray to fix, paint, or remodel."

Adele felt her face warm. "He needs the work. And I always have something that needs attention. He's the most reasonable handyman in Les Barbes." Adele smiled in spite of herself. "Are you going to let him in or not?"

"Yes, ma'am. I'm on my way."

Isabel left to answer the door.

Half a minute later Murray Hamelin came into the kitchen, holding his gold New Orleans Saints cap in his hands, his carrot-red hair showing a line where the hat had been. "Hello, Mrs. Woodmore. Little Miss Grace. I hope it's okay that I brought Flynn Gillis from Haven House to help me move furniture so I can paint."

"Of course it's okay." Adele held up the plate of cookies. "Better take a handful of these gingersnaps with you. Take some for Flynn."

"I wuv cookies!" Grace set her sippy cup down, using the back of her hand to wipe away a drop of milk that had escaped her smile.

"I knew that." Murray took a generous handful of cookies off the plate, his boyish grin and red hair reminding Adele of Richie on *Happy Days*.

"Were you able to get the paint I picked out?" Adele asked.

"Sure was. Should be enough to do the job and leave a little for touch-ups later on."

Touch-ups. Adele smiled to herself. That back bedroom would likely never be used. "Will you finish today?"

"I should. But I'll need to let it dry. I'd like to bring Flynn back tomorrow to help move the furniture back—if that's okay with you."

"It is. I'll be here."

"We'll go get started. Thanks for the cookies."

"You're welcome, hon. Come and go as you need to."

"Murray is nice." Grace's words were muffled by a mouth full of gingersnap.

"He *is* nice." Adele glanced up at Isabel. "And he's a fine handyman. It's always good to have someone I can trust."

"Murray seems nice enough," Isabel said. "But you really don't know anything about him. Just because Father Vince discovered that Murray's good with his hands is no guarantee that he's honest."

"I'm a pretty good judge of character, Isabel."

"Ma'am, with all due respect, a few months ago he was homeless. Don't you wonder why? How do you even know that he's who he says he is? Or that you can trust that Flynn fella he brought with him? I saw him standing out in the driveway. His hair is longer than mine, and he looks tough as nails. He could be casing the place."

Adele took a bite of cookie. "You let me worry about the people I hire. Murray's been nothing but polite and efficient. If he needs Flynn to help move furniture, who am I to second-guess him? He deserves a chance to get back on his feet."

"Maybe so. Just be cautious. You're so trusting and accepting of everyone."

Adele fingered the gold cross around her neck. "I don't necessarily trust everyone, hon. But I trust God. He brings people into my life for a reason." She smiled at Grace. "I take them as they come."

"Well, they're coming in the front door." Isabel arched her eyebrows. "Take a look at this Flynn character, and see if you're still comfortable letting him in your house."

Adele heard the front door open and close again. A second later the two men stood at the kitchen door.

"Mrs. Woodmore, this is Flynn Gillis." Murray nodded toward a man who reminded her of a young Willie Nelson.

"Nice to meet you," Adele said.

Flynn gave a nod and mumbled something, never making eye contact.

"We're going to get started now." Murray tipped the bill of his cap.

"Good. I'll be eager to see what a difference the pale blue makes."

Murray and Flynn turned and walked down the hall.

"Well?" Isabel whispered.

"I'm not in the habit of judging a man by the length of his hair, hon. If Murray asked him over here, he trusts him. And I trust Murray."

Isabel didn't reply.

Adele mused. Of course she trusted Murray. Hadn't he proven himself time and again? Yet something about Flynn *was* off-putting. Was it his long hair? His lack of manners? She couldn't put her finger on it, but it was a moot point. He was already here.

CHAPTER 2

Zoe Broussard stood on the gallery outside her apartment above Zoe B's Cajun Eatery. The late-morning breeze was thick with humidity and the melded aromas of ground coffee, chocolate, and caramel corn wafting from the quaint shops along *rue Madeline*. Across the street, Madame Duval waved from amidst a garden of blooming plants on the gallery that jutted out over the Coy Cajun Gift Shop.

A FedEx truck pulled up behind the horse-drawn carriage that was unloading passengers in front of the Hotel Peltier. Two little boys and a cocker spaniel raced down the sidewalk, chasing a runaway balloon.

Zoe glanced at her watch. She missed Grace and wondered how Adele was holding up with a lively two-year-old in the house. She went inside the apartment and slid the glass door shut, then went out the front door. She skipped down the wooden staircase and walked through the alcove, past the office, and into the cozy dining room at Zoe B's.

The breakfast crowd was long gone, the empty tables set with clean blue-and-gold fleur-de-lis tablecloths, a bud vase and yellow daisy in the center. The pervasive aroma of warm bread and rich seafood gumbo emanated from the kitchen, where her husband, Pierce, was busy preparing something delicious for today's luncheon special.

Could thirteen years really have passed since she opened this place? The same French country furnishings still flavored the ambience. Little had changed, other than the color scheme and laminated wood plank flooring, the addition of a dozen D'Arceau Limoges collector plates, and the for-sale oil paintings by local artists.

She headed for the window table where her head waitress, Savannah Surette, seemed lost in conversation with Tex Campbell, Father Sam Fournier, and Hebert Lanoux.

"Poetic justice, I'd say." Savannah filled Hebert's cup with coffee. "Normally, it's the people who don't deserve it who end up victims."

"Who's a victim?" Zoe said.

Savannah turned, her blue eyes wide and round, her ponytail swaying. "Girard Darveau, the president of Roux River Bank. I just heard on the radio he was found murdered this morning. It's hard to feel sorry for him."

"How'd he die?" Zoe said.

"It appears to have been a robbery. Someone cleaned out his safe and drowned him in the bathtub. The maid found him. He was dressed in a suit and tie."

"Goodness." Father Sam pushed a lock of white hair off his forehead. "What a gruesome start to the week. Every human life has value—even his."

"That might be a hard sell around here." Tex sat back in his chair, his thumbs hooked on his red suspenders, light from the window making his bald head shiny. "I don't see many people sheddin' tears over it."

"Why would dey?" Hebert leaned forward on his elbows, his mousy gray curls sticking up on one side, the ridges in his leathery skin made deeper by the intensity of his gaze. "Darveau lived high on da hog while workers were left wid nothing when dey got laid off. He foreclosed widout giving folks a chance to make good on dare mortgages."

"The man had ice in his veins." Tex wiped his forehead with a red kerchief.

"Well, if y'all will let me finish, there's a disturbing detail I haven't even told you yet." Savannah paused as if to make sure she had everyone's attention and then continued. "The killer spray painted the number one on the wall—that is, the pound sign followed by the numeral one."

"What does that *mean?*" Zoe felt a chill crawl up her spine.

"The killer numbered him. At least, that's what they said on the radio."

Hebert scratched the gray stubble on his chin. "So if Darveau's number one, dere must be a number two."

"The authorities won't say so," Savannah said. "But what else could it mean? Why else would a killer number the victim unless he plans to strike again?"

"Heaven help us." Father Sam took off his thick glasses and wiped his eyes. "You suppose the killer will go after someone else at the bank?"

Pierce Broussard came out of the kitchen, wearing his chef's hat and apron. He walked over to the table. "Did Savannah tell you what happened to Darveau?"

Everyone nodded.

"Do you know if there are any suspects?" Tex said.

"The sheriff won't comment during an open investigation." Pierce put his hands on Zoe's shoulders. "But if I had a close connection to Girard Darveau, I'd be hiring a bodyguard."

Zoe's heart sank. Darveau was the man everyone loved to blame. But murder? Who hated him enough to kill and number him? Was it someone she knew? A customer? A neighbor? Resentment ran deep in the community. It could be anybody.

Sheriff Jude Prejean sat at the oak desk in his office and looked across the street at the stately Saint Catherine Parish Courthouse, its proud white columns glowing in the hot July sun.

The old vendor, Andre Chauvin, stood on the sidewalk at Courthouse and Primeaux, serving up andouille corn dogs to a couple and three little boys.

People strolled round the courthouse grounds, some occupying the wrought-iron benches placed strategically in the shade of the giant live oaks.

The intercom buzzed and then Deputy Chief Aimee Rivette's voice startled him. "Excuse me, Sheriff. Chief Norman and Mayor Theroux have arrived and are waiting for you in interview room one."

"I'm on my way."

Jude got up and walked out of his office, across the detective bureau, and down the hall to the first interview room.

Mayor Oliver Theroux and Les Barbes Police Chief Casey Norman sat on one side of the oblong table.

Jude shook hands with each. "Good to see you. I wish it were under better circumstances."

"So do I," the mayor replied. "I understand your departments are working the Darveau murder as concurrent jurisdiction, with you taking the lead. Fill me in."

Jude sat across from them, his arms folded on the table. "Casey's officers and my deputies have done a complete sweep of Darveau's home and grounds, dusted for fingerprints, gathered trace evidence. We're processing all that now. So far, we have no prints that show up in the system. The maid's prints were all over the house, but no more abundant at the murder scene than anywhere else."

"Is she a suspect?" the mayor asked.

"Not at this time. We found a large opening cut in the wrought-iron fence at the back of the property. We believe that's how the killer gained access. The lock on the back door was also broken. Whoever did this either knew the combination to Darveau's safe or forced him to empty it. The preliminary evidence supports that Darveau was drugged, and then dragged to the bathtub where he was drowned. The maid weighs about a hundred and twenty pounds. There's no way she could've done this alone. And the woman was beside herself when she made that 911 call. The EMTs had to sedate her. We can't rule her out as a suspect, but she didn't react like someone who was involved."

"So Darveau was alive when he was put in the water?" the mayor asked.

Jude nodded. "That's what the medical examiner concluded. The cause of death was drowning. But he was drugged. The ME found a significant level of a veterinary sedative called ketamine, which is sold on the street as 'Special K' or cat Valium. It's likely the killer wanted Darveau to know he was being murdered and yet helpless to do anything about it."

"It shouldn't surprise us." Casey tented his fingers. "So many people in this area suffered because of Darveau's policy on foreclosures. Our concern now should be the number one spray painted on his bathroom wall and how we avoid a number two."

The mayor nodded. "What are you doing to protect the people who worked with him at the bank?"

"It's not possible to protect them all," Jude said. "Casey's got his officers staked out at the homes of Darveau's vice president, immediate staff, and board members. And my deputies are posted at Roux River Bank's main office and six branches. That's all the personnel we can spare. And we can't do it indefinitely and expect to adequately serve the rest of the community and the parish. If this guy is determined to strike again, he's probably smart enough to wait us out."

"So you're saying there's no way to stop him?"

Jude glanced over at Casey. "Probably not, if he's determined. We need to figure out who he is and catch him before he makes a move on whoever is number two on his list."

Murray Hamelin pulled his truck onto Jacquard Street and parallel parked in front of the gray frame house with the rocking chairs on the front porch. He walked up the steps, Flynn Gillis on his heels, and pushed open the oak and beveled-glass door of Haven House.

He stepped into the living room and was hit with a gust of refrigerated air.

Father Vince came out of the kitchen, a towel draped over his shoulder. "How'd it go? Did you get the furniture moved and the room painted for Adele Woodmore?"

"Yep," Flynn said. "Murray here's a whiz kid. All I did is move stuff. I took a nap while he did all the painting."

"I finished the job," Murray said. "We'll go over there tomorrow and move the furniture back."

Father Vince smiled at Murray. "You're getting quite a reputation. It's not easy to find a jack-of-all-trades these days. Every profession is so specialized and expensive. I've got a whole list of people who want you to do work for them. You can stay as busy as you want."

"Good. I'd like to stay busy." Murray inhaled the aroma of something that made his mouth water. "What's for dinner?"

"Blackened catfish, coleslaw, and dirty rice. Corn-bread pudding for dessert."

"Man, I'm starved." Flynn flopped on the couch. "Think I'll read the paper until you ring the bell."

"I could use someone to set the table," Father Vince said.

Murray glanced at the empty table in the dining room and then shot Flynn a crusty look. "I guess *I'll* do it."

"Thanks," Father Vince said. "I've got volunteers for the cleanup."

"Then I'm off the hook there, too." Flynn laughed.

"You're a real *bon rien*, you know that?" Murray said. "You're supposed to pull your weight around here."

"Hey, I helped you, didn't I—for a lousy thirty bucks?"

"You helped me for ten minutes and then took a three-hour nap.

I'd say you were well paid. You know, being lazy isn't going to win you friends around here."

"Hey, guys, lighten up," Father Vince said. "I've got some chores for Flynn to do that he didn't sign up for. He's going to do his share."

Flynn waited until Father Vince turned his back and then made an obscene gesture.

Murray didn't react. Flynn was such a loser. But what good would it do to get confrontational when he needed Flynn's help to move Mrs. Woodmore's furniture back? Unless Flynn changed his ways, Father Vince couldn't let him stay here anyway.

CHAPTER 3

Vanessa Langley sat on the floral Victorian settee, enjoying the ambience of the parlor at Langley Manor, finding it hard to believe it had been six months to the day since they opened the manor house as a bed-and-breakfast.

She could vividly remember her surprise when Ethan announced that his dad and uncles were giving them this family heirloom as a wedding gift. It was a generous gesture, but what were they supposed to do with it? It didn't take long for them to start the ball rolling to renovate the manor house and turn it into a bed-and-breakfast. And once they discovered the house had been used as a station on the Underground Railroad, drawing a steady stream of curious guests was easy.

The soft yellow walls trimmed with white crown moldings made this room elegantly warm and inviting. Above the white marble fireplace, the framed portrait of Josiah and Abigail Langley seemed so real she half expected them to blink.

The musty smell of the old plantation house was gone now, replaced by fresh eucalyptus—and the aroma of oatmeal cookies baking.

Out of the corner of her eye, she saw someone come out of the kitchen.

"Excuse me, Vanessa." Noah Washington spoke softly as if he were trying not to startle her. "I'm finished mowin' the grounds. I've got an errand to do in town. I'll be back this afternoon to weed the flower garden and put up those new birdbaths."

"No hurry." She turned to Noah. "Do it when you can. I've probably overstated it, but Ethan and I love what you've done with the landscaping. Our guests compliment us all the time, especially about the waterfall and the babbling brook."

His bright smile was a dazzling contrast to his polished dark skin. "It's an honor for me to help make this place beautiful again."

"It shows. Your ties to this place are as strong as Ethan's."

"So are yours."

Vanessa nodded. "Yes, but I wasn't a Langley until I married one. You two are descendants of heroes."

Noah smiled with his eyes. "I wonder how many times I heard my great-grandma tell the story of how her great-grandma Naomi gave up her chance at freedom to help the Langleys move other slaves up North? I'm proud to be her kin. Who'd have thought I'd be workin' here myself?"

Vanessa glanced up at the oil portrait. "Don't you wonder why Josiah and Abigail didn't keep a written record of what took place here? I guess the tunnels speak for themselves. If your family hadn't kept the story alive from generation to generation, we would never have made the connection to the Underground Railroad. And that's the *true* legacy of Langley Manor."

"And now it's our job to keep the story alive." Noah glanced at his watch. "I have to get goin'. I told Murray I'd meet him at Adele Woodmore's and help him move some furniture. Flynn flaked out on him."

"Flynn seems to flake out on just about everyone."

"You got that right. Sometimes I wish Father Vince would throw him out o' Haven House."

"Where? Back on the street?"

Noah shrugged. "Maybe that's what he wants. I've tried reachin' out, but he puts up a wall. No one can seem to get a straight answer outta this guy."

"Not even Murray?"

"Not really. It's hard to get along with Flynn. The guy's not serious about gettin' his act together. All he does is irritate the rest of us."

Vanessa heard the oven timer buzzing and rose to her feet. "Sounds like my cookies are done. Take as long as you need to help Murray, and be sure to tell Adele I said hello. At least you won't have to deal with Flynn much longer. The caretaker house will be finished soon, and then you can move out here."

⁂

Adele followed Zoe and Grace out onto the brick porch of the spacious white frame house with green shutters.

"I'm glad you could take a little time to visit, hon. I know you're busy at the eatery, but it's wonderful you're close enough to sneak by for a few minutes. I'm tickled to death to spend time with Grace."

"She loves you." Zoe slid her arm around Adele's waist. "We all do. I just hope you don't miss Woodmore too much."

Adele smiled. "I had sixty wonderful years living in that beautiful home Alfred built for me. What does an eighty-six-year-old widow need with a big mansion and all that property to maintain? The simpler lifestyle suits me just fine. And living close to you and Pierce and Grace is pure joy."

"For us, too. You're family now."

Grace tugged at Adele's skirt, the purple ribbons on her pigtails catching a glint of midday sun. "Bye, Addie!"

"Bye, darlin'." Adele cupped the child's face in her hands. "I'll see you soon."

"Thanks again for letting her come over." Zoe picked up Grace, and the little girl leaned over and put her arms around Adele's neck.

"You're my sunshine." Adele closed her eyes and relished the moment. She couldn't imagine that having a grandchild could be any better than this.

"I'll call you later in the week," Zoe said.

"Oh good. Let's plan on Grace and me having grilled cheese and pickles for lunch again."

"I wuv grilled cheese!" Grace flashed an elfin grin.

"Then it's a good thing I have plenty. Bye now."

Adele watched as Zoe carried Grace to the car and buckled her in her seat belt. She waved as they pulled out of the driveway and disappeared down the street.

Just as she turned to go inside, Murray's white truck pulled into the driveway, a red truck behind it. A few seconds later, both drivers got out. She was relieved the second man was Noah Washington and not Flynn.

"We came to move your furniture back," Murray said. "Is this a good time?"

"Heavens, yes. Any time is a good time. What else have I got to do? Come in."

Adele stepped inside and locked gazes with Isabel. "Would you make a pitcher of fresh-squeezed lemonade?"

Isabel glanced over at the two guests and managed a less-than-sincere smile. "Of course. Right away."

"Noah"—Adele took his hand in hers—"how are things at Langley Manor? Is it still drawing plenty of guests?"

"Sure is, ma'am. The history o' the place draws more guests than the Langleys can accommodate. They have a waitin' list."

"That's wonderful." She gave his hand a squeeze and let go. "I haven't really asked, but are you going to be able to keep your other customers once you move out there?"

"I'll keep a few favorites—you're one o' them." Noah's soft brown eyes lit up. "Don't you worry none about your yard and flowers. I'll take good care o' them."

"Oh, that's wonderful. I was afraid I was going to have to start over, trying to find someone."

"No, ma'am. Oh ... Vanessa asked me to say hello."

"Please give her my regards," Adele said. "I want to get out there soon. It's a pleasant surprise seeing you. I thought Murray was bringing that young man who came yesterday."

"Flynn's a deadbeat," Murray said. "And if he doesn't change his attitude, he's going to find himself homeless again."

Adele sighed. "He seemed troubled."

"Don't feel sorry for him," Murray said. "Father Vince has bent over backwards—and bent the rules. Nothing works with that guy."

"Perhaps I need to add Flynn to my prayer list," Adele said.

"Save your breath. I'm sure God doesn't like him either."

Adele winced. What an awful thing to say. That wasn't the first time Murray's cynicism had surfaced. What an unbecoming trait in such a nice young man.

"I'm going to leave you two to get the furniture moved back. When you're finished, we'll have a cold glass of lemonade out in the sunroom."

Adele watched the two men walk down the hall to the newly painted bedroom, aware that Isabel was put out with her for inviting them to stay for lemonade.

At least they didn't have to worry about that Flynn character.

CHAPTER 4

That afternoon, Sheriff Jude Prejean closed the Darveau case file and took off his reading glasses. No fingerprints. No usable trace evidence. No results back yet on DNA. The only thing they knew for certain was that the killer made sure Darveau was awake, aware, and helpless when he drowned.

The list of enemies was long. But Darveau's administrative assistant was not aware of any threats made. Nor was anything threatening found in Darveau's emails, phone messages, or text messages.

A knock on the door interrupted his thoughts, and he lifted his gaze.

"You look glum." Deputy Chief Aimee Rivette stood in the doorway. "You must be as frustrated as the rest of us."

"Whoever killed Girard Darveau covered his steps," Jude said. "There's nothing solid here—other than the victim had more enemies than most of us have friends. I doubt his own mother will mourn his murder." He winced. "I didn't mean that. Forget I said it."

"It's probably truer than we'd like to admit." Aimee came in and stood in front of his desk. "Gil and I have finished questioning Darveau's son and daughter. They drove up last night from New

Orleans with their families. We don't think either of them had anything to do with it."

"They're going to inherit a lot of money."

"True. But they're both wealthy in their own right. They seemed genuinely dazed. Though neither was surprised that someone would want to see their father dead."

"How can you be so sure *they* didn't want him dead?"

"I can't. But neither was in Les Barbes yesterday. And if either or both hired a hit man, we've got a long way to go to prove it. Besides, what hit man would've risked leaving evidence at the scene?"

"He wouldn't," Jude said. "He'd have made it quick and clean and certainly wouldn't have numbered his victim. This was personal. Have you caught up with his ex-wife yet?"

"Yes, I sent Stone Castille and Mike Doucet up to Lafayette to talk to her. She got a huge settlement when they split ten years ago and has remarried. According to the kids, the parents don't speak to each other. I think that's a dead end." Aimee glanced over at the window. "The press is crouched on our doorstep. Are you planning to talk to them again?"

Jude sighed. "Not until I have something new. Let them wait."

⚜

Adele stood on the porch and waved good-bye to Noah, glints of sunlight filtering through the deep pink blossoms on the crape myrtles that bordered her front yard. She smiled, noting that her entire property here on Magnolia Lane was smaller than her rose garden on the Woodmore Estates.

She walked back inside and out to the glassed-in porch where Murray sat at the table, his hands wrapped around a cold glass of lemonade.

"I'm sorry Noah had to hurry off," she said. "But I suppose he's got his work cut out for him now that he's the groundskeeper for the Langleys. They have a lot of property to maintain, and I haven't forgotten what's involved in that."

Murray took a sip of lemonade. "I hate that Noah's moving out there soon. There's really no one else at Haven House I hit it off with."

"You mentioned there are fourteen men all together."

"At the moment. Flynn Gillis should get cut, *if* Father Vince has the guts to do it. The guy's lazy and manipulates him. Honestly, I don't get it. I'd throw him out. I don't have patience for that."

"What's Flynn's background like?"

"Who knows? We don't talk about it. He'd probably lie anyhow. I just don't trust him. I know his type." Murray shifted in his chair. "I probably sound judgmental. But things have happened in my life that make it hard to trust people."

Adele fingered the gold cross on the chain around her neck. "The one person you can always trust is God."

"Why would I? He hasn't exactly been there for me."

"Maybe He's been closer than you think."

Murray clenched his jaw and didn't say anything.

"You think He's responsible for the pain you've suffered?"

"He could've prevented it. Isn't that the same thing?"

Adele could almost hear the door to Murray's heart slam shut. Time to change the subject. *Lord, help me to understand him. And show him Your love.*

Murray tilted his head back and downed the last of the lemonade. "Thanks for the cold drink. And the work. I'd better get down to Zoe B's and hook up their new computer."

"You know how to do that, too?"

"Actually, I'm good with computers." Murray's expression softened. "I wasn't always homeless."

"Well, I may hire you to help me get set up. I've been thinking about getting one of those little laptop computers. I want to send email. Zoe insists it's not difficult, but my eighty-six-year-old brain isn't so sure."

"It's the easiest thing in the world," Murray said. "Call me when you're ready. I'll set you up and show you how to use it. It's really simple."

"All right. I will."

Adele walked him to the front door and out onto the porch.

"Thank you for doing such a nice job of painting that back bedroom. The color is much more to my liking."

"I enjoy working for you, Mrs. Woodmore. Call me anytime." Murray started down the steps and turned around. "Oh … and if Flynn comes by looking for me, please don't tell him where I am. I'm done trying to help him."

⚜

Zoe took Grace by the hand and walked over to the table by the window at Zoe B's Cajun Eatery. The child crawled up in the booster seat in the chair next to Father Sam and across from Hebert and Tex.

"And who's dis *petite fille?*" Hebert leaned forward, his arms folded on the table.

"It's *me!"* Grace giggled.

"Me?" Tex looked at Hebert and shrugged. "Do we know anyone named Me?"

"Are you Me Broussard?" Father Sam asked.

"No, I *Grace Brew-sar!"* She giggled again, pointing to herself.

"*You're* Grace Broussard? Den we *do* know you."

Hebert tapped her on the nose, evoking a belly laugh that turned her topaz eyes to slits.

Zoe enjoyed this little ritual that had developed between her favorite customers and her daughter and couldn't quite remember what life was like before she had Grace.

"Is it okay with you fellas if Grace watches you play checkers while she has a snack? Her afternoon babysitter's going to be late."

"Okay wid me." Hebert picked up Grace's hand and kissed it. "I always win when Miss Grace watches."

"You always win—period," Tex said. "I've never seen anything like it."

The bell on the front door tinkled, and Murray Hamelin came inside, toolbox in hand. He caught Zoe's gaze and walked over to her.

"I'm all set. Where's your computer?"

"In the office," Zoe said. "Out in the alcove. I'll show you. Guys, if you need anything, tell Savannah I said it's on the house."

Zoe walked out of the dining room and into the alcove, and unlocked the door to the office.

"Normally, I'd call the Geek Squad." She went inside and flipped the light switch. "But Noah said you were good with computers so Pierce and I decided we'd rather give you the business."

"I appreciate that."

"The laptop is still in the box—there on the desk. Where'd you learn computers?"

"I had a life before things took a nosedive. Computers and I have always gotten along. I understand them. And I'm a lot more reasonable than the Geek Squad."

"And you stand behind your work?"

"Absolutely. I'll get you completely set up and running with all the software you purchased. I charge a flat rate of seventy-five dollars. I don't charge you extra if I have to come back and tweak it."

"Fair enough."

There was a knock on the door. Zoe looked through the peephole and saw her head waitress, Savannah Surette. She opened the door.

"Sorry to bug you." Savannah put her hands behind her head and tightened her ponytail. "There's a Flynn Gillis here to see Murray."

"Could you tell him I've left?" Murray said. "Or that you can't find me. I don't want anything to do with the guy. He can't be trusted."

Savannah locked gazes with Zoe. "He *is* a colorful character. Long, stringy hair. No shirt. The sort that better fits the clientele at the Den, if you know what I mean."

"Can you see Murray behind me?" Zoe said.

Savannah shook her head. "You're in the way. I hear his voice though."

"Go back and tell Flynn you looked for Murray and didn't *see* him, which is technically true. Suggest that he might want to check back at Haven House. If he gives you any trouble, come back and get me."

"Will do."

Zoe shut the door and turned to Murray, who was removing the packing from the laptop he had pulled out of the box.

"I'm uncomfortable telling lies," she said. "Even white ones. What's up with Flynn?"

"He's the one guy at Haven House I just don't like. Every time I give him a break and pay him to help me with a job, he blows it. Earlier today, he backed out of helping me move Adele Woodmore's furniture. That's it. I'm done helping him."

"He has to work to stay at the halfway house, doesn't he?"

"That's the rule. But he's shown no initiative. If he gets kicked out, it's his own fault."

⚜

At six fifteen that evening, Murray ran up the front steps at Haven House, pushed open the front door, and was hit with a delicious, spicy aroma that seemed to permeate the living room.

Father Vince came down the hall from the kitchen, still dressed in his cleric shirt, munching something crunchy. "There you are. I was afraid you were going to miss our Tuesday-night jambalaya."

Murray smiled. "After I finished setting up the computer at Zoe B's, I went down to Cypress Park and walked around—then sat on a park bench and fell asleep. I just woke up a few minutes ago. How's that for a confession?"

Father laughed. "Honest."

"I was scheduled to set the table. Am I too late?"

"Actually, you're just in time. By the way, do you have any idea where Flynn is? He borrowed my car."

"No. He came in Zoe B's looking for me this afternoon, and I told the waitress to tell him I wasn't there."

"Why?" A row of lines formed on Father Vince's forehead, his dark curls tighter from the day's humidity.

"Because I paid him to help me move Adele Woodmore's furniture, and he only did half the job. I had to call Noah to help me move it back because Flynn was nowhere to be found. That on top of all the other times he's flaked out, and I'm done. Flynn's lazy and dishonest. Please don't ask me to cut him any more slack."

"Not every homeless man readjusts to the real world as smoothly as you and Noah have."

"But the other guys are trying. Flynn isn't."

"Because he keeps messing up?" Father Vince sighed. "I think he's trying to do better and just can't get his act together."

"Tell yourself whatever you want. But it's not helping him that you make excuses for him."

Father Vince put his hands in his pockets. "I'm well aware of Flynn's shortcomings. I just don't believe it's time to give up on him."

"I don't have that problem. Flynn knows the rules. He's laughing because you let him manipulate you. Maybe that doesn't bother you, but it infuriates me."

"A lot of things bother me worse—like letting go of a man God put in my care." Father Vince took a step closer to Murray and patted him on the back. "There has to be a way to turn Flynn around. We're family here. We need to have patience and keep reaching out. Especially those of you who are good examples for him to follow."

Murray glanced at his watch. "I've got just enough time to go wash my hands and get the table set."

"So you'll do what you can to help Flynn?"

"All right, Father. I'll do it for you."

Murray walked through the living room and up the stairs. He turned into his dorm room—and ran headlong into Flynn.

"Where've *you* been?" Murray said. "Father Vince has been waiting for you to come back with his car. Why didn't you tell him you were here?"

"Oops."

Murray shoved him. "Thanks for flaking out on me again, moron."

"Sorry, man. I forgot about moving the furniture until it was too late. I tried to find you at Zoe B's and say I was sorry, but they told me you weren't there."

"Just don't expect me to share any more of my jobs."

"I said I was sorry."

"Yeah, we both know what your words are worth. You don't have any intention of bettering yourself. You're just working the system. You may have Father Vince fooled, but not me."

"Someone's touchy."

"*Touchy?*" Murray grabbed Flynn's T-shirt. "Try fed up! I've had all of you I can take."

"Now that really hurts my feelings." Flynn's tone was mocking, his smile irritating. "Father Vince said we're supposed to treat each other like brothers."

Murray remembered the promise he had just made to Father Vince and let go of Flynn's T-shirt. He held up his palms. "Sorry, *brother*. You just get on my nerves."

"Yeah, I had a *real* brother once," Flynn said. "I got on his nerves too. Know what happened to him?"

"Can't imagine."

"He went missing. Disappeared one day. Just like that." Flynn snapped his fingers. "No one's heard from him since. Tragic."

"Just stay away from me." Murray took a step backwards. "You're one sick dude."

"And don't you forget it." Flynn cocked his head and laughed.

Murray went into the bathroom and locked the door, his face sizzling with annoyance. Father Vince had better wise up about Flynn. He heard another voice in the hallway.

"You're a real jerk, you know that?" Noah said.

"I've been called worse." Flynn laughed. "If you came up here to lecture me, save it."

"You got a lot o' nerve threatenin' Murray."

"I was just messing with him, man. Get your stinking hands off me."

"Everybody here's had it with you."

"So?"

"So you'd better watch your back."

"What's that supposed to mean?"

"Anything you want, Flynn. I'm just sayin' you can't keep tickin' everybody off and expect them to roll over."

"I'm here to stay. Get used to it."

"Yeah, well. We'll see about that."

CHAPTER 5

What was that horrible ringing noise? Sheriff Jude Prejean lay dazed for a moment, then groped the nightstand for his cell phone. He stared at the lighted screen until he could make out the words *Chief Detective Gil Marcel.* His clock radio flashed the numerals 5:57. He remembered it was Wednesday morning.

Jude cleared his throat and put the phone to his ear. "Yeah, Gil."

"Hope I didn't wake you, Sheriff."

"That's all right. My alarm was just about to go off. What's up?"

"You're not going to like it."

"Let's hear it."

"Our killer claimed another victim: *Peter Gautier*."

"Gautier? That's *huge*." He looked over at his wife, Colette, who lay on her side facing him, her eyes open wide. "Same MO?"

"Looks that way. Gautier was drowned in the bathtub. Fully clothed. The medical examiner says he shows signs of being drugged. The pound sign and numeral two were spray painted on the tile behind the tub. His safe was cleaned out. The ME puts the time of death between five and seven last night. The killer must have caught him coming home from work."

"Any sign of forced entry?"

"A broken window in a back bedroom."

Jude sighed. "Who called it in?"

"Anonymous male caller on a prepaid cell. Spoke barely above a whisper, and said six words, 'Peter Gautier is dead. That's two.' The 911 dispatcher sent deputies out to Gautier's lake house, where they discovered his body. We retrieved a message his wife left on his answering machine. She's out of town, visiting their daughter. The area code is Providence, Rhode Island, and we're trying to reach her now. I imagine the entire parish will know within the hour that the president and CEO of Fontaine Sugar Refinery has been murdered."

"And I don't need to tell you that we can't afford any mistakes." Jude rubbed his eyes. "Make sure the crime scene isn't contaminated and everything gets done by the book. And get me a list of every employee, living or dead, who was laid off, fired, or who quit in the past five years, cross-referenced with the list of foreclosures by Roux River Bank. I also want to take a look at the security cameras at the sugar plant, especially the ones in the parking lot. Let's see if anyone followed him. I'll be out there in thirty minutes."

Jude laid his cell phone on the nightstand and turned his alarm off.

"I could hear what Gil told you." Colette fluffed her pillow. "Horrible as it is, you've been expecting the other shoe to drop."

"At least now we can see a logical connection between the two victims. The killer could be someone who was laid off at the sugar refinery and then lost his home to foreclosure. We should be able to narrow down those names." He kissed her on the cheek. "I need to shower and get going."

He started to get out of bed, and Colette clung to his arm.

"Jude, this is scary. What if the killer has a long list of people he's after?"

"I think that's a real possibility. I'm putting the executives and support personnel at all five branches of Roux River Bank and the sugar refinery on high alert. My department can work with police to help beef up security at each location, but it's impossible to keep them all safe twenty-four/seven."

⚜

Adele sat at the bay window in the kitchen, her hands wrapped around a cup of coffee, her heart relishing the streaks of blazing pink and purple that painted what little sky she could see through the tree branches out back.

Had it really been six months since she'd sold Woodmore Estates and moved here? It hadn't been an easy decision. But the huge old house and manicured grounds demanded constant attention, and just keeping good help was becoming too much for her.

But how she missed the magnificent magnolia trees that lined either side of the circle drive … the sweeping lawns dotted with weeping willows, dogwoods, crape myrtles, and hardwoods … the white gazebo where she stopped to rest and think and pray after strolling through the rose garden.

She smiled and looked across the quarter acre of backyard shaded by a mature live oak and two magnolia trees. All she needed these days was Noah to fertilize and mow and take care of her flower beds—and for the automatic sprinklers to supply whatever water

Mother Nature didn't. Her heart was her gazebo. It didn't take the beauty of Woodmore Estates to remind her that almighty God was on His throne, and His glory could be found in all of nature.

She heard a knock, and Isabel came into the kitchen, wearing the pink terry bathrobe Adele had bought her for her birthday. "Am I disturbing you?"

"Not at all. Come have a cup of coffee—and use the good china. It's a shame for it to just sit there looking lovely. It was meant to be used."

"Would you like a warmer?"

"Not just yet, thanks."

Isabel opened the glass door and took out a delicate Wedgwood cup and saucer—Florentine Turquoise pattern. She filled the cup with coffee, then sat at the table, her long, dark wavy hair framing her pretty face and puppy eyes. Why did she look so glum?

"What's wrong, hon?"

"The morning news was depressing. Did you hear there's been another murder?"

"Goodness, no. Who now?"

Isabel held tightly to her coffee cup. "Peter Gautier, the CEO of the sugar refinery. I went to high school with his daughter."

Adele sighed and shook her head. "Do the authorities think it was the same killer?"

"Sure looks that way. He was drowned in the bathtub, like Darveau. And the number two was spray painted on the tile behind the tub. Everybody's freaking out that there could be more victims. They're calling him 'the Bathtub Killer.'"

"Heaven help us."

"Mr. Gautier gave me a ride home from a football game once. He was really nice. I know people are upset that he's laid off so many workers, but that's happening everywhere. My dad says the economy's causing it. I can't believe somebody murdered him for doing what CEOs everywhere are doing."

Adele nodded. "It's a terrible thing. But it's complicated. And emotions run deep. Many families were hurt in the layoffs, and I understand that many lost their homes."

"Well, Renee just lost her dad. I think that's pretty horrible."

Adele put her hand on Isabel's. "Yes, it is. Did you know Renee well?"

"In high school. She went away to a girls' college in Rhode Island and married some guy she met on a ski trip. I think she lives in Providence and has a couple kids now. I haven't seen her in years."

"Did you hear whether authorities have any suspects?"

"I don't know. But they think the 911 call was from the killer. Maybe they can trace it."

Adele took a sip of lukewarm coffee. "I spent the biggest part of my life on a hundred-acre estate in the country and was virtually sheltered from all this. It was a different world."

"I grew up here in Les Barbes. We never had problems like this until three years ago when Remy Jarvis was lynched by that nutcase who came looking for Zoe."

Adele looked at her hands, remembering.

"Didn't you tell me Zoe worked for you once?"

Adele nodded. "She was a live-in member of my household staff at Woodmore many years ago."

"How did she go from working for you to owning Zoe B's?"

"It's a long story, hon. It's personal."

"You're too humble to say it, but I just know you helped her get started."

"It would be a mistake to make assumptions." Adele traced the pattern on her saucer. "Our paths crossed by divine appointment—and our friendship today is totally by God's grace."

"Well, speaking of Grace, you've got the cutest little godchild on the planet."

"Thank you. She's an angel—the granddaughter I never had. Relocating here was a bold move. But I'm adjusting to the simplicity—and I love living near Grace, Zoe, and Pierce. They're like family now." Adele glanced up at Isabel's somber expression. "I didn't mean to get sidetracked. I'm so sorry about Renee's father being murdered. I want you to feel free to take time off to go to the funeral or to be with the family."

Isabel nodded. "I appreciate that. I can only imagine how rattled the sheriff and police chief must be, waiting for a third victim."

⁂

Zoe stood at the work table in the kitchen at Zoe B's where Pierce had laid out small bowls, each containing ingredients he would need to make the breakfast entrées.

She popped the last of a beignet into her mouth, brushing the powdered sugar off her chin. "You outdid yourself on these today, *cher*."

"Think so, eh?" Pierce slid an omelet onto a plate, added two links of boudin, crispy potatoes, a thin slice of orange, and a sprig of mint. "What time is Grace's checkup?"

"Nine. I'll take her over to Adele's afterward and come back here until after lunch."

"I hope she's not wearing the poor woman out."

"Adele's got Isabel to help. They love having Grace there."

Pierce lifted his gaze, his eyebrows furrowed. "Babe, are you sure those guys from Haven House are not going to be over there working?"

"Positive."

"I'm just not comfortable with Grace being around them—or you and Adele being around them, for that matter."

"Murray's a really nice guy."

"But nobody knows anything about him, not even Father Vince. How is that different from Grace being around a stranger?"

"She isn't really *around* him. He's off working in another room—like he was when he was here hooking up our computer."

"What about that long-haired guy—Fred, Frank—"

"Flynn." Zoe took a sip of orange juice. "He just came to help Murray move Adele's furniture. He won't be doing any work for her."

Pierce bit his lip the way he did when he was irritated.

Zoe linked her arm in his. "It's not like we do a background check on the repairmen that come in here either. They're all strangers to us. At some point, we have to trust people."

"Trust isn't my strong point—especially where Grace is concerned."

"All right." She unlinked her arm, grabbed a mushroom, and popped it into her mouth. "I won't leave Grace with her when she's got Murray working over there."

"You don't have to look at me like I'm the bad guy."

"Actually, you're the good guy. You're just ultraprotective."

"You mean overprotective."

"I said what I meant, Pierce. You are extremely protective of Grace and me. I don't know if that makes you *over*protective—though it is a real pain once in a while."

He smiled sheepishly. "I know. Heaven help her when she starts dating."

Zoe kissed him on the cheek. "Let's just get her to kindergarten first, deal?"

"Deal."

"I'd better go make sure she hasn't gotten syrup on her dress before we leave. I'm sure she's charmed Hebert into sharing bites of his pain perdu."

Zoe pushed open the kitchen door and entered the cozy dining room. Every table was occupied with customers, the hum of their voices more pleasant than background music.

She walked over to the table by the window, where her hanging fern thrived and where Savannah was pouring coffee refills.

"Hi, Mama." Grace smiled from her booster seat, her face and dress surprisingly clean.

Zoe returned her daughter's smile and realized everyone else seemed somber. "Is … something wrong?"

"The FedEx driver just left," Savannah said. "He said there's been a second murder—Peter Gautier."

"The bigwig at the sugar plant?"

Savannah nodded. "Drowned in the bathtub, just the like the first. The killer spray painted the number two at the scene. So who's number three?"

Zoe locked gazes with Hebert as she processed the terrifying implications. "For heaven's sake, the killer had a grievance with the CEOs of the bank and sugar refinery. He must be someone who worked at the sugar plant, lost his job, and then his house. How hard can it be for the authorities to narrow it down?"

"Dey may not have enough time," Hebert said. "Dis guy's killed two people in two days."

Zoe's skin turned to gooseflesh. "Well, they'd better! I shudder to think he's already marked his third victim."

Sheriff Jude Prejean stood in the master bathroom at the Gautiers' lake house and watched as his deputies zipped the body bag that held Peter's waterlogged body.

"I'm going to head back to the office," Jude said to Gil Marcel. "As soon as we have the list of layoffs and foreclosures, we can start comparing names."

"I've got Castille and Doucet working on it right now," Gil said. "Somebody wanted these guys to pay—and wanted them aware of what was happening to them. It was cold and calculating of the killer to drug them and render them helpless. He probably hasn't been subtle about his feelings for them either. Once we start questioning family and friends, someone should stand out."

"I hope you're right." Jude stared at the body bag. "But we both know the bitterness that's prevalent in this community. I'm not sure that attitude alone will be a red flag."

"Maybe not. But the vocal ones can be a starting point."

Jude was aware of voices in the hallway, then Aimee Rivette came into the room with a thirtysomething Ivy-League-looking man who bore a strong resemblance to the victim.

"He's over here," Aimee said. "Your brother has already identified him. You don't have to do this."

"Yes, I do."

Aimee walked over to the body bag, bent down, and unzipped it enough that Peter Gautier's face could be seen.

The young man looked down at his father, then swallowed hard and remained silent for a few moments. "What are you doing to find his killer?"

"Let me answer that." Jude walked over and extended his hand. "I'm Sheriff Prejean. I'm so very sorry for your loss."

"Kevin Gautier." He shook Jude's hand, his palms sweaty, his handshake solid.

"We're in the process of getting the names of everyone who has been laid off from the sugar plant in the past five years," Jude said, "and comparing it to the names of foreclosures at Roux River Bank."

"There're plenty of people who have a bone to pick with my father," Kevin said. "He's had to lay off hundreds of people. Everyone blames him. But it was just business. That's what happens when the economy gets dicey."

"There's no justification for murder." Jude held Kevin's gaze. "We're going to get whoever did this to your father."

"I hope you mean that, Sheriff. I doubt you're going to get much public support."

"Public sentiment is what it is. It doesn't affect my judgment or my oath to uphold the law. I want justice as much as you do."

"Some might argue that this *is* justice." Kevin's eyes brimmed with tears.

"Well, son, I'm not one of them." Jude put his hand on the young man's shoulder. "Are you all right?"

"What do *you* think?" Kevin's taut face flushed, and then his expression softened. "So what happens next?"

"The coroner is about to take your father's body to the lab. We have to perform an autopsy to confirm the cause of death. According to the coroner's preliminary analysis, your father was drugged before he was drowned."

Kevin stared at the zipped body bag. "Like Mr. Darveau?"

"We'll know for sure after the autopsy."

"I sure hope you find him."

"Are you afraid we won't?"

"No, sir. I'm afraid if you don't, I'll track him down and kill him myself."

Jude studied the young Gautier. Was it grief that had made him so angry? Or was there more to it?

CHAPTER 6

Murray pushed open the door at Zoe B's, the tinkling of the bell causing a dozen pairs of eyes to look his way. He spotted Zoe moving in his direction. Her gait and her bobbed chestnut hair and blue-gray eyes bore a striking resemblance to his late mother. An unexpected pang of grief tightened his throat.

"Well, hi there," she said. "Are you here for lunch?"

"Actually I was on my way back to Haven House. I thought I'd check in here first to see how your computer's working."

"Perfectly." Zoe smiled. There was his mother again. Why hadn't he noticed it the day before? "I was able to get online using the laptop. Lightning fast, too."

"You're not having any problems?"

"None whatsoever. I don't know why we didn't go wireless sooner. Adele Woodmore said you're going to get her set up."

"I offered to. She's such a nice lady."

"One of my favorite people."

Murray nodded. "Mine, too."

"She doesn't need all the bells and whistles on a laptop. I doubt she would use it for anything other than email and browsing."

"I won't let the floor person sell her more than she needs."

"You seem to know a lot about computers. Do you have a degree in computer science?"

Murray smiled. "I'm mostly self-taught, like someone who instinctively knows how to play the piano."

"I know what you mean. My husband is that way with cooking."

Murray nodded and glanced at his watch. "If there's nothing you need me to do, I'm going to head out. Lunch at Haven House is come-and-go from eleven thirty to one. I'm starved. I've had a busy morning."

"Father Vince said you stay busy all the time."

"This morning I installed a new toilet and fixed an automatic garage door that was stuck." He winked. "This afternoon I'm fixing a sprinkler system. I don't think I'm going to run out of things to fix or install."

A man walked up to her, dressed in a chef's hat and apron—and a stony expression.

"Zoe, I need your opinion in the kitchen for a minute," he said.

"This is Murray Hamelin," she said. "Murray, this is my husband, Pierce—"

"I thought you were finished with the computer." Pierce's face was taut, his lips pressed together. His de Gaulle-like nose seemed out of joint.

"I came by to make sure everything was working properly," Murray said.

"And is it?"

"According to your wife, everything's great." Murray glanced over at Zoe and then held Pierce's intimidating gaze. "That's what I like to hear. Call if you have any problems."

"We'll do that." Pierce took a step forward but didn't offer his hand. "You don't need to stop by unless you hear from us. I'm sure you have plenty of other jobs that require your attention."

"This was just a courtesy call." Murray tipped the bill of his New Orleans Saints cap. "You folks have a nice day."

He pushed open the door and stepped outside and into the tide of tourists moving under the galleries that overhung the sidewalk. He moved past the coffee shop, the aroma of fresh-ground coffee beans replacing the foul vibes he got off Pierce Broussard. Talk about a control freak. What was *his* problem?

⚜

Zoe walked across the dining room at the eatery, Pierce behind her. She pushed open the door to the kitchen and went inside, then stopped and turned around, her hands on her hips.

"Pierce, what is *wrong* with you?"

"I needed you to taste the gumbo. My allergies are bothering me, and my taster is off."

"That is so lame." She hoped her gaze bored straight into his conscience.

"All right." Pierce threw his hands in the air. "I don't want Murray hanging around here."

"Hanging around? Are you kidding? He was here all of two minutes, just checking to see if the computer was working okay."

"He could've called."

Zoe took a breath and lowered her voice. "You're the one who's always complaining that the work ethic today is lousy.

Here's a guy who takes pride in his work, and you practically threw him out."

"No, I didn't."

"Not with your hands—with your hostility. How'd you even know Murray was here?"

"I came out to see which of the guys was winning at checkers. I saw you talking to him, and I just wanted him to leave."

Zoe rolled her eyes. "You're going to have to get a handle on your paranoia. Murray is a nice guy who is working hard to get his life back. He didn't deserve to be insulted. I was embarrassed for him—and for you for treating him that way."

Pierce's face turned bright pink. "I suppose I was abrupt."

"I told you I would keep Grace away from the men at Haven House, but I can't make them disappear. Murray's offered to help Adele pick out a laptop and get online, and I know she's going to have more jobs for him to do. And so is Vanessa. I don't want to cringe every time Murray's name comes up because I know you're uncomfortable."

"You won't, babe. I'll keep my thoughts to myself from now on. I'm sorry I embarrassed you." He put his hand on her shoulder. "Really."

"Do I need to remind you that when we put the Christian fish symbol on our front door, we knew we would be held to a higher standard? What do you think your attitude said to Murray and anyone else who overheard you?"

"I said I was sorry."

Zoe sighed. "You did. Apology accepted."

Murray parked his truck along Jacquard Street and Flynn pulled in behind him, driving Father Vince's Toyota Camry.

Murray got out and started walking briskly toward Haven House, Flynn catching up with him and keeping pace.

"Father Vince sent me on a job this morning," Flynn said.

"Good for you."

"Ain't you even curious what it was?"

"No."

Flynn jabbed him in the ribs. "Aw, come on, man. Cut me a little slack. I washed windows all morning at the public library—for only fifty bucks."

"It's fifty bucks more than you had yesterday."

"Thanks for the math lesson. What're you doing this afternoon?"

"None of your business."

"Think I'll watch the ball game."

"Why don't you ask Father Vince if there's something you can do to help around here?"

"Because I worked all morning, and I want to watch the ball game."

Murray shook his head. "Heaven forbid you should put in an eight-hour day, like the rest of us."

Flynn laughed. "So did you hear the Bathtub Killer struck again?"

"The who?"

"That's what they're calling the dude who killed Girard Darveau, now that he's drowned a second CEO in the bathtub."

"Who?"

"Peter Gautier—lord of the sugar refinery."

Murray glanced over at Flynn. "Where'd you hear that?"

"The padre's Toyota has a great radio." He flashed a toothy grin. "There was a day when I might've been tempted to steal it. But I'm getting my mind renewed now. That's why we're here, right?"

"We're here to work our way back into society, moron. But you still have the mind-set of a freeloader."

Murray bounded up the steps and went in the front door.

Father Vince was coming down the stairs. "Oh good, you're both back. Hope you're hungry. Chef laid out a nice spread. The blackened chicken pasta salad is amazing. So did you guys have a productive morning?"

Murray nodded. "I did. Got a garage door fixed *and* a new toilet installed. I've got a sprinkler system to work on this afternoon."

Flynn tossed the car keys to Father Vince. "I doubt the windows at the library have ever been cleaner, though that window cleaner isn't streakless like it claimed to be." He flopped on the couch, his arms folded across his chest. "I guess you heard there's been another murder?"

Father Vince suddenly looked somber. "Yes. I spoke with Monsignor Robidoux after he got back from administering last rites. It's looking more and more like revenge. Such a waste. The killer isn't going to feel better after he's eliminated the people who've hurt him. He's never going to find peace through violence."

"How can you know that?" Flynn said.

"Because I've heard confessions for a decade. People don't find peace by hurting others."

Flynn pursed his lips. "Not if they have a conscience. But what if they don't? What if this killer doesn't even believe in God?"

"If he doesn't believe in God, Flynn, he'll *never* find peace, no matter what he does. Either way, committing murder is an exercise in futility."

"Father, you're wasting your time trying to reason with this pin-headed *bon rien*," Murray said. "I'm going to go wash up."

Murray went upstairs and washed his face and hands, then left the bathroom and ran into Flynn at the top of the stairs.

"You really don't like me, do you?" Flynn said.

"What was your first clue?"

Flynn grabbed him by his T-shirt. "I'm fed up with your sarcasm. I said I was sorry for not helping you move the old lady's furniture. Let it go."

"Maybe I don't want to let it go."

"You want your lousy thirty bucks back?" Flynn reached in his pocket and pulled out a wad of bills. He took out a twenty and a ten and dropped them on the floor. "We're even. Now get off my back."

"I'll get off your back when you stop acting like a jerk, which is never."

"Keep messing with me, dude, and I'll shut you up."

"Good luck with that. I'm shaking in my boots." Murray shoved him aside, stepped on the bills, and went down the stairs.

When he reached the bottom, Noah Washington was walking out of the kitchen and into the dining room, his lunch buffet choices piled on a plate.

"Father Vince oughta kick that guy outta here," Noah said, "until he changes his attitude. He washes a few windows and thinks he's done his share for a while. He sure isn't tryin' to work his way back into society."

"Let's not ruin our appetites by talking about him." Murray grinned and snitched an olive off Noah's plate. "Save me a place. Let me load a plate, and I'll be right there."

⚜

Adele strolled arm in arm with Vanessa around the duck pond at Langley Manor, relishing the soothing sound of the babbling brook and the cool shade of the massive live oaks. They walked up on the wood bridge and stopped, leaning on the railing.

Adele looked out across the pond to the gently rolling green lawn and white antebellum mansion with its stately pillars and wraparound porch.

"You've done an amazing job turning this place into a bed-and-breakfast, hon. It's thrilling to know it was once a station for the Underground Railroad."

"Did Zoe ever tell you why it was named Langley Manor instead of Langley Plantation?"

Adele shook her head, her gaze fixed on a weeping willow, the eyes of her heart seeing Woodmore. "No, but I've wondered about that. I've never heard of a manor house in south Louisiana."

"According to what was passed down by word of mouth in Noah's family, Josiah and Abigail gave it that designation so everyone would think they were snobby Brits who clung to their own customs and refused to adapt to the culture here. The locals have told me how much the Cajuns resented them. And so did the other plantation owners. Living isolated would've made it easier for them to secretly provide shelter and safe passage for the slaves being ushered up North. No one knew what they were doing out here."

Adele smiled. "God knew. They'll be rewarded one day."

"We don't know much about them, except what I've pieced together from the diaries written by Ethan's great-grandmother Augusta Langley. We know that Josiah was Ethan's grandfather's great-grandfather. Neither he nor Abigail kept records of their involvement in the Underground Railroad—at least not that we can find. If it hadn't been for Noah, we might never have realized what happened here."

"Yes, he told me. It's amazing that the descendant of a slave and the descendant of a slave owner can come together to preserve a slice of history." Adele put her hand on her heart. "Honestly, it's a story that should be told on Oprah."

Vanessa's face looked radiant. "Ethan and I are content to tell it to one group of guests at a time. Though a feature writer from the Lafayette newspaper contacted us and wants to do a story sometime this summer. We feel honored to be entrusted with the history and beauty of this family heirloom, and it's always a privilege to share it."

"There's a lot to tell. And it's lovely here."

"We think so. Even our six-year-old—well, soon to be seven—loves it. Carter's a ham and likes the attention he gets from the guests. Plus he's energetic, and it's nice that he has room to run. We've fenced the property, so we don't worry about alligators. And our yellow Lab, Angel, is with him everywhere he goes and won't let him near the water. Do you ever miss Woodmore?"

"Oh, I try not to. I'm grateful to be close to Zoe, Pierce, and little Grace. That big estate was getting to be too much for me. Just keeping good people to run the place was starting to wear me out."

Vanessa nodded. "I can see how it might. We finally hired a lady who comes in at eleven to change out the rooms. And a laundry service that does the linens. My role is to prepare the breakfasts, conduct tours, and try to be available for guests. Ethan helps me on evenings and weekends. We hired Noah to be the groundskeeper. As soon as the caretaker house is finished, he'll move in there. It's the perfect size for one person and really nice—and private. I think he's ready to leave Haven House."

"He and Murray Hamelin seem to get along well."

"Noah likes Murray. In fact, he gets along with all the men at Haven House. But I don't think either of them likes that Flynn character." Vanessa arched her eyebrows. "I know I don't. He came out with Noah one day to help with the fertilizing."

"I met Flynn for the first time the other day when he came over with Murray and helped him move furniture in my back bedroom so it could be painted. Isabel doesn't trust him. I try to see the good in everyone, but he does seem dark." Adele sighed. "I've been praying for him. I haven't said anything to Murray, but I hope he doesn't bring him to my house again."

"Adele, you should be honest with Murray. I have to think about Carter and my guests. I didn't have any problem telling Noah I didn't want to see Flynn out here again. He gives me the creeps."

CHAPTER 7

The next morning, Adele dialed the number at Haven House. It rang three times, and she started to hang up when she heard a voice.

"Haven House. This is Father Vince."

"This is Adele Woodmore. I was trying to reach Murray before he got started for the day. I do hope I'm not calling too early."

"Not at all. The residents are just gathering for breakfast. Let me get him for you. Please hold...."

Adele looked out the kitchen window at the small swatch of earth she owned. Visiting Vanessa at Langley Manor had made her long for the beauty of Woodmore, but not for the upkeep. A Carolina wren landed on the bird feeder and puffed out its little chest and began singing. How could something that tiny let out a song that filled the backyard?

"Good morning, Mrs. Woodmore."

"Hello, Murray. I'm glad I caught you before you left. I just wanted to set up a day and time when we could go over to Best Buy and pick out a laptop. I'm totally flexible."

"I have tomorrow afternoon free. I usually keep Friday afternoon open for jobs that can't wait. There haven't been any this week, so why don't I put you down?"

"Splendid."

"Have you decided where you want to put the computer?"

"Yes, there's an empty corner in my den. I picked out a cherry computer desk that should fit nicely. It will be delivered in the morning."

"Sounds great," Murray said. "Do you think it will come before one?"

"The furniture store said they would deliver between nine and eleven." Adele glanced at the grandfather clock in the living room for no reason. "So that should be fine."

"Then one o'clock it is. I'll see you then."

"Murray … you won't be bringing Flynn, will you?"

"No, ma'am. I won't need help with this."

"I'd really prefer not to have him over here anymore. I know that might sound petty, but—"

"I can't blame you. He's a scary-looking guy."

"It's not his long hair," Adele said. "It's something I can't explain. He just makes me uneasy."

"No problem. You're not the first person to complain. I'm not planning to use him again for anything."

⚜

Murray glanced up as Father Vince walked into the dining room.

"Has anyone seen Flynn?"

Murray shook his head. "Not me."

"It's not noon yet, is it?" Pete leaned forward, his tattooed arms folded on the table. "He probably went back to bed to get his *beauty* sleep."

Daniel smirked. "It ain't workin'."

Everyone laughed.

"Did you check the lounge?" Jake grinned, exposing a huge gap where one of his teeth was missing. "He could be up there markin' his territory around the TV. I think he sleeps with the remote."

"He's probably in the bathroom," Noah said.

"I already checked all three." Father Vince went over to the big window in the living room and looked down the block. "Hmm … my car is gone. No one saw him leave?"

The residents all shook their heads.

Lines formed on Father Vince's forehead. "As I was going to bed last night, he asked to borrow my car and said he was going to the convenience store to get some snacks. Did anyone see him come back?"

"Now that I think about it," Murray said, "I don't remember seeing him in his bunk. You suppose he's been out all night?"

The dining room resounded with wolf whistles that stopped when Father Vince exhaled loudly. "All right," he said. "When Flynn gets back, I want to see him. Obviously I'm not going anywhere without my car."

Father Vince turned and walked toward the kitchen, his brisk gait a good indicator of his irritation.

Noah rolled his eyes. "Maybe Father Vince will kick Flynn outta here till he gets serious about bein' part o' the team."

Murray glanced at his watch. "I'd go looking for him, but I've got a whole list of repairs to do this morning. I can't stand how he treats Father Vince. He has a lot of gall, taking off with his car. Probably spent the night with some bimbo he picked up at the Den. Maybe this is exactly what needed to happen for Father Vince to get fed up. This is one time I don't think he's going to turn the other cheek."

"Then again"—Noah held his gaze—"maybe we'll get lucky and Flynn *won't* come back."

❦

Zoe walked out of the kitchen at Zoe B's and waited for Grace to climb into her booster seat in the chair next to Father Sam, then set a plate of dry Cheerios and cut-up fruit in front of her.

"As soon as you finish eating, Mommy will take you over to Addie's."

Grace giggled and stuffed a slice of banana into her mouth.

Tex flashed a smile the size of the Rio Grande, his thumbs hooked on his red suspenders. "Punkin' here sure does love goin' over there."

"It gives me a couple hours of freedom," Zoe said. "Today while she's at Adele's, I'm going out to Langley Manor to see Vanessa."

"How dey doing out dere?" Hebert fiddled with the button on his unironed yellow shirt.

"Just great. The place is booked seven days a week." Zoe sighed. "I'm happy for them, but I really miss having them living upstairs. Pierce and I never see them unless we go out there. They can't both be away at the same time as long as they have guests."

"Makes sense," Father Sam said. "I never really thought about it."

Savannah came over to the table and started pouring refills. "*All* the customers are talking about the Bathtub Killer. I'll tell you one thing: There's not a lot of sympathy out there for the victims."

Father Sam took off his glasses and wiped his eyes. "I know people are bitter, but those two men didn't deserve *that.*"

"Dere are some folks who tink dey did." Hebert took a sip of coffee. "Hearts are stone cold toward dose CEOs."

"Perhaps they should sit awhile with the grieving families," Father Sam replied. "The killer didn't make Girard Darveau and Peter Gautier pay. He made their families pay. The humiliating drama of drowning them in their business clothes and numbering them did far more to punish the families than the victims." Father Sam glanced over at Grace. "Enough said. It's cruel, that's all."

"I'm guessin' the killer would argue that what Darveau and Gautier did was cruel." Tex lifted an eyebrow. "I'm just sayin'."

"My aunt Nicole has a computer systems company," Savannah said, "and she's had to lay a lot of people off. She says we don't understand the pressure they're under to stay in the black—that layoffs are a necessity."

"So's eating and paying da mortgage." Hebert scratched the gray stubble on his chin. "Da reason people are cynical is dat CEOs still get whopping bonuses in spite of da layoffs. Dat's not right."

Father Sam nodded. "I agree. But none of it justifies murder."

"*I two!"* Grace held up two fingers and seemed to be speaking to anyone who would listen.

Father Sam smiled and turned his attention to Grace. "Do we know anybody who's two?"

"Me!"

"Me? Are you Me Broussard?" Tex asked.

"No, I *Grace* Brew-sar."

Hebert tapped her on the nose. "Den we do know you."

Grace bobbed her head, giggling with delight all the while.

"Eat your breakfast, sweetie." Zoe pulled one of Grace's blonde pigtails away from her mouth and looked over at Hebert and Tex. "With all the awful news we're hearing, Grace's sweet innocence reminds me there's still good in the world."

"There is," Savannah said. "But right now, all that innocence isn't going to help whoever's destined to be victim number three."

Zoe shuddered. Why hadn't the authorities figured out who was behind this?

❦

Zoe stood with Vanessa on the wooden bridge that spanned the duck pond at Langley Manor and took in the splendor of the rolling, velvet green grounds dotted with weeping willows, magnolias, and crape myrtles.

In the distance, shaded under the arms of a massive live oak, the stately white mansion with its four round pillars looked worthy of the cover of *Southern Living.*

"You have to love it out here." Zoe rested her arms on the railing. "It's gorgeous. Must seem surreal at times."

"It does. I know it's a privilege living here, but it's also a lot of work."

Vanessa wore a bright pink sundress, her long, dark hair tied back with a matching scarf. Did she realize her wardrobe matched the blossoms on the crape myrtles?

"Pierce and I miss having y'all next door," Zoe said.

"We miss it too. Ethan and I were just talking about how much we enjoyed living upstairs from Zoe B's. Especially standing on the gallery and watching the people on *rue Madeline*. That was a unique experience."

"I wonder how many times we came out here with Ethan and Pierce and had picnics while we watched the remodeling crews coming and going."

"And let Carter kick the soccer ball to his heart's content." Vanessa tilted her head back and looked up at a V formation of white ibis. "He's got so much room to play, and I don't worry about him as long as he doesn't go beyond the fence and Angel is with him."

"It's hard to believe a yellow Lab with her instincts ended up as a rescue dog at the humane society," Zoe said. "Speaking of Angel, where is she?"

Vanessa's eyebrows came together, her eyes the color of the summer sky. "I don't know. I don't remember seeing her this morning. With Carter at day camp, I haven't paid attention to what she's doing. She loves to roam as much as he does. You'll have to bring Grace with you next time and let her take a ride on Angel again. I'm not sure who enjoyed it more—her or the dog."

"Actually, I think Carter did." Zoe smiled. "He oversaw the entire operation and made sure she didn't fall off."

"You'd think they were siblings the way he watches after her."

"I know. It's cute." Zoe glanced at her watch. "I can't believe we're out of time. It's been so great catching up. Your next group of guests will be arriving soon, and I've got to get going. I'm sure Adele and Isabel are ready to give my little bundle of energy back."

"It's great that Adele has taken such an interest in Grace. What a wonderful godmother."

"She's absolutely a blessing," Zoe said. "Thanks for brunch. You've got your crepes down to perfection."

Vanessa beamed. "I have Pierce to thank for that. The guests are crazy about them, and I can offer them a lot of choices because they're so easy. Plus they look beautiful on the plate. A fine presentation always adds to the experience. Isn't that what you and Pierce always say?"

Zoe laughed. "I think we've cloned you."

As the two friends strolled back toward the house, Angel moved toward them across the grounds.

"Well, there you are." Vanessa bent down in anticipation of the dog jumping on her with excitement. But instead, Angel barked frantically and ran in circles. "What are you carrying on about?" Vanessa tried to pet the dog, but Angel kept pulling away.

"Does she want to play?"

Vanessa shook her head. "She's trying to tell me something. I'd better go see what she's fussing about. Let's talk soon, okay?"

"Definitely. Thanks again." Zoe gave her a quick hug. "Tell Ethan hello."

"I will. Give my love to Pierce and Grace."

Vanessa turned and walked briskly across the grounds, Angel already twenty yards in front of her.

Zoe trudged along the walkway that led back to the manor house, mulling over the morning's conversation and mentally savoring the shrimp and asparagus crepes Vanessa served her for brunch. Why didn't she get out like this more often? Few things were more energizing than having good conversation with a friend and sharing something delicious to eat.

She reached her car, which was the only vehicle parked in the guest lot, and had just opened the door when a scream echoed across the Louisiana sky and sent her heart racing.

"Zoe!"

Zoe turned on her heels and raced toward the sound as fast as she could, wishing she had on athletic shoes instead of sandals. She looked out across the rolling green and saw Vanessa waving her arms in the air.

Zoe pushed herself harder, and half a minute later slowed to a stop in front of Vanessa, a little short of breath. "What's … wrong?"

"He's dead!" Vanessa's face was ashen, her sandals covered in mud. "He has no pulse!"

"Who's dead?"

"The man in the bayou." Vanessa pointed beyond an open gate to a body lying faceup in shallow water. "Go take a closer look, and tell me if it's who I think it is."

CHAPTER 8

Vanessa pulled back the lacy sheers on the parlor window at Langley Manor and saw Zoe leaning against her car, waiting for sheriff's deputies to arrive.

She picked up her cell phone and dialed Noah's number. It rang several times. *Come on, Noah, pick up.*

"Hey there," he said. "How was your visit with Zoe?"

"Are you still on the grounds?"

"I'm out in the shed, organizin' my tools. You sound upset."

"Have you seen or talked to Flynn Gillis today?"

"Flynn? Why are you asking about him?"

"Have you?"

"No. He didn't show up for breakfast. He borrowed Father Vince's car and stayed out all night. He's on everybody's list right now."

"Not anymore. He's dead."

"Flynn's *dead?* How do you know that?"

"Angel discovered him a few minutes ago and came and got me."

"Are you sayin' he's here—at Langley Manor?"

"Yes, his body's down in the bayou." Vanessa sighed. "The sheriff's on his way. Do you have any idea who might have done this?"

"Not really. Nobody could stand the guy. But I don't know anyone who'd want to kill him."

Vanessa felt her face turn hot. "Noah, I have a feeling the sheriff is going to press you pretty hard—since you didn't like Flynn and his body was discovered out here where you work."

There was a long moment of dead air.

"I've got nothin' to hide. I'll just come up there to the house and talk to the sheriff."

"All right. Let's stay calm. Maybe we should call Father Vince and have him come out."

"I know how to tell the truth. You think havin' a priest sittin' next to me would make me sound more believable?"

She winced. "I'm sorry, Noah. My mom was a cop, and I grew up around this kind of thing. You're going to be a person of interest until they prove who murdered the guy."

"Do we even know it was murder?"

"I'm making that assumption—since he seemed to irritate everyone he came in contact with. What are the odds he just dropped dead in our bayou?" Vanessa wiped her upper lip. "I hate this."

There was a long pause. "You worried Sheriff Prejean's gonna look harder at me because I'm black?"

"I didn't say that. He's always been a fair man."

"Look, if I wanted to kill Flynn—which I *didn't*—why would I do it out here when I'd be the first person they'd suspect?"

"The sheriff is going to say it might've been a crime of passion—something you didn't plan. That maybe you two had an argument, and it just happened."

Noah exhaled into the receiver. "I'll be right there. There's no way the sheriff can hang this on me. I didn't do anything."

Vanessa saw a squad car pull up out front. "He's here."

"I'm on my way."

❧

Adele sat in the sunroom with Zoe, listening to her recount details of the awful ending to an otherwise wonderful morning with Vanessa.

"It helps to talk about it," Zoe said. "It was just so shocking to see Flynn's body lying in the muck. I told Jude's deputies what I know, but it's really not much. I'm sorry. I'm repeating myself."

"You go ahead and talk, hon. I don't mind listening." Adele glanced over at Grace, who had curled up on the love seat and fallen asleep.

"It seems like I should feel *something,* having just seen the body of a murdered man. But I'm numb."

"I'm not," Adele said. "I feel quite guilty for having judged Flynn. He made me uncomfortable. Vanessa and I talked about it yesterday, and she encouraged me to tell Murray not to bring him over anymore."

"Adele, you were probably nicer to him than you think. You're always nice to everyone."

Adele wrapped her hands around her Waterford iced-tea glass. "I could have done better—and should have. I suppose if I'd known—"

"Please don't tell me you're going to feel guilty because you didn't want Flynn over here. You were wise to listen to your instincts. He made most people uncomfortable."

"I should have been kinder when he was here at the house. But I avoided him." Adele pursed her lips. "Who do you suppose wanted him dead? Goodness gracious, there's entirely too much killing going on in this town."

"I doubt this is related to the bathtub killings either," Zoe said. "Jude is going to have his hands full with two separate investigations."

"I wonder how Murray's taking it."

Zoe shrugged. "Hard to say. Flynn was the least popular guy at Haven House, but this has to affect the others on some level. Father Vince, too. I feel sorry that Noah's in the middle. Just because he butted heads with Flynn doesn't make him capable of murdering him."

Adele traced the rim of her glass. "From what I understand, almost everyone butted heads with Flynn."

Isabel stood in the doorway with a pitcher of raspberry tea. "Yes, but his body was found on the property where Noah works. You have to admit it looks bad." She came to the table and refilled their glasses.

"Looks can be deceiving," Adele said. "Noah Washington is a fine man. I don't believe he had anything to do with Flynn's death."

"Neither do I," Zoe said.

"Saying it won't make it so." Isabel set the pitcher on the table. "He'll have to account for his whereabouts at the time the murder happened."

"What about Vanessa and Ethan?" Adele said. "Won't they have to do the same? Surely his being black won't be a factor."

"I doubt this is racial," Zoe said. "They questioned Vanessa pretty hard. And I'm sure they will do the same to Ethan."

"But they're not the ones who had issues with Flynn," Isabel said. "Noah is."

Adele bit her lip and glanced up at Isabel. "You've never been comfortable with my dealings with any of the men from Haven House."

"No, I haven't. I know you just want to give them a break. But it's risky, and I wish you wouldn't do it."

"Nonsense." Adele waved her hand. "Flynn gave me pause. But Noah and Murray are gentlemen and have been nothing but polite and efficient."

"You're not responsible for them," Isabel said.

"No, but I *am* responsible for how I respond to them." Adele looked out at the flower beds that Noah had so carefully tended. "If the Lord has opened this door, I don't need to shy away from it."

⚜

Sheriff Jude Prejean walked out on the back deck at Langley Manor after being briefed on the facts in the Gillis murder case by Deputies Stone Castille and Mike Doucet.

He spotted Noah sitting in a rocking chair, facing the cane fields, and walked up behind him. He coughed to avoid startling him.

Noah stood and turned around. "Sheriff, I've already told the deputies everything I know."

"Mind if we sit for minute?" Jude went over and sat in the rocker next to Noah. "First time I've been here since the deck was added. Pretty amazing view from back here."

"Yes, sir. I cleared out a few trees and opened it up. Now you can see a country mile."

"You've done an amazing job of landscaping."

"Thanks. But I had nothin' to do with those cane fields. They sure do make a nice backdrop though."

Jude looked out beyond the live oaks to a sea of tall green stalks bathed in sunlight and undulating in the breeze. He enjoyed the postcard picture for a few moments before continuing.

"My deputies tell me you have no idea how Flynn Gillis's body ended up in the bayou."

"That's right."

"The coroner places the time of death between eleven last night and one this morning." Jude turned to Noah. "Flynn didn't drown. He was strangled."

Noah's hands turned to fists.

"It takes a lot of pressure to break someone's hyoid bone, Noah. You have strong hands."

"A lot o' men have strong hands. And I imagine plenty o' them disliked Flynn as much as I did."

"My deputies just finished talking with the other residents at Haven House. They all agreed that Flynn was a real pain."

"That's right."

"In fact, Murray mentioned something that happened the other night. He said that Flynn smarted off to him, and right afterwards he overheard you tell Flynn to watch his back—that he couldn't keep ticking people off and expect them to roll over. Is that true?"

Noah wiped the sweat off his forehead. "Yes, but I was just mad that Flynn was hasslin' Murray, that's all."

"I see. Do you remember Flynn telling you to get your 'stinking hands' off him?"

"Somethin' like that," Noah said. "I didn't hurt him. I was up in his face, makin' my point."

"And when Flynn told you he was here to stay and that you'd better get used to it, did you say, 'We'll see about that'?"

"Yes, but I didn't plan to do anything 'bout it myself. I figured Father Vince'd get sick of his game playin' and throw him out."

Jude pursed his lips and linked his fingers together. "Murray also mentioned that the two of you talked about Flynn at breakfast this morning."

Noah nodded. "He stayed out all night with Father Vince's car. I figured it was just one more way he was thumbin' his nose at authority."

"Did you tell Murray that maybe y'all would get lucky and Flynn wouldn't come back?"

"Yes, sir. I meant it too. There's not a guy at Haven House who didn't feel the same way."

"But Flynn was found out here—where *you* work. Where you have easy access."

"With all due respect, Sheriff, it's easy to get in and out o' here. It's a bed-and-breakfast. People come and go all the time."

Jude stopped rocking and leaned forward, his hands clasped between his knees. "From what I understand, Flynn Gillis was about as obnoxious as they get. It's easy to see how this could happen."

"I didn't kill him."

"When's the last time you saw him?"

"Last night. I was in the lounge watchin' the ten o'clock news. He borrowed Father Vince's car to go to the convenience store. I went to bed when the news was over. That's it. Never saw him again."

"Anybody see you go to bed?"

"I doubt it. Murray was already asleep."

"You're sure about that?"

Noah nodded. "I saw him in his bunk."

"Well, the thing is, he didn't see you in yours. And neither did the other guys."

Noah turned, a row of lines on his forehead. "I was there, Sheriff. What do you want me to say? I only have two roommates. One was asleep, and the other was at the convenience store."

"Why didn't any of the *other* guys see you go to bed?"

"They're in different dorm rooms. Why would they notice when I went to bed?"

"You'd think with thirteen other residents and a priest, someone would've seen you go to bed—or to the bathroom. They didn't."

Noah closed his eyes and slowly shook his head, his lips curled with disgust. "And, o' course, why suspect any of *them* when you can go after the black man?"

"We're talking to each one of them at length. But Flynn's body was found out here—and right after you made that crack about him not coming back."

"I didn't do this."

"Noah, for what it's worth, I don't want you to be guilty. But you had a recent altercation with Flynn. I can't just ignore that. Or that fact that he was found dead out here, where you know the lay of the land."

Noah raked his hands through his hair. "Just curious, Sheriff: How do you think I lured him out here in the middle o' the night?"

"The coroner thinks he may have been killed elsewhere and his body dumped in the bayou. He showed signs of having died at least an hour before he was put in the water."

"So you think I strangled him somewhere else and dumped him out here—where you would be sure to discover his body and blame it on *me?*" Noah tapped his fingers on his knees. "You really think I'm that stupid, Sheriff?"

"I don't think it's stupid. Whoever left the body out here expected a gator to get him before anyone ever saw him."

"It wasn't me!"

Jude glanced at his watch. "We need to get the law enforcement presence away from the house before tonight's group of guests starts to arrive. I'm going to have to ask you come with me to the sheriff's department and answer more questions."

"Fine. But all you're gonna get from me is the same truth I already told you." Noah stood, a defiant spark in his eyes. "This home, sir, was a station on the Underground Railroad, and my ancestor Naomi gave up her chance at freedom to stay here and help free other slaves. This is holy ground! Even if I'd killed Flynn Gillis—which I did not—I would never, ever defile Langley Manor by dumpin' the likes o' him on this property!"

Vanessa stood in the doorway and looked questioningly at Noah and then at Jude. "Is everything all right?"

"Everything's fine," Jude said. "We're going to go down to the department and finish talking so you can get things ready for your guests."

"Sheriff, there's no way Noah did this. There has to be another explanation."

Jude locked gazes with her. "Then we need to find one."

"We will." She looked over at Noah. "Don't say another word. I'm getting you a lawyer."

"I don't want a lawyer, Vanessa." Noah's eyes narrowed. "I can speak for myself. They can't pin anything on me without evidence. And there isn't any evidence because I didn't do it."

"Trust me, Noah. You need someone to look out for your rights. Let me make some calls."

He shook his head firmly, his dark eyes now wide with resolve. "I said I can speak for myself."

"We just want to talk to him," Jude said. "If he has nothing to hide, there's no need for counsel. This is not a witch hunt."

"I sincerely hope not, Sheriff. Noah is like family. Ethan and I aren't going to stand by and let him take the fall for this."

"No one's accusing him of anything," Jude said. "But there are some serious implications that have to be resolved."

"Like what? He was asleep at Haven House when this happened."

"We haven't been able to establish that yet. None of the other residents remember seeing him between eleven and one—"

"Y'all know I'm standin' here, right?"

Jude ran his thumb along his badge. "Sorry, Noah. I didn't mean to talk as if you weren't present."

"I really think you need a lawyer," Vanessa said.

Noah held out his palm. "I can handle this. I just need to keep tellin' the truth. They can't prove somethin' that never happened."

"Then I have your permission to go over your truck for trace evidence?" Jude said. "And the clothes you wore yesterday?"

"Knock yourself out." Noah swatted the air. "You won't find anything."

CHAPTER 9

Zoe stood at the table next to the window at the eatery, where Hebert was shamelessly gloating after beating Tex at another game of checkers. She glanced outside and saw the florist van parked in front of the Hotel Peltier and the driver walking inside, toting a huge flower arrangement. For a split second she was a bride, walking hand in hand with Pierce into the Empress Ballroom, where their wedding guests applauded their arrival.

Father Sam stood, looking very authoritative in his black cleric shirt. "I hate to leave you two in the heat of battle, but I've got a physical scheduled this afternoon."

Tex glanced up. "Somethin' wrong?"

"You mean other than I'm old?" Father Sam laughed and patted him on the shoulder. "Don't worry. It's just routine."

"Wait till you're my age. Dey will poke and prod you in places you never knew you had." Hebert sat back in his chair, his arms folded across his bony rib cage. "Zoe, is dere any word on Noah?"

"He's still being questioned."

"Dey really tink he killed dat guy?"

"I don't see how. But why else would they question him all afternoon?"

Zoe sighed. "Vanessa's beside herself that Noah won't get a lawyer. He's determined to represent himself. Says he has nothing to hide."

"Maybe not. But it makes sense dey'd question him when he's da groundskeeper and knows every inch of da property."

"Hebert, anyone could've used the Langleys' property to dump Flynn's body," Zoe said.

"I know dat too."

Tex coughed as if to announce he was joining the conversation. "Don't you worry, Zoe. I'm sure the sheriff's just coverin' all bases. If Noah has nothin' to hide, the authorities will realize it. They're just doin' their job."

Zoe adjusted the blinds, her gaze fixed on the row of quaint buildings and lacy wrought-iron railings on the galleries overhanging the sidewalk. "I owe Noah my life. I'm not going to throw him under the bus."

"Of course not," Father Sam said. "Let's just pray Noah's name gets cleared."

Tex shot her a sympathetic look. "The sheriff oughta be more worried about the Bathtub Killer anyhow."

"Why?" Hebert pursed his lips. "Because da victims were rich CEOs instead of a homeless guy wid no friends?"

"No, because he's fixin' to strike again."

Zoe sighed. "All these murders … we might as well be raising Grace in New Orleans."

"Speakin' of Grace," Tex said. "Where is that little dickens?"

"The babysitter took her to Cypress Park to swing and feed the ducks."

"And on that happy note, I really must go." Father Sam pointed to his watch. "See you fellas at bingo?"

"I'll be dere."

"Not so fast." Tex raised an eyebrow at Hebert. "I'm not lettin' you outta here until I win at least one game of checkers."

"Oh dear." Father Sam laughed and headed for the door. "If I don't see you at bingo, I'll know where to find you."

Zoe's mind kept flashing back to the image of Flynn Gillis lying in the bayou. What a horrible ending to such a lovely morning.

"I know you're concerned about da violence." Hebert squeezed her hand. "But you can't let it drag you down. Dis, too, shall pass."

"When?" Zoe looked out through the blinds, her eyes following Father Sam across *rue Madeline*. "We're all just waiting for the other shoe to drop."

⚜

Jude paced in front of the window in his office, aware that the media presence was growing across the street in front of the courthouse. Scores of curiosity seekers milled about under the gigantic live oaks that shaded the grounds. And a long line had formed in front of Andre-the-vendor, who was selling andouille corn dogs on the corner of Courthouse and Primeaux.

It had been hours since Noah came in of his own free will and agreed to answer questions. How much longer could they keep at it before someone from the ACLU or NAACP was all over it?

A knock on the door caused him to look over just as Deputy Chief Aimee Rivette walked in, her tan uniform looking crisp and professional, her bleach blonde hair drooping from the humidity.

"We're getting nowhere with Mr. Washington," she said. "He hasn't budged on his story or given any inconsistencies."

"No one at Haven House can confirm he was there last night. We can't ignore that."

Aimee nodded. "No one remembers seeing him after the news ended. Each of the other men was seen by at least one other resident between eleven and one."

Jude sighed. "So Washington is the only resident without an alibi."

"But Washington says he saw Murray Hamelin asleep in his bunk, and that proves Washington was there, right?"

Jude glanced over at Aimee, the corners of her mouth twitching. "Now you're messing with me."

"Sorry." She flashed an ornery grin. "I couldn't resist."

"Where are we on evidence?"

"The lab is still testing the DNA on the clothes we found in Washington's laundry bag and in his truck, but so far it's just his. We found multiple sets of fingerprints, but none of them belong to Gillis either."

"So what you're saying is we haven't got squat?"

Aimee lifted her eyebrows. "Not on this case. Ask me about the Bathtub Killer."

"Speak to me."

"The lab just confirmed that the DNA from an eyelash found in Darveau's bathroom matches skin cells on a towel found in Gautier's bathroom. The DNA doesn't match anyone's in the system, but it's something solid."

Jude rubbed his hands together. "Good, we're making headway. We need to nail this guy before we get a call that someone's found another body in a bathtub."

"I want to catch him as badly you do. But we can't keep using up our manpower like we did today and hope to move ahead on finding the Bathtub Killer."

"You think we should make Flynn Gillis's murder investigation a low priority?"

"Don't you? No one's pressuring us to find his killer. Washington's our only person of interest, and all we really have on him is hearsay. I'm sure the people who were closest to Darveau and Gautier must be worried about who's going to be number three. That's where we should spend our resources."

Jude rubbed the sandpaper on his chin. "All right. Thank Washington for his cooperation and let him go for now."

"What will you tell the media? They know we've been talking to him."

"That he was merely a person of interest and that we don't believe Flynn Gillis's murder was in any way related to the bathtub killings. I think that's all the public cares about. No one is mourning Gillis. Once I tell the media we're making headway on the bathtub killings, they'll forget about this case."

⚜

Adele pressed the mute button on the TV and stared at the mocking-bird splashing in the birdbath in the backyard. Why couldn't she stop beating herself up for not being nicer to Flynn Gillis? Yes, he was a bit of an outcast. But weren't Christians called to love the unlovable in the name of Christ?

Noah would need reassurance that nothing had changed between them because he had been questioned by the sheriff regarding Flynn's death.

"You seem far away."

Isabel's voice startled her, and Adele turned and saw the young woman standing at the oven, checking the lemon chicken.

"I was just thinking, hon."

"Mrs. Woodmore, there's nothing you could or should have done differently toward Flynn Gillis."

"I'm not so sure, but it's too late to worry about that now. I can certainly do more to reach out to Noah and Murray."

"Are you kidding? You treat them like guests. They're just hired hands."

"So are you. And I regard you very highly." Adele realized by the blush on Isabel's cheeks that she had made her point. "Did I mention that tomorrow afternoon Murray is taking me to find a laptop computer?"

"I know your computer desk is being delivered in the morning between nine and eleven. You didn't mention Murray was taking you to get a laptop. Why don't you just have him pick one out for you and bring it here? Do you even know what to look for?"

"No." Adele smiled. "But it'll make him feel good to show off what he knows. I'm looking forward to it."

Isabel started to say something and then didn't.

"You've made it clear you're uncomfortable with me hiring men from Haven House."

"This is more than hiring them to do jobs, Mrs. Woodmore. Now you're letting Murray take you shopping."

"I let *you* take me shopping."

Isabel set the oven mitts on the counter and turned to her. “You did a background check on me first, and I don’t blame you one bit. You don’t know anything about these men except what they’ve told you.”

“Are you concerned that I’ve put you at risk?”

Isabel shrugged. “A little, I suppose. They could be sex offenders. Con men. Thieves. My point is we don’t know.”

“Have they ever been anything but polite?”

“You bring out the polite in people. I’m not sure that’s a true gauge of character.”

Adele picked up the notepad on the table and started to fan herself. “I hear what you’re saying, but I’m honestly not concerned about it. Maybe I should be. But I’ve always opened my home to those who work for me. Occasionally I’ve been taken advantage of, but it’s always worked out for good. I’m not going to live by fear.”

“I was pretty sure you’d say that.”

Adele studied Isabel’s face. “You’re not going to quit, are you?”

“No, ma’am. I prefer to stick around and make sure your luck doesn’t change.”

“I don’t believe in luck, hon. You know that. My life is ordered by the Lord.”

“I really doubt He’ll object if I make sure no one takes advantage of you.”

Adele tried to hide her amusement. “And You think He needs your help, do you?”

“No, but I need a job.”

Adele smiled. “Good answer.”

Murray sat in the living room at Haven House, listening to the ball game on the radio, when the front door opened.

"Noah!" Murray jumped up, rushed over to him, and slapped him on the back. "Man, am I glad to see you. Too bad about Flynn. What a mess."

"That's one way to put it."

"Did the sheriff finally come to the realization you had nothing to do with Flynn's murder?"

"Oh, I wouldn't go that far," Noah said. "But they couldn't trip me up, and I think I wore 'em out for now. They didn't have anything to charge me with."

"Come sit. Let me go get Father Vince."

"No." Noah's eyes had a spark of defiance. "I've answered all the questions I intend to for one day. But I've got one for you."

"What's that?"

"Why'd you tell sheriff's deputies that this mornin' at breakfast I made that comment about Flynn not comin' back?"

"It came up in the normal course of their questioning."

Noah's eyebrows came together. "No one would've known to ask you that, man. And you wouldn't have volunteered it unless you thought there was a chance I killed him."

"There's no way *you* killed Flynn."

"Then why'd you mention my offhanded crack to the cops? Didn't you know it would just make them suspect me?"

"I'm sorry." Murray sighed. "Look, they pressed us pretty hard too—one question right on top of another. I really don't remember how it came up—or even in what context."

"Really? Because you also told them you overheard me tell Flynn he'd better watch his back. You knew I didn't mean anything by it. I was just tryin' to get him off *your* back."

"I told the deputies that."

"Yeah." Noah rolled his eyes. "I'm gonna go crash."

"You should tell Father Vince you're back."

"You tell him. There's nothin' left to say."

Noah started up the stairs.

Murray called out to him. "Wait … I guess for a split second I thought it was possible you did it. But only for a split second. I swear."

"The deputies took you seriously."

"I told them I thought you were kidding."

Noah turned around. "Yeah, well. That's not how they took it."

"I'll go down there tomorrow and straighten it out."

Noah swatted the air. "Let it be. I said what I had to say."

"I guess we were all a little intimidated by the authorities," Murray said.

A row of lines formed on Noah's forehead. "I just thought you'd have my back, that's all."

"I'm sorry. Cops scare me. I didn't have time to think it through. I just told the truth. I figured I couldn't go wrong if I told the truth."

Noah shot him a crusty look and then turned around and started walking up the stairs. "We're about to find out."

CHAPTER 10

Vanessa sat in a rocking chair on the deck at Langley Manor, glad that the last of her guests had retired happily to their rooms and she finally had a moment to let go of the day's tension. She inhaled the smell of damp earth mingled with pine and let it calm her.

The full moon shone brightly, hiding the stars and exposing a layer of fine white haze that hovered ghostlike above the cane fields. An owl hooted from somewhere nearby and she mimicked its sound, enjoying the back-and-forth and wondering if the creature was really responding to her. A rustling noise interrupted her game, and she saw a white tail vanish into the woods. Probably a deer.

She glanced over at the pan of Critter Crunch she had set at the bottom of the steps and wondered how many raccoons, opossums, and foxes would help themselves once she had gone indoors. And whether the mother bobcat was out with her three kittens, teaching them to hunt for food.

It was magnificent here, raw and unspoiled. Had Ethan's ancestors enjoyed the wild beauty of the bayou—or were the hardships too great? It couldn't have been easy living in this climate without air-conditioning. Would they have felt safe keeping the windows open, knowing that a menagerie of hungry wildlife, including feral hogs, roamed these woods at night?

An uninvited flashback of Flynn Gillis's dead body invaded her peace, and she blinked it away. She could not let what had happened in the bayou defile how she thought of this place.

The door opened behind her, and she heard footsteps.

"Carter's out like a light." Ethan came over and sat in the rocker next to her. "Day camp wears him out. I read him *The Velveteen Rabbit,* or I should say he read it to me."

Vanessa smiled. "His teacher said he was the best reader she had. It'll be interesting to see what happens when he starts second grade in the fall."

"How are *you* doing?"

"Oh, fair. It feels good to be out here where I can finally get quiet and think. The guests have all retired for the night. That nice couple from Missouri stayed out here until a few minutes ago. I was so hoping we'd get a glimpse of the bobcats, but it didn't happen."

"You're amazing with the guests, you know." Ethan reached over and took her hand. "You make them feel as if they've known you all their lives."

"It's fun—most of the time. I'd like to leave today blank in my mind's diary."

He squeezed her hand. "I'm sure it was horrifying to see a dead body in our bayou. And I imagine it took you back to my cousin's murder."

"Actually it didn't. I guess I'm getting over Drew's death, though it's hard to believe it's been six years."

Vanessa sat with Ethan in comfortable silence for several minutes.

"Honey," he finally said, "we're going to have to talk about what happened today and what the implications are."

Vanessa shook her head. "Noah didn't kill Flynn Gillis. He's a gentle, kind human being and couldn't hurt anyone."

"Why do you think the sheriff grilled him all afternoon?"

"Noah went willingly down to the sheriff's department. No one forced him. He realized it could look suspicious that Flynn's body was found on the grounds where he's the groundskeeper."

"Do you think?" Ethan took off his glasses and rubbed his eyes. "Sweetheart, we have to consider the *possibility* that Noah might have killed Flynn. From what I understand, the guy was totally obnoxious. He ruffled a lot of feathers. Maybe something happened and Noah just lost control."

"He didn't."

"You can't be sure."

"I *am* sure," she said, more loudly than she had intended. "I wish he was already moved in at the caretaker house."

Ethan's silence said more than the words he was holding back.

"Just say it," she said. "I can tell you don't agree with me."

"It's not a matter of agreeing or disagreeing." Ethan pushed the dark curls off his forehead. "The circumstances have changed."

"Why—because someone dumped a dead body out here? In your heart of hearts, you can't believe Noah had anything to do with it."

"I'd certainly like to be sure."

Vanessa stopped rocking. "You have doubts? Good grief, Ethan! If you suspect Noah—have any doubt at all—there's no way we can keep him on!"

"You need to stay calm. I don't know *what* I think, but we can't just blow it off. We have to take a hard look at the facts and work through this."

"Don't use your counseling tone with me."

"I'm not trying to counsel you. It's just my tone, all right?" Ethan got up and stood at the railing, looking up at the moon. "We owe it to our son, to ourselves, and to our guests to feel a hundred percent sure that Noah wasn't involved."

"How are we going to do that?"

"First of all, we need to listen to Noah's explanation with a totally open mind."

"We agree on that. What else?"

"We need to remain objective and weigh whatever evidence the sheriff has."

"Ethan, he's not going to share it with us during an open investigation."

"But if he's concerned for our safety, I think he'll say so."

Vanessa blinked the stinging from her eyes. "I can't believe this is happening. I love Noah. He's like family now."

Ethan turned around and leaned on the railing. "Don't you think I feel the same way? I don't want to believe he could've done this. His family's story is as important to the history of Langley Manor as mine."

"Of course it is."

"I want to do everything we can to help clear Noah's name. But why do you suppose the deputies grilled him all afternoon and only spent thirty minutes talking with us?"

Vanessa bit her lip. "We don't fit the profile."

"And Noah does. So before we decide to move him out here, don't you think we should at least take a closer look at how this plays out?"

❧

Zoe stood on the gallery outside her apartment, listening to the lively Cajun music coming from Breaux's and looking down on the swarm of tourists that covered *rue Madeline*. It was a different world after dark when the city closed off the street to traffic. Colorful neon lights, horse-drawn carriages, and street entertainers created a carnival-like atmosphere. Vendors stood in the doorways of shops, trying to lure passersby with everything from authentic Cajun food to rubber alligators.

The sweet aroma of warm caramel corn flavored the night air and made her mouth water. She glanced at her watch. How hard would it be to walk over to Kernel Poppy's?

"There you are." Pierce came outside and stood next to her at the railing. "I thought you were reading."

"I was. I couldn't concentrate. I decided to let the smell of caramel corn tempt me instead."

"Why don't I go get you some?"

Zoe shook her head. "Thanks. But I need to exercise some willpower if I'm ever going to get my waistline back."

"You look great to me." Pierce patted her behind.

Zoe smiled. "Thank the Lord I'm married to a chef. I can blame it on your cooking instead of my sweet tooth."

"I'll gladly take the blame. So tell me why you couldn't concentrate on your book."

"Listen, mister." Zoe poked him with her elbow. "If you came out here to remind me you were right to be concerned about the men at Haven House, don't."

"Okay." Pierce folded his arms on the railing and seemed to be taking in the sights and sounds below. "It's beautiful, isn't it?"

"It still takes my breath away. I can't imagine living anywhere else. I'm so glad we decided to knock out walls and make the two apartments into one after the Langleys moved out."

Pierce slipped his arm around her. "Don't you ever dream about a house with a yard?"

"Never. There are some trade-offs to living upstairs from the eatery, but this is home. This is where I want to raise Grace."

"The gallery is hardly a yard."

"When she needs to run or climb, the park is just down the street. And when she's here with the babysitter, we can check in on her whenever we want."

Pierce's large nose suddenly looked aristocratic. "You think it'll be enough space when we have another baby?"

"Absolutely. We've got three bedrooms and a den. And a Jack-and-Jill bathroom separating the kids' rooms. That was the point of remodeling, right?"

"Right. I just want to be sure my woman is happy." Pierce flashed a toothy grin. "You said kids—*plural.* I like the sound of that."

Zoe linked her arm in his. "I haven't thought much about having a second one. I'm enjoying Grace so much."

"It'd be nice not to have too many years between them. Maybe we should start working on it. It might take a while."

"I'm certainly open to it." She bumped his shoulder with hers. "But not tonight, Bubba."

"That's *Chef* Bubba." Pierce chuckled, then got quiet and seemed far away for a few moments. "Listen, babe. I know I've been on your case about the men at Haven House. For what it's worth, I don't believe Noah killed Flynn. We know what Noah's made of. He risked his life to help us, and we'd probably be dead if he hadn't."

Zoe looked up at him. "Well, thanks for that much."

"I'm not comfortable with any of the other guys, but I'm sorry I embarrassed you when Murray what's-his-name came in."

"I let it go yesterday when you apologized."

"Good. Sure you don't want me to jog over to Kernel Poppy's and get you a bag of warm, delicious, chocolate-covered caramel corn that melts in your mouth and turns into the smoothest, crunchiest, most delectable—"

"Stop it!" Zoe put her hands over her ears.

"I could be back in fifteen minutes. It's only ten o'clock. It's open for another hour."

"All right. Maybe a small bag. What am I saying? No! I'm only craving comfort food because I'm upset about Noah." Zoe gave him a gentle shove and walked inside. "You're worse than the Devil! I'm trying so hard not to give in to temptation!"

"Could you say that a little louder? You have the attention of everyone on *rue Madeline*."

Zoe picked up a couch pillow and threw it at him, laughing all the while.

Pierce came over and pulled her into his arms, his voice suddenly low and sultry. "If you want to burn up some calories, we could get started on that long-range plan to add another Broussard to our family."

Zoe locked her arms around his neck, studying his expression. "Can't we just let it happen when it happens, instead of approaching it like a to-do list?"

Pierce smiled wryly. "I assure you, babe, that's not the way *I'm* looking at it. But yes. We don't have to start this minute. We can *plan* to be spontaneous."

"I want another child. But I really need to lose ten pounds first. I'm afraid if I start out ten pounds overweight, I'll never get rid of it."

"Let me get this straight: You want to lose ten pounds before you gain thirty?"

Zoe nodded. "Exactly. If I start out at my ideal weight, I'll be more inclined to lose afterwards."

"Then I need to make you salads for a while and get you trimmed down. We don't want Grace to start kindergarten before we have another one."

Zoe unlocked her arms and flopped on the couch. "Maybe I should start walking again to boost the weight loss. I just don't know if I can take an hour out of every day to do it."

"Sure you can. You're the boss. Savannah can take charge. She loves it." Pierce sat on the couch next to her and was quiet for a minute. "I wonder how Vanessa and Ethan are handling Noah's situation."

"Interesting choice of words." Zoe sighed. "Why is it *Noah's* situation?"

"You know what I meant."

"Pierce, what if his name never gets cleared? What if the Langleys don't go through with their plan to make him caretaker? There's a lot riding on Noah's presence there."

"Definitely," Pierce said. "It would be truly historic if a descendant of one of Josiah Langley's slaves were to become caretaker. The history of Langley Manor is the town's claim to fame. It would be a shame if Flynn Gillis's murder cast a shadow over that."

Zoe sighed. "I'm more worried about Noah. Langley Manor can stand on its own merit. He can't."

"Yes, but don't be so sure the Langleys won't take a financial hit. How many people will want to stay out there until the murderer is caught? In fact, I'd be surprised if Vanessa and Ethan weren't feeling unsettled—especially about letting Carter roam freely unsupervised. We're all speculating that Flynn Gillis was murdered because he stepped on someone's toes, but we really don't *know* what the motivation was or if the killer will strike again. Or if it's somehow related to the bathtub killings. It's not safe right now."

"Pierce, you're scaring me."

He pulled her closer. "I'm sorry, but I don't think it would hurt for us all to be a little scared. And if the sheriff doesn't put a stop to these murders, tourism is bound to suffer. We could take a big financial hit too."

Zoe held tightly to Pierce's arm. Could she ever have imagined things getting this frightening—or this complicated?

CHAPTER 11

Late Thursday night, Adele sat in the window seat in her bedroom and looked up at the moon, which shone brightly through the live oak branches and formed strange shadows on the back lawn.

She glanced across the moonlit room at the delicate poster bed—so different from the bulky seventeenth-century English oak canopy bed she and Alfred had bought in the Cotswolds on one of their antiquing trips.

She had sold most of the Woodmore antiques in an estate sale and bought furniture more suitable for this smaller home. She settled on French Country decor—mostly because Zoe and Vanessa seemed so drawn to it. The new look proved warm and inviting, and everyone seemed comfortable and relaxed in her home. Why didn't she? Perhaps it was because all the tangible reminders of Alfred were gone now—except for the wedding portrait she kept on her nightstand.

She moved her gaze to the framed sepia photograph, barely visible by the light of the moon but vivid in her memory. Adele in her ivory peau de soie gown and lacy veil and Alfred in his gray morning coat and ascot—standing in the archway at the front door of Saint Francis Xavier Cathedral in Alexandria. Weren't they a sight to behold—young, passionate, so full of themselves? They had little need of anyone besides each other. By the time they decided they wanted a child, they had trouble conceiving. And when they finally did, Adele lost the baby in the third trimester—a girl. Her anger and disappointment with God was even more crippling than the grief. Why had He taken from her the thing she wanted most—the one thing money couldn't buy? She and Alfred mourned until they had no tears left. They wanted to conceive again, but it never happened, so they traveled the world, rubbing elbows with the rich and famous and living the life others only dream about.

Adele sighed. Hadn't the Lord known all along that her anger over not being able to bear a child would drive her away from Him for a time—but that she would return to Him spiritually barren and needy and ready for a relationship with Him?

Would she have ever given her heart to Jesus and trusted Him as her Lord and Savior if she hadn't experienced the emptiness that nothing else could fill? She'd had it all—the finest designer fashions, the richest food, the most exotic vacations. A husband who adored her. Perfect health. A magnificent home on a sprawling estate. Servants to tend to her every need: a maid, a chauffeur, a cook, a seamstress. Anything she wanted was hers—except a child.

She went over and sat on the side of the bed, feeling a twinge of the shame that she had given to God long ago. How many people had she hurt in the years that followed her baby's death? It had been hard to accept that she lost an infant daughter she would never know. Her attitude turned caustic—not with Alfred, but with the hired help. She was impatient with anything less than perfection. She didn't fire people. She tormented them. Belittled them. Alfred had to pay a high price to keep people willing to put up with her relentless perfectionism.

And then he died of a heart attack. He kissed her good-bye one morning and went to play golf. She got a call later that he was gone. Died on the way to the hospital—while she thumbed through the latest issue of *Better Homes and Gardens,* totally unaware that her soul mate had taken his last breath.

Adele turned on the lamp. She picked up the picture and looked for a moment into Alfred's eyes, then held the frame to her heart. If her baby's death had driven her away from God, wasn't it Alfred's death that had brought her back? One night, while she was in the throes of grief and despair, she had watched a Billy Graham crusade on TV. His message of hope touched something deep inside her, compelling her to confess her corrosive attitude and all the emotional wounds she had inflicted on others—and ask God's forgiveness. She invited Jesus into her heart and was filled to overflowing with His grace.

Adele was a changed woman. Was it anything short of a miracle that her critical spirit had turned to genuine affection? Over time, she sought out the people she had hurt and apologized for her harsh words. And instead of pointing out the faults of those in her employ, she began to bring out the best. She came to regard them as extended family, even though her peers cautioned that fraternizing with the help was foolish and that someday it would cost her. But she hadn't seen it coming—and certainly not from Zoe, the most trusted member of her household staff.

Adele dismissed a pang of sadness. Why dig up unpleasant memories? She had forgiven Zoe's transgression. And hadn't the Lord used the painful truth to teach everyone involved the depths of His grace?

Grace. Adele smiled without meaning to. It was significant that Zoe and Pierce named their daughter Grace, and perhaps, when the child was old enough to understand, they would tell her why.

Adele yawned and captured it with her hand. How could she be this tired and still unable to fall asleep? Her treatment of Flynn Gillis was weighing on her. Isabel and Zoe had absolved her of guilt, but would the Lord agree that there was nothing more she could have done to show kindness to this young man?

She could still see Flynn helping Murray move her furniture out of the bedroom. He was cocky. And unkempt. But he had been a soul in need of love, just like everyone else. Why hadn't she reached out to him with kindness instead of keeping her distance and feeling relieved when he finally left? Hadn't she promised the Lord that she would extend to others the amazing grace He had bestowed on her—the most unworthy of all?

A knock at the door startled her.

"Mrs. Woodmore? Are you all right?"

"Come in, Isabel."

The door opened, and Isabel, dressed in her yellow nightgown, filled the doorway. "I noticed your light was on. Is everything okay?"

"Yes. Yes. I'm fine. I just can't sleep."

"Why don't you take something on nights like this? You're having entirely too many of them."

"I've gone eighty-six years without being dependent on pills. I don't intend to start now."

"I could get you a cup of warm milk," Isabel said. "That's *my* drug of choice."

Adele didn't especially like warm milk, but she didn't want to deny Isabel the blessing of helping her.

"Very well, hon. Maybe it will help. I really do need to sleep. I have to be up and presentable by nine, since the computer desk is being delivered. And I really don't want to be exhausted when Murray comes to take me shopping."

A long moment of silence registered Isabel's disapproval, and then she turned and walked toward the kitchen.

Adele slipped on her robe and slippers, trying not to be annoyed with Isabel's stubbornness and remembering their earlier conversation.

"You did a background check on me first," Isabel had said, *"and I don't blame you one bit. You don't know anything about these men except what they've told you."*

Isabel had a point. Perhaps doing a background check on Noah and Murray couldn't hurt. After all, she had done that routinely with live-in staff over the years. No one needed to know, and everything she learned would be kept in strictest confidence. In the meantime, she wasn't going to distance herself from Noah and Murray the way she had with Flynn Gillis. Isabel would just have to live with it.

CHAPTER 12

Adele floated somewhere between sleep and wakefulness, aware of a chirping sound that kept getting louder. She turned over in bed and looked on the windowsill. *A Carolina wren.*

She smiled. Who needed an alarm to wake up when nature was so willing to be involved? She sat up on the side of her bed and held out her arms and stretched. By the end of the day, she would own a computer and know how to send email. Not bad for an octogenarian.

Good morning, Lord. Guard my words today and help me to be kind to all those You put in my path.

She spotted a note she had written to herself just before she went to bed. It was almost eight. Danny would already have been up for hours. She picked up the phone and dialed his number.

"Danny Clinton."

"Hello, Danny. It's Adele."

"Well, hello, my queen. What can I do for you today?"

"I've befriended two men who currently live at a halfway house here in Les Barbes. One takes care of my lawn; the other does odd jobs for me. Both were homeless and are getting back on their feet, and neither is eager to talk about his life. And since they're both at my home quite often, it probably couldn't hurt for me to know more about them."

"Of course," Danny said. "How deep shall I dig?"

"I'd like to know where they've worked. And whether they have any family. I'd like to know if they've ever been arrested, though they couldn't be living at Haven House if they were convicted felons."

"Should be easy enough to find out."

"When can you start, Danny?"

"I've got a few irons in the fire, but I'll try to have something for you in a week or so. It's always a pleasure working for you."

"How many years has it been now?"

"Twenty. I know this because you called while I was on my way to my fortieth birthday bash."

Adele smiled. "Oh, that's right. I had forgotten."

"So who am I investigating?"

"The first man is Noah Washington. Middle-aged African-American. He says he lived in the ninth ward in New Orleans and lost everything in Katrina. Claims he had his own landscaping business there. Are you getting this?"

"Yes, ma'am, I'm recording. Go ahead."

Adele looked at the notes she'd made. "Now he's working at Langley Manor for Vanessa and Ethan Langley, the proprietors. One of his ancestors was a slave there. I know the Langleys, but I don't feel comfortable asking them about him and don't want them to know anything about this."

"Understood. Who's the other fellow?"

"Murray Hamelin. He's much younger—about thirty. Caucasian. Single. I'm pretty sure he's from Lafayette. He's a whiz with computers.

Very good with his hands and can do just about anything around the house—paint, repair, install. If only I'd had someone that versatile working for me at Woodmore. That's really all I know about him."

"Do these men drive?"

"Yes. But I'm no good with vehicles. They both drive older-model trucks. Murray's is a white Ford, I think."

"Good. Anything else?"

Adele doodled stars on the notes she had made. "Perhaps you heard about the young man from Haven House who was found murdered yesterday?"

"I didn't make the connection until just now. But yeah. I sure did."

"Of course, Noah and Murray knew him. And since his body was discovered on the Langleys' property where Noah works, the authorities questioned Noah at length."

"I heard that. The sheriff told the media he was just a person of interest."

"I'm never quite sure what that means," Adele said. "But all the men at Haven House were questioned by sheriff's deputies."

"Anything else I should know?"

"I can't think of anything."

"Well, if you do, call. Otherwise, I'll get back to you as soon as I know something."

"Thank you, Danny. I know you'll be discreet."

"Always."

As Adele hung up the phone, her cheeks burned. Why did she feel as if she was snooping? She had paid Danny to investigate dozens of potential employees over the years. It was good business.

But she wasn't doing this to satisfy Isabel or to feel safer. She didn't consider Noah or Murray to be a threat. Wasn't she doing this was because she was curious about what had caused them to become homeless?

❧

Jude headed for his office after the Friday-morning briefing and planned to tackle the mound of paperwork that had been piling up since Monday when the first murder victim was found.

Just as he anticipated, the community seemed relatively disinterested in the victim from the halfway house. But there was heavy speculating—even bets being placed—on who the next victim of the Bathtub Killer might be. As offensive as that was, it wasn't surprising. Who in Les Barbes hadn't been touched in some way by the layoffs and foreclosures? Cynicism ran deep, even among his detectives.

He spotted Chief Detective Gil Marcel at the water fountain and hurried over to him.

"I've been looking for you!" Jude said, aware that his voice had gone up a decibel.

"Sorry, I just got back from the lab," Gil said. "What's up?"

Jude got right in Gil's face. "What's this I hear about your detectives placing bets on who's going to be the next victim of the Bathtub Killer?"

"They were just clowning around."

"*Clowning around?* We're public servants. Our job is to protect the public so there *isn't* another victim! For crying out loud, Gil. Your people take their cues from you. What were you thinking?"

Jude could feel his own breath bouncing off Gil's face. "I want you to put a stop to this right now. Any personal disdain for the victims is irrelevant and should be kept to ourselves. You're a professional! Either you start acting like it, or I'll find someone who will. Is that clear?"

"Yes, sir."

Jude stormed down the hall and into his office. He flopped in his desk chair, his temples throbbing.

Half a minute later, there was a knock at the door. He looked up and saw Aimee standing in the doorway. *Not now.*

"You okay, Sheriff?"

"I will be." Jude wiped the perspiration off his upper lip. "Is it too much to expect my chief detective to set a good example?"

"No," Aimee said. "He was out of line. You were right to call him on it. I was just about to talk to him myself when you stepped in."

"How Gil—or any of us—feels about the victims is irrelevant! We need to stay focused!"

"Yes, sir. You made that abundantly clear."

Sir? Jude took a few moments to calm down, then lifted his gaze. "Look, I know I'm edgy. It's going to be a long day unless we get something useful back from the lab. Did you need anything else?"

"Not really. I overheard your run-in with Gil and was just checking on you."

"I'm sure everyone on this entire floor heard my run-in with Gil. You think I was too hard on him?"

Aimee came in, shut the door behind her, and sat in the chair next to his desk. "You were right to set him straight. Allowing deputies to bet on who the next victim might be is over the top. He's lucky you didn't suspend him. But you should know that Gil's brother was laid off at the sugar refinery and has been without a job for eighteen months. And Deputy Castille's sister—a single mom with three kids—was laid off ten months ago and is still looking for a job that pays her a living wage. The majority of people in this town and in this department aren't going to shed a tear that these two CEOs are dead."

Jude bit his lip. *Let her have her say.*

"But as you pointed out, Sheriff, it's not our job to voice our opinion or express our sarcasm. Our job is to do everything in our power to see that the killer is stopped and brought to justice. And to help protect those who are high-probability targets."

"That's right. And I need your help to keep everyone focused." Jude glanced out the window at the white pillars on the courthouse. "We need to brace ourselves for the likelihood that the Bathtub Killer isn't done. We're assuming he's targeting CEOs—but we don't know that. All we really know for sure is that no one is safe until the killer is locked up."

⚜

Murray came downstairs from his dorm room at Haven House and saw Father Vince in the living room.

"Did you sleep well?" Father Vince asked.

"Not really." Murray put his hands in the pockets of his cargo pants. "I can't shake what happened to Flynn. The guy was irritating, but I sure didn't wish him dead. How's Noah?"

"He could use some encouragement." Father Vince nodded toward the dining room. "He's hardly said a word to anyone."

"Probably embarrassed, don't you think? Having the cops grill him all day for a murder he didn't commit couldn't have been easy."

"I'm sure it wasn't," Father Vince said. "And even though the sheriff let him go, he's still considered a person of interest."

"Noah's not capable of murder."

Father Vince's eyebrows formed one bushy line that almost disappeared under the dark, wispy curls that lay on his forehead. "I'm glad to hear you say that, Murray. Maybe you should say it directly to him."

"I did. He's upset with me for telling the deputies about his run-in with Flynn and for joking around about Flynn not coming back."

"Yes." Father Vince met his gaze. "He thinks you should've had his back."

"He's right. I explained to Noah that I was intimidated by the authorities. I've never been questioned about a murder before. But there's no way he's capable of killing anybody. I did tell the deputies that."

"A kind word would probably go a long way." Father Vince glanced into the dining room where Noah sat alone.

"I doubt he's speaking to me."

Father Vince patted his back. "He may not speak, but he'll listen."

Murray went out to the kitchen and filled his plate with scrambled eggs, sausage, hash browns, and biscuits, then grabbed a banana and went out to the dining room.

"Mind if I sit with you?" he said to Noah.

"Suit yourself." Noah took a bite of sausage, his plate almost empty.

Murray set his plate at the end of the table, pulled out the chair, and sat across from Noah. "I didn't sleep. How about you?"

"If you didn't sleep, then you already know the answer. Don't patronize me."

"I'm just making small talk. Isn't that what we always do?"

Noah put down his fork, his angry dark eyes glaring. "The last time we small-talked, you used it against me."

"I said I was sorry, man. Cops intimidate me."

"Try bein' black."

"Look, I'm sorry they were tough on you. I wasn't thinking about how the deputies would use what I said. I was just trying to make them understand that none of us liked Flynn. That's all."

"Well, you succeeded." Noah stuffed half a biscuit into his mouth.

Murray sprinkled salt and pepper on his eggs and let a long moment of silence pass before continuing. "So are you still working for the Langleys?"

"Yeah. At least *they* believed I had nothin' to do with Flynn's death. Vanessa kept tryin' to get me a lawyer."

"Not a bad idea."

Noah waved his hand. "I don't need a lawyer. I'll speak for myself. I've got nothin' to hide."

"If push comes to shove, everyone here will stand by you. There's not a man here who thinks you did it, including Father Vince. That's got to mean something."

Noah's eyes suddenly glistened, and he kept eating.

"There's no way we're letting you go down for this."

"There's nothin' you could do about it if the sheriff thinks I'm guilty."

"He let you go, didn't he? The sheriff wouldn't have done that if he had anything on you."

"How much do you think he needs?" Noah shot him a defiant look. "I'm a black man with strong hands, and there's a strangled white victim—that everyone knew I didn't like, and I'd just told to watch his back—found on the property where I work."

"It's all circumstantial."

"Plenty o' black men have been convicted for less."

"But *nobody* liked Flynn. He could've had an altercation with anyone—even someone at that bar where he hangs out."

"Well, his body ended up in the bayou, just 'bout a football field away from my toolshed."

"You're going to get through this," Murray said. "The sheriff has to follow protocol. But in the end, your name will be cleared."

Noah buttered the other half of his biscuit. "Did you hear they found Father Vince's Camry?"

"No. Where?"

"In the back parking lot at the Den. No big surprise."

"Good," Murray said. "They ought to get some DNA or something that'll help them find whoever killed Flynn. Do they think he was killed in the car?"

"Father Vince didn't say. Just that the authorities have his car and are checking it for trace evidence and fingerprints."

"If you weren't in the car, they can't nail you for it, right?"

"Just can't resist those *ifs*, can you?" Noah stuffed the last bite of biscuit into his mouth and stood.

"Come on, man. You know what I mean."

"I've got to go to work," Noah said. "Do me a favor and don't try to defend me to the cops. Every time you open your mouth, I sound guilty."

CHAPTER 13

Vanessa finished setting out a generous breakfast buffet for her guests and making preparations for andouille sausage and shrimp crepes that lived up to the advertisement posted on the Langley Manor website. She had plenty of fresh blueberries, strawberries, bananas, and fried apples for those who preferred fruit crepes. For the less adventuresome guests, she provided scrambled eggs and bacon and a variety of cereals, including her own special granola mix. She was also set up to make beignets.

Breakfast would be served on the Villeroy and Boch tableware—Cottage pattern—that Ethan's family had gone in together and bought them for their grand opening. The luscious design of cherries, blueberries, and raspberries on a white background made it a homey complement to the elegant navy walls and white crown molding in the dining room.

The anniversary clock on the mantle chimed eight times. She smiled. Carter would be saying the Pledge of Allegiance, starting another fun morning at day camp. Ethan would be sitting down for his first counseling session.

Noah was late. Had he decided he needed the day off to recover from yesterday's interrogation? Poor guy. Anything that needed to be done on the grounds could certainly wait a day or two. Should she call him? Or just wait until he was ready to venture out?

She heard the kitchen door open, and a few seconds later, Noah stood in the doorway of the dining room.

"You *did* come!"

"Mornin', Vanessa."

She went over and put her arms around him. "I'm so glad you're here. How're you doing?" She pushed back and looked into his sad brown eyes. "Is the sheriff finished questioning you?"

"Far as I know. I told him everything I told you—over and over and over. I was so glad to finally get out o' there."

"Have you had breakfast?" Vanessa took a step back. "I'll be glad to make you crepes."

"Thanks, but I had a big breakfast. I'm goin' to prune the roses. I'll be in the flower garden, if you need me." He turned to go.

"Noah, wait …" She gently gripped his arm. "I don't know what happened to Flynn. Or why his body was put in our bayou. But I know *you.* You're a gentle, hardworking, honest man who couldn't possibly have had anything to do with it."

"I appreciate your confidence, Vanessa. Unfortunately, the authorities aren't that interested in your opinion o' me. Truth is, I didn't like Flynn one bit."

"Did anyone? That doesn't mean you killed him."

"The suspicion's been raised. It's not just goin' away."

"I have to wonder if they'd be as suspicious if you were white."

Noah shrugged. "It'd be easy to blame it on race. But I doubt the sheriff would care if I was purple. The facts are what they are. He's just goin' to have to sort them out."

"You should have legal counsel."

"That'd just make me look more suspicious."

⚜

Zoe took Grace's tiny hand and walked across the dining room at Zoe B's and stopped at the table by the window. Grace climbed into her booster seat in the chair next to Father Sam and across from Tex and Hebert.

"Ah, dere's our *petite fille."* Hebert reached over and tickled her chin. "How's our little girl dis morning?"

"I not little girl." Grace pointed to herself. "I *big* girl."

Tex laughed. "Atta girl. Talk that Texas talk."

Zoe set a bowl of fruit and cheese slices on the table in front of Grace. "She wanted to have her morning snack down here so she could watch you fellas play checkers."

"She likes to see ol' Hebert whip everybody. Isn't dat right, *honeychile?"*

"Her babysitter will be here in thirty minutes." Zoe glanced out the window and saw Savannah standing on the sidewalk, talking on her cell phone. "Which is good because she really needs a nap."

Grace shook her blonde curls. "No *fais do do*. I not sleepy."

"You need your beauty sleep," Hebert said. "All princesses need lots o' sleep. Dat's how dey stay so pretty. I don't take naps—and jus' look at dis wrinkled face."

Tex laughed out loud. "Think pushin' a hundred had somethin' to do with it?"

"By da way"—Hebert looked up at Zoe—"is dere any news on Noah's situation?"

"Just that Jude let him go. He can't possibly be a serious suspect. He wouldn't hurt a flea."

"You're partial," Tex said. "I don't think you can say that with any assurance. Don't get me wrong, I like Noah. I can't see him doin' it either. But the facts have to be addressed."

"It's all circumstantial," Zoe said. "There's not a shred of evidence that Noah was even with Flynn the night it happened."

"No one at Haven House remembers seein' him," Tex said. "That's not in his favor."

Savannah came in the front door, the color gone from her face. She walked past the table as if she didn't see them.

"Excuse me, guys." Zoe followed Savannah into the kitchen and finally caught up with her. "Hey, you okay?"

Savannah stopped. She seemed to stare at nothing and didn't acknowledge Zoe's presence.

"What's wrong, honey? What is it?"

"Aunt Nicole … she … she's dead. He killed her … just like the others." Savannah's eyes were blue pools. "He spray painted the number three on—"

Savannah's knees buckled, and Zoe grabbed her arm.

"Pierce! Dempsey! Somebody! We need help."

Within seconds, Pierce and Dempsey Tanner, the sous-chef, came running toward them, each wiping his hands with a towel.

"Can you get Savannah a chair?" Zoe said. "She's about to collapse."

Dempsey helped hold Savannah up while Pierce darted over to the utility closet, took out a folding chair, and placed it behind the distraught waitress. Zoe and Dempsey lowered her into a sitting position.

"What *happened?"* Pierce said.

"I think her aunt Nicole was the third victim of the Bathtub Killer."

"What?" Dempsey put his hands to his temples. "Man, what's going on in this town?"

"Was she the aunt who always orders my Cajun shrimp?" Pierce said. "And who works for Aubry Computer Systems?"

Savannah gave a weak nod. "She owns it."

Zoe's gaze met Pierce's. "Nicole's in here at least once a week. The last time, she had Father Sam in stitches."

A tear spilled down Savannah's cheek. "I just saw her over the weekend. She took me shopping. She loved buying me clothes. But she would never let me tell anyone that she did it. I need to call Benson and tell him before he hears it on the news."

Zoe sighed, her heart aching for Savannah, her mind flashing back to the last time Nicole Aubry came into Zoe B's. She sat at the table across the aisle from Father Sam, Hebert, and Tex. She was dressed in designer jeans and a pink tank top. Unpretentious. Funny. She told a joke about a priest and a mule that made Father Sam laugh so hard he lost his breath. Such a delight.

"We were all waiting for the other shoe to drop," Zoe heard herself say. "But I never dreamed it would be so close to home."

⚜

Adele hung up the phone and sat at the table in the sunroom, her hands folded, her heart heavy. She realized someone was talking to her and looked up into Isabel's face.

"The new computer desk looks really nice. Are you pleased?" Isabel handed her the mail.

"Yes, I believe it's going to work out nicely, hon." Adele pushed the mail aside. "That was Zoe on the phone—with horrible news."

"What now?"

"The Bathtub Killer has claimed another victim. This time it was Savannah's aunt Nicole."

"Savannah at Zoe B's?"

Adele nodded. "Nicole was divorced. No children. But she and Savannah were close. Zoe said the poor thing just found out and is devastated, as you might imagine. I met Nicole at Zoe B's when I first moved here. She and Savannah invited me to join them at their table for dinner." Adele smiled. "They ordered all kinds of fancy hors d'oeuvres I'd never even heard of before. I sampled them all. Nicole was hilarious. A ball of fire. We giggled like a bunch of schoolgirls. I can't imagine anyone wanting to kill such a delightful lady."

"Was her aunt killed the same way as the others?"

"Yes." Adele sighed. "Nicole was drugged and then drowned in the bathtub, while still dressed in her business clothes. Her safe was empty. No one seems to know how much the killer made off with. Goodness! If I thought money would stop him, I'd pay him off myself. I wonder if the killer has any idea what he's taken from Savannah. The two of them were so close. I had a favorite aunt growing up. I can't imagine how I would've felt if something this horrible had happened to her."

"Do they know what time she was killed?"

"Between five and six last night. Nicole lived alone. Her assistant got worried when she didn't show up for work and didn't answer her phone or call back. She went over to her house and found the door ajar and her boss dead. It's dreadful. Simply dreadful. Sheriff's deputies are there now, investigating."

"I don't feel safe in this town anymore," Isabel said.

"It doesn't seem to me that the general public is being targeted. All three victims were executives in their businesses."

"No one really knows who he's after—or why. It's all speculation."

"I suppose you're right."

"Doesn't it scare you—just a little? He's targeting the wealthy."

Adele waved her hand. "I'm the Lord's. I can't worry about all the dangers that might be lurking. I don't want to spend what's left of my life in fear."

"Neither do I." Isabel folded her arms. "I'd feel a lot better if we had deadbolt locks on the doors."

"All right. When Murray takes me computer shopping this afternoon, I'll see if he'll stop by the hardware store and get deadbolts for the front and back doors."

Jude watched as the men from the coroner's office zipped up the bag holding Nicole Aubry's body. Her lifeless eyes held a blank stare, and yet they seemed to look right through him. If only she could tell him what happened.

"She wasn't a high-profile CEO," Aimee said. "Why go after her?"

"I want the names of everyone who's worked for her for the past five years. And let's single out the names of those who quit, got fired, or were laid off. Let's compare names with employees and customers of the other two. There has to be a connection."

"That's a tall order, Sheriff. It's possible the killer is just choosing his victims at random."

Jude pursed his lips. "Maybe. But more than likely, we've got a serial killer whose rage is tied to *these* specific victims. There has to be a connection beyond the obvious. I mean, he could be a disgruntled employee, but I would expect him to walk in shooting and take out as many people as he could before he turned the gun on himself. This perp drugs his victims so they're awake and aware that he's drowning them. He wants control, yet he doesn't torture them—at least not physically. We didn't even find defensive wounds on the victims."

Aimee folded her arms across her chest. "So what are you thinking?"

"I'm thinking he drugs the victims and renders them helpless so he can unload his grievances and make them understand what they're being punished for. He wants these people to pay."

"Pay for what?"

"That's what we need to find out. Get that list, and let's get a team together to match names. Maybe we'll get a break."

⁂

Adele sat on the torn passenger seat of Murray's Ford truck, relishing the scenic ride past the courthouse and thinking back on the many Jeep rides she'd enjoyed with Alfred.

"I would've tried to borrow Father Vince's Camry," Murray said, "but the sheriff still has it. I hope you're not too uncomfortable."

"I'm fine," Adele said. "I *like* the view from up here. Until I moved here six months ago, I rode in the backseat of a Rolls-Royce. Not terribly scenic."

"You had a Rolls?"

Adele smiled. "A Silver Shadow. Alfred bought it in 1970, and it still ran just fine when I sold it in the estate sale. Come to find out, it was a collector's car."

The corners of Murray's mouth twitched. "You've probably sunk to an all-time low, riding around in this old rattletrap. I bought it for next to nothing. And once I get on my feet, I'll get a newer one."

"Nonsense. This is an adventure." Adele chuckled. "Alfred is probably laughing his head off. We always loved doing things our friends didn't."

"Like what?"

"Skydiving. Scuba diving. Deep-sea fishing. I was much younger then. Oh my, we did have a glorious time at the barrier reef in Australia. We even backpacked in the outback."

"Wow," Murray said. "I'd love to have those adventures under my belt. What else?"

"Well, let see … we hiked in the jungles of Costa Rica and Brazil—and took a houseboat trip on the Amazon River. We rode the donkeys down to the bottom of the Grand Canyon. We went mountain climbing in the Rockies, the Andes, and the Himalayas." Adele smiled without meaning to. "You don't want to hear all this."

"I do! Tell me more. What adventure did you enjoy the most?"

"Oh my. How can I compare them? They were all so different. I think our African safaris were the most memorable because we saw so many beautiful animals in the wild. The lions were my favorite. Nowadays, everyone is privy to these magnificent sights because of the fine nature documentaries. But in our day, it was a privilege, and only those wealthy enough to pay for a guide and a crew got to see such things." Adele paused for a moment and let an unexpected pang of grief pass. "My Alfred had an insatiable wanderlust. I picked up the bug, and we just never got weary of traveling. We even took a yearlong cruise around the world."

Murray turned the truck onto Primeaux. "I can't imagine having that kind of money to spend."

"We had far more than we could ever spend on ourselves. Alfred started a foundation so we could give some of it away. After a while, there just wasn't much left that could *oooh* and *ahhh* us, if you know what I'm saying. It became just as exciting to give money to people or causes that were special to us. Alfred liked having hospital wings and college buildings named after him. So did I. But after he died, I lost interest in everything for a long time—until I found a relationship with God. I started giving again, but I stopped letting the recipient know where the money came from. It was much more fun imagining their surprise—or seeing it firsthand and playing dumb. Truly a joy."

"You're an amazing woman, Adele."

"Hardly. God has given me much, and much is required. It's quite simple, really."

"So you believe in God?"

"I most certainly do. Do you?"

Murray's hands gripped the steering wheel. "I believe He's there. But He doesn't seem to care much about human suffering."

"I felt that way—after I lost my baby. I was eight months pregnant and went into labor. The baby was stillborn. She had a heart defect."

"Sorry. That must've been hard."

"Devastating. It took Alfred and me three years to get over the debilitating grief. We wanted children, but I never conceived again. We talked very little about it. We filled that void with our adventures. And we did have fun. But underneath the smiles was an aching void. It seemed cruel to me that God gave me anything I wanted, except the one thing I wanted most—to have a baby. I would have traded it all for a child."

"Did you ever consider adopting?"

"*I* did. Alfred didn't. His family put a lot of stock in bloodline. I never quite understood why, but I accepted it."

"Do you regret it?"

Adele felt a tinge of sadness. "Yes and no. I've often wondered if his family would have overcome the bloodline issue, especially if we'd adopted a daughter, who would have probably married and changed her name. But everything happens for a reason."

"You really believe that?"

Adele looked over at Murray. "Yes, I do."

"What good reason could there be for you losing a baby and going through all that heartache?"

"Only the Lord knows for sure. But I'm pretty certain that I wouldn't have looked for God if I'd had everything my heart desired."

Murray didn't say anything, but she noticed his jaw was clenched.

"Do you feel God has let you down, hon?"

"He let my parents die. So yeah. I guess I do."

"Would it help to talk about it?"

"It never does. I just get depressed. Ah, here we are." Murray pulled into the parking lot at Best Buy. "We're in luck. I see a spot right by the door."

Adele bit her lip. She had a million questions but didn't want to press him. She would just wait and see what Danny found out.

CHAPTER 14

Adele sat at her new desk and studied the screen on her laptop, wondering if anything Murray taught her would make sense an hour from now.

"All right, then," she said. "How do I send email?"

Murray smiled. "First you click on the email icon. It's that little envelope. Go ahead."

Adele clicked the icon, and the screen changed. "What happened? Oh dear—I'm not sure I'm cut out for this."

"Sure you are. Let me show you. It's really easy."

She let Murray have the mouse and watched as he clicked on Create Mail. The screen changed again. He inserted Zoe's email address on the line marked *To*.

"There you go," Murray said. "Just type your message."

Adele placed her hands on the keys. This was nothing like her old Royal typewriter. "I do hope I remember how to type. I believe it's a bit like riding a bicycle. My mind hasn't forgotten how. Now if these wrinkled old hands will just cooperate."

"You don't have to press hard at all. The touch is going to seem different. Go ahead. Try it. If you make a mistake you can just back it up and erase it."

Adele moved her fingers gingerly and typed the words as she spoke them. "'Dear Zoe, I guess if you are reading this, you know what I am doing. Murray is sitting here with me, teaching me how to use my new laptop. Why don't you be the first to send me email? Love, Adele.' Well, forever more. I did it! How do I send it?"

Murray seemed both amused and pleased. "You click the Send button up there on the left side of the screen."

Adele did as Murray told her, and the message disappeared. "Oh no! What happened?"

"You sent it. It's supposed to disappear. Zoe will probably be reading it any moment."

"Well, if that doesn't beat all!" She looked over at Murray. "Thank you for everything. This has been the best adventure I've had in years."

"I'm glad. I'll turn on the spell-check once you have this mastered. But for now, you're good to go. You can send Zoe or Vanessa email. Once you have more addresses, we can add them to your address book."

"This wasn't nearly as hard as I envisioned," Adele said.

"There's so much more I can show you once you're comfortable with it. Before long, you'll be shopping online."

"Heavens to Betsy, I never thought I'd live to see the day when *I'd* be working at a computer. I do believe I have *arrived.*"

Murray laughed, his face beaming. "I haven't had this much fun in a long time. You remind me so much of Grandma Sophie. She was my dad's mom. I was an only child, and she let me stay with her after school and in the summers when my parents had to work. She was a blast. I preferred her company to just about anybody."

Your father's mother was named Sophie. That's a start. "Has she passed?"

Murray's grin flatlined. "Yes. She caught the flu and developed complications. Everyone in my family had it, but I think she caught it from me. Mom said she could've gotten it anywhere. But I know she didn't."

"How old were you when she passed?"

"Twelve. I remember because it was my birthday. That was eighteen years ago, and I still get sad on my birthday."

So you're thirty. "Yes, I could see how you would. I'm so sorry you had to experience that. And then your parents' dying too."

It seemed as though a dark cloud enveloped Murray, and he seemed far away for half a minute. Finally he said, "Would you mind if we change the subject? This kind of talk always drags me down."

"Of course it does. What was I thinking?"

The computer made a dinging sound.

"Oh dear, is something wrong?" Adele said.

"Absolutely not. See that?" Murray pointed to the name in the inbox. "Zoe Broussard. You've got email."

Adele saw Isabel standing in the doorway. "Come in and take a look. I've got email. Can you believe it?"

"Dr. Carey's office called. They can work you in for a physical at nine a.m. on the twenty-ninth. I wrote it on the calendar," Isabel said.

"Thank you, hon. You should come sit with us and see how this works. We're having a grand time."

"I can't." Isabel's tone was flat. "I need to go fold the bed linens while they're still warm. You should have Murray fix the leak in the sprinkler, as long as he's here."

"No need," Adele said. "Noah can do that."

"I'll be happy to take a look at it," Murray said.

"Let's have our praline cake and lemonade first." Adele locked gazes with Isabel. "Would you bring it to us now—in the sunroom?"

"Yes, ma'am."

Isabel's scowl was insulting. Adele refrained from correcting her in front of Murray but decided she couldn't let the matter go unaddressed.

⚜

Zoe sat at her desk in the office, texting Pierce. *Just got an email from Adele. How fun is that?*

She sat back, her arms folded, and looked at the framed picture of Adele holding baby Grace. Adele was dressed in an ivory silk skirt and jacket, Grace in her christening gown. What a joy it was—and a miracle—that Adele was living here in Les Barbes, not only a beloved family friend but the perfect godmother for Grace. If Adele had been less of a person, mightn't Zoe's stealing from her have turned her into a bitter, vengeful woman? Instead, she was the dearest, most forgiving and accepting person Zoe had ever known.

Zoe's cell phone rang. She read the screen, then pressed the Talk button. "Hey, sweet lady."

"Isn't this fun?" Adele said.

"Definitely. You're a modern woman now."

"Murray took me to Best Buy and we picked out a laptop and some paraphernalia to go with it." Adele sounded almost giddy. "Then we came home, and he set everything up. I just typed an email and clicked the Send button. Heavens, if I'd known it was this easy, I would have gotten a computer long ago."

"Has Murray left?"

"Not yet. He's offered to take a look at my sprinkler before he leaves. But right now, we're in the sunroom, enjoying a cold glass of fresh-squeezed lemonade and a piece of your praline cake Isabel picked up earlier."

"So Isabel's there?"

"She's in the kitchen. Did you need to talk with her?"

"No." *But Pierce is going to ask me.* "I'm just glad she's there to help you. It's so wonderful having you living here in Les Barbes."

"For me, too. All right, I guess I'd better get off, lest I seem rude to my guest."

"I'll talk to you later," Zoe said.

"Bye for now, hon. Hug Pierce and Grace for me."

"I will."

Zoe ended the call and promptly got another. It was Pierce. "Hey there."

"So Adele is up and running," Pierce said. "It'll be fun for her to play online. Are you going to show her how?"

"Murray's doing just fine without my help. Those two have really hit it off. He's teaching her everything she needs to know. She said they were enjoying lemonade and a piece of your praline cake. And then he's going to check her sprinkler before he leaves."

Pierce's silence registered his disapproval. Finally he said, "Is Isabel home?"

"Yes, she's there. You should've heard the excitement in Adele's voice, Pierce. She sounded like a schoolgirl."

"That's because she's sweet and naive and trusts everyone. You know how I feel about her socializing with guys from Haven House."

Zoe's voice went up an octave. "Excuse me, but Noah's from Haven House. And he's a gem."

"He's also the person of interest in Flynn Gillis's murder."

"You don't believe for one minute he had anything to do with that."

"Not really. But it just reinforces my point that even law enforcement is suspicious of those men. I wish Adele would keep her distance."

"So noted. I need to finish the ordering." Zoe hated that she sounded terse.

"And I need to go make more gumbo. I'm not working tonight. Dempsey's running the kitchen. Maybe we can go out somewhere for dinner."

"Sure. You decide. I'm just here in the office, finishing up. Maddie's got Grace until five. They went to the park."

"You're comfortable with her taking Grace out of the building?"

"Pierce, don't you dare get paranoid on this. Maddie Lyons is a student at the junior college. I interviewed her *with* her parents present. She's just a nice, responsible kid who would love to babysit and earn some college money. If you'd spent any time with her at all, you'd agree with me."

Pierce sighed. "Am I that bad?"

"You're *worse* than bad. If you choose *not* to be involved in the process of selecting a babysitter, at least have the courtesy not to second-guess my decision. I think Maddie is perfect for the job, and I don't worry for a moment when I leave Grace with her."

"I do trust your judgment. I'm sorry. I don't know why I get like this."

"You need to trust Adele's judgment too. If she hadn't taken a chance on me, just think how different our lives would be."

⚜

Adele went in her bedroom and shut the door. She picked up the phone and called Danny Clinton's number. She let it ring four times, and the answering machine went on.

Hello, this is Danny. I'm not available. Leave—"This is Danny."

"Is that really you?" she said.

"It's me." Danny sounded out of breath. "I heard my phone ringing and realized I'd left it in the other room. What can I do for you, Adele?"

"I have some information on Murray Hamelin that might help you do the background check."

"Great. Let's have it."

"I was right about his age. He *is* thirty. And his parents *are* deceased. He also told me his paternal grandmother's name was Sophie. She died eighteen years ago of complications from the flu."

"Can I ask you a dumb question?" Danny said.

"You don't ask dumb questions, hon. But go ahead."

"Why would a guy you hired to do odd jobs be talking to you about his grandmother?"

"Oh, we had the best time talking this afternoon. We went to Best Buy so I could buy a laptop, then he came back and set it up for me. We just chatted on and on about all sorts of things. He said

I remind him of his grandma Sophie. I don't know that she's the key to anything, but it's information I didn't have yesterday."

"Thanks. It might help."

"Why does it feel as if we're spying on Murray?"

"Because we are?" There was a smile in Danny's voice.

"Is it really considered spying that I want to know more about a person so that I can understand him? I'm not doing this to be nosy."

"Of course not. It's a safety issue." There was that smile in his voice again. "I haven't had a chance to start checking on Noah Washington or Murray Hamelin just yet. But soon. I'll get back with you when I have something. Now that you have email, do you want to get updates that way?"

"Heavens, no. I'm not that good at it yet," she said. "Let's just do this the way we always do. When you're finished doing the background checks, call me."

"Good enough. I'll be in touch."

"Thanks, Danny."

Adele sat quietly on the side of the bed, the aroma of Isabel's homemade chicken and dumplings wafting under her nose. Hadn't God always brought people into her life for a reason? Some, like Zoe, had taken advantage of her and caused her sorrow. But hadn't her sorrow been turned into joy?

She was inexplicably drawn to Noah and Murray. Should she be worried they were going to take advantage of her too? Did God want her to play it safe? Or was He testing her faith?

CHAPTER 15

Murray pushed open the beveled-glass door at Haven House and was hit with a delicious, tangy aroma that made his mouth water.

"Hey there. You *did* make it in time for dinner." Father Vince walked toward him from the kitchen, a hand towel draped over his shoulder, his dark curly hair framing his face. "Hope you're hungry. We're having blackened catfish, coleslaw, and Chef's Cajun pinto beans. How'd your computer setup go?"

"Great. I enjoyed getting to know Adele, too. She's an interesting woman."

"I'm glad you had a good day. Did you hear there's been another murder? It happened last night between five and six."

"No way," Murray said. "Now who?"

"A fifty-two-year-old *female* CEO. Murdered when she returned home from work."

"What company?"

"Aubry Computer Systems. She was the owner and CEO."

"This is so sick. I hope they get whoever's doing this and give him the death penalty." Murray looked around the room. "Where is everybody?"

"They're up in the lounge playing Wii bowling. I was on my way up to tell them dinner's about ready."

"I'll tell them. I need to go change." Murray laughed and, with his thumb and forefinger, pulled his T-shirt away from his chest. "I got into a fight with a sprinkler head on Adele's lawn. It didn't take long to fix."

"I'm proud of you, Murray. Don't tell the others I said so, but you're my superstar. I wish I had thirteen more just like you."

Was he serious? "Why?"

"You're an example for the others. I've embarrassed you. You're blushing."

"I'm not really comfortable with compliments." Murray stuffed his hands in the pockets of his cargo pants. "I'm nobody special. I don't deserve to be singled out for doing what I should've been doing all along."

Farther Vince patted his back. "The point, Murray, is you bounced back. And that's saying a lot. Not every guy who comes to Haven House leaves with a bright future."

Murray smiled wryly. "Are you hinting that it's time for me to leave?"

"I'm just saying you're an asset. If you have to spend time in a halfway house, I'm glad it's mine."

"Thanks." Murray glanced at the clock on the mantle: 6:25. "I'll go change and let the guys know that dinner's ready."

Vanessa crossed another name off the guest list and picked up the ringing phone.

"Langley Manor." *Put a smile in your voice.* "This is Vanessa Langley speaking. How may I help you?"

"Vanessa, this is Marjorie Stuart. Some weeks ago, I made a reservation for tomorrow night. But after this fourth murder in Les Barbes, my husband and I have decided to postpone our trip for a while. I know our fee is nonrefundable, but surely you can work with us, considering how unsafe it is there right now. I mean, we really want to come. It's just that—"

"I completely understand, Mrs. Stuart."

"Well, good. So I can get my money back?"

"We aren't able to refund cash, but I would be very happy to give you a credit and leave your reservation date open until you're ready to reschedule. Would that work?"

"All right. But unless things take a turn, it might be a while. Are things really as bad as the media makes it sound?"

"I suppose it depends on which ones you listen to." Vanessa glanced over at the morning headline—*Bathtub Killer Still at Large.* "This is normally a very peaceful community."

"What about that man from the halfway house? Wasn't his body discovered right there at Langley Manor?"

"No. It was discovered in the bayou—a considerable distance from the manor house."

"But wasn't your hired help implicated in the murder?"

"First of all," Vanessa said, "Noah is much more than hired help. He's our full-time groundskeeper and he's practically family, since his ancestral ties to Langley Manor are almost as tight as ours. But to answer your question, he's merely a person of interest in the case. Nothing more. Since he works out here and knew the victim, the sheriff was compelled to question him as he did my husband and me. But he's not being held."

"One of the cable shows made it sound like he was about to be arrested."

"That's not the case."

"Hmm. Never know who to believe these days. Well, good luck dealing with all the murders. I'll be back in touch."

"Thank you, Mrs. Stuart. We look forward to having you stay with us."

Vanessa hung up the phone and felt as if she could throw up.

The phone rang again. She took a deep breath, then picked it up.

"Langley Manor."

"This is Rodney Williamson from Liebersville, Vermont. My wife and I have been watching the news about what's happening there. I'd like to know what we can do to cancel our reservation and see about a refund."

Vanessa explained to Mr. Williamson everything she had explained to Mrs. Stuart and two others before her.

"Very well, then," he said. "If that's your policy, that's your policy. I'm just disappointed. We were led to believe Les Barbes was a nice little town and a wonderful place to bring the family. So much for believing the Chamber of Commerce."

"Les Barbes has always been a peaceful community, Mr. Williamson. Whatever is going on here must be the actions of one crazy man. Once the sheriff locks him up, we can go back to being that great place to bring the family." *I hope.*

Vanessa hung up the phone harder than she intended. If this pattern continued for long, they would have to borrow money to keep the place going—or go back to Ethan's dad and uncles and ask for more.

She decided to let the answering machine take the calls for a while. She went out to the kitchen and popped two Excedrin, then went out on the deck and sat in a rocker, where she could watch a sea of tall green sugarcane stalks swaying in the breeze. Carter was down on all fours at the far end of the deck, playing with his Matchbox cars, Angel lying next to him. She heard footsteps coming up the deck steps.

"I'll be leavin' now," Noah said. "I've done all the trimmin' I can handle for one day."

Vanessa looked at her watch. "Dinner will be over by the time you get back to Haven House."

"That's all right. I'll stop and get a double cheeseburger. Sounds great, actually. Sittin' around the table in silence with thirteen guys who won't ask the questions everyone's thinkin' drives me nuts. I'll give it a few days before I try *that* again."

Vanessa glanced over at Carter and then back again. She lowered her voice. "No one thinks you killed Flynn."

Noah sighed. "They don't know what to think. It's not like we're close. Sure, we share the meal table and dorm rooms. But most of us don't talk 'bout why we were homeless. For all they know, I'm a black Charles Manson."

Vanessa rolled her eyes. "Oh, please. Anyone who's spent five minutes with you knows you couldn't hurt a flea."

"I never let those guys see that side o' me. What you consider an asset, they'd consider a weakness. In the homeless culture, the weak are easy prey. You learn not to let down your guard."

"I was under the impression the guys at Haven House have a special camaraderie—since you've all been through similar things."

"Not really. The only person I have any connection with is Murray. And he and I don't talk 'bout the past."

"Not at all?"

Noah shook his head. "I don't need to know what he's done or where he's been. And I sure don't want to talk 'bout myself."

"Then why are you friends?"

Noah shrugged. "I like him. But I have no desire to rehash Katrina and the busted levees that took everything from me. I just don't."

"Regardless, they can tell you're one of the good guys."

Noah's eyes widened. "No, they can't. None of us knows what the other is capable of—and we all have trust issues. Anyhow, I'm just fine with keepin' my distance at Haven House till the dust settles. Whoever killed Flynn is the least of everyone's worries."

Even yours. Vanessa watched Noah go down the steps and out to his truck. How were they going to keep him on as groundskeeper if the cancellations kept coming in at this rate?

⁂

Jude took off his reading glasses, his stomach rumbling in protest of his having been too busy to eat lunch. He looked out the window in his office. Friday evening had brought the usual onslaught of week-end tourists.

His cell phone rang, and he cringed. *Go away. I just want to go home and relax.* He took his phone off his belt clip, relieved to see it was his wife.

"Hi, honey."

"I've got grilled shrimp and homemade dirty rice with your name on it," Colette Prejean said. "Are you coming home, or do I have to feed it to the dog?"

He laughed. "Don't you dare give it to Keeper. I'm on my way."

"Seriously, I'll understand if you need to work. I can't believe you have another murder to deal with."

"I need to take a break—for dinner anyway. I might come back later when the media presence thins out. Did you know today's victim was Savannah Surette's aunt?"

"No." Colette sighed into the receiver. "But there seems to be no public outcry. I've heard remarks that the killer should get a medal—as if he were some kind of vigilante."

"I know. I even to had pull Gil aside for letting his deputies make bets on who would be the next victim. He knows better than to allow that kind of thing to go on."

"Feelings run so deep. Almost everyone in town, on some level, has been touched by the layoffs and foreclosures. It's easy to blame these wealthy CEOs for all their financial woes."

"They'd better get over it. You don't just sanction the murder of the boss because you get caught in the cutbacks."

"Not to defend it, Jude, but those cutbacks have destroyed lives."

"My job is to find out *who* killed these CEOs, not to be the judge of *why*. Please tell me you're not discussing the case with anyone."

"Give me a break. I know better. I've been doing this as long as you have. But I hear things. I've never known the people in Les Barbes to be so cold and indifferent."

Jude switched the phone to his other ear. "Not toward the victims anyway. Maybe public sentiment will soften some with this latest murder. I got the impression that Nicole Aubry was well liked."

"Somebody didn't like her. Are you any closer to finding the killer?"

"We have his DNA, but he's not in the system."

❧

Adele sat at her computer desk, wishing she had the email addresses of more people so she could practice her newfound skill. She wanted to try browsing, whatever that meant. Murray promised to come back and teach her more. He had showed her which icon to click and said to type in any subject and see what happened.

She clicked on the icon that looked like a blue lowercase e with a halo and saw the space next to the word Google. She typed in Zoe B's Cajun Eatery and pressed the Enter key. A page of results came up, and Zoe B's was the first name listed. She clicked onto it, and, almost magically, a colorful page appeared, with a picture of Pierce and Zoe standing in front of Zoe B's. She scrolled down the page and read everything but was afraid to click on anything else, fearing she might do something that would mess up her email.

She heard a familiar cough and looked over at the doorway and saw Isabel standing there.

"You wanted to see me when I was finished cleaning the kitchen," Isabel said.

"Yes, come in, hon. Sit here next to me."

Isabel walked softly across the room and sat in the chair next to the desk, avoiding eye contact.

"I didn't want to talk about this over dinner, but we need to come to an understanding."

"What understanding, ma'am?"

"Oh, I think you know what this is about. Let's not play games."

"I'm not sure I do."

Adele looked over at Isabel and waited until she met her gaze. "I cannot run my household to suit you. I hired you to suit me."

"I'm not following you."

"Isabel, I like Murray, and I like Noah. I intend to keep hiring them as long as they are available and continue to do good work. While I cannot tell you how to feel about them, I can demand that you treat them like you would any guest in my home."

"Did I say or do anything out of line?"

"You were icy polite, which, in my book, equates to rude. I promise you Murray was well aware that you do not approve of his being here."

The color of Isabel's cheeks told Adele she understood exactly what she was saying.

"Are we clear?" Adele spoke softly. "I like having you here. I think we do very well together, and I don't want this to become an issue between us. Should that happen, I would find it impossible to keep you in my employ."

"You're asking me to just ignore my instincts?"

"You're not ignoring them. You made your feelings known. I considered what you said. I simply don't share your point of view.

God seems to have given me the gift of mercy, and I'm drawn to people others aren't."

"But it's dangerous mercy, ma'am. Would He really call you to that?"

Adele fingered the gold cross around her neck. "Perhaps the Lord's idea of dangerous differs from ours. After all, He knows the ending of the story."

Isabel blew her bangs off her forehead. "Well, getting to the end of the story is the scary part. Sometimes I wish He would tell me what's going to happen. Don't you?"

Adele smiled. "It might frighten me to death, if I knew what He knows. I try to take it a day at a time." Adele gently gripped Isabel's wrist. "I'm not asking you to understand my choice of acquaintances. But I do expect you to accept those that God has brought to me."

"How can you be sure it's God?"

"Simple. Not one thing happens in my life that He doesn't either orchestrate or allow for a greater good."

"You have a lot more faith than I do. I think He gives us a brain and instincts and expects us to use them."

"Of course He does. And we need to use them. But faith, by its very nature, requires belief in the unseen—that which we have to trust Him for. He's called us to love others as we love ourselves. That requires a great deal of acceptance of those we aren't drawn to naturally."

"I'm sorry my attitude was disappointing. It won't happen again. I really want this job. I like working for you."

"Then we shouldn't have any problem. Simply treat Murray and Noah as you would anyone else I've welcomed into my home. Can you do that?"

"Yes, I think I can. I'll give it my best."

"Very well." Adele studied the computer screen, then turned to Isabel and smiled. "I would sure like to have another piece of that praline cake. Would you like to join me in the kitchen?"

"Sure. I'll go cut us each a piece."

Adele let out a sigh of relief. How she hated confrontation! Was she really willing to fire Isabel because the girl found it difficult to accept a couple of reformed vagabonds? Then again, if everyone reacted the way Isabel had, how would Noah and Murray be encouraged to stay on course?

But it's dangerous mercy, ma'am.

Adele considered Isabel's words. Wasn't all mercy dangerous? Wasn't there always a chance it could be abused? Noah and Murray had been nothing but kind and hardworking. What cause did she have to believe either would take advantage of her?

CHAPTER 16

The next morning, Jude sat at the desk in his office, his hands wrapped around a mug of coffee, and began reading Saturday's issue of the *Les Barbes Ledger*.

Bathtub Killer Strikes a Third Time

> Sheriff Jude Prejean and Police Chief Casey Norman are shaking their heads after the discovery Friday morning of a third victim of the Bathtub Killer. Nicole Aubry, 52, the owner and CEO of Aubry Computer Systems, was found drowned in the bathtub in her home in the upscale neighborhood of Magnolia Blossom.
>
> Reba Chapin, Aubry's personal assistant, became concerned when the CEO missed an important meeting and failed to return her phone or email messages. Chapin finally drove to Aubry's home and found her fully clothed in business attire and submerged in the bathtub. The pound

> sign followed by the numeral three had been spray painted on the wall.
>
> The medical examiner confirmed the victim had been drugged with a veterinary sedative called ketamine, sold on the street as "Special K" or cat Valium. The ME also placed the time of death between five and six Thursday night, which suggests that Aubrey might have been killed when she returned home from work.
>
> The victim's safe had been emptied. It's unknown at this time what was taken—

A knock at the door broke his concentration. "Come in."

Aimee walked to his desk and handed him three colored folders. "Here's the preliminary list of all the foreclosures at the Roux River Bank in the past five years. And the list of employees at Fontaine Sugar Refinery *and* Aubry Computer Systems who either quit or were laid off or fired in the same time frame. Gil has a team cross-referencing any names that appear more than once. They're going to create a comprehensive list. In the meantime, he knew you'd want a copy of all three."

"I do. Thanks."

Aimee's gaze seemed to probe his thoughts. "What time did you finally get out of here last night?"

"I hung it up about one. I probably shouldn't have stayed that late just going over the same information. I'd have been better off getting a good night's sleep and hitting it fresh this morning. I feel like I've been run over by a semi."

"I think the same truck ran over me."

He held up the folders. "Anything in here stand out to you?"

"Not at first glance. But we know these murders were personal. Well thought out. Calculated. I agree that it's significant the killer didn't torture his victims. There's not a scratch on any of them—no defensive wounds either. Makes me think the victims didn't find him threatening. Maybe they even knew him. Your theory that he wanted the chance to vent before he killed them makes sense, especially if we're right about the murders being related to a layoff and foreclosure."

"I just really want to catch this guy before he strikes again."

"We're too late, Sheriff." Gil Marcel filled the doorway. "Castille just called. We've got another body."

Jude pulled up behind Aimee and Gil in front of a three-story brick and stone mansion in the new Park Heights development. A media van was already parked down the block and a camera crew set up on the sidewalk behind the barrier his deputies had set up.

Jude got out of the car, and Deputy Stone Castille ran over to him.

"What do we know about the victim?" Jude said.

"Name's Jeanette Stein. Thirty-one. *Not* a CEO, but the wife of that hotshot defense lawyer Barry Stein. The front door was unlocked, the security alarm off, and no sign of forced entry. The victim was drowned in the bathtub in the master suite—same MO as the first three, except she was wearing a nightgown. The ME puts the time of death between nine and eleven last night."

"Where was her husband?" Jude said.

"In New Orleans on a court case. Mrs. Stein's sister got worried when she didn't return her calls last night or this morning, and she came over here about thirty minutes ago and found her dead. The victim's eight-month-old twin boys were next door in the nursery, screaming in their cribs. Hungry. Scared. Diapers dirty. The sister is packing their things now and taking them to her house. Doucet is going to get her statement there."

"Any chance this could be a copycat?" Jude said. "It's odd that Mrs. Stein is the only victim that wasn't a CEO."

Castille shrugged. "Too soon to tell. The safe wasn't robbed this time. But the way she was positioned in the bathtub with her hands crossed on her chest—like a body in a casket—wasn't something we told the press. This one looked just like the first three."

"Has Barry Stein been notified?"

"Yes, he's driving back from New Orleans."

"Don't miss a step—not one—or he'll be all over this. You know his reputation." Jude looked up at the yellow crime-scene tape across the front door. "Find out if Stein represented Roux River Bank, Fontaine Sugar Refinery, or Aubry Computer Systems. There must've been numerous lawsuits filed after all the layoffs."

"You're reading my mind, Sheriff."

"And find out if Mrs. Stein worked for her husband or had a personal connection to any of the other victims. I want to know what kind of relationship she had with her husband. And whether she might have been seeing someone else. We need to find out how she fits the puzzle."

"Yes, sir. We will."

"We're really spread thin," Aimee said.

Jude nodded. "I'll ask Chief Norman to request additional manpower from other police departments. I've utilized all the deputies I can spare without disrupting necessary parish operations."

Jude heard babies crying and turned toward the sound. Two young women walked from the house to the Dodge Caravan parked in the driveway, each carrying a shoulder bag on one arm and a baby in the other.

The brunette, her face red and swollen, opened the sliding door of the minivan and buckled the unhappy baby in his car seat. The blonde woman got the second twin situated in the other car seat, but he cried all the louder. Deputy Mike Doucet opened the hatch and set two suitcases in the back.

"The dark-haired woman with the long braid is Mrs. Stein's sister, Bonnie Lonigan," Castille said. "I don't know who the blonde is. She looks like money."

The two women embraced and held tightly to each other for several seconds. Then Stein's sister slid into the driver's seat, backed out of the driveway, and drove away, the heartrending sound of the babies' wailing finally growing mute.

"That tears my heart out," Aimee said. "If I didn't know better, I'd swear those poor little boys know exactly what's happened."

Jude coughed to cover the tightness in his throat, glad that he wasn't the one who had to tell Mr. Stein that the mother of his children had been murdered.

The classy blonde woman, her face streaked with mascara, walked over to them. "How many people have to die before you stop this monster?"

"I didn't catch your name," Jude said.

"Madison Vermilion. I live next door." She dabbed her eyes. "Jeanette was my closest friend."

"I'm very sorry for your loss." The words sounded rote. But would anything he said really make her feel better?

"Sheriff, I realize there are those in the community who are convinced the killer is doing us all a favor." The woman's lower lip began to quiver, a tear spilling down her cheek. "But Jeanette wasn't a CEO and never hurt a soul in her life. She was just a wife and—" Madison let out a sob and stifled it with her hand. "She had two little boys, for heaven's sake."

Aimee put her hand on Madison's shoulder. "We're going to do everything in our power to find out who killed your friend and bring that person to justice."

Jude noticed a diamond-and-sapphire ring on Madison's left hand. "Mrs. Vermilion, did you notice any unfamiliar vehicles parked in the driveway or at the curb? Or any unusual activity at her place?"

Madison shook her head. "I didn't. You might ask the other neighbors. Surely someone saw something."

⚜

Adele turned off the TV and went into the sunroom, where Isabel was cleaning.

"I'm sorry to tell you this," Adele said, "but there's been another murder."

Isabel stopped and looked up, her eyes wide. "This is so out of control. Who's the victim?"

Adele sighed. "A young mother—Jeanette something. Stein, I believe. Yes, that's it. Stein. She was the wife of a prominent defense attorney."

"Yes, I know who he is. He's in the news a lot. What happened?"

"She was found drowned in the bathtub. She'd been drugged and—well, you know what this killer does. She was number four. Her husband was out of town, and she was home alone with eight-month-old twin boys. Thank the Lord they weren't harmed."

Isabel's eyebrows came together. "This just proves what I've been saying all along. We shouldn't presume to know who this killer is targeting. We could all be at risk. Can the sheriff even connect this woman to the other victims?"

"I doubt they would give the media that information while the investigation is in progress," Adele said. "But your fears might not be unfounded after all. Maybe this killer *is* striking at random. It's tragic. Simply tragic."

The phone rang.

"Let me get that." Adele reached over and picked up the receiver. "Hello."

"Adele, it's Murray. I hope I'm not bothering you."

"Not at all."

"How's the email coming?"

"Oh, I believe I've just about got it mastered. I'm eager to learn a little more about *browsing*."

"Great. But first things first. If it's okay with you, I'd like to come back over there and put on those bolt locks we picked up yesterday. I'd feel a lot better after this latest murder. You heard about the young mother, didn't you?"

"Indeed I did." Adele pulled out a wicker chair and sat at the table. "I was just talking with Isabel about it. I think we would both feel safer if those locks were in place."

"I should've put them on yesterday before we got distracted with the computer and I had that little run-in with your sprinkler head." He chuckled. "At least I got it fixed."

Adele smiled. "Noah will be surprised. It's one less thing for him to do. Taking care of the grounds at Langley Manor is really a full-time job. He's phasing out almost everything else."

"Would it be convenient if I came over around four?"

"Absolutely. Why don't you allow time to have another piece of that praline cake? Isabel and I certainly can't eat all of it ourselves, and we wouldn't want something that delicious to spoil."

Isabel's facial expression didn't change, but Adele could see her jaw tighten. At least she was subtle about it.

"Okay," Murray said. "I'm doing a paint job today, but I'll be at your place around four."

⚜

Zoe stood next to the table by the window at the eatery, watching Hebert win his seventh consecutive game of checkers.

Tex groaned and sat back in his chair, his thumbs hooked on his red suspenders. "I don't know how you do it, Hebert ol' buddy, but I sure can't beat you. Let Father Sam give it a try."

"Dat's all you got?" A grin tugged at the corners of Hebert's mouth. He began resetting the checkers. "Come on, Père Sam. I not goin' to *let* you win. You got to earn it."

Grace stuffed a piece of apple into her mouth, wiggling and giggling in her booster chair.

Savannah came over to the table and started pouring coffee refills.

"I really wish you'd take some time off." Zoe gently tugged her ponytail. "I can schedule one of the other girls to take your shift for a few days."

Savannah shook her head. "It's better if I stay busy. If I have time to think about what happened to Aunt Nicole, I'll just get depressed."

"I tink you already dere," Hebert said, not quite under his breath.

"I'm fine. It'll be much easier if I can stay focused on my job." Savannah put two tiny tubs of creamer next to Tex's cup. "It's not affecting my job performance."

"I know," Zoe said. "I'm just concerned for you. You need to give yourself space to grieve."

"I'd like to have the day of the funeral off. But other than that, I'd really appreciate it if you'd let me work. I'll do my grieving in private."

Zoe slipped her arm around Savannah's waist. "Whatever you need, sweetie. You just have to be honest with me."

Pierce came out of the kitchen, wearing his chef's hat and apron—and a scowl.

"What's wrong?" Zoe said.

"The Bathtub Killer struck again—last night. Another woman, but she wasn't a CEO. She was the wife of a high-powered defense lawyer. And a stay-at-home mom."

Zoe's heart sank.

"Dat's a disgrace." Hebert looked up from the checkerboard. "A *mère?*"

"Of eight-month-old twin boys," Pierce said. "I think we all have to take a second look at what's going on. I'm not convinced this is totally related to the layoffs and foreclosures."

Tex took a red kerchief and wiped his bald head. "It's a wonder the creep didn't kill those babies."

"Dis ting makes me *moitié fou."* Hebert shook his head.

"It makes us all half crazy," Father Sam said. "And now we have the uncertainty of just who this killer's targeting. I don't see how this latest victim ties in with the others. And it makes me wonder if that man from Haven House was murdered by the same killer."

"The MO was different." Tex took a sip of coffee. "But I guess it's different in this case too."

"Not really," Pierce said. "The victim was drugged and drowned. And the number four was spray painted on the bathroom wall. None of those variables was present when the Haven House guy was killed. Listen, I've got to get back to the kitchen. I just thought you'd want to know the latest, in case you hadn't heard."

Pierce went back in the kitchen, and no one said anything for half a minute.

Finally Grace started bouncing up and down in her booster chair. "It's *meeeee,"* she said, obviously trying to engage the guys in their daily ritual.

"Me?" Tex looked at Hebert and shrugged. "Do we know anyone named Me?"

"Are you Me Broussard?" Father Sam asked.

"No, I *Grace* Brew-sar!" She pointed to herself, giggling all the while.

"*You're* Grace Broussard?" Hebert tapped her on the nose. "Den we *do* know you."

Zoe relished the little game and drew comfort from its predictability and innocence. Five murders in less than a week was enough to turn her stomach. And if the Bathtub Killer took out the mother of two babies, was anyone safe?

CHAPTER 17

Jude walked in his office and closed the door, trying not to think too hard about the eight-month-old Stein twins left alone and crying while their mother was drowned in the bathtub. He doubted his deputies would feel indifferent or sarcastic toward *this* victim.

Jude went over to the window, unwrapped a stick of gum, and stuffed it into his mouth. The pillars of the stately Saint Catherine Parish Courthouse reflected the sunlight and looked as if someone had flipped a switch and turned them on. People hurried up or down the front steps, and one school-age boy was sliding down the railing. On the corner, Andre-the-street-vendor sold andouille corn dogs to tourists dressed in matching T-shirts.

The Bathtub Killer was still out there somewhere. Had he targeted his next victim? Why had he chosen Jeanette Stein? Was there a grievance with the husband? Was her murder a payback? If so, how was it connected to the other victims? What was the common thread?

The intercom beeped and startled him.

"Yes."

"Sheriff, something's come up." Aimee's voice filled the room. "When you have a few minutes, I'd like to talk to you about it."

"I'm free now. I'm just trying to catch my breath. This latest victim threw me for a loop."

"I know what you mean. It's not that Jeanette Stein's life was more valuable than anyone else's. There's just something so sad about robbing two little babies of their mother."

Jude watched a young couple pushing a double pram down the sidewalk. "Do we know when her husband is coming in for questioning?"

"Gil said one thirty. You want to sit in on it?"

"Absolutely. Stein's a powerful guy—and vocal. We want to make sure he knows we're *on top* of this." Jude glanced at his watch. "So what's come up?"

"Let me come to your office. I'll be right there."

Jude went over to his desk and sat. He picked up the framed picture of Colette and their three grown kids. He couldn't imagine being in Barry Stein's shoes. How would he have dealt with losing his wife and raising their kids on his own?

There was a knock at the door and Aimee came inside, her tan uniform looking crisp and pressed, her bleached hair short and sassy.

"You want the door closed?" she said.

"Not unless you do. What's up?"

Aimee left the door open and sat in the chair next to his desk. "A few days ago, a young woman called here and reported that she had found a thousand dollars—ten one-hundred-dollar bills tucked inside a note card left in her mailbox. The note was handwritten and unsigned and merely said, 'This belongs to you.' She wanted to know if it was legal to keep it."

"And she had no idea who it was from or why he or she would say it belongs to her?"

"No. She'd been laid off from the sugar refinery and wondered if someone felt sorry for her. But before she spent it, she wanted us to tell her it was all right to keep it. Of course, not knowing anything more than what she told us, we couldn't tell her not to spend it."

"So what's your point?"

"It happened again just a few minutes ago. We got a call from a man who's been out of work since he was laid off last year from Aubry Computer Systems. This morning he found a note in his mailbox with ten one hundred dollar bills. The same thing was written in his note."

"'This belongs to you'?" Jude said.

"Yes. But he's afraid to spend it because if it turns out to be a mistake and someone wants it back, he could never repay it."

"Does he have any idea how the money could be his?"

"Not really. He wondered if someone at Aubry felt guilty that he got laid off and was trying to compensate him. Deputy Doucet took the call and said it sounded to him like the guy was just trying to justify keeping it."

"Does he still have the note?"

"We don't know. Either he got cut off, or he hung up. He hasn't called back. But I'm wondering if a pattern is emerging. What if the killer is distributing the money he's stealing from his victims and giving it back to the people who've been hurt in the layoffs?"

"Robin Hood?" Jude raised an eyebrow. "That's a new twist."

"I doubt most recipients of the thousand dollars would come forward and question the source, especially if they're hurting for money. They'd just keep quiet and spend it. But if we knew who they were, we might be able to put the pieces together and figure out who the killer is."

Jude sat back in his chair, his hands clasped behind his head. "Check the phone records and find out who made the calls. Let's question those folks and see if we can shed some light on this."

"We're already on it."

"Good." Jude pursed his lips and thought for a moment. "If our Bathtub Killer is targeting CEOs who are responsible for the layoffs and stealing their money to give back to people who got hurt, what's the connection to Jeanette Stein—a stay-at-home mom married to a successful defense lawyer?"

Aimee shrugged. "It's baffling."

"I want you to find out everything you can about her. She's the one victim that doesn't seem to fit, and even less so with this new development."

⚜

Vanessa Langley looked at the computer screen and spoke into the phone. "All right, Mrs. Phelps. Your reservation is canceled."

"I hear annoyance in your voice," Mrs. Phelps said. "Surely you understand why we don't want to come there for vacation right now?"

"Yes, ma'am. And I'm not annoyed. I'm sad. The murders are disconcerting to all of us here on a number of levels."

"I think it's absurd you won't refund my money."

"I'm sorry. Our refund policy is clearly stated on our website. You can reschedule for up to a year and won't pay more, even if the rate goes up. And because of the unique circumstances, we'll even give you two free dinners at Zoe B's, one of our authentic Cajun eateries. We want your business. And look forward to booking you later on."

"You'll be hearing from me again. Good-bye."

Vanessa hung up the phone on her kitchen desk and rubbed the back of her neck. How many more cancellations would they be getting now that the news was out that a stay-at-home mom had been added to the list of victims? At least when it was CEOs, there was a pseudo sense of safety for everyone else. But if he could kill a mother with two babies in the next room, was anyone safe?

She heard a man clear his throat and turned her swivel chair around. How long had Noah been standing behind her?

He held up a glass. "Didn't mean to bother you. I just came in to get a drink o' water and see if there's somethin' in particular you want me to do this afternoon."

"Have you been out to the caretaker house today?"

Noah nodded as he downed the glass of water. "It's nearly done. They have some finish work to do, but they're talkin' like it'll be ready in a week or so." He seemed to study her. "Vanessa, I'll understand if you and Ethan want me to hold off movin' in until after things calm down. I overheard you on the phone just now. I know you're gettin' cancellations. And that it's been unpleasant for you, havin' to deal with negative publicity."

Noah gave her an opening. Why couldn't she just tell him?

"You're right about the cancellations," she said. "And it *has* been unpleasant. But it's not your fault. I know you had nothing to do with Flynn Gillis's murder."

"I believe *you* know. How does Ethan feel 'bout it?"

"He knows too. But he's methodical and wants us to take things a step at a time."

"In other words, he wants to see what the investigation proves?"

"Ethan just likes to see everything through to the end." Vanessa felt her cheeks warm. Could she get the words out without crying? It was so unfair of Ethan to ask her to do this. "Noah—"

He held up his palm. "I can see that my bein' here is not in the best interest of Langley Manor. I think I should leave—at least until the sheriff is convinced I didn't kill Flynn."

Vanessa struggled to find her voice. Had Noah figured out that Ethan had asked her to get his keys back?

"We *know* you're innocent, Noah."

"Doesn't sound like Ethan's so sure."

"He would just like the facts to agree with us. So we could reassure guests."

"Doesn't matter." He swatted the air as if he were dismissing the implications.

His fallen countenance belied his comment.

"I'm absolutely confident that everything will work out at the right time." She wasn't. Why did she tell him that?

Noah buried his hands in the pockets of his cutoffs. "Thing is, my time's up at Haven House. Father Vince has already let me stay longer than the two-year policy rule because I was waitin' to move into the caretaker house. If that's not happenin', I need to find somewhere else to live. And I need to find other work."

"Noah, we've had eight cancellations in the past two days. I hope it's just temporary. But if our business continues to be impacted this way, I don't know what we're going to do. We have some cash set aside for emergencies, but it's not going to last long at this rate. If we have to go to Ethan's dad and uncles to ask for more money, they may ask us to cut operating expenses."

Noah raised his eyebrows. "Like forget about the on-site caretaker?"

"It certainly wouldn't be *our* choice. But this is the first time since we opened that we've had to deal with multiple vacancies, and we're not sure what it will mean to the future of the business. It's not just Flynn's murder. It's the other four too. People are afraid to come to Les Barbes right now. Five murders in less than a week. Can you blame them?"

"O' course I don't."

Vanessa got up and took his hand, a tear trickling down her cheek. "It'll all work out. I just don't know how long it will take. You waited two years for this position. I hate that it's come to this."

"Me, too." Noah pulled the key ring out of his pocket and held it in the palm of his hand, staring at it for a moment. "Feels a little like givin' up a part o' myself. I've grown fond o' Langley Manor. So much of me's invested in this place—where my people were, where my roots are."

"That's exactly right." Vanessa gripped his wrist. "That's why it's going to work out. It has to. I know you're innocent. We're going to work through this."

"Only if Ethan agrees with you. The sheriff's got his hands full with the bathtub murders. When's he goin' to find time and manpower to investigate Flynn's death? The truth is nobody really cares that Flynn's dead. He's bein' put in the church's cemetery today, but no one knows if he had family or if Flynn Gillis was his real name. Murray offered to go with Father Vince when he reads the burial prayers, but he didn't like Flynn either."

"That's really sad," Vanessa said. "I would hate to die without anyone coming forward to say a kind word about me."

"Don't go feelin' sorry for Flynn. He brought it on hisself." Noah's voice was suddenly cold, his expression stony. "He didn't even *try* to make friends and went outta his way to irritate people."

"He didn't deserve to be murdered, Noah."

"I'm not sayin' he did." Noah's eyes narrowed. "But he pushed people too far and had to know that eventually someone would push back."

"Is that what you think happened?"

Noah shrugged. "Can't say fuh shore. But regardless, Flynn's laughin' his head off that he's still keepin' things stirred up, even from the grave."

Vanessa was unaccustomed to the bitterness she heard in Noah's tone and could only imagine how much he was hurting.

"You're a big man to step up and make the hard choice here. But it's only until the sheriff sorts things out and business is thriving again. Then you can come back and pick up where you left off."

Noah put the key ring in her hand, avoiding eye contact. "We'll see."

CHAPTER 18

Adele Woodmore sat in the parlor at Langley Manor, sipping sweet tea and studying Vanessa's demeanor.

"You really didn't have to come out here," Vanessa said.

Adele patted her hand. "When Noah came to mow and told me he turned in his keys, I just knew you'd be as distraught as he was."

"Of course I am. But what Noah doesn't know—and you can't tell him—is that I was just about to ask him for the keys when he volunteered them."

"Oh?"

Vanessa wiped her eyes. "I didn't want to. It wasn't my decision. Ethan thinks it's unwise to give Noah access to the manor house until his name is cleared—for the sake of the guests. But people are canceling right and left. If this keeps up, we'll be ruined."

"Trust the Lord, Vanessa. He's brought you this far."

"I know. But at the rate things are going, our cash reserves won't last long." Her blue eyes brimmed with tears. "You have no idea how hard it would be for Ethan to have to ask his dad and uncles for money after all the pains we've taken to do this right. I mean, we researched everything thoroughly before we started the renovation and were so careful to stay on budget. We got off to a great start and have been booked solid since we opened. Now all that's about to go south."

"You don't know that. And no one can blame you for this sudden downturn. I'm sure the cancellations are just temporary."

Vanessa sighed. "It's hard to believe that the future of Langley Manor could be in jeopardy—all because of a dead man no one really knew or liked."

Adele remembered thinking that Flynn looked like a hippie right out of Haight-Ashbury when he came with Murray to move her furniture. "I had the opportunity to be kind to him, but I essentially brushed him off because he made me uncomfortable. I'm not proud of myself."

"He made everyone uncomfortable. No one would blame you."

"I blame me. The Lord expects better. I could have at least approached him as a real person instead of someone I wished would leave. That certainly wasn't an example of loving my neighbor as myself." Adele took a sip of tea. "I have to wonder what Flynn might have been like if he'd had someone who really cared about him. There's no point in beating myself up over it, but I'm not making the same mistake with Noah and Murray."

Vanessa plucked another tissue from the box. "I don't know Murray very well, but Noah's easy to like."

"Yes, he is. So is Murray. He wouldn't let me pay him for going with me to get the computer. The two of us must have been a sight to behold, riding up high in his old truck." Adele smiled, remembering. "What a delightful adventure."

"So, you actually *enjoyed* it?"

"Oh my, yes," Adele said. "We both did. Murray said I remind him of his grandma Sophie. Isn't that sweet? Isabel's uneasy that I'm becoming friends with Murray. She thinks I should keep my distance since I don't know anything about him. How else can I get to know him if I don't open my heart and my home?"

"Zoe mentioned that Pierce doesn't want Grace at your house when any of the guys from Haven House are there."

"Oh?"

Vanessa's cheeks went from peachy to crimson. "I'm sorry. I just assumed Zoe told you."

"She didn't." Adele's mind raced in reverse. "I do remember her asking me the other day if I was expecting any of the workers to be there. I thought she was being sensitive—not wanting to overwhelm me by bringing Grace over on the same day."

"For what it's worth, it's Pierce, not Zoe. He doesn't want Grace around any of the men from Haven House. He said that even before Flynn was murdered. Of course that just strengthened his resolve."

"Goodness, I would never put that sweet Grace in any kind of danger." Adele shook her head. "Why didn't Pierce just come to me? I would have at least vouched for Murray."

"He knew you would. He respects you too much to get into a disagreement over it, and Zoe had already agreed to honor his wishes so it was a moot point."

"I wonder why *she* didn't tell me."

"I don't know." Vanessa sighed. "And here *I* am telling you her personal business. I really thought you knew, Adele. I'm not usually a gossip."

Adele squeezed her hand. "We both love Zoe. And you know this conversation won't go anywhere else."

"I appreciate that."

"So what will you do without Noah?"

Vanessa's eyes brimmed with tears. "We can't let things go. We'll have to hire someone to mow and do the basics, just until his name is cleared and the business picks up again."

"And what if Flynn's murder is never solved? What then?"

"I don't know. Maybe it'll all blow over in the months to come, and we'll feel good about rehiring Noah and having him move into the caretaker house." Vanessa dabbed her eyes. "But we're losing business and need to do whatever it takes to regain the confidence of potential guests—or our bed-and-breakfast business won't survive and Noah won't be the only one out of work."

"It's sad, isn't it?" Adele said. "Noah is caught between a rock and hard place. Nothing he can say will dispel that flicker of suspicion that he might have killed Flynn. His good name is totally dependent on the sheriff's investigation and how the media handles it."

Vanessa nodded, a tear spilling down her cheek. "Noah saved my life. I can't tell you how awkward and painful it was when he handed me his keys. You should have seen the look in his eyes."

"I did, hon. That's why I'm here."

⚜

Sheriff Jude Prejean sat next to Deputy Chief Aimee Rivette and across from Barry Stein at an oblong table in the largest interview room. Stein's face was drawn and pallid, his shoulders limp. Except for the silk suit and tie he was wearing, he bore little resemblance to the fierce defense lawyer who was always mouthing off in the media. Jude had little respect for the man after being subpoenaed on several occasions to testify for the defense in ways that Stein manipulated in his client's favor. But who could not feel sorry for this shell of a man who sat across from him—a widower with two little babies?

Or was Barry Stein's grief an act? Could he have seized the opportunity to do away with his wife by hiring someone to make it look like another bathtub killing? Was he capable of it? Did he have a motive? Nothing seemed to tie Jeanette to the other victims.

Jude folded his hands on the table. "Mr. Stein, I'm very sorry for your loss. I can only imagine how you're feeling. I would put this off if I could. But I'm sure you know we need to ask you some questions."

Barry gave a nod. "Go ahead. Please call me by my first name."

"You were in New Orleans last night and the night before and stayed at the Hotel Charette. Is that correct, Barry?"

"Yes."

"What was the nature of your business in New Orleans?"

"I have a client there. His court case comes up next week, and I was prepping him."

I'll just bet you were. "Were you with this client last night?"

"I was. We had dinner in the hotel dining room at six thirty."

"It says on the report"—Jude put on his reading glasses—"that you had a business dinner with this client and then went up to your room a little after eight."

"That's right."

"Can anyone confirm you were in the hotel dining room all that time?"

Barry lifted his gaze. "Yes, of course. My client and the waiter. I charged the two meals to my room. It's on the bill."

"Did you leave the hotel for any reason last night?"

"No. But I did leave my room to go down to the gift shop and get my wife"—he choked back the emotion—"a box of truffles. She loved Godiva chocolate."

"It says here you spoke with her on your cell phone at eight fifteen."

"Correct. After we hung up, I went down to the gift shop. That's the last … the last time I spoke to Jeanette."

Jude paused to let Barry regain his composure and then continued. "Were you in your room between nine and eleven p.m.?"

"I was."

"Can anyone confirm that?"

"Yes and no. I didn't see anyone after that, but I watched a movie and charged it to my room. And I called the front desk around ten thirty and asked for a six a.m. wake-up call. The hotel can confirm that."

"Okay, good. And according to the report, you had breakfast with the same client this morning at eight in the hotel coffee shop?"

Barry nodded. "It was during that meeting that a New Orleans police officer found me and told me about—" He put his fist to his mouth and just shook his head.

"Would you like to take a break, Barry?"

"Just give me a moment."

"Take your time."

Barry took a sip of water. "Okay. What else?"

"Can you think of anyone who would want to hurt your wife?"

"Everyone loved Jeanette."

"Is it possible that someone wanted to get back at *you* by hurting her?"

"I suppose it's possible."

"But no one comes to mind?"

"Not offhand." Barry seemed to be thinking. "Maybe someone will come to mind when I can think more clearly. But it's generally the good guys I make mad, not the bad guys."

No kidding. "What about the other six lawyers you have working in your firm—ever get sideways with any of them?"

"Sure. But nothing out of the ordinary and nothing unresolved. We're a team."

"Is it usual for you to leave town to prep a client? Isn't that the kind of thing you'd have your associates do?"

Barry loosened his tie. "This is a high-profile case. I wanted to do it myself."

"Isn't that hard on your family—having you gone?"

"Sheriff, what's your point?"

"You have to admit that it's odd you just happened to be out of town on the day your wife was murdered."

Barry's eyes glistened. "How dare you! I resent the insinuation! I have no idea how or why the killer knew I would be gone. All I can think about is if I'd been home, Jeanette would still be alive."

"I'm just trying to cover all bases, counselor. Don't read into this. So how would you describe your marriage?"

Barry sighed, his gaze moving from Jude to Aimee and back to Jude. "Let me save us all some time and just cut to the chase. I loved Jeanette with all my heart. I wasn't cheating on her. She wasn't cheating on me. I didn't pay someone to kill her. I didn't stage a copycat murder to throw off the authorities. I had no knowledge of her death prior to the police officer informing me."

"Sir, can you think of any connection—anything—that would tie you or your wife to the other victims?"

"Not off the top of my head. I never represented Fontaine Sugar Refinery or Roux River Bank or Aubry Computer Systems. I didn't know any of the other victims. I'm not sure what connection there could be."

"Did your wife know the other victims?"

"No. We were just as shocked as everyone else when each victim's name was given to the media. But we had no personal connection. At least not until now—" Barry's voice failed. His hands were shaking. Was that from grief—or guilt?

"Barry," Jude continued, "I'm sure it's no surprise to you that some people find your line of work distasteful." *Present company included.* "Have any of your mutual friends—or your wife's friends—ever vocalized this or seem fixated on it?"

"Lawyer jokes are huge in our home, Sheriff. We can't get together without my wife's brothers telling the latest ones. Our friends have told plenty of lawyer jokes too, but it's all in fun."

"Is that a no, counselor?"

"Yes, that's a no. I can't always tell if the jokes are meant as a dig or just to get a laugh—or both. But if you're asking if I have enemies who hate me enough to *kill my wife* ...?" Barry's voice cracked. "It would take someone really sick to kill a beautiful young woman with two little babies."

"And you don't know any sick people?"

"The sick people I know are the people I defend. Since I usually get them a good deal or get them off, I sincerely doubt any of them want to get back at me."

"Let's get back to your marriage for a minute," Jude said. "So you and Jeanette were getting along?"

"We were great. Close. She was everything to me—" Barry buried his face in his hands for a moment and then folded his hands on the table. "Yes, we were getting along."

"And there wasn't anyone else? Not even during the times you were away on business?"

"Absolutely not. I take my vows seriously."

"Was Jeanette as committed as you were?"

"I'm sure she was."

"If we question her girlfriends, are they going to tell us the same thing?"

Barry's eyebrows formed a bushy line. "Jeanette and I were great together. Ask anyone."

"I'm asking you."

"And I answered you."

"Getting used to caring for twins can't be easy," Jude said. "It had to change things in your marriage."

"It did. But it was a good change."

"Sometimes couples grow apart when the demands of raising kids enters the relationship."

"We didn't."

Jude locked gazes with him. "Why did you need a million-dollar life insurance policy on your wife, Barry?"

"I took that out when the twins were born." Barry rolled his eyes. "I make a *lot* of money, Sheriff. That policy amount was totally in line with our lifestyle. If I'd planned to kill Jeanette to collect the money, I'd have insured her for three times that."

"Insuring her for a lower amount might've been one way to avoid suspicion."

"I didn't need the money, Sheriff. I've got more money than I'll ever spend." Barry raked his hands through his thick, dark hair. "Look, I know you have to ask these questions. The husband is always scrutinized when the wife is murdered. But I'm telling you, Jeanette and I loved each other. And I had nothing to do with her murder."

"Don't get defensive, counselor. We're just doing our job."

"I'm sure you're enjoying being on the questioning end. And you could grill me all night, but you'd end up with the same information. Why don't you save us time and stress and just take my statement so I can go home to my boys?" Barry's bottom lip quivered, and a tear spilled down his cheek. "Please ... you know there's no way I had anything to do with Jeanette's murder. If you're trying to break me, my heart is already broken. You don't have to do this."

Jude shifted in his chair. Hadn't he, on one level, enjoyed making Barry Stein answer the questions for a change? He glanced over at Aimee, hoping she hadn't noticed. "Anything you want to ask Barry?"

"I think we have what we need," she said.

"All right, sir. You can go. If we have more questions, we know where to find you."

Barry got up, and a deputy outside the door escorted him away.

Jude sat for a moment, feeling both sheepish and baffled.

"I believe him," Aimee said.

"I'm not sure yet." Jude turned his pencil upside down and bounced the eraser on the table. "It really bothers me that we can't connect Jeanette Stein to the other victims. The killer changed his MO slightly, and the victim had nothing at all to do with the layoffs or the foreclosures."

"You're still thinking this was a copycat?" Aimee said.

"It was a perfect opportunity for Barry to do away with his wife, if he wanted to cover his tail."

"He said they were getting along fine."

"I know what he said. I want us to dig into Jeanette's background. Someone wanted her dead. Why?"

CHAPTER 19

Adele stood at the front door and waved to Murray as he got out of the old truck that had been a source of entertainment the day before.

"I'm a little late," he said. "It took longer to clean up than I planned, but the painting is done, and my customer is happy."

"I have a feeling all your customers are happy." Adele held open the front door and let Murray inside, aware that Isabel had walked the other way and disappeared into her room.

Murray turned and went into the kitchen. "Are the locks still in the pantry?"

"Yes, right where you left them. Why don't you take a break before you change the locks and have a slice of praline cake with me?"

Murray flashed a boyish grin. "You don't have to ask *me* twice."

"Me either. I've had a craving for this all day." Adele opened the refrigerator. "This is the last of it. It's all ready. Let's sit here in the kitchen."

She reached in the refrigerator and handed Murray two plates, each with a slice of cake and a fork, and then took out two glasses of milk and sat across the table from him.

"I had such an enjoyable time picking out the computer," she said.

"I did too." Murray took a huge bite of cake. "So you've mastered email?"

"I don't know that I've mastered it, but I'm comfortable now. I'd like to learn how to browse."

"That's easy enough. I'll be happy to show you how it works."

"I'd like that." Adele took a bite of cake and savored it a moment. "Did you happen to see Noah this afternoon?"

"He stopped by the house where I was painting. Told me he quit his job at Langley Manor until Flynn's murder is solved and that he could use my help to drum up more business. He's been living at Haven House for two years, and that's the limit. He's going to have to make other living arrangements."

"Poor man thought he was going to move out to Langley Manor. This change of plans was quite a blow."

"Tough break, all right." Murray was quiet and seemed lost in thought. Finally, he said, "You trust Noah?"

"I wouldn't have him working for me if I didn't. Why?"

Murray seemed hesitant to answer and then replied, "Just curious. You probably know him better than I do. He and I talk about surface stuff, but I don't really know him."

"Did he tell you that his ancestors were slaves at Langley Manor when Josiah Langley was using the house for the Underground Railroad?"

"Yes, he did tell me that. Just nothing about himself."

Adele let the icing melt in her mouth. "His ancestor Naomi was a slave there and gave up her chance for freedom to help the Langleys shelter the slaves on their way up North. It's just amazing that, six generations later, Noah is working with Langleys to keep the history alive. It would be tragic if that was marred by the suspicion surrounding Flynn Gillis's death."

"It doesn't bother you that Flynn's body was found out there?"

"Well, of course it bothers me," Adele said. "But not because I think Noah had anything to do with it. The Langleys are getting cancellations right and left. It's like a dark cloud hanging over them. The sheriff needs to get to the bottom of it."

"Father Vince says the sheriff is too busy trying to get the Bathtub Killer to worry about Flynn's case."

"That's probably true," Adele said. "It's such a shame. It might be a long time before the truth about Flynn's murder is uncovered. In the meantime, Noah won't be able to totally shake the suspicion, even though the sheriff doesn't have anything on him."

"Might make it hard for him to find work." Murray took a gulp of milk. "I like the guy, but I'll admit to you *I* have doubts. Why would an innocent man just turn in his keys and walk away from a job he loves? Don't get me wrong, even *if* it's true that Noah killed Flynn—and I'm not saying it is—that doesn't make him a dangerous person. Flynn pushed a lot of people to the edge. It could've just been a crime of passion."

Adele felt hot all over and was rendered mute for a moment. "You can't be serious. Noah doesn't have a mean bone in his body."

"I believe that, Adele. But Flynn might've pushed him too far."

"Have you said this to the sheriff?"

"Of course not. It's just a gut feeling. I don't have any proof, and I like the guy. I don't think he's dangerous or anything. But I can't help but wonder if Flynn pushed him over the edge."

"And you don't think a man that can be pushed to kill someone out of anger isn't dangerous?"

"Not necessarily. Not if his anger was only directed at one person."

Adele mashed the cake crumbs with her fork, trying not to show how disturbing she found Murray's comments to be.

"For example," he said, "Moses got mad and murdered a guy who was abusing an Israelite slave. And he wasn't a violent man."

"I'm not sure I'm comfortable with that analogy. Are you suggesting that Noah had grounds to kill Flynn?"

Murray shook his head. "I'm just suggesting that sometimes the murderer isn't a violent person, and the deed could've been a one-time thing—a crime of passion. But again, I don't have proof that Noah did *anything* wrong. There're just unanswered questions in my mind. I probably should've kept it to myself."

Yes, I wish you had. "I think we should probably not go down this line of conversation. It's unfair to speculate on something neither of us knows anything about."

"You're right," Murray said. "I'm sorry. That was really out of line."

Zoe stood outside the eatery, under the gallery that overhung the sidewalk, and smiled at passing tourists, handing them two-for-one dinner coupons for Zoe B's.

A limousine pulled up in front of the Hotel Peltier, and the doorman helped the new arrivals to climb out while the bellman unloaded their bags. On the gallery above the Coy Cajun Gift Shop, Madame Duval stood amid a jungle of greenery and flowers, holding her white poodle and watching the bustling activity on *rue Madeline.* The bright orange sale sign in the front window of Sole Mates seemed to draw shoe-loving ladies like a magnet.

The aroma of bread baking beckoned Zoe back inside. She walked over to the table by the window where Grace was seated next to Father Sam and across from Hebert and Tex.

"You fellas ready for me to take Grace off your hands?"

"*My eye!"* Hebert glanced up at her. "I'm jus' about to beat Père Sam at dis game o' checkers. I always win when Grace is watching. Isn't dat so?"

Grace gave a nod and giggled.

"Shoot, you just win—period," Tex said. "I've never seen anything like it."

"So you goin' to *make a babine?"* Hebert grinned, exposing a row of stained teeth. "Or you goin' to man up and play?" Hebert took his red king and jumped three of Father Sam's pieces.

"Mercy, I'm the one who should pout." Father Sam sat back in his chair, his arms folded.

"Dat all you got?" Hebert's tone was playful.

"Absolutely. You've shamed me enough for one day."

Savannah appeared at the table with the coffeepot, and the mood instantly turned somber.

"Y'all don't have to stop enjoying yourselves on my account," she said.

Tex set his mug where she could reach it better. "Doesn't seem right for us to be laughin' and carryin' on when you're hurtin' so bad."

"Sure it does." Savannah filled Tex's mug and set a few tubs of creamer on the table. "Aunt Nicole loved to laugh. She was the most positive person I've ever known. She wouldn't want the rest of us to be morose and gloomy because of what happened to her."

"When's the family coming?" Zoe said.

"Different times. They all live in Louisiana and don't have far to drive. Mother and Daddy are helping my grandparents plan the funeral."

Hebert looked up, his faded gray eyes full of compassion, his voice tender. *"Ça viens?"*

"It's coming together fine, all things considered. Aunt Nicole's casket will be placed in the family mausoleum. We're having a private service there before the funeral at Saint Catherine's. Police Chief Casey has promised to keep the media away so we can lay her to rest with just family and close friends present."

"How's da family doing?"

Savannah patted Hebert's stubbly cheek. "Not well, but thanks for asking. My grandparents keep saying they never expected to outlive any of their children. But murder? How do they even begin to deal with what their daughter might've been thinking and feeling in her last moments?"

"Dey can't. Remember how it was when Remy was hanged? His papa and all o' us suffered when we dwelled on it. Dat didn't change what was."

"I know." Savannah filled Hebert's cup. "But right now, they don't know how to stop thinking about it."

"Dey will. *Un jour à la fois.*"

Savannah nodded. "One day at a time." Her eyes were suddenly blue pools. "Great. That's exactly what I didn't want to happen. It's better if I don't talk about it here at work."

"It might help to talk about it with friends," Father Sam said. "We all love you and thought the world of Nicole. We'll help you through it."

Savannah wiped her eyes. "I can't help but wonder how that attorney is handling his wife being murdered. At least Aunt Nicole didn't have a husband or kids."

"I'll say one ting," Hebert said. "Most folks will change dere tone, now dat a young *mère* was murdered. Dey gonna want da man responsible put away."

"Hebert's right," Savannah said. "The public didn't care when they thought the victims were just greedy CEOs. Aunt Nicole wasn't like that, though she's been lumped in with the others. The victim who's going to draw attention is the young mother who left behind a husband and twin babies. I have to believe everyone is outraged over that."

"I sure am." Zoe helped Grace out of her booster chair and picked her up. "I wonder how Jeanette Stein is connected to all this."

"Maybe it's her husband," Savannah said. "It could've been a payback for something he did."

Hebert shook his head. "Dis is da reason I never wanted to live in New Awlins. But now da violence is here, too."

⚜

That night after dinner, Adele sat in the overstuffed chair in her bedroom, mulling over her earlier conversation with Murray. She had never doubted Noah's innocence until now. What if Flynn had pushed him too far? What if he *was* capable of murder? Should she be so trusting when even his closest friend wasn't?

Adele picked up the phone and keyed in the numbers to Danny Clinton's cell phone and then hung up. Had he ever failed to get back with her in a timely manner? What good would it do to push him? On the other hand, when had it ever been this critical? Adele rekeyed the numbers. Danny knew her well enough to know she wouldn't press him if it wasn't important.

"Hello."

"It's Adele Woodmore, Danny. Is this a good time to talk?"

"Sure. What's on your mind?"

"I know you said you'd get back to me in a week or so, but I was just wondering if you'd found out anything yet on Noah Washington."

"I'm finishing up another job. So no, I haven't."

Adele sighed. "Oh dear. I don't want to seem pushy. But when you start, I need you to look into Noah's background first. I'm interested in everything you can find and would appreciate your starting on this as soon as you're able."

"You sound worried."

"I have concerns."

"You want to share them with me?"

Adele played with the bottom button on her blouse. "I told you that Noah had been questioned by the sheriff in the death of Flynn Gillis. Murray Hamelin, who lives at Haven House with Noah, is beginning to question his innocence. Naturally, that bothers me."

"You think Washington is capable of murder?"

"No, I don't. But I can't afford to be naive either." Adele picked up a pencil and notepad and began doodling. "Danny, do you think it's possible a man can murder someone and not be a danger to anyone else?"

"I suppose so. There've been plenty of people who've committed murder and then gone on to live out their lives without killing again. And plenty more who've killed a bunch of folks before anyone has a clue."

Adele sighed. "I know you have other clients, and I wouldn't normally ask for special treatment. But if you can fast-track this, I'll pay you double."

"It's that important to you?"

"It really is."

"Then I'll get right on it, but there's no way I'm charging you double. Just give me a couple days. Some of Washington's records may have been lost in Katrina. Especially if he lived in the Ninth Ward, like he told you."

"I'm convinced he did."

"We'll see. I'll get back to you just as soon as I have anything."

"Thank you, Danny. I know you will."

Adele hung up the phone and stared at the open Bible on her nightstand. *Lord, it's no accident that Noah has come into my life. So what role am I to play?*

CHAPTER 20

Jude sat at the conference table in his office at the sheriff's department, going over all the evidence they had so far in the bathtub killings. He glanced at his watch. It was already 10:00 p.m. He had planned to spend the evening with Colette, getting absorbed in a movie and forgetting about the case. She had called twice and must have finally given up hope that he would make good on his promise.

He sensed someone had entered the room and then felt a pair of hands kneading his shoulders, the scent of White Diamond carrying his thoughts back to his Memorial Day weekend with Colette in New Orleans.

He reached up and took hold of a soft forearm. "So you decided to come rescue me, eh?"

"Someone had to do it." Colette Prejean put her lips to his ear. "You've been working fifteen hours straight. Enough is enough. You can't possibly be thinking clearly at this point."

"You're right. Why do I do this to myself?"

"I don't know, but you've been doing it for twenty-five years. You should know by now that once you pass a certain point, your mind shuts down and you're wasting your time trying to make headway."

"You know me too well."

"I do. You need to rest your mind. Get a good night's sleep. Go to early Mass in the morning. Then you can hit it again."

Jude rose to his feet and pulled Colette into his arms, savoring her scent and the peace that always settled over him when she decided to intervene.

He pressed his lips to her cheek. "I stood you up tonight. I'm sorry. Time got away from me."

"You've stood me up before." She pushed back and looked up at him, her voice surprisingly void of annoyance and sounding almost playful. "You can make it up to me."

"Sounds like you have something in mind."

She flashed an elfin smile. "I looked into renting a cabin in Colorado—near Telluride. They're running a promotion right now, and the rates are outrageously reasonable."

"Outrageously?"

"Absolutely. We could book now for the third week of September and lock in the price. We can do the entire vacation for almost five hundred dollars less than we budgeted. And it's the ideal time frame if we want to see the aspens after they've turned gold."

"I see. Are you trying to manipulate me because I've neglected you?"

"*Me?*" She giggled. "Of course I am. But the only way you're going to take a vacation is if you're coerced."

He relished the look of sheer delight on her face. She was obviously enjoying this. "All right, sweetheart. Book it. Then give me the dates so I can mark it on the schedule."

"See how easy that was?"

"It'll be fun," he said. "Something to look forward to."

"Are you about ready to call it a day?"

"I suppose. I'm hung up on Jeanette Stein. She doesn't seem to be connected in any way to the other victims."

"Maybe the other victims aren't connected either. Maybe it just looks as if they are."

Jude sighed. "Without that premise, I'll really be stymied."

"Sorry."

"I'm probably just trying too hard." He put his arm around Colette. "Come on, sugar. Let's go home. I know it's late, but why don't we pop some popcorn and watch a movie? You up for that?"

"I could be. If you were to *bribe* me."

Jude winced in jest. "Please. We don't use the B word around here."

"My terms are nonnegotiable—a pint of Scoops Chocolate Chocolate Chunk ice cream."

"You drive a hard bargain, ma'am. But I'm willing to meet your terms for an evening of exceptional company."

Jude walked toward the door with his arm around Colette and turned off the light. Maybe for a few hours he would be able to forget the image of Jeanette Stein's sister driving away from the murder scene with two crying babies in the backseat.

Vanessa stood out on the back deck, the thick night air seeming damp enough to wring out. A curious raccoon started up the steps then scurried away when it saw her.

She heard the door open and close. Did she want to have this conversation? Did she have a choice? She knew better than to let the day end before dealing with her anger at Ethan.

"There you are," he said. "Carter's sound asleep, and the guests are settled in for the night. Can we talk now?"

"I suppose so."

"You didn't end up asking Noah for his keys," Ethan said. "So why are you angry?"

"Because you asked *me* to do it. That was really unfair, especially since it was your decision and you knew I didn't agree with it. Do you think that just because Noah made the first move I wasn't stressed out? I worried all morning about how I was going to approach him. My neck is still so tight I've got a splitting headache."

"I didn't realize it would affect you this way. I'm sorry."

Vanessa heaved a sigh. "You should've seen the look on his face when he put the keys in my hand. It was like he was giving away part of himself. This is where he belongs, where his ancestors …" Her voice failed, and she didn't try to finish her sentence.

"I respect Noah for having sense enough to leave until things are settled," Ethan said. "I want to believe he didn't kill Flynn Gillis. But we need to be *sure* before we expose our son, our guests, and ourselves to someone who'll be living on the premises. You know I'm right."

"Doesn't it boil down to trust? How we can ever be sure?"

"We need to be a lot more sure than we are today."

"All I know is that Zoe, Pierce, and I would probably be dead if it hadn't been for Noah. He put his life on the line for us. And this is how we repay him?"

Ethan tilted her chin until she met his gaze. "We can never *repay* him. His bravery at that moment in time was a gift. But he can have a good heart and still be guilty of a bad deed—a lapse in judgment or control."

"Oh, stop being a psychologist for a moment. He didn't kill Flynn and you know it."

"No, I don't. Not yet."

"I believe him."

"And I *want* to. More than you know." Ethan's eyes were wide and filled with resolve. "But it's my job to protect this family. It would be irresponsible of me not to insist we put a little distance between us and Noah until Flynn Gillis's killer is found. Or at least until Noah's no longer a person of interest. Apparently he agrees since he chose to leave. Besides, you told me earlier that the deciding factor for his decision was all the cancellations—that he didn't want to jeopardize the future of Langley Manor."

"That's what he said. But he also asked me how *you* felt about him. I tried to cover for you and put things in the best possible light. But Noah could see through me."

"All right. So he knows I'm the bad guy. I don't know what you want from me. You know how fond I am of Noah. And you know the bond I have with him because our ancestors worked together to help free the slaves. But none of that changes the present. Fair or not, Noah has to ride out the investigation of Flynn Gillis's murder. Once he's cleared, business will pick up again, and things can go back to normal."

"But will they? Noah will never be able to forgive you for not trusting him after he saved our lives. Could you blame him?"

Ethan brushed the hair out of her eyes and wiped her tears with his thumbs. "Look, why don't I go talk to him? Man-to-man. I'll commend him for having the courage to leave while Flynn's murder is in question and assure him I want him cleared as much as you do. Would that help?"

"It might."

She turned away from Ethan and placed her hands on the deck rail. The moon shone brightly, illuminating the landscape and the ghostly haze that hovered over the cane fields that lay between Langley property and the neighboring plantation.

How would Josiah and Abigail Langley have handled the situation with Noah? Would they have stood by him—or waited until the law had proven his guilt or innocence?

Ethan stroked her hair. "Vanessa, I love you. I really don't want this to be an issue that divides us."

"My feelings matter too."

"Of course they do. It was insensitive of me to saddle you with the responsibility of getting Noah's keys back. Thankfully, it didn't come to that. But I really don't want to cause a rift between Noah and me either. Our families' history together is too important."

"I agree. And I think he needs to hear that from you."

⚜

Adele sat in the overstuffed chair in her room, her Bible clutched to her chest. She opened her eyes. How long had she been sitting there, hoping for a word of knowledge? Did she really think that God would speak audibly and tell her what to do? She had to rely on His Word and whatever wisdom she could find there.

It wasn't right to prejudge people. She knew that much. But Isabel made it sound as if her way of reaching out was irresponsible and risky. That both irritated and concerned her. Where did she draw the line? Wasn't she supposed to love her neighbor as herself? Noah had been nothing but kind to her and the Langleys and efficient in his work.

She put the Bible on the table and rose to her feet. She shuffled over to the window seat and sat, looking up at the moonlit sky, words from the Psalms instantly coming to mind.

Be exalted, O God, above the heavens; let your glory be over all the earth. Find rest, O my soul, in God alone; my hope comes from Him.

Murray's uneasiness about Noah and his reference to Moses' act of murder wouldn't leave her alone. Given the right circumstances, wasn't anyone capable of being pushed over the edge? How could she discern such a thing?

What good would it do for her to worry about it? She belonged to God. Wasn't every breath and step she would take known to Him? How could she be salt and light unless she was willing to shine and to bring out the best in those around her? Without that, her life didn't have much meaning and she was just taking up space.

Was she naive for trusting people? Was she leaving herself wide open for someone to take advantage of her? Was she putting Isabel at risk?

Lord, I don't know what to do. It's just not my nature to distance myself from people. You didn't.

She heard the floor creak in the hallway and then the door to Isabel's room close. Isabel had been quiet all evening. If it came down to letting Noah and Murray go—or losing Isabel—what would she do?

CHAPTER 21

Adele sat at her computer and checked for new messages just as Murray had taught her. She saw one from Zoe and clicked on it.

Hi Adele. If you would like to have Grace for a couple hours this afternoon, let me know when, and I'll have Maddie adjust her schedule accordingly. Love, Zoe

Adele smiled. Email was fun. She put her hands on the keys and then hesitated. What time should she tell Zoe? She had called Murray earlier this morning, and he was supposed to come by this afternoon and fix her dishwasher. What if he came by when Grace was there?

How could she respond to Zoe without revealing that Vanessa had slipped and told her Pierce didn't want Grace there if any of the men from Haven House were around?

"What do I do?" she mumbled to herself. This was beginning to get complicated. She shouldn't have to run her life to suit others. But wasn't it important to be sensitive? Honesty was always the best policy. Tell Zoe what her schedule was, and let her work around it.

She began typing. *Dear Zoe, I would love to have Grace anytime that works for you. I am expecting Murray to come by and fix my dishwasher (which decided to stop working last night after dinner). I don't know for sure what time he's coming because he's going to work me in. Isn't email handy? I don't know why I didn't do this sooner. Love, Adele*

There. That was easy. Zoe could decide what she wanted to do. Adele clicked on Vanessa's name, and a blank email page came up. She began writing a message. *Dear Vanessa, I'm thinking of you and praying that the authorities get to the bottom of Flynn Gillis's murder so Noah's name will be cleared. I'm here if you need some encouragement. With much love, Adele*

Adele pressed the Send button and got up and walked out to the kitchen.

Isabel had a cup and saucer in hand and was about to sit at the table. "Good morning, Mrs. Woodmore. Can I get you a cup of coffee?"

"Yes. Thank you."

Isabel brought Adele's coffee to the table and then sat across from her. "Did you remember that Peter Gautier's funeral is today at one?"

"Yes, I remember. I want you to take the afternoon off." Adele took a sip of coffee and held Isabel's gaze. "I called Murray this morning and asked him to come fix the dishwasher. I don't think either of us can do without it for long. He'll be by sometime after lunch."

"You're okay here by yourself?"

"Of course. Why wouldn't I be?"

Isabel started to say something and then didn't. Just as well. Adele was in no mood to spoil a perfectly glorious day.

Zoe read Adele's email and then put her phone in her pocket. So much for letting Grace go over there today. She would need to handle it delicately so Adele wouldn't figure out that her change of plans was because Murray was coming over.

"Come on, sweetie. Let's go see your uncles."

Grace clapped her hands with delight, her topaz eyes wide and bright, her blonde curls pulled into pigtails tied with yellow ribbons.

"You want to walk or ride?"

"I walk."

Zoe helped her slip on her Hello Kitty backpack and opened the front door. "Let Mommy help you down the stairs."

Grace ran out of the apartment and down the hall, waiting at the top of the stairs, looking adorable in her sunflower sundress and matching sandals.

Zoe held tightly to her daughter's hand as they walked together down the steps. When they reached the bottom of the stairs, Zoe said, "Remember not to run."

Grace let go of her hand and showed as much restraint as a two-year-old could, walking briskly through the alcove, past the office and the customer restrooms, and into the dining room. She squealed when she spotted the three men sitting at the table by the window. At that point, she forgot her manners and took off running.

By the time Zoe arrived at the table, Grace had shed her backpack and climbed into her booster seat and was already into her verbal routine with her adopted uncles.

Hebert leaned forward on his elbows, his mousy gray curls thick and unruly, his plaid shirt wrinkled. The adoring look on his face was priceless. How many more days would they have to enjoy his company? He was about to turn ninety-seven, though Zoe would have guessed him to be eighty.

"No, I *Grace* Brew-sar!"

"*You're* Grace Broussard?" Hebert grinned and tapped her on the nose. "Den we do know you."

Zoe took a beignet out of the basket, broke off a piece, and handed it to Grace. "Daddy's making you something healthy and yummy. It'll be ready soon." She looked around the table. "How's everyone this morning?"

Father Sam folded Monday's issue of the *Les Barbes Ledger* and pushed it aside. "We were just talking about Jeanette Stein. What a tragedy."

"Sure is," Tex said.

"Everyone's waiting for news dat dere's been anudder murder, but dere hasn't been any in two days. Dat's good."

"Maybe the killer did what he set out to do," Father Sam said. "We can only hope it's over."

"I thought I heard somewhere the authorities have the killer's DNA." Tex hooked his thumbs on his red suspenders. "If so, all they need now is the killer. I haven't heard anybody mention suspects."

"I still think the bathtub killings are related to the layoffs," Zoe said. "Though I don't know how Jeanette Stein fits in with the CEOs."

Father Sam took a sip of coffee. "Maybe the killer did away with the wrong person. Is that possible?"

"Highly unlikely," Tex said. "Someone that set on *gettin' even* for somethin' isn't gonna miss his mark. Hard to say how long he's been plannin' these murders."

"Have there ever been serial killings in Les Barbes before?" Zoe said.

Hebert shook his head and scratched his unshaven chin. "Nope. Dere's been more murders in Les Barbes in da past week dan dere's been in two decades. Dis is out o' control."

"I'll bet every CEO in the region is nervous." Savannah stood at the table with a fresh pot of coffee and started pouring refills. "There's no indication this killer is finished. Maybe there's just too much media attention after Jeanette Stein's murder, and he's decided to lay low for a while."

"I hope and pray he's done," Zoe said. "But Savannah may be right. He numbered the last victim. There was no indication it was over."

Jude sat at the conference table in his office with Deputy Chief Aimee Rivette and Police Chief Casey Norman. He took a sip of the Starbucks coffee Aimee had picked up and read through the report on trace evidence gathered at the murder scenes of Jeanette Stein and Nicole Aubry.

DNA was found on a Kleenex in a trash can at the scene of Jeanette Stein's murder—and it matched DNA from the eyelash found in Girard Darveau's bathroom and skin cells on a towel found in Peter Gautier's bathroom. The DNA didn't match anyone's in the NCIC database.

No conclusive DNA was found at Nicole Aubry's murder scene. But a muddy right shoe print was found on the wet bathroom floor—a man's size ten. Not distinguishable enough to identify the brand. But the soil analysis indicated soil consistent with south Louisiana and contained Broadleaf Buster Plus, a weed killer that could be bought at any garden center but was not found in samples taken from any of the victims' yards. But it was present in soil samples collected from the floor at each murder scene.

"I think we can reasonably conclude we're looking at the same perp," Jude said. "Even though we didn't get viable DNA from Aubry's murder scene, her body was positioned in the bathtub as if she were lying in a casket—same as the others. We never released that detail to the media."

"Ironic, isn't it?" Casey said. "We've nailed this guy, but we don't know who he is."

"He's bound to get careless." Aimee pulled the box of doughnut holes closer and examined the choices. "They all do. I cringe to know he's still out there. I really don't want to conduct another interview like the one we did with Barry Stein."

"I pushed him pretty hard." Jude looked over at Casey. "I had to be sure he wasn't involved in his wife's murder. The guy's certainly shrewd enough to pull off a copycat murder."

"That's for sure." Casey set his copy of the report on the table. "Guess it's a moot point now though. Stein volunteered his DNA, and it doesn't match the lab results. And his shoe size is nine."

"I didn't need the lab results to know that man didn't kill his wife," Aimee said.

Jude didn't either and was still ashamed that he had taken pleasure in making Barry Stein answer uncomfortable questions at such a gut-wrenching time.

"I suppose we should go out there and update the media," Casey said. "It couldn't hurt for people to know that their sheriff and police departments have been working round the clock. The lab put aside everything else and got us those results."

Jude closed the report and rose to his feet. "Let's go do it. We can conclude with relative certainty that the same person or persons were involved in the four serial murders."

"Think we should get an FBI profiler involved?" Aimee said.

Jude shook his head. "We don't need the feds to tell us these murders are related to the layoffs."

"What about Jeanette Stein?" Aimee said. "The media's going to ask you how she's connected to the other victims."

Jude arched his eyebrows. "We'll just tell them the truth: We don't know yet, but we're connecting the dots. And while Casey and I talk to the media, why don't you find out from Gil if his team has uncovered anything that would tie her to the others."

⁂

Adele pushed aside the day's newspaper and tried to put the disturbing headlines out of her mind. She looked out through the bay window at her nicely mowed and trimmed lawn. Noah's suggestion to resod the yard with Saint Augustine grass had solved the problem of growing grass in limited sunlight—at least for now.

She smiled, thinking back on how she had enjoyed watching Noah as he plunged his hands into the damp, rich soil, creating a beautiful border garden along her fence. Pansies, jasmine, begonias, snapdragons, daylilies, and others she couldn't remember the names of—colorful confetti, celebrating the Giver of life. Could the same gentle hands that had tenderly planted and cared for such delicate beauty also have brutally strangled another man to death? She shuddered to imagine it.

Why should she give in to the what-ifs that had bothered her since her conversation with Murray? As far as she could tell, Noah was a good and decent man. A creator of beauty. A man who worked with the earth and didn't mind getting his hands dirty. Any thought that he might have killed Flynn Gillis was pure speculation. The sheriff let him go. Obviously there was no evidence. Who was she to entertain such thoughts?

She sighed. Zoe had decided not to bring Grace over. She said it was because having a toddler there would be too much for Adele when Murray came to fix the dishwasher. Obviously, Zoe was honoring Pierce's insistence that Grace be kept away from the men at Haven House. Zoe would never volunteer that information and would likely be embarrassed if she thought Adele knew. Better to say nothing and plan to keep Grace on another day.

All this suspicion was dizzying. She hated that she was feeling suspicious of Noah simply because others were. Perhaps Danny's investigation would revive her initial feeling that Noah was a good person, worthy of her trust and her business.

But if Danny couldn't dispel the doubt—what then?

The doorbell rang. She got up and went to the door, surprised by her almost giddy response to seeing Murray on the porch, toolbox in hand. How fond she had grown of this young man.

She held open the door and let him in. "I'm so glad you could work me in."

"I'll always work *you* in, Adele. You're my favorite customer. And you feed me well." He laughed and patted his middle. "I think I've gained a little weight since I started working for you. So what's your dishwasher doing?"

"Nothing. It won't go on."

"Let me take a look." Murray turned and went into the kitchen.

"It amazes me that you know how to fix things," she said. "It takes a certain mind."

"I was just born that way. I could fix things even when I was a kid." Murray sat on his heels and began fiddling with the dials.

"I'll bet you were a happy child."

Murray glanced over at her, a smile on his face. "What makes you say that?"

"I don't know. You have a cheerful, boyish side that I like. Though I never had a grandson, I often imagine what it might have been like."

"Grace is like a granddaughter, though, right?"

"Oh yes. Loving her satisfies something that nothing else has. Didn't you tell me you were an only child?"

"Uh-huh. I always wanted a younger sister. Don't really know why."

"After your parents died, did you have extended family?"

In the silence that followed, she could almost hear the door to Murray's past slam shut. Why wouldn't he let her in?

"Aha, here's the problem," he said, raising his voice slightly. "You need a new switch."

"Is that an easy thing to fix?"

"Pretty simple. I'll probably have to order the part. But if I have it sent overnight, I could put it on tomorrow afternoon."

"That's such good news. I'll pay the shipping, of course."

Murray put a screwdriver back in his toolbox and stood. "Why don't I go order the part right now?" He glanced at his watch. "If I hurry, I might still be able to catch the noon buffet lunch at Haven House."

"No need to rush. Have lunch with me," Adele said. "That way we could visit. And you could relax before you go back to work."

"I don't want to put Isabel out. I don't think she likes me."

"Isabel's not here, hon. She went to Peter Gautier's funeral."

"I didn't realize she knew him."

"She and Gautier's daughter Renee went to high school together."

"Small world," Murray said. "In that case, thanks. I'll take you up on your offer, but I don't mind making myself a sandwich. You don't have to wait on me."

"Nonsense. It would be fun to serve you."

Murray removed his New Orleans Saints cap, his face almost as red as his hair. "That's really sweet of you. You're always looking out for me."

"I've grown fond of you, Murray. I enjoy your company very much. I'm hoping we might try another adventure. I haven't had a banana split since Alfred passed, and Zoe told me Scoops makes something called a Banana Mountain. Maybe some afternoon when you're not too busy—or maybe even a Sunday—we could go indulge ourselves—if you're not embarrassed to be seen with an old woman."

"Of course I'm not embarrassed to be seen with you. You're fun. I would think it would be the other way around. It's not every day that a dignified, refined woman like yourself would lower the bar and hang out with the likes of me."

"I don't believe that God has a bar for measuring social status. I certainly don't."

"Are you serious?" Murray's blue eyes widened, his freckles pronounced from exposure to the sun. "What would your friends say? It's one thing for me to go with you to pick out a computer. A social outing is entirely different."

"I'm eighty-six. I can do what I want. You're like the grandson I never had. And I don't see that it's anyone's business if I want you to accompany me to the ice cream parlor, do you?"

"Not really, no. But we'll hardly be inconspicuous in my old truck. It's certainly not sophisticated."

Adele chuckled. "That's what made our last adventure so much fun. I thought it was great riding up high and getting to see the world from a whole new perspective. I rode in the back of that Rolls-Royce for over forty years. Never could see much."

"You're a hoot, you know that?" The corners of Murray's mouth twitched. "I'm game. Let me check to see what I've got on tap this week. I'll make some time."

Adele saw a spark in Murray's eye—something she couldn't quite read. Was he agreeing to the outing just to please an old woman itching for adventure? Did he feel sorry for her? Or did he enjoy her company as much as she enjoyed his?

CHAPTER 22

Late Monday afternoon, Vanessa Langley hung up the phone and fought back the tears that threatened to turn her mascara into black streams. When she and Ethan opened Langley Manor as a bed-and-breakfast, it never crossed their minds that they would ever have to deal with cancellations on this scale—or a murder on the property. And now she was getting calls from well-meaning friends who questioned whether it was safe for Carter to be staying out there while the killer was at large.

"Mom, what's wrong?"

Carter's voice startled her, and she quickly wiped her eyes and pasted on a smile, then turned around. Her son's cheeks were flushed and sweaty and his mop of strawberry blond hair windblown. Angel sat next to him, panting.

"Where have you two been?" she said. "I asked you to stay close to the house. I want you where I can see you." An image of Flynn Gillis's dead body lying in the bayou popped into her head.

"I was out back, throwing the Frisbee for Angel."

"Good." Vanessa brushed the hair off his damp face. "I baked peanut butter cookies. Would you like some?"

"Yes, I'm starved! I could eat a hundred thousand million."

Vanessa chuckled in spite of herself. "How about two—and a glass of milk? I don't want to spoil your dinner."

Carter flashed a jack-o'-lantern grin. "When's the last time *I* didn't want dinner?"

"You have a good appetite, all right. But that's partly because you have a mother who spaces out your snacks."

"Can Angel have *her* cookies too?"

"Sure."

She followed Carter into the kitchen.

He raced to the pantry and took out the familiar green and white bag and gave two dog treats to Angel. "Mom, where's Noah? He loves your peanut butter cookies."

"He's not here right now. Use the hand sanitizer, please."

Vanessa poured Carter a glass of milk.

He cleaned his hands, and then, with his elbows, he lifted his upper body onto the counter and took two cookies out of the cookie jar. "When is Noah moving into the yellow house?"

"I don't know, Carter. It's not finished yet."

"Mr. Jack said he would have it all done by this time next week. That's only seven days. That's even before my birthday."

"When did you talk to Jack?" Vanessa turned and held his gaze. "Carter, did you go to the caretaker house? You said you were out back, throwing the Frisbee."

"I went there *before* I went out back," he said sheepishly.

She took him by the hand, led him over to the table, and sat facing him. "A half-truth is just a different way of telling a lie."

"Sorry."

"I wish I didn't have to keep you close to the house," she said.

"Then why *do* you?"

Vanessa studied his innocent face and questioned whether she should tell him. How could she not? People were talking. He was bound to find out. Wouldn't she rather he heard it from her?

"Carter, when you were at day camp the other day, something happened. I haven't said anything to you because I don't want you to worry. But now I think it's more important for you to know so you'll obey me about not roaming the property until I give you permission."

"What happened?"

"Angel found a man's body down in the bayou. He was dead. Sheriff Prejean said someone killed him."

Carter's bright blue eyes were round and wide. "Did someone *shoot* him?"

"No. Someone choked him."

"Who did it?"

"Well, that's just it, sweetie. We don't know yet."

Carter went over and sat on her lap. "You think he might hurt *me?*"

"I think he probably just wanted to hurt Flynn Gillis. That's the dead man's name. But until we know more, I want you to play close to the house, where I can see you. I mean it." She gently squeezed his wrist. "Do you understand?"

"Yes, ma'am."

"You're not to go outside without Angel."

"I know, Mom."

"If you disobey me again, you'll have to play indoors."

His gaze met hers, lines forming on his forehead. "Have any *kids* been killed here before?"

"No." She wet her thumb and wiped a speck of dirt off his cheek. "Daddy and I think the bad man is gone. But until we're sure, I need you to do what I ask. Do you understand?

He nodded. "Why do you look sad?"

"I'm just disappointed. Another couple just canceled their reservation."

"Oh, man. That's a bummer."

Vanessa forced herself not to smile at her son's sincere attempt at empathy.

Carter broke a cookie in two and stuffed half into his mouth. "Why do people keep doing that?"

"I think, before they stay here, they want to know as much as Daddy and me about why the dead man was found in our bayou."

"Because whoever hurt him might hurt them?"

"They're being careful, Carter. Just like we are."

"But Noah will protect us. He showed you the slave's tunnel so you could get away from that bad man."

Vanessa blinked, but the tears came anyway.

"Mommy?" Carter cupped her face in his hands.

Vanessa resisted the impulse to turn away. She swallowed the ball of emotion that tightened her throat and struggled to find her voice. "I … I'm fine, sweetie. Even mommies have days when too many things go wrong. This has been that kind of day."

"Did you pray and ask Jesus to help you?"

She hadn't. Normally that was the first thing she would do. She took one of Carter's hands and pressed it to her cheek. "I didn't. I don't know why either. Maybe that's what's wrong."

"I always pray like you showed me, and Jesus always helps me when I ask Him."

"Me, too." She brushed the hair out of Carter's eyes and managed a smile. The last thing she expected today was spiritual counsel from her not-quite-seven-year-old.

Lord, why didn't I come to You with this? Is it because I'm still angry with Ethan? Help me to handle this so that I don't scare Carter and so that it doesn't divide Ethan and me. And please take care of the bed-and-breakfast business. We can't keep taking these financial hits and expect to survive.

⁂

Zoe sat with Pierce and Grace, having dinner at the table in the kitchen at Zoe B's. She took a spoonful of seafood gumbo, blew on it, and then put it into her mouth, savoring the shrimp.

Pierce seemed to study her. "I'd like to win the Copper Ladle again this year, but don't you just know that Marie Nadeau is working overtime, trying to top my gumbo?"

"I'm not sure that's possible." Zoe took another bite.

"You seem preoccupied tonight," Pierce said.

"Do I?"

"Zoe, don't punish me because I don't want you-know-who around those men at Haven House. I'm just being a responsible dad."

"I know. I think you're overreacting."

"Be that as it may, I would be wrong not to speak my mind."

"It was embarrassing backing out of my offer to leave Grace with Adele. The woman's very astute. I'm sure she's starting to figure things out."

"That's probably a good thing. Adele knows we love her. She won't blame us for being protective."

"Except that it undermines her judgment."

Pierce's eyebrows came together. "That's not my intention. But the fact is, Adele is tenderhearted and a bit naive. She would likely invite Jack the Ripper to stay for tea." He reached over and put his hand on hers. "That's part of what's so endearing about her. But I'm just not wired that way. I'd rather be safe than sorry. Deep down, you know it's the best thing for Grace."

Their daughter beamed and pointed to herself. "I Grace."

"Yes, you are." He tilted her chin. "And Mommy and I love you most of all."

"I talked to Vanessa just before we came downstairs for dinner," Zoe said. "They had three more cancellations today. Right now, their occupancy is less than fifty percent."

"Unreal." Pierce shook his head. "Let's just hope they can afford to stay in business until Jude figures out if Noah's innocent."

"I wish you would stop saying *if.* All the suspicion around Flynn's murder has done irreparable harm. I would never have thought in a million years that you would doubt Noah on any level—not after he saved our lives."

"Noah's a good man. He's not a perfect man. I have no idea what his relationship was with Flynn or what might've happened between them."

"Noah said he didn't do it. I'm willing to give him the benefit of the doubt."

"You make it sound so simple, Zoe. Do you think if Noah killed Flynn he's going to admit it to you or to anyone else?"

❧

Adele sat at her computer, thinking back on the enjoyable lunch she'd had with Murray. What had happened to this young man to cause him to end up under a bridge, penniless and homeless? He certainly hadn't given her a hint and seemed to shut down completely anytime she tried to get him to talk about his parents.

Not that it was any of her business. But she really was fond of Murray. Was it so wrong to want to know what had caused a bright, skilled, polite young man to withdraw from society? Murray was neither helpless nor a freeloader. He was hardworking, honest, and considerate. So was Noah, for that matter. Entering the homeless scene had been a choice for both men—why? Each was so capable of taking care of himself.

Lord, I'm such an unlikely person to befriend these men. And yet You've allowed our paths to cross for a reason. Help me not to judge them but to show them Your love and kindness.

Adele held the gold cross that hung from the chain around her neck, her mind wandering back three summers ago when Zoe came to her and confessed her darkest secrets. How different her life would be now if she had judged Zoe instead of reaching out to her.

Adele's cell phone rang and brought her back to the present.

"Hello."

"Adele, it's Danny. I'm in New Orleans and would like to pass on what I've got so far on Noah Washington."

"Oh good. Let me go to my room so we can keep this conversation private."

Adele walked down the hall and into her bedroom. She closed the door and sat in her overstuffed chair.

"Okay, Danny. I'm listening."

"Looks like Noah was telling the truth about losing everything in Katrina. He lived in the Ninth Ward with his wife, Rachellyn, and teenage daughters, Tasha and Teena. According to the police report, their home was flooded, and the four of them waited on the roof for rescuers. When the floodwaters covered the roof, they clung to a heavy wood beam that floated by. His wife and daughters couldn't hold on and were swept away."

"How dreadful." Adele paused for a moment, remembering how it felt to lose a baby and wondering how a person could cope with losing his entire family. "What happened to Noah?"

"Someone in a bass boat found him a few miles from his home, clinging to a street sign."

"What happened after that?"

"Don't know yet," Danny said. "I have a copy of the police report, including Noah's statement, but I don't see where he was housed in the aftermath. About a million people left New Orleans, either just before Katrina or right after. Finding out where Noah was taken is next to impossible. The police report indicates he didn't have flood insurance. Also that he was in business for himself. His company name was NW Landscaping. Noah didn't file income tax returns after Katrina—not until two years ago when he moved into Haven House and started working for the Langleys and you and other folks in the region. Probably didn't have a steady job in those years he didn't file. It's hard to say at which point in time he joined the ranks of the homeless. But it could have been right after Katrina. The man lost everything."

"He must have been desolate." Adele moved her gaze over to the nightstand, to the wedding picture of Alfred and her. "I withdrew from everyone for three years after Alfred died of a heart attack. I was devastated."

"Before you feel too sorry for the guy, keep in mind his sorrow could've turned to anger and bitterness. That's a recipe for violence if I ever saw it."

Adele's heart sank. "But Noah seems so gentle and kind. I've never even seen him lose his temper."

"Have you ever provoked him? I don't think you can afford to assume he's incapable of violence. In his mind, the government let him down. The rescuers failed his family. He was helpless to do anything. All that anger has to go somewhere."

"Not everyone who experiences a tragic loss turns violent. And he's not wanted by the law, or he couldn't be living at Haven House."

"This is true. But like I said, what happened to him is a recipe for violence."

Adele sighed. "Danny, I'm right back where I started. Noah had already told me he lost everything in Katrina."

"I know. But this confirms he told you the truth. I'm not done digging. I want to find out where he went and what he was doing in those years he didn't file income tax."

"You said that would be next to impossible."

"*Next* to impossible, but not impossible." Danny had a smile in his voice. "I've got contacts in FEMA, the Red Cross, Salvation Army, Catholic Charities—just about every agency that might have a list of victims and what shelters they were sent to. Those records are out there somewhere because many of the victims were trying to get reconnected with family members in other shelters. Do you want me to keep digging?"

Adele thought for a moment. As sympathetic as she was to Noah's misfortune, the facts Danny confirmed didn't relieve her suspicion that Noah might have a dark side.

"Yes," she said. "Keep digging. See what else you can find."

CHAPTER 23

Murray sat on the floor in front of the big-screen TV in the lounge at Haven House, watching the six o'clock news. He spotted Noah in the hallway and got up and followed him into the dorm room they shared.

"You okay?"

"Not really. My head hurts from thinkin' about how I can get more work. I've got a few yards to mow, but I was makin' most o' my income from bein' the groundskeeper for the Langleys."

"Are you any good at painting?" Murray said.

"I can paint with the best o' them. Always did my own, inside and out."

"Why don't you take all my paint jobs? I've got plenty of other work to keep me busy."

"You serious?"

"Sure. It's the least I can do."

Noah's face softened, and he swallowed hard. "That'd sure help me out. I've gotta move fast and make some plans. My time's up here. I need a place to hang my hat, and I need to make enough money to pay for it. I don't wanna be homeless again."

"So take the paint jobs. It might not be enough in the long run, but in the short run, it should help."

Father Vince appeared in the doorway. "Noah, I spoke with Monsignor Robidoux, and he's granted you a six-month extension."

"He's lettin' me stay?" Noah's eyebrows came together. "Does he know I'm a person of interest in Flynn Gillis's murder?"

"I didn't bring it up. I told him there's been a delay in your moving out to Langley Manor. That's true. And he knows your family tie to the Langleys."

"It means a lot that you went to bat for me." Noah's eyes glistened. "I really wasn't sure where I was goin' if I had to leave here."

"Well, the pressure's off."

"That's *great* news, Father." Murray slapped Noah on the back. "We were just talking about Noah taking my painting jobs until Flynn's murder is solved and he can move out to Langley Manor."

Father Vince turned to Noah. "Do you have experience painting?"

"Shore do. I always did my own. It's like ridin' a bicycle. You don't forget how."

"There. That's another problem solved. God is good."

"Why do you always say that?" Murray asked. "I don't mean any disrespect, but what did God have to do with this? Shouldn't we be thanking Monsignor Robidoux and ourselves for working out the details?"

"God's always involved in the details."

Murray pushed his hands deeper into his pockets. *Not always.*

Jude wadded up an old phone memo and tossed it in the trash, deciding to call it a day, when he heard a knock at the door.

Gil Marcel stood in the doorway.

"Come in, Gil. How come you're still here?"

"I could ask you the same thing, Sheriff. I thought you were meeting Colette for dinner at Zoe B's."

"I was just about to leave," Jude said. "What's up?"

"We've found something that might connect Jeanette Stein to the case."

"Talk to me."

Gil handed him some papers stapled together. "This is the list of former employees at Aubry Computer Systems. It goes back five years. Look on the next to the last page at the name highlighted in yellow, second from the bottom."

"Jeanette LaBelle?"

"That was Jeanette Stein's maiden name. We checked it out. The Social Security number and date of birth match. She worked in Aubry's Lafayette branch for thirteen months."

Jude lifted his gaze, his mind racing in reverse. "And Barry Stein, the hotshot defense lawyer, who never misses a trick, didn't think that was *relevant?* Get him back in here. Now. I'll call Colette and tell her to meet me later. I want to be here when he's questioned."

"Yes, sir."

"And call Aimee back in. I want her here for this."

Gil nodded and left.

Jude sat back in his chair, his hands linked behind his head, trying not to let his anger boil over. Why would Barry Stein conveniently not mention that his murdered wife had worked for the murdered CEO of Aubry Computer Systems? What was he hiding? Stein was a cunning man who knew how to manipulate the facts in his favor. He wasn't dumb enough to think the authorities weren't going to find out his wife worked for Aubry.

He sat looking out at the Saint Catherine Parish Courthouse, remembering the times he'd been subpoenaed by Barry Stein to give testimony that worked in favor of his good-for-nothing client. All the guy cared about was making money and growing his ego. But this wasn't about getting back at Barry. This was about holding the man accountable for knowingly withholding evidence in the case. Why would he do that—unless he had something to hide?

Jude picked up the phone and dialed home.

"Hey there."

"Colette, honey, I'm going to have to stand you up again."

"Okay. So I'll get new luggage to go with that trip to Colorado. It could be worse."

"Seriously, I'm really sorry. We're bringing back someone we questioned before in the bathtub killings, and it might be a break in the case. I doubt I'll be more than a couple hours. You want to plan on meeting me for a late dinner?"

"Sure. Zoe B's is open until eleven. They'll serve until ten thirty. I've got nothing planned. I can be on call."

He smiled. "I love you."

"See if you still feel that way after I've priced a new set of soft luggage."

"You're kidding, right?"

"Of course I'm kidding. I'm so excited about the trip to Colorado I'd throw my clothes in paper bags, if I had to."

"Do you need luggage?"

"I was kidding, Jude. I'm fine with a late dinner. Do what you need to do there. Can you tell me what's going on?"

"Not yet. Let me see how this goes. I'll call you when it's over."

⁂

Jude stood on one side of two-way glass and watched as Gil and Aimee brought Barry Stein into the interview room and shut the door. They seated Barry on one side of the table and then sat facing him.

"You'd better have a good reason for dragging me down here," Barry said.

Gil folded his hands on the table. "You were escorted. Believe me, you'd know if you'd been dragged."

"Why am I here? I told you everything before."

"Is that so?"

Stein rolled his eyes. "Stop with the intimidation tactic, detective. It won't work on me. I can dish it out better than you can. So let's don't go there."

Gil flashed a phony smile. "Fine, I'll cut to the chase. Are you aware your wife worked for Aubrey Computer Systems before you two were married?"

Barry's eyebrows furrowed. "What are you talking about?"

"Is that a yes or a no, counselor?"

"No. Jeanette was a software programmer for Davidson Software Solutions. To my knowledge, that's the only job she ever held. Other than she worked part-time as a receptionist in the dean's office at Wentzel College when she attended there."

Gil turned the list of names to the last page and pushed it across the table. "That's her name—Jeanette LaBelle. The Social Security number and date of birth match. Your wife worked in the Lafayette branch of Aubry Computer Systems for thirteen months. Look at the dates."

"That was before we met," Barry said. "I knew her when she worked for Davidson. She never mentioned working for Aubry."

"Are you telling me that never, in all the time you two shared personal histories, did she mention working for Aubry Computer Systems?"

"That's exactly what I'm telling you."

"I don't believe you."

"I don't care. It's the truth."

"You'd better care, counselor. You could be charged with giving a false report to law enforcement, which is a Class A misdemeanor. Even if you got off with probation, I don't have to tell you that being convicted of a crime of *moral turpitude* could get you disbarred or put on probationary status."

"How dare you threaten me!" Barry slammed his hands on the table. "That's totally bogus. I answered all your questions. I didn't withhold anything. I didn't know Jeanette worked for Aubry."

"Makes me wonder how well you knew your wife."

"I knew Jeanette better than anyone on the planet."

Gil leaned forward and held Barry's gaze. "Why would she lie to you?"

"She didn't lie. It never came up."

"Never came up?" Gil smirked and shook his head. "How long did you and Jeanette see each other before you married?"

"Four months."

"And you must've had a lot of time to talk in those four months."

"What's your point?"

"What conceivable reason would Jeanette have for not telling you she worked for Aubry, especially when she told you she worked in the dean's office at the college? That means she deliberately hid it from you."

"I have no idea. She led me to believe she worked for Davidson immediately after she graduated from college. I can't recall if she ever actually *said* that, but that's the impression she gave me. I have no idea why she would choose not to tell me about her working for Aubry. I really don't."

Jude leaned on the glass and studied Barry. He didn't look like a man who was hiding something. Then again, he could convince entire juries his lowlife clients were innocent. Could he be using those same skills now?

Jude watched his every movement. Barry was slick, but there was no way that man killed his wife. So why would he lie about her working for Aubry—to protect her reputation? Had she been in some kind of trouble? Done something that would be embarrassing to her—or to him?

Jude spoke into the mike so Gil could hear through his earphone. "Gil, push him about Jeanette's employment at Aubry. See if he's covering for her—if she had something to hide."

Gil coughed to buy a few moments and then said, "Maybe it was Jeanette who had something to hide? Is that why you didn't want us to know she worked for Aubry? You might as well tell us. We're going to find out anyway."

"It's not that I didn't want you to know," Barry said. "*I* didn't know."

"I don't believe you."

"That's unfortunate, detective. I can't tell you what I don't know."

"Well, you've got to do better than that, counselor." Gil's voice went up an octave. "Or things are going to start getting ugly. I know you're hiding something."

Barry seemed furious, then folded his arms and sat back in his chair. "No. I'm not. And you don't have enough to hold me. Look. I can play this game better than you and Sheriff Prejean hiding behind that mirror. I don't want to play games. I want Jeanette's killer brought to justice, and I'll cooperate any way I can. But I'm telling you the truth. I didn't know she worked for Aubry. Have you talked to employees? I'm sure some of them were working there when Jeanette was. Maybe they can help you figure out if Jeanette's working at Aubry is significant."

"Oh, it's significant, counselor. It's just a matter of figuring out *how* significant."

"Well"—Barry rose to his feet—"while you're busy trying to figure out *how* significant, I need to go home and take care of my twins, who no longer have a mother to rock them to sleep…." His voice cracked. "Am I free to go?"

Gil hesitated, seemingly surprised at Barry's sudden show of emotion.

Jude spoke into the mike. "Let him go, Gil. We know where to find him. Let's see if we can find out more about Jeanette's employment at Aubry. Let's go talk to her sister again."

❧

Adele sat in the sunroom, flipping through the July issue of *Better Homes and Gardens*. Why was Isabel so quiet at dinner? She didn't have much to say about Peter Gautier's funeral, other than his family seemed devastated, the church was half empty, and she thought there was more media outside than mourners inside.

Isabel didn't ask about Murray's visit, other than wanting to know what he discovered about the dishwasher and what it would take to fix it. Just as well. She would not have taken kindly to Adele's fixing lunch for Murray. And how was she going to react when Murray came to take Adele to Scoops for one of those Banana Mountains? Pity they couldn't just invite Isabel to come along. Then again, a third party would change the dynamic. They interacted so well. She was growing very fond of him and wondered, more than ever, about what had caused him to enter the homeless lifestyle.

Isabel walked into the sunroom. "I need to go to the grocery store."

"Really? I thought you just went."

"We're low on smoked turkey and Swiss cheese. I know how much you enjoy that for lunch. Grace does too. If she comes tomorrow, there won't be enough."

Adele glanced up and turned a page of her magazine. The look on Isabel's face told her that she'd figured out Murray had stayed for lunch. Why didn't she just ask about it?

"All right, hon," Adele said. "We could use more milk, too."

"I saw that. I also need chocolate chips so I can bake more cookies. I can't believe they're almost gone already."

Adele didn't comment. Why should she feel guilty for having Murray stay for lunch and sending him off with a baggie full of cookies? She wasn't going to volunteer that information to Isabel as if she were confessing some wrongdoing. If she wanted to know why they had gone through the grocery items so quickly, let her ask the question.

"I'll be back in a few minutes." Isabel turned and left.

Adele set down the magazine. It was unpleasant enough sensing disapproval from her friends. She didn't have to tolerate it from Isabel.

Lord, You've brought Isabel into my life for a reason, just as You have Noah and Murray. I'm irritated with her. Help me not to be. I do believe she has my best interests at heart.

Adele sighed. It occurred to her Isabel might have been sent to warn her, but she immediately dismissed the idea. She would just wait and see what Danny had to say.

CHAPTER 24

Vanessa sat on the couch in their private living quarters at Langley Manor, aware of footsteps moving across the hardwood floor in the guest room above. What if the cloud surrounding Flynn Gillis's murder didn't lift for a long time? Or what if his murder was never solved? Would Ethan ever agree to hire Noah back? Could they afford to? The home's historical tie to the Underground Railroad would not be nearly as attractive to guests without the opportunity to meet a real descendant of the slave Naomi who was now a working partner with the Langleys in keeping the history alive.

Vanessa heard the back door open and close. A few seconds later, Ethan came into the living room and closed the door. He walked over and kissed her on the cheek, then sat beside her on the sofa.

"Well?" she said. "How did Noah react?"

"It's obvious he's hurting, but he seems confident he did the right thing by leaving until he's cleared. I supported his decision and commended him for wanting to preserve Langley Manor's reputation as much as we do."

"But I don't support his decision to leave!"

"I told him that, too."

"What did he say?"

Ethan pushed his glasses up higher on his nose, his dark curls tight from the night's humidity. "He said he knew that."

Vanessa didn't say what she was thinking. "What's he going to do for money? A place to live? He can't stay at Haven House."

"Actually, Father Vince took care of that."

Vanessa listened as Ethan told her about the six-month extension and Murray's sharing his painting jobs.

"Honey, the minute Noah is no longer a person of interest in the case, he can move into the caretaker house. I promise."

"Maybe he won't want to," Vanessa said. "Why would he want to work for someone who doesn't trust him?"

Ethan tilted her chin and looked into her eyes. "Noah chose to turn in his keys and leave, Vanessa. And unless *you* told him I wanted him to, he did it of his own accord and because he thought it would be best for the business. I happen to agree with him. One thing all three of us agree on is that we won't survive long with only half our rooms filled in peak season."

Vanessa pulled away and stared at her hands. "What are we going to do if this trend continues? The last thing either of us wants to do is tell your dad and uncles that we're in trouble and need money. They'll be so disappointed, especially after we've been booked almost every night for six months."

Ethan sighed. "We'll find a way to hold it together. Have you contacted the people on the waiting list?"

"Every last one." Vanessa's eyes clouded over. "None of them are interested in booking right now."

Ethan didn't say anything.

Vanessa plucked a tissue from the box on the end table. "If anyone had told me a week ago that Noah's reputation would be in question and we'd be facing financial problems because people were afraid to stay here, I'd have laughed."

"Me, too, honey. But things are what they are. We have to deal with it a day at a time."

Vanessa wiped the tears off her cheeks. "This afternoon, when I told Carter that Angel found a dead body in the bayou and why people are canceling, do you know what he said?"

Ethan shook his head.

"He said Noah would *protect* us. That he showed me the slave's tunnel so I could get away from that bad man." She looked over at Ethan. "I think Carter got it right."

⁂

Jude sat across from Colette at a corner table at Zoe B's, a candle flickering between them. The soft light was flattering to his bride of twenty-six years, her shoulder-length brown hair highlighted with golden strands that hid the gray she wasn't ready to own. Why was she so hung up on hair color when he still saw her as she was the day he married her? Time had only deepened his love and given him new eyes to see beyond the aging shell that housed a soul so lovely he often wondered what it was she saw in him.

Jude picked up his stemmed glass filled with peach iced tea and held it up in front him. "To us."

Colette touched his glass with hers, then took a sip of tea, her deep brown eyes peering over the top of the glass. "We're going to be the last ones out of here."

"Someone has to be. I'm just glad we were able to keep our date."

"So am I." She took the last bite of Cajun shrimp and rice pilaf and wiped her mouth with a napkin. "That was amazing. I don't know how Pierce makes the batter with just the right kind of spicy. No matter how hard I try, I just can't duplicate it."

"That's how I feel about the crawfish étouffée. Love this stuff."

Jude put down his fork and picked up the stainless-steel basket of French bread and offered Colette a slice, then took one and buttered it.

"*Now* you can talk shop," she said. "What's going on?"

Jude told her about the latest lab report concerning DNA and about the muddy print and the soil analysis.

"Based on all that," Jude said, "and the toxicology report that indicated all four victims were drugged with cat Valium, *and* the handwriting analysis that shows the same angle on the spray-painted numbers, *and* the fact that all four bodies were positioned exactly the same in the tub, we can say with almost a hundred percent certainty that the same perp is responsible for all four murders."

"You suspected as much."

"Yes, but there's more." Jude held her gaze. "We're not talking to the media about this, so you need to keep it to yourself. We found Jeanette Stein—actually she was Jeanette LaBelle at the time—on a list of employees that worked for Aubry Computer Systems. She worked for their Lafayette branch for thirteen months, nearly five years ago. We confirmed the name with her Social Security number and date of birth."

"Why didn't her husband mention it?"

"That's what I wanted to know. So I had Gil bring Barry Stein back in for questioning."

"I'll bet that went over big. What did he have to say?"

Jude told her everything he had observed during Gil and Aimee's questioning of Barry Stein.

"Truthfully," Jude said, "I didn't bat an eye when he got upset. I confess it felt a little satisfying, having him on the answering end for a change. But this isn't about my opinion of Stein. I want justice for his wife's murder. In my gut, I don't think he had anything to do with it. I'm not even sure he was a factor at all. I'm just trying to figure out why anyone would want her dead."

"She *and* her boss were both murdered. That's the closest connection so far in the case."

"Yes, and we're after it," Jude said. "Gil was sending a couple detectives over to talk to Bonnie Lonigan again. She's Jeanette Stein's sister. For some reason, she didn't mention Jeanette worked at Aubry either. Maybe she can shed some light on Jeanette's employment there to help us add another piece to the puzzle."

The waitress came over to the table. "Would you like dessert? Coffee?"

"Thanks, but we're done." Jude winked at Colette.

"I'll bring the check."

As the waitress left, the corners of Colette's mouth twitched. "I feel like I'm in high school again, going to Kernel Poppy's to get caramel corn this time of night."

"We can walk off our dinner on the way."

Colette tucked her hair behind her ear. "Do you remember the first time we ate at Zoe B's? It was our thirteenth anniversary. Zoe had just opened the place, and it was hard to get a reservation. But you managed somehow."

"I did indeed." He wiped his mouth with his napkin and picked up her hand. "Anything for my lady."

"You spoil me."

"Every chance I get. It's the least I can do. I'd hate to guess how many times I've stood you up over the years."

"Who's counting?"

He kissed her hand. "That's one of things I love about you most."

⚜

Jude walked out of Zoe B's and was hit with a blast of thick, moist air that smelled faintly of the mesquite smoke coming from the Texas Cajun Grill on the corner. He took Colette's hand and crossed *rue Madeline,* which had been closed to traffic since 7:00 p.m. Tourists swarmed the warm street, even at this late hour.

Jude strolled hand in hand with Colette, enjoying the anonymity of being lost in the crowd. Neon lights flashed all up and down the street, and vendors stood at the open doors to the shops, beckoning passersby.

Street vendors danced, played musical instruments, and did mimes, adding to the carnival-like atmosphere, but without the sleazy side attractions of the Big Easy.

Jude looked up at the galleries, where people stood amidst a jungle of plants and flowers, waving to those on the street.

"I love it that parents can bring their kids out here, day or night," Colette said. "And never have to cover their eyes."

Until the news comes on. Five murders in one week—on my watch. Jude held his gaze on a young pregnant woman coming out of Brissette's Nursery Nook. What kind of heartless maniac would kill a mother of baby twins?

"You're thinking about the case again," Colette said.

"How'd you know?"

"You tensed up." She squeezed his hand. "There's nothing you could've done to prevent the murders."

"But why can't I catch the killer?"

"You will."

Jude sighed. "I can't shake the sound of Jeanette Stein's twins wailing as their aunt drove them away. It was heartbreaking."

"I know, *cher*. But they didn't know what was happening. It would've been so much harder if they had been old enough to understand."

"As obnoxious as Barry Stein can be, I felt sorry for his loss."

"You'll catch the killer, Jude. He's bound to make a mistake. And the more evidence you gather, the better chance you have of making sense of it. Plus this new discovery that Jeanette Stein worked at Aubry could end up being a big break."

Jude smiled. "Why don't *you* do the morning briefing? We could use a cheerleader."

"You're too good at what you do for him to elude you for long."

"I hope you're right, sugar." Jude spotted the gray building and red-and-yellow neon light flashing *Kernel Poppy's*. "What do you say we put everything on hold and go pig out on caramel corn?"

As they approached the popular establishment, Jude let his gaze move across the crowd and the many faces of adult males. The Bathtub

Killer could be any one of them. He held Colette's hand a little tighter. He couldn't imagine losing her—and in such a horrible way.

⚜

Jude walked into his office and flipped the light switch. He heard footsteps behind him and turned around just as Gil Marcel stopped in the doorway.

"What are you doing back here?" Gil said.

"I had a nice evening with Colette. Now I want to hear how your interview with Bonnie Lonigan went. Come sit. Fill me in."

"You want coffee, Sheriff?"

"Is it made?"

Gil nodded. "I'll go get us both a cup. Be right back."

Jude looked out the window. Lit up at night, the Saint Catherine Parish Courthouse reminded him of a mini Lincoln Memorial. How could the city council, in 1965, have been foolish enough to propose the tearing down of this historic icon and building a modern courthouse? That made about as much sense as stripping the trees of the Spanish moss for which the town was named—Les Barbes, French for "beards."

Gil breezed through the door, holding two mugs, and set them on the conference table. "There you go, Sheriff. Extra cream. The way you like it."

"That's perfect, Gil. Thanks."

Jude sat at the table across from him and took a sip of coffee. "So what did Bonnie Lonigan have to say?"

"It was all she could do to think through the questions," Gil said. "It was obvious her sister's murder and her concern for her nephews is tearing her up. It was even more evident this time than when we questioned her immediately after the murder. She and her sister were close."

"Then she must've known Jeanette worked for Aubry Computer Systems. Why didn't she say something?"

"Says she didn't make the connection. At the time, she was a student at the University of Texas and living in Austin. She remembers Jeanette worked for a computer company but didn't pay much attention to the name."

"But does she remember anything that could shed some light on this case? Did Jeanette ever mention her boss?"

"Bonnie said that Jeanette seemed happy with her job but it just wasn't a topic of conversation. They only saw each other a couple of times that year. Both were seeing someone and preoccupied with their own lives."

"Who was Jeanette seeing? Maybe he knows something useful."

Gil shook his head. "Bonnie never met him. Said they only dated a short time, and she can't even remember his name."

"Did you get *anything* useful out of her?"

Gil sighed. "Not really. Like I said, she was having trouble putting thoughts together. But I got the feeling that Jeanette's time at Aubry was uneventful."

"I'm not satisfied with that," Jude said. "Is there someone else in the family—or a friend—we can ask?"

"We've got a list," Gil said. "Their father and both sets of grandparents are deceased, and their mother has Alzheimer's. We'll start talking to other family members, girlfriends, boyfriends, employees at Aubry. We're bound to get something."

CHAPTER 25

Adele opened the front door and walked out to the curb, awed by the lava-and-purple-colored streaks that painted Tuesday morning's sky. She walked slowly down the sidewalk, steadying herself with her cane and hoping she could make it to the end of the block and back. Her new Nikes felt good on her feet, though they were hardly an attractive accessory with her flowered shift.

Why had she abandoned her daily walks since she moved to Les Barbes? Trying to keep up with little Grace had tested her stamina. If she wanted to maintain her mobility, she would have to be intentional about pushing herself on a daily basis—and *before* it got too hot outside.

"Goodness, it must be ninety already with humidity to match," she heard herself say. With each step, she was encouraged to take another. She just needed to take it slow.

A young woman in short shorts and a tank top jogged past her on the other side of the street. For a split second, Adele was a young wife running along the lake at Woodmore, Alfred at her side, keeping pace. Those morning runs were always so invigorating. The two of them were in great shape in those days. How else could they have gone mountain climbing? Scuba diving? Skydiving? Traipsing through rain forests and African jungles?

Adele smiled. What a sight she must be now. A wrinkled, white-haired woman hobbling down the sidewalk with the help of a cane and a good pair of athletic shoes. Though she was an octogenarian on the outside, her girlish love of adventure had not been squelched by the aches and pains of growing old. What she wouldn't give to get around like she used to.

At least Murray didn't coddle her as if eighty-six were merely a terminal disease. He got a kick out of her adventuresome spirit. She could tell. And she was growing quite fond of him. Why should she let the disapproval she knew would come from others keep her from enjoying his company?

She stopped walking and tried to catch her breath. How had she gotten so out of shape? She simply had to walk more. Isabel wanted her to get a treadmill and exercise in the house, where it was cool. But would she be as faithful to it if she couldn't see the splendor of the morning sky and the flocks of ibis and egrets flying back and forth to the rookery? Hear the chirping of birds? Smell the damp earth and the honeysuckle? There was a lot more to taking a walk than just ambulating. One needed to use the senses and enjoy the Creator's handiwork.

She glanced at her watch. Noah was coming over this morning to weed her flower beds and trim her shrubs before he started a paint job Murray had passed on to him. She still didn't believe he was capable of killing Flynn Gillis, but she would feel a lot better once Danny finished looking into his background.

She heard the distinct squawking of a great blue heron as it passed overhead. She was glad she decided to venture out this morning—the first day of a new routine.

⚜

Jude was sitting at his desk, sorting the stack of papers in his inbox, when Aimee breezed through the doorway and sat in the chair next to his desk.

"Please don't tell me the Bathtub Killer struck again."

"He didn't," Aimee said. "But a laid-off employee of Fontaine Sugar Refinery got ten one-hundred-dollar bills in his mailbox this morning—inside a note card, just like the others."

Jude lifted his gaze. "I assume the note said, 'This belongs to you'?"

"Exactly. He's here now, and I'm about to question him. You want to sit in on it, or should I get Gil?"

"No, I'd like to be there. Let's go."

Jude got up and followed Aimee through the detective bureau and into the hallway, keeping pace as they walked toward the interview rooms.

"Who's the guy?"

"James Simon, a fifty-four-year-old supervisor who was laid off at the sugar refinery four years ago. He's working at Walmart now."

"Let's cross-reference him with the other two who called and reported receiving money. Maybe that will tell us something."

Aimee nodded. "Castille and Doucet are already on it. But there have to be others who haven't come forward. I think you should talk to the media and tell them we believe the Bathtub Killer is distributing money stolen at the time of the murders, and that our knowing who he's giving the money to could be a clue to his identity. Ask anyone who has received money from an anonymous source to contact us. And let them know we're not asking for the money back. We just want to talk."

"Agreed. I'll take care of it. But I'm not going to tell the media about the ten one-hundred-dollar bills. Only the killer will know that."

Aimee stopped in front of the second interview room. "He's in here. Do you want to take the lead—or should I?"

"You take the lead," Jude said. "I want to eyeball him."

Jude followed Aimee inside and saw a balding man with square glasses sitting at the oblong table. They walked around to the other side and sat facing him.

"Mr. Simon, I'm Deputy Chief Aimee Rivette, and this is Sheriff Jude Prejean."

Mr. Simon shook their hands. "Call me James."

"Just relax, James," she said. "Tell us how you came into possession of the money."

"It was in my mailbox last night—inside a white note card with a pelican on the front. But I didn't get home from work until ten p.m. That's when I found it. I'm not comfortable keeping it since I don't know who it's from."

"Do you have a hunch?" Jude said.

"Not really. But a thousand bucks is a lot of money. Why wouldn't the person just say who they were? Seemed suspicious to me."

Aimee nodded. “You were right to contact us. So you didn’t recognize the handwriting in the note?”

“It was printed in block letters with blue ink. And no, I didn’t. I gave the note to Deputy Doucet.”

“No one owes you money?”

“No, ma’am.”

“But you could use the money?”

“You bet I could. Like I told the detective over the phone, I was a supervisor at the sugar refinery and got laid off four years ago. I drew unemployment for over a year and finally got a job unloading incoming freight at Walmart.”

Aimee leaned forward on her elbows, her voice sympathetic. “A comedown in pay, I assume?”

“You got that right. My wife was a waitress, but we couldn’t make it, even with both of us working. We were slipping behind on our bills. She finally got burned out with creditors hounding us and filed for divorce and moved to Arizona to live with her mom. Our son was in college at the time. He got a second job and managed to graduate. I filed for bankruptcy and started over. Some life.”

“Did Roux River Bank foreclose on your home?”

“Yeah, and they didn’t waste any time either.”

“Did you talk about your situation to anyone?”

“Just my son. I’m a private person. I was ashamed of losing the house and filing for bankruptcy. I didn’t even tell my mother.”

“No one at the sugar refinery knew?”

“I suppose it’s a matter of public record. But I didn’t stay in touch with anyone there after I got laid off.”

"Do you know a Peggy Royer or a Lloyd Wilson?"

"Their names don't ring a bell. Should I?"

"They also received money from this anonymous source."

James seemed deep in thought for a moment. "I can't place them. I was responsible for fifty workers, and I don't remember either of those names."

"Of the people you knew at the refinery, does anyone stand out who was especially vocal about the layoffs?"

James rolled his eyes. "You're kidding, right? Almost everyone was vocal. Not a day went by that we didn't wonder if we were next."

"Anyone mad enough to make threats against Peter Gautier?"

"I heard a few idle threats. Just frustrated workers blowing off steam."

"Can you remember any names?"

James sighed. "If you provide me with a list of the workers I supervised, I'll probably remember. But like I said, they were just letting off steam."

"Well, the Bathtub Killer might be a disgruntled employee or someone who got cut. We don't have the luxury of assuming they were just blowing off steam."

"I'm not comfortable pointing a finger at anyone. Just because someone couldn't stand Peter's guts doesn't mean they killed him."

"Hardly anyone liked Peter Gautier. We know that." Aimee folded her hands on the table. "We're just gathering information. You came to us with suspicious money. We just want to find the source. See if there's any connection to the murders."

"Why would you think there was a connection to the murders?" James said. "What aren't you telling me?"

"Three of the victims had a safe that the killer cleaned out. I'm sure you heard about that in the news. We think the killer took the money and might be returning it to some of the people he thinks deserve it."

"So you think it's someone who knows I got laid off?"

"And that you lost your wife and your house and went through bankruptcy. That's why I asked if you confided in anyone."

"I didn't."

"Maybe your son did. Or your ex-wife."

James exhaled. "Yeah, that's a possibility."

"Would the people at the refinery know you were laid off as opposed to quitting?"

"Yeah, the layoffs were posted."

"Who were you closest to when you worked there? You must've had a peer you shared your frustrations with."

James's face went expressionless—and turned bright pink. "Yeah, another supervisor—Mona Johnson. We talked a lot over lunch. We had a fling. It only lasted a couple months, then we cut it off. We were both married and felt guilty."

"You think she was angry that you got laid off?"

"More like scared. She quit and went to cosmetology school."

"How do you know that, if you didn't stay in touch with anyone at the refinery?"

James cracked his knuckles. "Mona and I picked up where we left off after my wife left. Neither of us was working for Fontaine at the time. Look, she didn't send me this money. You asked who I was closest to, and I answered truthfully. I wasn't close to anyone else, and I didn't confide in anyone."

Aimee nodded. "We appreciate your honesty."

"Listen, if the money I got came from the Bathtub Killer, I sure want to help you. It's one thing to kill Peter and those other CEOs. It's an entirely different thing to kill an innocent mom. He's got to be stopped."

"Thanks. I'll tell you what, why don't I get you some coffee while we get that list of employees for you to peruse? Maybe seeing the names will trigger a memory."

"Okay. I don't have to be at work until two."

Jude stood and shook James's hand. "I need to be at a press conference in a few minutes. Thanks for coming in. We appreciate your helping us."

Jude left the room, Aimee on his heels. He stopped out in the hallway and leaned against the wall. "Well?"

Aimee shrugged. "Hey, it's possible he'll remember something important. It's worth a try."

"Be sure to find Mona Johnson and talk to her."

"We will. You don't sound as if you think this is a viable lead, Sheriff."

"I didn't say that. But everyone at Fontaine resented Gautier. I guess the question is, who resented him enough to kill him, two other CEOs, and a stay-at-home mom? And how is Jeanette Stein connected to all this?"

"We should know something soon," Aimee said. "Gil's got a team looking into her background as we speak."

⚜

Jude finished addressing the media and then went down the hall to Gil Marcel's office. He knocked on the open door, and Gil looked up from his desk and put half a doughnut back in the Krispy Kreme sack.

"Come in, Sheriff. I was just finishing my lunch."

"You really should do something about that doughnut addiction. You need brain food."

"Yeah, I know. When I'm involved in a case, my self-discipline goes out the window."

Jude walked over and stood in front of Gil's desk. "Found anything on Jeanette Stein?"

Gil wiped his mouth with a napkin. "You mean other than she's a good wife, mother, friend, neighbor, and a weekly volunteer at hospice?"

"I was hoping you uncovered some deep, dark secret that would help us connect the dots."

"Afraid not. We've talked to a number of coworkers at Aubry. But the two who knew her beyond a *hi-how-are-you?* don't work there anymore. We're looking for them now."

"The coworkers who are still there—what did they tell you?"

"Just that Jeanette was pretty. Nice dresser. A little shy. According to the HR director, Cecilia Nunn, her male coworkers tripped over themselves being nice to her, but she wasn't a flirt."

"Her sister said she was dating someone."

"Her boss thought so too but never saw Jeanette with anyone. She appreciated that Jeanette was modest, hardworking, and competent—and that she kept her private life out of the office."

"Did she say why Jeanette left?"

"She took a job with Davidson Software Solutions. For considerably more money. Aubry wasn't willing to pay her that much so they wished her well and hired a replacement."

"That's it?"

Gil pushed the sack of doughnuts to the side. "I'm afraid so. But we're still looking for the two coworkers she was closer to. They might know something that would help us."

"What do the people at Davidson say?"

"Same thing, basically. She was good at what she did. During the time she worked there, she was very private. They didn't even know she was dating someone until she got engaged to Barry Stein. She gave notice when she married him."

Jude sighed. "Don't tell me this is a dead end, Gil. It can't be a dead end. Jeanette Stein is connected to these other murders. Keep digging."

CHAPTER 26

Just before lunchtime, Adele sat in the sunroom, thumbing through the latest issue of *National Geographic* and watching Noah, who was down on all fours, working in the flower beds. He looked sad. It must be so hard on him, not working for the Langleys while the suspicion surrounding Flynn Gillis's murder seemed to settle over him like a cloud. Vanessa seemed as sad as he. Surely the sheriff would clear his name soon?

Isabel's voice startled her.

"The phone is for you, Mrs. Woodmore. It's Murray."

"Thank you, hon. I'll take it right here." She picked up the extension. "Well hello, Murray." She glanced up in time to see the scowl on Isabel's face before she left the room. "I was just sitting here with a magazine, enjoying a glass of lemonade and watching Noah work outside. He's doing such a wonderful job with those flower beds."

"Is this a bad time?"

"Not at all."

"I'm getting back to you about setting up a time to go to Scoops. I'm free tomorrow afternoon around three thirty. I know that's late in the day. And eating all that ice cream is liable to spoil your dinner." His voice was playful.

"No doubt it will." She laughed. "I'll tell Isabel to take the evening off."

"All right, then. I will pick you up at three thirty."

"This time I'll know to wear a pair of slacks and my Nikes."

"You have Nikes?"

"Indeed I do. I ordered a pair over the phone. I've started walking again. I used to walk outside every day when I lived at Woodmore. It'll be a little easier getting in the truck if I'm dressed for the big step up. I'm really looking forward to our outing."

"Me, too. I'm bringing a footstool to make it easier for you getting in and out."

"How thoughtful."

"And if you have errands to run, we could do those at the same time."

"We'll see," she said. "Right now, I'm just eager to try the Banana Mountain at Scoops."

"Then I'll see you tomorrow afternoon."

"I'm looking forward to it. Good-bye, Murray."

Adele hung up the phone, feeling a bit giddy. It was nice having something fun to look forward to—something out of the ordinary. Something that made her feel alive and not like an old prune. But even more important, she welcomed the chance to get to know Murray better.

Lord, thank You for this chance to touch his heart in whatever way I can. I sense he's been very wounded and blames You.

Adele looked at the stained-glass dove hanging on the window. Maybe the conversation would be relaxed enough that she could broach the subject of God again.

She smiled. Regardless, it was going to be a fun afternoon. And Isabel had better keep her negativity to herself.

Zoe picked up the coffeepot and walked over to the table by the window, where Grace sat in her booster seat next to Father Sam and facing Hebert and Tex.

"Hi, Mama." Grace flashed an elfin smile with giggles to match.

"Hi, sweet girl." Zoe started pouring refills. "Pierce said your lunch orders are up next."

"You handle this waitressing thing pretty well," Tex said, looking uncharacteristically handsome in his dark sport coat and yellow shirt.

Zoe put two tiny tubs of creamer in front of Tex. "I can manage through the lunch hour—until the second shift takes over. It's the least I could do so Savannah could be off today for her aunt Nicole's funeral."

"Us guys are goin' together," Tex said. "You wanna come with us?"

"That's so sweet." Zoe patted his cheek. "But I have to get Grace situated with her babysitter and run a few errands. Why don't I meet y'all at the church? Maybe you could save me a place."

"Be glad to. Talk about déjà vu—all of us gettin' together for a funeral. Can't believe it's been three years since Remy died."

"And here we are again." Father Sam took off his glasses, breathed on the lenses, and wiped them with his napkin. "This time Savannah has lost someone tragically. And it shouldn't lessen the blow to our community because her aunt was a CEO." He held Hebert's gaze, his black cleric shirt lending authority to his words. "Each of these victims had friends and family who mourn their loss."

"But most folks here tink da CEOs got what dey deserved."

"It's not for us to judge them." Father Sam put his glasses back on. "No one *deserves* to be murdered—certainly Nicole didn't. She was a fun-loving, delightful person. I can't remember when anyone made me laugh the way she did."

"I know dat," Hebert said. "Da massive layoffs in da past few years was bound to make *someone* to go off, dat's all."

"Someone went off, all right." Tex took a sip of coffee. "I'm hopin' that since he hasn't killed anyone since last week, maybe he's done. Maybe whatever grievance he had with these folks has been satisfied."

"I certainly hope so," Father Sam said. "It was one thing to lash out against the CEOs. But the killing of this young mother really has people afraid."

"Dat's fuh shore." Hebert pulled at a snag on the sleeve of the brown leisure suit he bought at Goodwill and had worn to Remy's funeral.

"The sheriff will piece things together," Zoe said. "The killings have to be related to the layoffs and foreclosures."

"What about Jeanette Stein?" Tex arched his bushy silver eyebrows. "She doesn't seem to fit that scenario one whit. There's just somethin' that tilts with me about her bein' lumped in with the others."

"But that unnamed source close to the case told someone in the media she worked at Aubry a few years back." Zoe set the carafe of coffee on the table. "That could be significant. I'm sure Jude is looking into it."

"I tink dey should put dat Barry Stein under a microscope," Hebert said. "He's da one dat's ticked people off—not his poor dead wife."

⚜

Adele walked into the kitchen, surprised that Isabel hadn't prepared lunch yet and was instead standing at the kitchen sink, staring out the window.

"What is it, hon?"

Isabel didn't answer for what seemed an eternity, and then she turned around, her face expressionless. "Mrs. Woodmore, I think the world of you. But this arrangement just isn't working for me."

Adele bit her lip. So it was finally coming to a head. "What you mean is my association with Noah and Murray isn't working for you."

"I thought I could handle it. But I can't." Isabel neatly folded a hand towel and set it on the countertop. "I'm sorry. I quit. I'll go pack my things and leave."

"Because I choose to be kind to these young men?"

"You are the dearest, kindest woman I know. But leaving yourself open to these guys is careless. And it's painful to watch. I can't tell you what to do. But I'm not opening myself up to the men from Haven House."

"I see. And it doesn't impress you at all that they're hardworking and honest and have been nothing but kind and thoughtful?"

"It's irrelevant to me how they act. I don't trust them. They're manipulative, and they're working you. I can't just sit back and watch. I don't have mercy on people like that. I'm not willing to be that vulnerable."

"I suppose by its very nature mercy leaves us vulnerable. That can't be helped."

"It's not for me." Isabel glanced up and then stared down at her hands. "I'm sorry for letting you down like this. But I think both of us will do better if I leave. I tried, but I can't hide my feelings about this."

"I'm disappointed, Isabel."

"I'm disappointed too. I wanted to settle into this job. I really like it here. I resent feeling the need to leave because of these guys. It was difficult enough when you hired Noah and Murray and they were around here all the time. But now you're even willing to give up time with Grace to spend time with Murray."

"Were you eavesdropping on me, Isabel?"

"I wasn't trying to." Isabel lifted her gaze. "But you haven't exactly tried to hide any of this. I can read between the lines. Zoe's excuse for not bringing Grace over was bogus. Since when have you been too overwhelmed to have her here—especially when I'm here to help? It's obvious Zoe doesn't want her daughter over here when Murray or Noah's around. And Vanessa didn't argue with Noah when he gave his keys back. That tells me there are trust issues there, too."

"Well, you certainly have everything figured out."

"My point in all this is I'm not the only one who's uncomfortable with the men from Haven House."

"No. I suppose not."

"And I'm concerned for you. I think it's a *huge* mistake to befriend Murray. I did overhear today's conversation. That was the final straw."

"You're quitting because I'm going to the ice cream parlor with Murray?"

"I don't think you should go *anywhere* with him."

"You made that clear once before. You called it dangerous mercy."

"Yes. I did."

Adele held Isabel's gaze. "Mercy *is* risky. I guess that's what makes it mercy. There's always a chance someone will abuse it. Am I just supposed to stop reaching out to these young men—even though they haven't done one thing that gives me pause?"

"There are others trained to deal with these types of people. Father Vince knows what he's doing. He isn't going to let anyone take advantage of him. You're a sweet, trusting, wealthy widow. With all due respect, ma'am, you're an easy mark for guys like that."

Adele smiled. "For heaven's sake, you make me sound like a helpless numskull who wouldn't know if someone had his hand in my proverbial cookie jar. I didn't stay rich by being foolish, Isabel."

"Just be careful. Find out who these men are before you invite them to sit down at your table. And please don't feel sorry for them and give them money."

"I've given them only what they've earned. They worked hard for it."

"You've *invented* jobs for Murray to do. Isn't that the same thing?"

"Not if the jobs benefit me."

Isabel sighed. "Believe me, they have their sights on your money, whether you think they do or not. I feel obligated to warn you. That's all I can do. I'll go get my things now. I'm very sorry things between us had to end this way."

"So am I. I owe you for half a month. How would you like me to pay you?"

"If it's all right with you, just send it to my parents'. That's where I get my mail."

Isabel brushed past her and disappeared down the hall.

Adele sat at the table. She hated that Isabel was so unhappy here. And that she would have to dig out the employment applications she'd tucked away and see if she could find a suitable replacement.

I don't have mercy on people like that.

Isabel's words echoed in her mind. On some level, weren't we all "people like that"? Yet how could she expect Isabel to understand mercy unless she had been the recipient of it? Adele remembered all too well what she herself had been like before the Lord saved her and forgave the cruel words she had used to control those desperate enough to work for her in the years following the loss of her baby. The thought of it still made her squirm.

She couldn't undo the past. But she promised the Lord she would show compassion and mercy to every person He put in her path. What gave her the right to single out those who were worthy of it and those who weren't? Wasn't she to love her neighbor as herself? What kind of person would she be today, if the Lord hadn't allowed her to start with a clean slate? If there was ever a person unworthy of mercy, it was she.

Noah and Murray had proven to be honest and hardworking. And they were pleasant to be with. Wasn't it foolish to end that arrangement because of the unfounded suspicion of others?

Footsteps in the hallway broke her concentration, and she looked up just as Isabel walked into the kitchen, pulling a rolling suitcase.

"I cleaned out my closets and drawers and packed my car."

"Goodness, that was fast."

"I still had the boxes. I guess I'll be leaving now."

"Wait." Adele rose to her feet with the help of her cane and took Isabel's hand. "I so wish it hadn't come to this. I really like you, hon. I want you to know I appreciate all you did. And your companionship."

"Aren't you angry I'm leaving you high and dry?"

"Not angry. Disappointed. And sad. Are you okay financially until you can find something?"

"There! See what I mean?" Isabel threw her hand in the air. "You're already concerned for my well-being. If I told you I needed five hundred dollars, you'd probably give it to me."

"I might, if I felt it was warranted. After all, it was the oppressive environment here that caused you to flee. But let me emphasize again that I didn't manage to stay wealthy by being foolish."

Isabel shook her head. "You've missed my point entirely."

"I really haven't. I could count on two hands the times I've loaned or given any individual money. My wealth has been entrusted to me by God. I don't waste it. But I don't worry about it either."

"It's not just money, Mrs. Woodmore. I worry about your safety."

"Don't. I have angels for that." Adele put her arm around Isabel's waist and pulled her gently to her side. "I *will* miss you. You're always welcome here."

Isabel's eyes glistened. "You're not making this easy for me."

"I don't want there to be hard feelings between us, just because we don't see eye to eye. You were efficient and trustworthy. And I loved your cooking. Most of the time we spent together was very nice."

Isabel nodded.

"If you need a reference," Adele said, "I'll be happy to give it. I imagine anyone who wants to hire you will understand the reason you felt compelled to leave."

"Do *you?*"

Adele brushed the wispy hair out of Isabel's eyes. "Of course I do. You've been forthcoming with your feelings all along. We've just reached an impasse. Your leaving, as much as I regret it, is probably the only viable solution."

"Just be careful. A little more caution wouldn't cost you anything. The lack of it could. Bye, Mrs. Woodmore." Isabel tilted her suitcase and rolled it toward the front door.

"Good-bye, Isabel." *I really hate to lose you.*

Adele walked to the front door and watched as Isabel stuffed the suitcase into the trunk of her car, the backseat already filled with boxes and hanging clothes. Isabel slid in behind the wheel and pulled away from the curb. Adele waved but couldn't see whether or not Isabel waved back.

"Hello?"

The male voice startled her and sent a cold chill up her spine. She turned around, her hand over her heart, and saw Noah standing there.

"Goodness, you frightened me! Why didn't you cough or something so I would know you were there?"

"Sorry, Mrs. Woodmore. I thought you heard me come in. You told me to let you know when I was finished."

"Well, I *didn't* hear you. I was engrossed in something. Heavens, my heart's nearly pounding out of my chest."

"Maybe you should come out to the kitchen and sit for a spell. Let me get you somethin' cold to drink."

She took in a slow, deep breath and let it out. Then did it again. "You look hot. Why don't you have a glass of iced raspberry tea with me?"

"Don't mind if I do."

Adele walked out to the kitchen, holding tightly to her cane, suddenly feeling awkward about being in the house alone with Noah. Why was she letting Isabel's paranoia play on her? What nonsense. The dear man had lost everything in Katrina. And now even what he had gained back had been taken from him. The least she could do was offer him something cold to drink.

CHAPTER 27

Vanessa arranged fresh-cut potatoes, carrots, and onions around a pot roast, then secured the lid and slipped the roasting pan into the oven. She set the temperature so that it would slow cook all afternoon, allowing the aroma to permeate the house.

The phone rang, and she grabbed it, cradling the receiver. "Hello."

"Mrs. Langley, it's Jack Joyce. You need to come down to the caretaker house. There's something you need to see."

"Can it wait? Ethan knows a lot more about the specs."

"No, ma'am. It can't. It's not about specs. We've got a real problem."

"All right. I'll be right there."

Vanessa wiped her hands and hung up the phone. She put the sign on the front door—*Proprietor will return shortly*—and then turned the bolt lock.

She breezed through the kitchen, out the back door, and down the deck steps, then climbed into the old Chevy truck they used to drive around the property.

She started the engine and headed down the winding road that was overhung with a basket weave of leafy branches. What was so important that Jack would pull her away from the manor house? He knew she was preparing for the arrival of today's guests.

A couple minutes later she pulled up behind the caretaker house, which had been painted a homey shade of yellow, and saw four vehicles, one of which was Jack Joyce's red Dodge Ram. She pulled up next to it, got out, and walked toward the back door of the house.

A man dressed in jeans and a T-shirt came outside, his tall, lanky frame and full beard making him easy to recognize.

"Jack!" She hurried to meet him halfway. "What's this about?"

"Follow me," he said. "I'll show you."

Vanessa followed Jack through the side yard and around to the front of the house—and stopped cold. A single word had been spray painted in black between the picture window and the front door:

Liar

"Liar?" she said. "What's that supposed to mean?" *That he killed Flynn Gillis?*

Jack shrugged. "It's none of my business, other than my paint job is wrecked. I'd like to get my hands on whoever did this."

"When did you discover it?"

"About a minute before I called you." Jack hooked his thumbs on his jeans pockets. "We just got here. We were doing finish work at the Thompson place all morning and came here right after lunch. I walked around to the front of the house to put the second coat on those shutters. That's when I discovered it. I called you right away."

"I have to report this to the sheriff." Vanessa's heart sank. "If this is an accusation, I wonder why the person didn't go directly to the authorities."

"Can't answer that. But there's no point in my crew hanging around, doing nothing, while sheriff's deputies are making a report."

"Actually, there is," she said. "They're going to need your statement."

"What statement? I walked up and saw what you're seeing. End of report."

"They're going to want to hear that from you."

"Why can't you tell them what I said? It's just graffiti. Could be a prank."

"If it's a prank, it's a serious one. You know what the implication is here," Vanessa said. "Do you need me to spell it out?"

"With all due respect, Mrs. Langley, I don't have time to get in the middle of Noah's problem." He made a sweeping motion with his hand. "You're seeing what I saw. Can't you just tell them?"

"Jack, my mom is a cop. I know how this works. The sheriff will need your statement."

Jack lifted his blue cap and wiped his forehead. "Then he can come over to the Thompson place. I've got serious work to do. Time is money. You know that."

"I'm really sorry, Jack. I know it's the last thing you need, but I'd appreciate it if you'd stay—just until they get your statement."

"Whatever you say, ma'am." His voice dripped with annoyance.

Vanessa moved her gaze to the word someone had spray painted, her mind racing with the implications. Just when she thought Noah might be in the clear. Who wanted to stir things up—and why?

❧

Deputies Mike Doucet and Stone Castille finished taking pictures and getting statements. Jack and his crew had left.

Vanessa glanced at their patrol car in the driveway and dismissed the notion that it was a bad omen that theirs was the first vehicle to park there.

"All right," Stone said. "I think we're done here. You can go ahead and paint over it anytime you like."

"I'm not sure why someone did this," Vanessa said. "But Noah is not a liar."

"I see here in your statement that Mr. Washington isn't working for you at the moment. May I ask why?"

Vanessa sighed. *Lord, only You know for sure if Noah's telling the truth. I believe him. If I'm wrong, show me.* "He thought it would be better for business—just until you solve Flynn Gillis's murder."

"I see."

"It's just temporary," Vanessa insisted. "Noah's going to move into this house. We've planned for a long time for him to be the caretaker and our full-time groundskeeper."

Stone arched his eyebrows. "But you're not going through with it until you're sure he didn't kill Flynn Gillis. Is that what you're saying?"

"Not because we think Noah did it. It's simply a matter of dealing with the cloud of suspicion. Naturally, our guests are concerned that a murdered body was found on our property. In fact, it's greatly impacted business. Occupancy is way down."

"I'm sure the fact that your groundskeeper is a person of interest in the case doesn't help matters."

Vanessa folded her arms across her chest. "People only know what they hear in the media. They don't know Noah like we do."

"How well *do* you know him?"

"I know he saved Zoe, Pierce, and me when he didn't even know us. He could've been killed. Yet he didn't hesitate."

"That's not in dispute, Mrs. Langley. But what else do you know about him? Has he ever opened up about where he's been since Katrina?"

"He had some kind of emotional breakdown after his wife and daughters were swept away. He lost his home, too. And his landscaping business, since most of his customers never came back after the hurricane. Truthfully, it seems too painful for him to talk about."

"Or convenient?"

"Meaning what?"

"There may be another side to the Boy Scout you know. Perhaps a more violent side."

Vanessa pursed her lips. "I've never seen any indication of it. And I've seen him almost every day for over two years. We've had many conversations about many subjects. Noah is a trustworthy, hardworking, gentle man."

"But he never talks about those missing years?"

"Missing years? Those are your words, Deputy Castille. He's not hiding anything. He readily admits he gave up on life for a while and 'bummed it.' He didn't think he had much to live for."

"Or much to lose?"

Vanessa locked gazes with him. "What is it you're implying?"

"I'm not implying anything. I'm just pointing out the fact that no one really knows this man—at least not until he showed up here, claiming his ancestors were slaves at Langley Manor. Can that even be documented?"

"No. It's all word of mouth. But how else would he have known about the secret tunnels? Not even Ethan's dad and uncles knew about them. Everything Noah told us makes perfect sense."

"But all we're *sure* of," Stone said, "is that he used the tunnels to gain access to the house so he could live there while it sat vacant. He could have discovered the door in the woods, followed the tunnel into the house, and made up the story."

"That's a lot less likely than what he told us."

"Don't you think it's odd that neither Josiah nor Abigail Langley kept a diary of what happened out here? Something as important as the Underground Railroad?"

"They may have and we just haven't found it. But they didn't know how significant the Underground Railroad would be in American history." Vanessa put her hands on her hips. "What's your point?"

Stone nodded toward the front of the house. "Maybe *liar is* meant to discredit his claim to be a descendant of the slave Naomi. It might not have a thing to do with Flynn Gillis's murder. We just don't know. The man could be a complete fraud. If he is, you'd want to know, right?"

"Are you going to talk to Noah again?"

"Yes. Father Vince located him and told him what's going on. He volunteered to come back in and talk to us."

Vanessa locked gazes with him. "I'm not going to sit back and let you pin Flynn Gillis's murder on him."

"We're just trying to get at the truth, ma'am. If he's lied about who he is, what's to stop him from lying about what he's done?"

Vanessa felt emotion constrict her throat. Had she been wrong about Noah? Was she too close to him to be objective?

Her cell phone rang, and she read the screen.

"Excuse me. I need to take this." She walked over and leaned on a magnolia tree. "Hello, Adele."

"Noah and I were having something cold to drink when he got a call from Father Vince, saying the sheriff wanted to talk to him about some graffiti at Langley Manor. What's going on, hon? Did someone deface that beautiful house?"

"Someone spray painted the word *liar* on the caretaker house." Vanessa told Adele everything that had happened since Jack called her and told her to meet him at the caretaker house. "Sheriff's deputies are still here, Adele. I really can't talk. I've got guests checking in soon, and Carter will be home from day camp in a little while."

"At least tell me your assessment. Do you think the graffiti was intended to be an accusation?"

Vanessa sighed. "I don't know what to think. This could be in reference to Flynn's murder. It could be about Noah's claim that his ancestry connects him to Langley Manor. Or something unrelated to either. I haven't talked to Noah, and I really don't think it's fair for me to have an opinion yet."

"You're such a good friend to him. I know he appreciates your support."

Vanessa glanced over at Deputy Castille, who was writing something on his clipboard. "Maybe now he'll let me get him a lawyer."

❧

Zoe walked out of the kitchen at Zoe B's and over to the table by the window, where Father Sam, Hebert, and Tex were setting up for a game of checkers. The dining room was almost empty of customers, and the second-shift waitresses had already vacuumed the wood floor and changed out the tables with blue-and-gold fleur-de-lis tablecloths and put a fresh yellow daisy in each bud vase.

"You fellas want a snack to tide you over until we serve dinner?" she said.

"Nothin' for me, thanks." Tex took off his sport coat and hung it on the back of his chair.

Hebert shook his head. "Seeing Savannah so upset at da funeral stole my appetite. Dat was hard to see."

"Indeed it was," Father Sam said. "I baptized that girl when she was still a babe in arms. Her aunt Nicole was her godmother and was probably the age Savannah is now. Doesn't seem that long ago either."

"It's strange how the resentment about her bein' a CEO went right out the window when we all saw her as a real person." Tex folded his arms on the table. "I imagine Jeanette Stein's funeral will be packed out—and emotional."

"No doubt," Zoe said. "Listen, I came out here to tell y'all something I just heard. Adele talked to Vanessa. Someone spray painted the word *liar* on the caretaker house the Langleys are having built for Noah."

"Liar?" Lines formed on Tex's forehead. "Referrin' to what—that Flynn fella's murder?"

"Hard to say for sure what it's implying, but that's the first thing everyone will think of."

Hebert leaned forward on his elbows. "We all know what dis guy means to you, Zoe. But dis doesn't look too good. What does Noah have to say?"

"What *can* he say? This just feeds the suspicion that he had something to do with Flynn Gillis's murder. It's certainly not proof. But it'll keep the sheriff looking at him as a person of interest." Zoe sighed. "The truth is, we really don't know why someone would call him a liar."

Tex looked up and held her gaze. "Maybe it's high time we paid attention."

CHAPTER 28

Adele sat in her room, trying to read from her devotion book but distracted by the events of the day. She had locked the front and back doors and checked them several times. When was the last time she was alone overnight—without help if she needed it? Not that she was incapable. She'd warmed up leftover meatloaf for dinner and washed a load of towels. But what if she stumbled and fell? Or spilled something she couldn't clean up? How long could she go without a companion to assist her? She could always contact an agency and get someone to come out. But that seemed so impersonal.

She sighed. Zoe was not going to like it one bit when she found out that Isabel had quit and Adele was by herself. And she would like it even less when she found out the reason. How could she keep it from her? Zoe was like the daughter she'd never had. All the money in the world couldn't buy the kind of love and devotion Zoe had shown her. Adele had no doubt Zoe would make sure she was cared for, should the time come when she needed more help than a live-in companion could provide. She had given Zoe power of attorney to make those kinds of decisions. If she could trust her with that, surely she could tell her why Isabel quit.

She closed her devotion book. Was she prepared to stand her ground concerning Noah and Murray, when she knew Zoe and Pierce were going to fight her on it? Was it worth it? Why did she feel a personal responsibility to open her heart to these men? The words from Luke resounded in her head.

Love the Lord your God with all your heart and with all your soul and with all your strength and with all your mind; and, love your neighbor as yourself.

Weren't Noah and Murray her neighbors? Wasn't she trying to be like the Good Samaritan—touching wounded people who needed help? It wasn't that risky. All she was doing was providing work—paying them for a needed service. And extending kindness. Was she willing to be disobedient to this biblical directive, just to keep the peace?

But it's dangerous mercy, Isabel had insisted.

Was she supposed to withdraw in fear and spend the last years of her life doing nothing of significance because someone might take advantage of her? She'd been a good steward of the fortune the Lord had given her. When she died, a healthy sum was going to Zoe and Pierce and Grace, but most of it was going to charity.

Adele laid the devotional on the nightstand. Since when did she shy away from a challenge? It wasn't her nature to take the easy way—whether it was climbing a mountain or standing for something.

She would call Zoe in a day or two and let her know the circumstances. And then she would begin the process of replacing Isabel.

❧

Jude sat at the conference table in his office, looking through the files on the victims of the Bathtub Killer. Why couldn't they connect Jeanette Stein to the other victims? This killer was intentional about picking the CEOs of three major companies. What did Jeanette Stein have in common with them? Was it even significant that she had worked briefly at the Lafayette branch of Aubry Computer Systems? Had she ever even *met* Nicole Aubry?

Jude got up and went over to the window. The lights around the courthouse had come on, and the western sky was painted with streaks of glowing-hot crimson.

On the corner of Primeaux and Courthouse, a shirtless man, covered in tattoos, placed a donation jar on the sidewalk and began juggling what appeared to be colored balls.

A crowd had gathered on the sidewalk in front of the courthouse, where street musicians played zydeco music.

How he loved Les Barbes—his boyhood home. Why couldn't he find the killer who threatened its peace? Any minute he expected someone to come tell him that another victim had been found.

A knock on the door caused him to turn to where Aimee stood in the doorway.

"What's happened?" he said.

"Nothing, believe it or not." She smiled. "I'm going to call it a day. I'm beat."

"Me, too."

"How much time do you want us to spend trying to get to the bottom of the graffiti incident at Langley Manor?"

"None," Jude said. "We need to focus on catching this Bathtub Killer before he strikes again."

"*Liar* could mean a lot of things." Aimee pursed her lips. "And it may have nothing at all to do with Noah. It could be directed at the Langleys."

"Except that Castille and Doucet talked with Vanessa at length. She can't think of any reason why someone would call her or Ethan a liar. There are a number of reasons why they might call Noah a liar. At any rate, in and of itself, it's nothing more than vandalism. We can't spare manpower right now to pursue it." Jude fingered the badge on his shirt. "Let's stay focused on finding out how Jeanette Stein fits the puzzle."

"Maybe she doesn't, Sheriff. Maybe she merely represents something to the killer—something we'll never understand."

Jude shook his head. "I'm not willing to accept that. Not now anyway. He chose Jeanette Stein. Let's find the connection."

"Do you think we could use the FBI's help on this one? Maybe a profiler?"

Jude lifted his gaze. "I've thought about it. I hate inviting the feds into this though. You know how they are. They treat us like we're from Mayberry. The condescending attitude gets old."

"I know. But they have a lot at their disposal we don't. I'd sure like someone to give us a profile of who we're looking for."

"It has to be someone striking back at the CEOs because of the layoffs and foreclosures," Jude said.

Aimee captured a yawn with her hand. "I thought so too. But explain Jeanette Stein."

"We will. We just need to keep digging."

"The feds might help us do it faster. Before he kills someone else."

Jude winced. She was right. Was he going to let pride get in the way?

"All right." He walked over to his desk and sat. "I'll call the field office in New Orleans and see what they can do to help us."

⁂

Vanessa sat in a rocker on the deck at Langley Manor, a cricket serenade soothing her frazzled nerves. Two more cancellations on top of the accusatory graffiti that seemed to be aimed at Noah. Why would someone feel the need to accuse him of being a liar in such a public and destructive way? Had he made up the entire story about his great-grandmother's great-grandmother Naomi and the Underground Railroad? Or worse yet, had he killed Flynn Gillis? Was that possible? Was she being naive—blinded by her affection for Noah? He had saved her life. Was she just supposed to distance herself from him and let him fight this battle alone?

A raccoon boldly scurried to the bottom of the steps and went straight for the bowls of apple slices and crunchy dog food she had set out. She sat quietly and watched him help himself. She loved it out here. The woods teemed with wildlife emboldened by the shroud of night. If she sat here long enough, how many animals might she see besides raccoons? Opossums? Skunks? Rabbits? Bobcats? Deer? Or perhaps even quail or wild turkeys? They were all out there. Not to mention that playful barred owl that sometimes got close enough to the edge of the forest that she could *who* back at him.

The deck door opened and closed, and Ethan's silhouette moved toward her and sat in the chair next to her.

"Carter's out like a light. He read me every word of *The Velveteen Rabbit*. I have such mixed emotions. I love it that he's a good reader, but I miss reading to him. He insists on reading it himself." Ethan took her hand. "What happened to our toddler? When did he get so grown up?"

"It seemed to happen overnight." Vanessa heard the flatness of her tone.

A long moment of silence finally became uncomfortable.

Ethan spoke. "Look, I know this is not what you want to hear. But with the graffiti on top of everything else, I don't think we can afford to assume Noah's coming back here anytime soon, so"—he held out his palm as she started to respond—"we need to be thinking about who we can hire in the interim. The grounds have to be maintained for the guests we *do* have."

Vanessa's eyes stung, and she let go of Ethan's hand. "This is so unfair. Someone has it in for Noah. He's being set up."

"You don't know that."

"Yes, I do!"

She heard Ethan sigh. "Honey, you really don't. We both want to believe Noah. But while the sheriff is sorting things out, we've got a bed-and-breakfast to run. We can't let the situation with Noah consume us. There's too much at stake."

Vanessa wiped a tear off her cheek. "Without Noah, even the history of Langley Manor changes."

"Not really. He just won't be here to greet guests. I don't think that's a big deal in the grand scheme of things. The *history* is what it is."

Vanessa folded her arms across her chest. "Then what do you think the graffiti means?"

"Truthfully? My first inclination is that someone is warning Noah that his lying about Flynn Gillis's murder won't work—and that he'd better own up to it. It could also be someone trying to negate what Noah told us about his ancestry. Either way, it's a little depressing."

"Do you think?" Vanessa wiped a runaway tear off her cheek.

"Sweetheart, please don't treat me like I'm the bad guy. I didn't create this mess. With all my heart, I want to believe Noah is telling the truth about not being involved in Flynn's murder."

"But you don't believe him."

Ethan cracked his knuckles. "I'm trying."

"But you don't?"

"Why are you so determined to trap me into admitting I don't believe Noah? I told you I'm trying. That's better than just *not believing* him."

"He's been nothing but honest, creative, and hardworking."

Ethan didn't say anything.

"Now what? Just say it."

Ethan cleared his throat. "Not *completely* honest. Don't forget that, when this house was vacant, he snuck in through one of the secret tunnels and decided to come and go as he pleased. He knew he was breaking the law, and he did it anyway."

"He didn't have anywhere else to go."

Ethan shook his head. "You can't make excuses for someone trespassing like that. He could have found a shelter. He refused help from the government after Katrina. He was responsible for not having anywhere else to go."

"You make it sound like that's what he wanted. He was devastated when his wife and daughters were swept away. He doesn't even remember the months following Katrina."

"Says he doesn't, anyway."

"I believe him."

"Well, we're not talking months. We're talking years."

Vanessa rolled her eyes. "I'm wasting my breath."

"Honey, I'll talk to Noah face-to-face. But trust me, he already knows that the graffiti makes him look even more suspicious. And that he's probably not coming back anytime soon."

"It's wrong, Ethan. I'm telling you, he's being set up. Someone is trying to hurt him—to wreck his chances at getting a fresh start."

"Maybe so. But until we get to the bottom of it, he can't be seen out here."

❦

Adele sat in her chair in the bedroom, wondering how long it would take her to replace Isabel. She already missed her. And not just because Isabel helped her with things she found difficult to do. Isabel was pleasant company.

The phone rang, startling her. She glanced at the clock: 9:05. She reached over and picked up the receiver. "Hello."

"Adele, it's Danny. I know it's late, but I'm just now getting back to my room, and I knew you'd still be up. I'd like to tell you what I found out today."

"Wonderful." Adele grabbed a pen and pad of paper. "Go ahead, Danny."

"I've exhausted every means I have, and I can't figure out where Noah Washington was after Katrina. There's just a big blank there. The first record I have of him after Katrina is when he showed up there and went to work for the Langleys. He definitely didn't file income tax in that time frame. I don't know whether he didn't work, didn't earn enough to file, or just didn't file. But I couldn't find a record of him signing in at any of the designated shelters after Katrina.

"Prior to that, he was a model citizen. Good credit record. His business had a good reputation. I found a couple customers that he did landscaping for. They had good things to say about him. I'm not sure where else to take this. There are a number of blank years there, but he doesn't have a criminal record. Are you satisfied, or do you want me to keep after it? Truthfully, I'm not sure I can find out anything else. A lot was lost after Katrina. Makes for a pretty cold trail."

"I don't need you to push this any further," Adele said. "Thanks, Danny. You can go ahead and send me that report."

"Wait ... don't hang up yet. I've got something on Murray Hamelin, too."

"Oh, good. Go slow. Tell me everything."

"Well, first off, his name is Robert Murdock Hamelin Jr. Murray is his nickname. You're right about his age. He's thirty—or will be. His birthday's tomorrow, in fact. Was raised in Lafayette. His parents are both deceased. His father was a supervisor at the Fontaine Sugar Refinery for twenty-two years and then was laid off four years ago. His mother cleaned houses."

Adele made notes as fast as she could. "Do you know how they died?"

"Let's see … his mother had a heart attack. Three months later, his father died of a self-inflicted gunshot wound."

Adele's heart sank. "How dreadful."

"That's all I could find out about the parents. Murray was some kind of computer geek for Aubry Computer Systems. As far as I can tell, that's the only place he ever worked. I got someone to look into his personnel file for me. He was terminated three years ago after months of bad employee evaluations. The supervisor's report indicated that his parents had moved in with him, which had created a lot of stress. His girlfriend broke up with him. Then both parents died. Bottom line: He couldn't do his job, and he was terminated."

"Poor boy," Adele said. "Did it say why his parents moved in with him?"

"No. But both parents died the same year Murray was fired. They were both in their early fifties."

Adele tried to take it all in. "So, if I'm hearing you correctly, Danny, Murray lost both parents, his girlfriend, and his job—all in the same year?"

"That about covers it."

"Goodness. Did you talk to anyone who knew him?"

"One coworker who still works at Aubry's Lafayette branch. She said he was a really nice guy, good at his job. Prior to the year his parents died, his career was going forward. And then it tanked."

"Is he an only child?"

"Yes. Grandparents are deceased too. If you want, I'll locate some relatives and get more information."

"That won't be necessary. This tells me all I really need to know. Thanks so much, Danny. Send your invoice with the report, and I'll get a check right out to you."

"Will do. Pleasure doing business with you. Call on me anytime."

Adele hung up the phone, satisfied with Danny's findings. Nothing he found on Noah contradicted what Noah had told her. He said he wandered homeless during those years after Katrina. Since Danny couldn't track him, he was likely telling the truth.

As for Murray ... no wonder he walked away from life for a while. If only she could get him to talk about it, maybe it would be less painful. But these were intensely private matters, and she had to give him space to open up when he was ready. She could never let him find out she'd hired Danny to look into his personal life. At least now that she knew *why* he was secretive, she could gently draw him out.

She laid her head back on the chair, her mind racing with this new information. She'd done her homework. Zoe and Pierce would just have to trust her with these two.

CHAPTER 29

Adele stood in the kitchen, fiddling with the timer on the coffee-maker she had set the night before to go on at 6:30 a.m. She never could make the fool thing work without it giving her a headache. She finally saw the red light go on and waited for a few moments until she heard it purring, the enticing aroma of freshly brewing coffee wafting under her nose.

A smile tugged at her cheeks. One more thing she could do by herself. All those years of having household staff to do everything for her hadn't rendered her completely helpless. The coffee would be waiting for her when she came back.

She walked to the front door and opened it, then, holding tightly to her Black Forest cane, stepped into the humid, honeysuckle-scented morning. She slowly descended each of the four brick steps, then walked toward the blossoming crape myrtles that lined the sidewalk, eager to start day two of a healthy new exercise regimen.

She turned right and headed up Magnolia Lane, her Nikes seeming to grip the sidewalk, propelling her along. Was there any neighborhood in Saint Catherine Parish that had charmed her more than Lafayette Gardens? She loved the generous, manicured lots and the interesting architectural mix of homes: Georgian and French Colonials, French Eclectic, Colonial Revivals with magnificent wraparound porches—and Greek Revivals, like hers. The longleaf pines, hardwoods, and live oaks were mature and provided abundant shade. Nothing here had the sprawling splendor of Woodmore. But Lafayette Gardens had its own character and beauty and was as wide open as she was going to find in a residential setting.

She passed by the red-brick two-story next door and gave a polite wave to her neighbor Abe Nolin, who was out trimming the hedges. Tall, muscular, and white-haired, the widower looked enough like Alfred to be his brother. And wasn't he fit as a fiddle for a man his age? She was sure he had tried to flirt with her after she first moved in. But her heart had room for only one man.

Thinking of Alfred just reminded her that she was alone and would have to deal with finding someone to replace Isabel. But today the most important thing on her list was her outing with Murray to go to Scoops and get a Banana Mountain.

She heard herself laugh as she thought of climbing into Murray's old truck and crossing town. Only this time, she knew his secrets. She wasn't entirely comfortable knowing that she had paid Danny to uncover things about Murray he hadn't volunteered. But she didn't intend to tell anyone what she had found out, not even Murray. And having the information would enable her to help him—and wasn't that the point?

⚜

Zoe lay in Pierce's arms, her heart still pounding, hoping their lovemaking hadn't awakened Grace. She really wasn't ready for this moment to end. She and Pierce hadn't had a day off together in a long while.

Pierce gently stroked her hair, a smile of contentment tugging at his cheeks. "I think you're prettiest first thing in the morning when you don't have makeup on."

"That's because your desire is off the charts, *cher.* And you're not wearing contacts."

"I'm nearsighted, remember? I just prefer natural beauty. Thank God Grace has your facial features. No girl should get my nose."

"I love your nose." Zoe traced it with her fingers. "Decidedly French and befitting a true Cajun."

"I guess. I'm just glad Grace's features are feminine like yours."

Zoe nestled in the warmth of his arms, glad the house was still quiet. Once Grace was up, she would have to shift gears from lover to mom.

"How are you doing on losing the ten pounds?" he said. "You look great to me, but I know you don't want to get pregnant until you lose it."

Zoe smiled. "I've lost five. It was easier than I thought. No beignets. No gumbo. No rice. I won't have to do it forever, but it's working."

"Good." He kissed the top of her head. "I'm really serious about having another child. I think it would be better if we don't have too much space between them."

"If we have another girl, I hope you're serious about stopping. I can't handle three and keep working."

"I'm fine with two girls or one of each. I like us running Zoe B's together. I would hate for that to change."

"Me, too," she said. "Though I don't think with two I can plop them down with Hebert and the guys every morning at breakfast, like I've done with Grace."

"Or drop them off at Adele's. She won't be able to handle two."

Will I? Zoe tried not to feel overwhelmed by the thought of having two children under the age of three. "Grace will be in preschool by then. I'm sure it would work out, once we get our rhythm."

"People do it all the time, babe. Two is doable. And you know I'll help. We'll hire a part-time chef to help Dempsey so I can take more time off."

"Speaking of Dempsey, is he working your shift today?"

"Yes. He's pulling a double so I don't have to go downstairs and check on anything. I'm all yours. What do you want to do today?"

"I already promised Grace we would take her to the park. But other than that, I haven't really thought about it. I'm thoroughly enjoying just lying here, not having to do anything."

"Maybe this would be a good day to drop by Adele's." Pierce smoothed her eyebrows with his finger. "I haven't seen her in a few weeks. We could take her some lemonade bread pudding. You know how she loves it. We wouldn't have to stay long. But it would be nice to see her."

Jude sat in on the morning briefing and then got a cup of coffee and went back to his office to tackle his overflowing inbox before

Special Agent Kyle Duffy arrived from the New Orleans field office. He didn't need to be distracted by Jeanette Stein's funeral today. Aimee asked Chief Norman to request extra help from other police departments in the region. It was being handled. Why was it so hard to turn loose of it? Either he trusted his people or he didn't.

A knock on the door caused him to look up. Aimee came in, carrying a file folder, and stood in front of his desk.

"Gil finished the comprehensive list." Aimee handed him the folder. "It includes only those employees at Fontaine and Aubry who—in the past five years—either quit, were fired, or were laid off *and* lost their home to foreclosure by Roux River Bank."

"Good work." Jude opened the folder and thumbed through the list. "*Five* pages? Are you kidding me?"

"I'm afraid so. It's easy to see why the resentment runs so deep in the community."

"Anything stand out to you?"

Aimee shook her head. "Not yet. It's a little overwhelming. It's going to take time and manpower to follow up with each one of these. We're already spread thin."

"We don't have a choice, Aimee. Do it. There might be someone who has a connection to each of the victims. Also"—he locked gazes with her—"I called the field office. They're sending us a profiler. He should be here by early afternoon. I need you to work with Chief Norman's people to make sure everything goes smoothly for Jeanette Stein's funeral. I need to be here. You're in charge."

"I'll handle it."

Jude glanced down at the list of names. "Since their homes were foreclosed on, do we even know how to find these people?"

"The hard way. We can check with the post office and utility companies. But since many of them are dodging creditors, they may not have left a forwarding address. We'll probably have to go back to the neighborhoods and see if anyone knows where they are. Like I said, I need time and manpower to tackle it."

"All right. After we get today's funeral behind us, I want you to turn your total attention to this list. Find these people, and see where it leads."

Murray sat at the dining room table at Haven House, finishing up a hearty breakfast he hoped would hold him until his outing with Adele.

He looked across the table at Noah. "You need any supplies to start the paint job for the Millers?"

"Yeah, I'll pick up what I need at the building center."

Murray reached in his back pocket and took out his wallet. He flipped through a stack of bills and handed Noah a hundred. "I'm flush right now. Let me get it."

"I've got money," Noah said. "You've already forfeited what you would've made on this job. I can't let you pay for the supplies, too."

"Why not? I've got no real expenses right now. My truck's paid for."

"Yeah, but you're savin' for a new one."

Murray took Noah's hand and put the bill in it. "A hundred bucks isn't going to make or break me right now. But it should take care of everything you'll need. Let me do this, man. You're going to have all kinds of expenses you hadn't planned on."

Noah played with the edges of the hundred. "Why are you bein' nice to me?"

"Because you're a decent guy who's in a tight spot. I don't know why someone is trying to make you out to be liar, and I don't care. I just want to help, okay?"

Noah folded the bill and put it in his pocket. "Thanks. So what've you got on tap today?"

"I'm installing new kitchen sinks for several units in those old brick apartments on Ninth."

"How'd you learn to do all this stuff?"

Murray shrugged. "I never really learned it, per se. Just always had a knack for it. I can figure out how to do most anything."

"Same here." Noah took a bite of a biscuit. "But landscaping … now that's my passion. Though I'm thinkin', if I have to start over, I might as well leave Les Barbes and go back to New Awlins. The city's recovered enough from Katrina that I should be able to start up my landscapin' business again."

"Where would you live?"

"Father Vince could get me a place in a halfway house there."

"You already talked to him about this?"

Noah shook his head. "But I got to be thinkin' ahead. More and more it's not lookin' like I have much of a future here. Only reason I came *up the bayou* was to see where my ancestors were slaves. Only reason I planned to stay was because the Langleys asked me to be groundskeeper. I was honored to do it. I wanted to be a part o' history. But the way things are goin', I don't think I'll be workin' at Langley Manor anymore."

"You don't know that. Give it time. Besides, I thought the sheriff asked you not to leave town."

"Asked. But unless he's got somethin' on me, I can do what I want."

Murray stuffed a slice of bacon into his mouth. "How old are you, man?"

"Fifty-four. Don't let the gray in my hair fool you. I got a lot o' workin' years left. And I'm plenty fit."

"Maybe so. But how many years did it take you to get your landscaping business off the ground? Do you really want to start over?"

"I'll tell you what I don't want: I don't want to live in a town where folks think I could be a murderer."

"People will forget about it after a while." Murray leaned forward, his hands folded on the table, and lowered his voice. "To tell you the truth, it wouldn't bother me if you *did* do it."

"I told you I didn't."

"I know what you told me. I'm just sayin' ..."

"Keep your doubts to yourself, Murray. I got enough trouble."

"I never said I doubted you. I just said it wouldn't bother me."

"Well, it bothers me." Noah's face was taut, his eyes scolding. "It burns me that people will believe what they want, even though there's no evidence."

"Like I said, they'll forget about it after a while."

"Well, I won't. And neither will the Langleys."

CHAPTER 30

Jude walked down the long hallway, his rubber soles squeaking on the newly polished floor. He opened the door to the lounge and saw a pretty blonde woman about forty, dressed in a white skirt and navy blazer, sitting at a round table, sipping a Coke and thumbing through a magazine.

She looked up and smiled, a dead ringer for Julia Roberts. "Sheriff Prejean, I'm Special Agent Kyle Duffy."

He stood mute for a moment, trying to erase the image he'd had of a thirtysomething stiff in a dark suit and tie. He shook her hand. "We've been expecting you."

Her smile was suddenly as wide as the Mississippi. "It's okay that you're surprised I'm a woman. I get that a lot. Kyle was my mother's maiden name, and my parents were determined to give it to their firstborn."

Jude returned her smile. "Thank you for coming, Special Agent Duffy."

"I'd really prefer first names, if that's okay with you."

"Sure, call me Jude. Let's go to my office and get started."

Kyle threw her empty can in the recycle bin and picked up a black leather briefcase.

Jude walked toward his office, Kyle keeping stride, her straight blonde hair falling over her shoulders and down her back. Her pleasant attitude and relaxed demeanor were very different from the last fed he had worked with.

"I've reviewed everything your office faxed to the field office," she said. "I believe this killer has given us a road map that leads right to him. We just have to read the signs."

"We've been trying to do that, but we're stumped at the moment."

"That's why I'm here."

He led the way into his office. "Why don't we sit there at the conference table? Can I get you something to drink?"

"No thanks, I just had a Coke."

He reached into the small refrigerator next to the file cabinet and pulled out a bottle of water, then sat at the table across from her.

"How was your drive up from New Orleans?"

"Uneventful. A lot of tourist traffic. This is my first time in Les Barbes. What a pleasant-looking community."

"Thanks. We're pretty proud of it. Murders are rare here. Or at least they were. We've had five in just over a week—one wasn't related to this case. I want this guy's head on a stick."

"I understand." Kyle opened her briefcase and pulled out a tape recorder. "I'd like to record your comments, if it's okay with you."

"Sure."

"Sheriff, tell me in your own words what you know about this case."

Jude unscrewed the cap on the water bottle and took a sip. "The Bathtub Killer, probably acting alone, has targeted four victims so far. Three were CEOs of major companies who have been responsible for layoffs that also resulted in numerous foreclosures. The fourth victim was a wife and stay-at-home mom. Married to a high-profile defense attorney. We've been unable to establish a connection between her and the other victims, other than, a few years back, she worked for Aubry Computer Systems for thirteen months. On the surface, it appears to be a coincidence, but we're digging deeper."

"Tell me about the killer's MO."

"He drugs his victims and drowns them in the bathtub—the three CEOs were still dressed in business attire and the fourth victim in her nightgown. No defensive wounds. No sign of sexual assault. The victims were found submerged in water, their hands folded on their chests as if they were positioned in a coffin." He opened the file and laid photographs of the crime scenes on the table. "The killer spray painted—in black—the pound sign followed by a numeral, beginning with number one on the first victim and ending with number four on the last victim. The CEOs each had a safe that was found open and empty of valuables. The fourth victim had a safe, but it was not unlocked, and the surviving spouse indicated the contents were intact. The murder scenes have been mostly clean, but we have been able to piece together enough evidence to conclude the same person was present at all four. Handwriting analysis determined that the spray-painted numbers were formed by the same person. And the brand of spray paint was Rust-Oleum, which can be bought almost anywhere paint is sold."

Kyle lifted her gaze, her deep brown eyes reminding him of Colette's. "Tell me about the evidence."

"We got matching DNA from the bathrooms of three murder scenes: a Kleenex found in a trash can in Jeanette Stein's, an eyelash found in the sink at Girard Darveau's, and skin cells on a towel found at Peter Gautier's. Unfortunately, the DNA did not match anything in the NCIC database.

"There's something else." Jude picked up the latest evidence report and thumbed through it until he found what he was looking for. "No useful DNA was found at Nicole Aubry's murder scene. We did find a muddy right shoe print on the wet floor—a man's size ten. But the sole pattern wasn't distinct enough to identify the brand of shoe. The soil analysis showed soil consistent with this area and containing a broadleaf weed killer that can be purchased at any garden center but was not present on the lawns of any of the four victims. However, high traces of that same broadleaf weed killer was found in soil samples collected from the floor at each of the murder scenes. That's about it."

Kyle pulled her hair back and put a rubber band around it. "Jude, you said the victims were drugged. Was the same substance used in each case?"

"Yes. The toxicology report indicated that each victim's blood contained a significant level of the veterinary anesthetic ketamine, known on the street as 'Special K' or cat Valium."

"I'm familiar with it," Kyle said.

"Oh, one more thing … We've had several people contact us after receiving an anonymous note containing ten one-hundred-dollar bills. The message in the card was the same in each, 'This belongs to you.'"

"You think this is money stolen by the killer?" she said.

"I do. I think he's attempting to give back some of the money he feels the CEOs got in bonuses in spite of the layoffs."

"Were the notes signed?"

"No, but they were printed by hand. We have them in evidence. The only fingerprints we found on any of them are the recipient's."

Kyle seemed to be deep in thought. Finally she said, "You've given me a great overview. Thanks. I'd like to spend some time in the files and go through the evidence. Is there someplace quiet where I could work?"

"Sure, I can put you in one of the interview rooms. In your opinion, is this guy through killing?"

"It's too early to give you an opinion. I need time to review the facts. I should have a profile worked up for you yet today—tomorrow morning at the latest."

"I really appreciate whatever you can tell us."

She flashed him a knowing smile. "Look, there's no need for you to feel territorial in any way. I'm here at your request to profile your perp. I don't have jurisdiction, and I really don't want it. So let's make sure we're both on the same page."

"We are. I'm eager to hear what you come up with. Once we have some idea who we're looking for, maybe all this evidence will start to click."

⚜

Adele heard a vehicle pull in the driveway and looked out just as Murray got out of his truck. She walked to the front door and stepped out on the brick porch.

"Hello, Murray. My goodness, it's exactly three thirty."

He flashed a boyish grin, his fiery red hair catching glints of the afternoon sun and looking uncharacteristically in place. He was dressed in khaki pants and a green golf shirt. Was he quietly celebrating his birthday?

"Well, Adele. You've climbed a mountain or two. Are you ready to tackle a Banana Mountain?"

"Oh my, yes. I've been craving it all day. You look very nice, Murray."

"I thought it might be helpful if I didn't embarrass you."

"For heaven's sake, if you embarrassed me, I would never have invited you to go with me."

Murray folded his arms across his chest, his grin widening. "Look at *you* in pants and those spiffy Nikes."

"I dressed for the climb up into your truck."

"I brought the step stool. Come on. It'll be much easier."

"I'll be ready in just a moment."

Adele went inside, grabbed her purse, and came out and locked the front door.

"Here we go," Murray said.

"I wonder what a Banana Mountain looks like." Adele giggled. "In this heat, we can't get a to-go box."

"Something tells me we won't need one." Murray opened the passenger-side door and pulled out a sturdy-looking step stool and set it on the ground. He took Adele's hand. "Ready?"

"I've tackled steeper in my day. Let's do this." Adele held tightly to Murray's hand and climbed the steps, using her cane. She slid right into the passenger seat. "Not bad for an octogenarian."

"Not bad at all," Murray said. "I wish you'd known my grandma Sophie. You two would've gotten along famously."

"I'd love to hear more about her."

Adele remembered him saying that his grandmother had died on his twelfth birthday and birthdays made him depressed. Maybe today's would be different.

Murray walked around to the driver's side of the truck and climbed in behind the wheel.

"We're off."

"I love being up so high," she said. "I may not want to get out at Scoops."

Murray laughed. "Tell you what. I'll take the long way and we can enjoy the ride."

Adele looked out the window and took in the world from this vantage point. It was hard not letting on that she knew Murray was turning thirty today.

What a shame not to celebrate this milestone in his young life.

⚜

Zoe stood with Pierce and Grace on the brick porch at Adele's and rang the doorbell a second time.

"We probably should've called first," Pierce said. "But it'll be fun to surprise her."

"I want to see Addie!" Grace said. "I give her *big* hug."

Zoe pushed the doorbell again. "Why isn't Isabel answering? Maybe they went out to run errands or something."

"I'll check the garage window," Pierce said, "and see if Isabel's car's in there."

Pierce jogged over to the garage, cupped his hands around his eyes, and looked in the window. He turned to Zoe and shook his head. "The garage is empty. They must be out."

Zoe spotted something under the brick next to the front door. She bent down to see what it was. It was an envelope with Adele's name handwritten on it—from Danny Clinton, Professional Investigator.

Pierce came up on the porch. "What are you looking at, babe?"

"I thought it was a flier. But it's something for Adele from a professional investigator. I know this name. Adele used this same guy back when I was working for her. She always checked out her household staff, and she's probably done that for Isabel. Seems unprofessional of a PI to leave personal information out here instead of dropping it in the mail slot."

Pierce put his hand on her shoulder. "I thought you said Adele had Isabel checked out before she hired her."

"She did." Zoe pushed the envelope through the mail slot on the front door, then brushed her hands together. "It's none of our business. I really hate that we missed her though."

"Not to worry. The lemonade bread pudding will keep in the cooler," Pierce said. "Let's go to Target and finish our shopping. We can come back later."

Zoe turned and took Grace by the hand and helped her down the steps. "I'm positive Adele told me she had Isabel checked out weeks ago. Why do you suppose she's hired a PI?"

"I don't know," Pierce said. "But I hope he told her she's playing with fire by hiring the men from Haven House."

CHAPTER 31

Adele stepped carefully across the black-and-white checkered floor at Scoops, sat at a round red table, and then leaned her cane against an empty chair. It seemed crowded for four o'clock in the afternoon. She glanced out the window at the digital numbers displayed on the bank. Ninety-nine degrees. Was it any wonder this place was busy?

Red ceiling fans whirred overhead. The entire back wall was covered with a painted mural of the quaint shops along *rue Madeline*—an amazing likeness of the buildings and overhanging galleries lush with blooming plants, greenery, and flowers.

The walls on either side of Scoops were painted red, and each featured poster-sized framed photographs of happy, adorable children eating a variety of ice-cream delights.

Along the front of the store, colorful bins of small toys and trinkets were strategically displayed next to a glass freezer showcasing two dozen flavors of ice cream.

She studied a mother with three small children and admired her patience with the messy fidgeting.

Murray arrived at the table carrying two red bowls, each containing a tall mound made of five scoops of banana-cinnamon ice cream smothered in slices of fresh banana and topped with hot butterscotch, pecans, and whipped cream. The peak was the two-inch end of a banana, topped with more whipped cream and a cherry.

Adele put her hands to her mouth and started to laugh. "We really did it, Murray. Banana Mountains. How am I ever going to eat all mine?"

"I promise you"—Murray sat across from her and handed her a spoon—"nothing's going to waste. Eat as much as you want, and if there's any left, I'll take care of it."

She realized people were staring. "Are we the only ones here who got this?"

"No. Half the people in line ordered it. I think it's so impressive looking, it always gets a double take."

Adele ate the cherry and then took a bite and savored it. "Oh my. This is heavenly."

"Or as my generation would say, it's to *die for*."

Adele enjoyed bite after bite, feeling completely comfortable with Murray's silence and hoping he wasn't dwelling on his grandma Sophie's death on this very day eighteen years ago.

"I like being with you," Murray said. "I haven't had time to make new friends."

"I'm sure it must be difficult to start over."

"Yeah. It is."

"Where do young people go these days—to meet other young people?"

"I'm not into bars," he said. "I prefer social networking. There are a few gals I like talking to online. But it's hard to have any privacy at Haven House. Once in a while I take my laptop to Boucher

Bookshop, where I can get free Wi-Fi. I can access the Internet that way without someone looking over my shoulder."

"Where do you keep your laptop?"

"In my backpack. It's called an iPad. It's really small. I bought it used, right after I bought the truck. I couldn't believe how much technology had changed since I'd been away from it."

Adele waved her hand. "Goodness, everyone I know uses computers these days. Zoe and Vanessa couldn't do without theirs. Even Noah said he kept all his financial information on computer when he had his landscaping business."

"I don't know how people ever managed a business without them."

"Tell me again exactly what it was you did for a living." Adele felt her face get hot. Would he remember that he'd never told her?

"I was a computer systems analyst. I helped businesses set up their individual computer systems and keep them current."

"Can't you go back to doing that?"

Murray put a big bite of banana in his mouth. "Not really. I've been out of it too long. I'd need to take a refresher course to learn how to implement the current technology. I loved it though. Speaking of loving it, isn't this Banana Mountain amazing?"

"It's terrific. Better than I even imagined." Adele put her hand over her mouth and giggled. "I just might finish mine after all. I won't want to eat for a week."

"I imagine Isabel will enjoy the break from cooking and can get caught up on something else."

Adele picked up a slice of banana with her spoon. "Murray, since you brought up Isabel, you should know she quit."

"I didn't even realize she had given notice."

"She didn't. We had some differences we couldn't resolve. She thought it best if she left."

"Pretty unprofessional to leave with no notice," Murray said. "Isabel always seemed tense. It was obvious she didn't like me."

"She had trust issues, hon. It was difficult for her to accept that I allowed strangers into my home."

"Me?"

"It wasn't just you. She was uncomfortable with Noah as well. What I thought to be hospitable, Isabel considered to be reckless. I don't think we would ever have come to terms on it."

The corners of Murray's mouth curled. "You're not afraid of me, are you?"

"I should say not."

"I could be a serial killer, for all you know."

"And I could be the Queen of Hearts from *Alice in Wonderland.* Off with their heads!"

Murray laughed. "You're a fun lady. I like being with you. Would you believe me if I told you it was my birthday?"

Adele arched her eyebrows and managed to put a questioning tone in her voice. "You're serious?"

"Yes. I'm thirty today. I haven't celebrated my birthday for a few years. But it's nice being here with you."

"Well, forevermore! Happy birthday, Murray." She reached over and squeezed his hand. "I'm so glad you decided to share it with me. Thirty is somewhat of a milestone."

"It's also a reminder that the clock is ticking and I haven't done anything with my life yet."

"There's still plenty of time to do anything your heart desires." Adele leaned forward and looked into his eyes. "You're smart. And you already have a profession with computers. You just need to brush up. If you want to get your life back, it's right there, just waiting for you."

"I do want my life back. I've had some serious pain to deal with, but today I've put that behind me. I'm ready to move on."

"That's the spirit," she said. "If there's anything I can do to help, you know I will."

Isabel's words instantly came to mind. *Just be careful. Find out who these men are before you invite them to sit down at your table. And please don't feel sorry for them and give them money.*

"You're sweet to offer, Adele. But you're already helping me—just by being a friend and letting me work for you."

If he was after money, wasn't that the perfect opening? So much for Isabel's overactive imagination.

"I like being with you, too, Murray. I don't have many friends in Les Barbes. I lived in Alexandria all my life until six months ago. I've outlived most of my family. And so many of my friends have died now."

"But you have cool memories of the adventures you had with Alfred. Do you realize how lucky you are?"

"Indeed. But nothing in my life was luck. It was all a blessing from God."

"What about the loss of your baby? And Alfred's sudden death? Were those from God too?"

"He certainly allowed them. He used them as opportunities to bring me into a personal relationship with Him. That part was a blessing."

Murray put a big bite of ice cream into his mouth and didn't say anything.

"I know you struggle with God, perhaps even blame Him for the troubles you've had."

"You're right. I don't trust God. Not after what He threw my way."

"A lot of bad things happen in this life. God allows them, but He certainly doesn't enjoy seeing us suffer. He's there to comfort us and guide us through it."

"Really? Where was He, I wonder, when my dad lost his job at fifty-three and no one would hire him? When my parents went bankrupt, lost their home, and had to move in with me? When my mom died of a heart attack from the stress? And Dad put a bullet through his head to end the humiliation?"

Adele felt her throat tighten with emotion. The reality seemed so much worse hearing it from Murray than it did getting a report from Danny.

"I'm sorry you've had all that heartache," she said. "I don't pretend to know exactly how you felt. But I know how I felt when I lost the baby. And when I lost Alfred. I was desolate."

Murray lifted his eyes. "I could've handled it. But my parents were so bitter and depressed. Living with their pain, day in and day out in a one-bedroom apartment, was torture for all of us. I slept on the couch for six months and hated going home."

"Did you have anyone to confide in?"

"Just the girl I planned to marry." Murray bit his lip and seemed lost in thought. "Our relationship was never the same after my parents moved in with me. We had been talking about getting married, but when I surprised her with an engagement ring, she gave it back the next day. Said she loved me but my family situation was just too *oppressive,* that she couldn't handle the gloom and doom. She broke it off—just like that. I felt like half of me was gone."

"I'm so sorry, Murray. I really am."

"Yeah, me, too. After my parents died, I tried contacting her and found out she had gotten married. She didn't waste any time."

"Is that what caused you to enter the homeless lifestyle?"

Murray shook his head. "Not exactly. I got so depressed when I realized I had no chance of ever getting her back that my performance at work slipped even more. I made a big mistake that cost us a valuable client. Long story short, I got fired. I tried to explain what I was going through. The big boss didn't care that the bottom had fallen out of my life. My performance had been slipping for months. She needed a good systems analyst—and that was no longer me."

Adele didn't know what to say and decided just to listen.

"I was in no shape to find another job. Plus, there was no way I'd get a good reference. I just stayed in my apartment and cut myself off from everyone and everything. I had used up my savings to bury my parents, but I still had my 401(k). It didn't last long. My truck was repossessed, and I was evicted from my apartment. Truthfully, I didn't even care. *That's* when I entered the homeless lifestyle."

"You've suffered a great deal in your young life, Murray. But perhaps turning thirty is a good time to change directions. You've got all the makings of a bright future."

"Yes, today is a turning point. Now I can get on with my life." Murray sat quietly for a few moments, a faraway look on his face.

Finally he looked up. "Thanks for listening. It felt good getting that out. I've never told anyone before. I hope it didn't depress you."

"No. I'm looking at it from *this* side of the pain. I'm very sorry you had to suffer all these things, but it's over now."

"I'd really appreciate it if you kept this between us," he said.

"Of course I will. There's no reason anyone needs to know your personal business." Adele took a bite of ice cream. No wonder Murray had been reluctant to talk about his past. "I'm not going to quit working on you to make peace with God, though. He can make all the difference in how you go forward."

"Trust me, God doesn't want me any more than I want Him."

"Oh, I beg to differ," she said. "I think God's been trying to get your attention for a long time."

"He got my attention. The question is: Did I get His?" Murray almost sounded amused.

Adele studied him, wondering what he meant but not wanting to debate the sovereignty of God. All in good time.

"Well, here's to a wonderful future." Adele held up a spoonful of ice cream, and Murray did the same. "I wish you every perfect blessing. Happy birthday, Murray."

CHAPTER 32

Adele leaned back in the passenger seat of Murray's truck and enjoyed the ride along Ascension Boulevard. This main thoroughfare was lined on both sides with mature live oaks draped with Spanish moss. Beyond the expansive green lawns stood elegant antebellum homes owned by the Les Barbes Historical Society and open to the public.

Murray turned onto *rue Evangeline,* its quaint double-gallery houses now shops of all kinds. Above the shops, the galleries were thick with potted trees, plants, and flowers, and some were furnished with tables and chairs and used by eating establishments for guest dining.

"Les Barbes is truly a beautiful little city," she said.

Murray glanced over at her, wearing a pleasant smile. "I grew up in Lafayette. But I remember my parents bringing me over here when I was a kid. They were Cajun to the core, and Cajun culture was becoming popular around the country. Les Barbes was just starting to take its place in all that. Today its economy is about fifty percent tourist driven."

"It's lovely. The Cajun influence is much stronger here than in my hometown of Alexandria. That's where Alfred and I were married—at

Saint Francis Xavier Cathedral—and we lived in Alexandria until Woodmore House was built. That was Alfred's wedding gift to me."

"Some wedding gift."

Adele smiled. "I've always been blessed with more lavishness than I deserve. In my younger days, I took it for granted. But since Alfred set up the foundation, I've been very much involved with what I have and how the wealth is being distributed. My fortune is a gift from God, and I feel a responsibility to share it where it can do the most good."

"I can see that," Murray said. "I doubt I'll ever be rich, but I made good money as a computer systems analyst. I hope to get back to it. I should be able to make a good living."

"Would you like to marry and have a family?"

Murray nodded. "For a long time, I was bitter that my fiancée broke off the engagement and bailed when I needed her most. But starting today, I'm putting it all behind me."

"I'm so glad to hear you say that. Turning thirty does seem like the perfect time to start fresh."

In the next instant, a red car with out-of-state plates pulled out in front of them from a side street and Murray slammed on the brakes.

Lord, help us! Send angels! Adele prayed as she was thrust forward, her seat belt holding her securely, her eyes clamped shut in anticipation of a collision.

Instead the car stopped short of a crash, and Murray pulled the truck over to the curb, his face flushed, his hands shaking.

"You okay?" he said faintly.

"Yes. I ... I think so. I didn't think there was any way to miss that car." *Thank You, Lord.*

Adele felt something roll on the floor against her foot. She looked down and saw a can of spray paint.

Murray snatched it and stuffed it under his seat. "Sorry about that. Your purse fell over too. Here, let me get it for you." He reached down and picked up her purse and handed it to her, along with a tube of lipstick and a compact that had fallen out. "There you go."

"Thank you, hon. Looks like we're both fine. That was close."

"I've got to be on my toes every second with all these tourists. Half the time, they have no idea where they're going." Murray gripped the wheel with both hands and turned to her. "You want to keep going, or did that do you in?"

"I'm fine. I'd like to continue our drive, if you would. I hope that sun won't be in our eyes the whole time."

"I can fix that." Murray pulled down her visor and then his own. A piece of paper fell into his lap.

Adele saw the words *In Memory of Jeanette Elise Stein* printed on the front and realized it was a memorial folder from her funeral.

"You went to Jeanette Stein's funeral. No wonder you're dressed so nicely."

Murray's face was suddenly crimson. "I didn't say anything because it's hard to talk about. Her death really touched me. Maybe because my ex-fiancée is her age, and I have some idea what Mr. Stein is going through. Why would anyone want to hurt someone like her? I mean the woman had two little babies."

"The Bathtub Killer has a twisted mind. We can't understand his reasoning, so there's no point in trying."

"In a strange way, going to her funeral helped me to accept my own loss." Murray looked over at her, his eyes glistening. "It's been a long time coming, but I've finally accepted that I'm not going to get her back."

"That's one good thing that came from this present tragedy. I'm so glad you can finally put yours behind you."

⚜

Zoe rang the doorbell at Adele's a third time. "She's not home, *cher*. Must be having dinner out."

"I'm so disappointed," Pierce said. "I really wanted to surprise her with the lemonade bread pudding. I doubt I'll get a chance to see her until we have another day off together. Oh well."

"It's unlikely she would've taken Isabel out to dinner," Zoe said. "Then again, she's so generous I wouldn't put it past her."

"Maybe she's just expanding her horizons like we suggested."

Zoe rang the bell again. "She would've mentioned it to me."

"I think that's a stretch. She's not going to check in with you if someone asked her over for dinner—or took her out. I kind of hope she decided to join that neighborhood mah-jongg group. It'd do her good."

"I think so too. But Adele didn't seem interested."

"Maybe she changed her mind." Pierce put his arm around her. "It takes time to acclimate. This was a very difficult move. She was totally self-contained at Woodmore—like living in another country. Being out in the real world again has to be a culture shock."

"I suppose you're right."

"We'll call or come back later, depending on how Grace holds up. Let's go to Louie's and have a steak burger."

Zoe laughed. "A fine Cajun you are. Every chance you get, you want a burger."

"I get my fill of Cajun cooking in my own kitchen. Going out for a steak burger is a treat."

"I love Louie's steak burgers." Zoe smiled wryly. "But I'll settle for a salad. I want to drop those last five pounds so we can get serious about working on that little addition to our family."

"I *am* serious." Pierce winked and patted her behind.

Zoe laughed. "You need to help me lose five more pounds."

"I will. Okay, Gracey Racey"—Pierce lifted Grace onto his shoulders—"let's race Mommy to the car and help speed up her metabolism."

⚜

Adele looked out the passenger-side window of Murray's truck and took in the sights around Les Barbes.

"This reminds me of Sunday drives I used to take with Alfred. After we wandered around the countryside, we would end up in Alexandria and drive through the neighborhoods." She turned to Murray. "You're awfully quiet. I guess my chattering doesn't give you much room to comment."

"That's not it. I'm just enjoying listening to you. I learn a lot about you in bits and pieces. I wish I had known you before."

"Before what, hon?"

Murray turned onto *rue Madeline*. "I just realize how much I've missed Grandma Sophie. She was there for me in ways my parents couldn't be. I mean, they tried. But with both of them working long hours and even weekends, it was Grandma Sophie I spent the most time with. Her dying hit me harder than either parent. I guess, in a way, she was both a mother and father to me."

"Perhaps it was your age, too," Adele said. "Twelve is fragile, even without something traumatic to deal with."

"I was never the same after that," Murray said. "She caught the flu from me. I was convinced I killed her."

"But you know better now."

"Sure. If God's in control, then *He* did it."

"Murray, we live in a world where germs thrive. You weren't responsible, and neither was God."

"Then who was? *Someone* has to take responsibility!"

Adele was taken aback by his harsh tone. The poor young man was still hurting terribly. She remembered all too well what grief was like.

Lord, he needs You. Help me to say the right thing.

Murray's face was red again. "I'm sorry. I … I didn't mean to snap at you, Adele."

"You don't have to apologize. But maybe it's time you talked more about your grandma Sophie's death. It's obvious to me that you're still hurting a great deal."

"There's nothing more to say. She died of the flu. And I gave it to her. I have to live with that."

"But you don't," she said. "If only you would let the Lord have your pain. He wants to take it away."

"That's big of Him." Murray's face grew taut, his expression dark. "He's in control and caused it—and now He wants to come to the rescue and take it all away? What kind of sick God is that? That's like a father abusing a child and then expecting the kid to warm up to him—and trust him."

"No, Murray. It's like a father allowing his child to live in complete freedom, while He follows at a safe distance. And, when the child gets hurt, picking him up and taking care of the injury. There's a big difference."

Murray's jaw clenched. "I don't see God the way you do. I've been through this a thousand times in my mind. And I don't think He cares about anyone but Himself."

"Goodness gracious, Murray. He died in our place so we can live with Him forever. Whether or not you believe Jesus' death has the power to save you, how can you possibly see it as caring only about Himself?"

"He sure didn't care about *me.* I lost everything. *Everything!* You still had your fortune. I know you went through a lot. But you didn't lose everything. So don't judge me."

Adele grew increasingly uncomfortable with Murray's agitation. Why was he twisting the conversation into something she never intended?

"I'm not judging you," she said softly. "I'm honestly trying to understand your pain. The last thing in the world I want to do is upset you."

A minute passed without either of them saying anything. Adele wondered if their lovely afternoon was going to end on a sour note. Should she have refrained from telling him that God wanted to take away his pain? What good was friendship without honesty?

Finally Murray said, "I have an idea: Why don't we go to the rookery and watch the flocks of birds come in to roost?"

Adele didn't sense any anger in his voice. It was as though the unpleasant exchange hadn't happened.

"I'd really like that. I've never been."

He smiled, the tension gone from his face. "You're in for a treat. I've gone down there a few times. It's quite a sight."

Adele settled into her seat and enjoyed the ride. Murray was complicated. But someone had to draw him out.

CHAPTER 33

Jude sat at his desk, reviewing the evidence they had so far in the bathtub killings. He heard a knock on the door and looked up, happy to see Special Agent Kyle Duffy in the doorway.

Jude rose to his feet. "Come in, Kyle. I was just about to have a Coke. Would you like one?"

"I would, thanks. I've come up with a rough profile. I was hoping to run it by you before you left for the day."

"I was hoping the same thing. You think it's someone who's working alone?"

"I do." She pulled out a chair and sat at the table. "Is there anyone else you want to sit in on this?"

"Not yet. I'd like to hear it first and get a feel for what we're dealing with."

Jude took two cans of Coke out of his minirefrigerator, went over to the table, and popped the tops. He handed one to Kyle and then sat across from her.

She folded her hands on the table. "Let me start by saying there was a lot to consider. The perp's MO changed with the fourth victim—but just enough to tell us his story. Or what I believe is his story."

"Go on," Jude said.

Kyle took a pair of round glasses out of her briefcase and slipped them on. "The perp is male, thirty to thirty-five years of age. He's physically strong. Left-handed. He's highly intelligent but plays it down as part of his cover. He's likely self-employed so he can control his time. Early in his life, he suffered the loss of someone close to him. He has control and abandonment issues. This is a man filled with rage and who's a master at concealing it. He's friendly, but only to mask the anger that's eating him up. He's on a mission to take back control of his life by destroying those who have controlled him—those whom he holds responsible for his pain."

Kyle turned the page and took a sip of Coke. "His MO with the first three victims tells us a lot. He cleaned out their safes, which symbolized his stripping them of their wealth. He drowned each of them while they were dressed in business attire, symbolizing his washing away the injustice done under their authority. He drugged them just enough to render them helpless, yet leave them fully aware that he was taking back the power they once held over him by taking their lives. That's why he made sure their eyes were open when he drowned them. He made sure he had their full attention. It was essential to him that his victims understood what he was doing—and why."

Jude leaned back in his chair. "So you concur that he targeted these CEOs because they were behind the layoffs and foreclosures?"

"Not necessarily. His grudge is personal. Each of these victims caused some kind of trauma in his life, real or perceived. I believe he numbered them to humiliate them. Having the power to turn them into murder statistics and knowing that's the way they will be remembered was more satisfying to him than the brief but excruciating pain they experienced in a wet drowning. I haven't been able to establish that the order in which he killed them represented anything specific. It's possible. But more important is the matter of how Jeanette Stein figures into this."

"Go on."

"She wasn't a CEO. She was wearing a nightgown, not business clothes when he drowned her. He didn't sexually assault her. He didn't take her money. Or take the lives of her children. All he wanted was to take back control—like he did with the CEOs."

"What control did *she* have over him?"

"I'm guessing romantic. Either they were involved or he fantasized that they were. Your report indicates Jeanette LaBelle Stein had a boyfriend when she worked at Aubry."

"Yes," Jude said. "And we've talked with the employees who knew her. She was private about that relationship. No one remembers meeting him. Not even her sister, who was away at college. Unfortunately, we can't question her parents. Her father's dead, and her mother has Alzheimer's. We're talking with relatives, but so far, no one can remember the guy's name or what he looks like."

"Someone does," Kyle said. "You need to make finding that someone a priority. The boyfriend could be our killer."

"So what was the stressor that set him off? Do you think he was laid off?"

Kyle shook her head. "He's young. I'm not sure being laid off at this age would be devastating enough to trigger this kind of reaction. He didn't have a lot to lose yet. He wouldn't have had time to build up a pension. And if he owned a home, he probably hadn't had it long."

"So what are you thinking?"

"I'm thinking that someone close to him was laid off and lost their home. Possibly a parent or a close relative. It was likely tragic and affected him deeply."

"I don't get where Jeanette LaBelle Stein fits into this."

"I'm still trying to piece it together. But I believe she broke his heart."

"Based on what?" Jude took a sip of Coke.

"They were almost the same age, considerably younger than the other victims. Romantic involvement would be the perfect stressor if she ended it and he didn't want to."

"And what makes you think that's what happened?"

"Because no one close to Jeanette can remember ever meeting the guy. That tells me that perhaps the relationship meant more to him than it did to her. I think the stressor was her ending it."

Jude scratched the stubble on his chin. "Makes sense."

"There's more. It's significant that, before he drowned her, he didn't defile her."

"Why is that significant?"

Kyle's eyes grew wide. "Because unlike the others killings, ending Jeanette's life wasn't about revenge, it was about it being *his choice* to break it off with her. It wasn't his choice before. She left him and broke his heart. But this time, he was totally in control. He wanted her to know that he didn't need her anymore. That he was no longer dependent on her emotionally. That he was no longer in bondage to the debilitating pain that had controlled him since she ended the relationship. Her death—his act of letting her go—was the finale. He had to take her life in order to get his life back. It's complicated."

Jude combed his hands through his hair, his elbows planted on the table, his mind racing with the implication. "So you think he's done killing?"

"I didn't say that. He's dangerous. He's already killed four people to exact his justice. He would certainly kill again to keep from getting caught."

"So it's *not* over—at least not if he feels threatened." Jude looked over at Kyle. "I'm still not clear on how Jeanette Stein is connected to the other victims."

"Neither am I. Maybe she isn't. Maybe the only connection is that she added to his pain and was last on the list of people to eliminate."

Jude pushed back his chair and rose to his feet. "I'd better go tell my people to step up the questioning of everyone who knew Jeanette LaBelle when she was working at Aubry."

"Jude, wait." Kyle seemed deep in thought. "I want to talk to Jeanette's mother. Even if she has Alzheimer's, her long-term memory might kick in if we ask questions about Jeanette's boyfriend."

"You really think the boyfriend is the key?"

"I'm convinced he could be our killer."

He glanced at his watch. "I don't know what time they put the patients to bed at the Alzheimer's center."

"I don't think we can worry about that. We need to find this guy. And we need to do it now."

Adele unlocked the front door and went inside, Murray right behind her. She spotted an envelope on the floor. Before she could bend down to get it, Murray picked it up and handed it to her.

She saw it was from Danny, and her pulse quickened. Why didn't he mail it? Did Murray notice the return address on the envelope? If he did, he didn't react.

"Thank you, hon." Adele stuck it in her purse and walked out to the kitchen. "I've still got some chocolate chip cookies that Isabel baked. Would you like some?"

"I don't know where I'd put them." Murray put his hands on his middle. "But I wouldn't mind something cold to drink."

"I've got a whole pitcher of raspberry iced tea."

"That sounds great. I'd love some."

"I had such a wonderful time," she said. "And the rookery was amazing. I'd like to go back with my camera."

"I had a feeling you'd enjoy it."

"I've never seen that many shore birds gathered in one area. Goodness, the ground looked like snow."

"It's pretty amazing." Murray glanced at the purse tucked under her arm. "Would you like me to put that somewhere for you?"

"I'll just set it over there on the counter. I'll get our tea."

Murray sat at the kitchen table, seeming to avoid eye contact, his finger slowly tracing the floral pattern on the tablecloth. He was quiet. Too quiet.

"Are you feeling all right?"

Murray folded his hands on the table. "I couldn't help but notice the envelope I picked up was from a private investigator. Are you having someone investigated?"

She felt the heat scald her cheeks. What should she say? Should she lie? How could she?

"I routinely get background checks on my household help."

"Isabel?"

"Yes."

"So, if I were to read that report, would my name be mentioned?"

Adele carried the glasses to the table and sat across from Murray. "For twenty years, I used Danny Clinton to do a background check on every person I put on the payroll at Woodmore. When I moved here, I hired you and Noah on a fairly routine basis. I invited you into my home. I didn't know a thing about you."

"So you had us investigated?"

"You make it sound like a bad thing, Murray. It really isn't."

"Then why don't you read the report?"

"I already know what it says. This is just the written confirmation of my conversation with Danny on the phone. Neither you nor Noah had anything in your backgrounds that gave me cause for concern. But I had Danny do a background check for another reason too. I thought if I could understand what had hurt you, I could help you get your life back."

"You couldn't have just trusted me and waited until I *chose* to tell you personal information?"

"I didn't think you were going to open up. But you did, and I'm glad."

"But earlier, when I was spilling my guts, you sat there, already knowing everything I told you and just played me?" Murray's voice sounded gruff.

"I certainly did not *play you*. Reports don't tell the whole story."

"But you already knew today was my birthday?"

"Yes, I did. I also know your given name is Robert Murdock Hamelin Jr."

Murray tapped his fingers on the table. "Did your PI tell you where I worked?"

"Yes—for that big computer outfit that's been in the news. I wasn't surprised. It's top-notch, and you're very smart with computers."

"Did he mention my fiancée?"

"Not by name. But I'm so glad you told me about her. It helps me to understand some of the choices you made."

Murray threw his hands in the air. "Don't presume to understand me. You don't even know me."

"But I do."

"You don't, Adele! You just think you do. I have a side you wouldn't like very much."

"So do I. Just ask Isabel." Adele wrapped her hands around the cold glass of raspberry tea. "I accept you for who you are, Murray. I care about you. Surely you can see that."

"Then why didn't you just ask me this stuff, instead of hiring a PI to sneak around behind my back?"

"I did ask you," she said softly. "I tried several times to get you to open up about your parents and your grandma Sophie, and you shut down."

"But that was *my* choice," Murray said.

"Yes, it was. I'm sorry. I truly am. I overstepped. I should have just trusted you to tell me when you were ready."

"Which is exactly what I did." His intense blue eyes narrowed. "Have you told anyone else what you found out about me?"

"Oh no. I would never do that. I hadn't even planned to tell you. I just wanted to know enough about you so I could help you get on with your life." Adele sighed. "Have I lost you as a friend, Murray?"

Jude held open the front door of the Alzheimer's center and let Kyle go in first. The blast of cold air felt great as the evening's heavy, humid air seemed to push him indoors.

He went over to the check-in desk, where a twentysomething woman stood.

"May I help you?"

"I'm Sheriff Jude Prejean. I called and spoke with a Marla Monet, and she told me to ask for her when I arrived."

"Yes, she's expecting you. I'll get her."

Jude stole a glance at Kyle and wondered how many of the elderly patients here once looked as vibrant and lovely as she did.

A middle-aged brunette in a business suit and heels walked up to the desk. "I'm Marla Monet, the administrator here."

Jude introduced himself and Kyle.

"You said it was imperative that you speak with Mrs. LaBelle. What's this about?"

"She may have information crucial to a murder investigation," he said. "I promise we won't upset her. But we need to ask her a few questions."

"Have you been around Alzheimer's patients, Sheriff?"

"I have."

"Then you know that Mrs. LaBelle may not be able to give you any reliable information. Her short-term memory is tentative on a good day."

Jude nodded. "I understand. My questions have to do with someone she knew a few years back. I'm hoping we can jog her memory."

"She's one of our newer patients and still has moments of lucidity. But I wouldn't get your hopes up. I just checked on her. She's still awake. Come this way."

Jude and Kyle walked down the hall, keeping step with Marla.

"I must insist that I be allowed to remain in the room when you question her," Marla said.

Jude nodded. "That's fine."

Marla stopped at room 109. She knocked and then slowly opened the door.

"Clara, I brought the nice people we talked about earlier."

Clara LaBelle sat in bed, dressed in her nightclothes, her head propped on a pillow. She made eye contact with Jude and instantly smiled. "There you are! Mother said you were coming to take me to the fair."

"Clara, this is Sheriff Prejean. And Special Agent Duffy of the FBI. They need to ask you some questions."

Jude and Kyle moved to the side of her bed.

"We're friends of your daughter Jeanette," Jude said.

Clara stared at him but didn't say anything.

"We know your husband, Ken, and your daughter Bonnie."

Her eyes widened. "Has Bonnie brought blueberries for my cobbler?"

"Ken, Jeanette, and Bonnie can hardly wait to have some of your cobbler."

Clara cast a scolding glance his way. "Ken *hates* blueberries."

"But Bonnie loves your cobbler. She said you could help us."

The elderly woman seemed miles away and infatuated with the hem on her bedsheet. Then she suddenly seemed present again. "Who are you?"

"Clara," Jude said. "We're looking for Jeanette's boyfriend."

"Jeanette quit. She went to the farmer's market to get tomatoes."

"We don't need to see Jeanette. We need to see her boyfriend."

"The redhead?"

"Yes. Yes. The redhead."

"He fixed my toaster. And my waffle iron." Clara smiled with her eyes. "He can fix anything, that one."

"Clara." Kyle gently took her hand. "What's the redhead's name?"

"Jeanette gave the ring back. She's not going to marry him. Pity."

"You sound disappointed," Kyle said. "You like him."

"Well, of course I like him. He spends enough time over here."

"What's his name?"

"Who?"

"The young man with the red hair?"

"He's not here. Jeanette gave the ring back. Bonnie's picking blueberries. She'll be home soon. I need to make my crust!"

Clara tried to get out of bed, and Marla gently restrained her. "Your crust is made, sweetie. It's okay."

"Clara, who did Jeanette give the ring to?"

Marla stood. "This seems to be upsetting her. I don't think she—"

"Please." Jude held up his palm. "Just a few more minutes. This is crucial."

Clara locked gazes with him and lay back on her pillow. "What do *you* want? Jeanette doesn't want to see you."

"I promise not to stay long," Jude said.

"She won't take the ring back."

"But *you* want her to marry me."

"Her mind's made up, Murray. You're too sad. Go home."

"Where's home?"

Clara sighed and looked at Jude as if it were a trick question. *Come on, Clara. Give me something.*

"Jeanette's grounded." Clara folded her arms across her chest. "She needs to bring her grades up."

"This is going nowhere," Marla said. "I can't let you upset her any further."

"Please, we're so close," Kyle insisted. "We need to know where to find Murray."

"Third and Audette." Clara sat up straight. "I already mailed his Christmas card."

Clara stared at Kyle for several moments, and then began babbling. "Who are you? Where's Ken? Where's my husband? He won't eat the cobbler! I need to fry my shrimp. We'll be late for the fireworks!"

Clara tried to get up, and Marla gently took her arm and stroked her hair. "Come on, sweetie. It's time for bed. Sheriff, that's all. She's my responsibility. You've pushed her hard enough. She's getting agitated."

"We're going," Jude said. "Thanks. This was invaluable."

Jude hurried down the hall, Kyle keeping stride.

"Let's see what's at Third and Audette in Lafayette," he said. "And hope it will lead us to a redheaded guy named Murray."

CHAPTER 34

Jude followed Kyle into the lobby of the Mabry Arms Apartments at Third and Audette in Lafayette. A huge bouquet of fresh flowers graced a glass table in the center of the lobby. Behind a rich wood counter was a well-groomed young man dressed in a white short-sleeved shirt and black tie.

Jude glanced around the room at the wood floor, Oriental rugs, and oil paintings. Quite a place. Definitely upscale.

"May I help you?"

Jude walked over to the counter, Kyle standing next to him, and read the young man's name badge. "David, I'm Sheriff Jude Prejean of Saint Catherine Parish, and this is FBI Special Agent Kyle Duffy. We're following up on a lead and need to talk to the manager."

"I'm sorry, he's gone. He'll be back in the morning. Is there something I can do to help you?"

Jude leaned on the counter. "Do you have a male resident with the first name Murray—thirty to thirty-five, red hair?"

"I don't know anyone who fits that description," David said. "But I just work nights. Let me call Tim Fraser. He's the owner and manager. He knows all the residents. Would you excuse me?"

"Sure." Jude held David's gaze. "Please tell your manager this is a matter of utmost importance, and it can't wait."

"I will."

Jude turned to Kyle. "I hope this pans out. I think we're on to something, and I don't want to let it go. I'll check with Aimee. Maybe her team has found something." Jude keyed in the speed dial for Aimee and got an answer on the first ring.

"Hello, Sheriff."

"How's it coming?" he said.

"We've located the director of human resources at Aubry Computer Systems. We're at her home now. She said they did have a Murray who fits the description. He worked as a computer systems analyst in the Lafayette branch, but Murray was a nickname. She's trying to remember his last name so she can go into the office and pull up his personnel file. She doesn't recall ever seeing Jeanette LaBelle with him though."

"I'm not sure that means anything," Jude said. "Everyone who knew Jeanette LaBelle said she kept her personal life to herself."

"I'll let you know as soon as we have something."

"I'll do the same."

Jude disconnected the call and told Kyle what Aimee had said.

"We're closing in on him," Jude said. "I can feel it."

"Me, too."

Jude wandered around the lobby, aware of the expensive rugs under his feet and looking at the oil paintings of famous New Orleans landmarks. He could smell the flowers on the glass table—and burnt coffee coming from the almost-empty pot still on the burner.

"This is an upscale apartment complex," Kyle said. "If Murray lived here, he probably made a good salary."

Jude glanced at his watch just as David came back to the front desk. "I reached Tim. He's coming right over. He just has to walk across the courtyard."

"Thanks."

Jude paced in front of an oil painting of the French Quarter. He used to feel proud that life in Les Barbes was so much simpler and safer than the Big Easy. Not this week.

A couple minutes later, the front door opened, and a man who appeared to be in his fifties came into the lobby and walked over to them, his hand extended.

"Tim Fraser. I'm manager here. David tells me you're looking for a resident."

"That's right." Jude shook his hand. "I'm Sheriff Prejean of Saint Catherine Parish, and this is FBI Special Agent Duffy. All we know is his first name: Murray. Thirty to thirty-five, red hair."

"Sounds like Murray Hamelin. He lived here for several years. What's this about?"

"Do you know where he is now?"

Tim shook his head. "His circumstances were tragic."

"Tell us," Kyle said.

"He was some sort of computer geek at Aubry. He was dating a knockout. Joyce, Jean, Jenna—something like that. They seemed real happy together. She was over here all the time, until Murray's dad got laid off out at the sugar refinery and the bank foreclosed on his parents' home. I made an exception to the rule and let Murray's parents move in with him, even though he only had a one-bedroom.

His girlfriend stopped coming over. I don't think I ever saw Murray smile after that. His parents lived here six, seven months. Murray's mother died of a heart attack. Shortly after that his father committed suicide."

"That's got to be him," Kyle said. "Can you describe the girlfriend?"

"Yes, she was about five seven. Brown hair and eyes. Beautiful smile. A figure that would stop a clock."

"Have you seen the pictures of Jeanette Stein in the news?" Kyle said.

Tim nodded. "Sure. Who hasn't?"

"Does she bear any resemblance to Murray's girlfriend?"

Tim's face lit up. "Now that you mention it, she sure does. Her hair was a lot longer when Murray was dating her. But that could be her."

"Was her name Jeanette?"

Tim shrugged. "Maybe. I honestly don't remember."

"Do you have any idea where Murray might have gone?" Jude said.

"No. He stopped paying rent. I gave him all the grace I could, but eventually I presented him with an eviction notice. He left all his stuff behind—furniture, clothes, everything—and just disappeared."

Jude put his hand on Tim's shoulder. "Thanks. You have no idea how important this is."

Jude hit the speed dial, and Aimee answered on the first ring. "Murray's last name is Hamelin. He sounds like our guy."

"Great," Aimee said. "Maybe the personnel director can tell us his given name. We'll head over to Aubry with her. Are you going back in?"

"Yes, we're leaving Lafayette right now. Call me when you have something."

Tim looked from Jude to Kyle and back to Jude. "Could someone please tell me what's going on?"

"We really can't," Jude said. "But if we're right, you'll be hearing about it in the news."

⚜

Jude flipped the light switch and walked into his office, Kyle on his heels. When was the last time he had experienced an adrenaline rush like this? His cell phone rang. He glanced at the screen and put it to his ear.

"What have you got, Aimee?"

"Murray's given name is Robert Murdock Hamelin Jr. That's the name on his driver's license and Social Security card and in his personnel records."

"What can you tell me about him?"

"He was a computer systems analyst. Hired by Aubry right after grad school. He was an employee in good standing until family issues began to affect his work performance. He was fired three years ago."

"Anything that connects him to Jeanette LaBelle?" Jude said.

"Other than he worked here at the same time she did—nothing. Sorry."

"Everything points to this guy. And Jeanette LaBelle's mother

ID'd him. Murray gave Jeanette an engagement ring. She either refused it or gave it back."

"Sheriff, just before you called, Deputy Castille remembered questioning a Murray Hamelin at Haven House—after Flynn Gillis was murdered. He fits the description."

"Now we're cookin'. Get a warrant to search his room and his vehicle. And pick him up for questioning. Make sure Police Chief Norman is apprised of these latest developments."

"I will."

Jude put his phone on his belt clip and told Kyle what Aimee had said.

"Do you have a contact at Haven House?" Kyle said. "If Murray gets even a hint that we're on to him, he might bolt."

"Good point. I'll call Father Vince." He keyed in the number and put it on speakerphone.

"Haven House, Father Vince speaking."

"Father, it's Sheriff Prejean."

"Yes. What can I do for you?"

"My deputies are on their way with a warrant to search Murray Hamelin's room and vehicle. I need your help to keep him there so we can question him."

"In Flynn Gillis's murder?"

"I can't get into it just yet, other than to say it's serious. Could you try to keep him there for a few minutes? Maybe distract him so he doesn't run?"

"I could, if he were here. He's been gone all day. Can't you tell me what this is about?"

"Do you know what his schedule was?"

"Murray took the day off. Said he had some personal business to take care of. And he had plans to take Adele Woodmore to Scoops this afternoon at three thirty."

"Father, if he comes back before my deputies arrive, I need you to act completely natural."

"I can't believe Murray's done anything wrong. He's the *example* around here. The others look up to him."

"Please just cooperate with my deputies when they arrive with the warrant."

"All right, Sheriff. I'm eager to get to the bottom of this."

Jude disconnected the call, his mind reeling. "Kyle, why would a serial killer take an elderly woman out for ice cream? I need to call her and give her a heads-up."

"Wait," Kyle said. "What if he's still with her? If she reacts and he picks up on it, we could lose him. She could end up his next victim."

Jude's mind raced with the implications. "I have an idea."

He began scrolling his cell phone directory. "I know someone who could call her without alarming her." He found the number and entered it. "Let's hope I get a person and not an answering machine." The phone rang three times. "Come on, pick up …"

"Hello?"

"Zoe, it's Jude. Just listen, this isn't a personal call. I need you to do something for me."

"Sure, what is it?"

"We're trying to locate Murray Hamelin from Haven House. He wrote on his schedule that he was going to take Adele Woodmore to Scoops this afternoon. Do you know anything about that?"

"No." Zoe sighed. "She wouldn't have mentioned it to me because she knows Pierce doesn't approve of Murray. He doesn't trust any of the guys from Haven House."

"Okay, listen carefully. Here's what I need you to do ..."

Adele finished the last of her raspberry tea and noticed that Murray had hardly touched his refill.

"Are you sure I can't get you a sandwich or a cookie or something?"

He seemed miles away, and her voice appeared to startle him. "Uh—no thanks. I probably should get going."

"Murray, if it would make you feel better, I'll let you read the report Danny brought by—except the part about Noah. I think I should keep that confidential."

"So it's okay for you to sneak around behind his back and get information he didn't choose to tell you—but it's not okay for me to know what it says?"

Adele winced at Murray's caustic tone. Was this the side of his personality he had warned her about? "I don't obtain this information to share, Murray. I already explained that I've done it for twenty years. As a result, with few exceptions, I've had people I can trust in my employ."

"Just an observation from a friend: I don't think you should trust Noah."

"There was nothing in the report that led me to believe he couldn't be trusted."

"Your friend Danny doesn't live with him. I do. I'm pretty sure he killed Flynn Gillis. I just can't prove it."

Adele put her hand over her heart. "Goodness, that's a horrible accusation. Why am I just hearing about this?"

"I didn't want to alarm you. But I told you once before I didn't trust him. Like I said, I can't prove he killed Flynn. It's just a gut feeling based on a conversation I had with him the morning of the murder. And his attitude. He couldn't stand the guy."

"Did you tell the sheriff?"

"Yes. He knows. He must have doubts. Maybe you should ask him."

"It's my understanding that no one really liked Flynn," she said. "Why do you think *Noah* killed him?"

"I know things. That's all."

"You're scaring me, Murray. Why are you just now telling me this?"

He sighed. "I guess because you're digging into areas that could reveal things you're better off not knowing."

"I told you the report didn't reveal anything that gave me pause. But if there was something to fear, how could I be better off not knowing?"

Murray cracked his knuckles. "Even a private investigator can't find out everything about a person. You're too trusting."

"So I've been told. But the fact is I do trust Noah. And I trust you. I'm basing it on more than the report from Danny. I have a feeling about people. And my trust is based on more than a piece of paper."

"Then why pay someone to look into private matters?"

Adele traced the rim of her glass with her finger. "Though I think I read people pretty well, it's probably best for me not to rely strictly on my own instincts in such matters."

"Have you ever been burned?"

"Yes, a couple of times. Once a trusted employee stole a valuable ring and I didn't find out for many years. But even that resolved itself in time. I just don't believe I need to stop being kind to people because I might get burned. What kind of adventure is that?"

Her cell phone rang. "I'd better see who it is, hon. I haven't checked my messages all afternoon."

"I should go."

"Wait just a moment," she said. "I'd like to give you some chocolate chip cookies to take with you." She picked up her cell phone and put it to her ear. "Hello."

"Hi, Adele, it's Zoe. Are you busy?"

"Just sitting here having a glass of raspberry tea."

"By yourself?"

"With a friend."

"Adele, I want you to act completely normal and not react to anything I say. But I need to know if you're with Murray Hamelin."

"Yes. As a matter of fact, I am."

"Is Isabel there?"

"No, she quit. I haven't had a chance to tell you."

"Okay," Zoe said. "Listen carefully. I want you to smile while I'm talking to you and remain calm. Sheriff Prejean asked me to call. He didn't want to alarm you, but he's looking for Murray. They want to question him."

"I see. And why is that?"

"Adele, he's a murder suspect. Smile and say you understand what I'm telling you."

"I understand exactly. I can't imagine that's accurate, though."

"You have to trust me. I don't have time to explain except to say that as soon as I confirm with the sheriff that Murray is there with you, deputies are coming to take him in for questioning. Do you understand?"

"Uh-huh."

"I need you to keep him from leaving. Can you do that?"

Adele felt as if her heart would pound out of her chest. She glanced over at Murray. Was she smiling? She wasn't even sure.

"I … I don't know. I think so."

"Try. They'll be there shortly."

"All right, Zoe. I'll put that on my calendar for Monday afternoon. Good-bye."

Adele disconnected the call, aware that her hand was shaking. There must be some mistake. Stall. She needed to stall. Take her time getting the cookies. How could she act normal? How could she deceive Murray?

"Who was that?" he said. "Why do you look upset?"

"It was just Zoe."

"Is something wrong?"

"Everything's fine." Adele stood. "Let me get those cookies for you."

A second later, Murray jumped to his feet and grabbed her wrists. "I heard what she said, Adele. You had the phone on speaker."

"I did?"

"Looks like you're not the only one who's been digging into my personal business. I need to get out of here *now*. And you're coming with me."

CHAPTER 35

Jude slowed his squad car in front of the corner house at Magnolia Lane and Cypress Way and then pulled into the driveway. The July sun had dropped low in the western sky, but the temperature and humidity still hovered in the upper nineties.

He scanned the tall hedge in back and didn't see any sign of Chief Detective Gil Marcel's team.

"Where's Hamelin's truck, I wonder?"

"Maybe it's in the garage," Kyle said. "I'll go check."

Jude got out, glanced up and down both streets, and then spoke into his shoulder mike. "Gil, are you in place?"

"Copy that. We've got the back covered. We have a visual on the house but don't see any sign of movement inside."

"Do you see Hamelin's truck?"

"Negative."

Kyle waved from the garage window. "It's empty."

"He must've parked it somewhere else," Jude said to Gil. "He has to be here. It hasn't been five minutes since Zoe called Adele Woodmore. Stay in place. I'm going to ring the doorbell. Be prepared in case he tries to run."

"Copy."

Jude walked up on the brick porch of the neat-as-a-pin white frame house with green shutters and rang the bell. Kyle came up the steps and stood beside him.

"If Hamelin spots us out here," she said, "he might not let her answer the door."

"Let's just hope she's still alive to answer the door." Jude rang the bell a second time. "Come on, lady. Open it."

"Think you should call and see what's keeping Zoe?" Kyle said.

He glanced at his watch. "She should be here any second with the key. But if Mrs. Woodmore doesn't answer this door, we're not waiting for Zoe."

Jude rang the bell a third time and then put his hand on the doorknob, surprised when it turned.

"It's unlocked." He pushed open the door about a foot. "Mrs. Woodmore? It's Sheriff Prejean, are you there? Mrs. Woodmore?"

The house was pin-drop still except for the pendulum swinging on her grandfather clock.

"I don't like the feel of this." Jude spoke into his shoulder mike. "Gil, we're going in."

"Copy that."

Jude drew his gun and took a step inside the house. "Mrs. Woodmore, it's Sheriff Prejean. Are you here? Mrs. Woodmore?"

He walked softly into the kitchen and saw two glasses on the table with ice cubes and motioned for Kyle to take note.

They walked ever so stealthily from room to room until the entire house was cleared.

Jude lowered his weapon and spat out a swear word under his breath. "Gil, there's no one in the house. Do you copy?"

"Copy that, Sheriff. Nothing out back either."

"What's wrong? Has something happened to Adele?"

Jude turned to the familiar voice just as Zoe rushed through the open front door.

"Adele isn't here," he said. "The door was open, and we've searched the house."

"But she was here less than five minutes ago. She wouldn't have just left without telling me." Zoe walked up to him, her blue-gray eyes wide and animated. "Has Murray taken her *hostage?*"

"We don't know." Jude put his hand on her shoulder. "There's nothing here to indicate a struggle. You said she'd made friends with him. She might've gone willingly. We have to assume they're together. Are you sure Adele wouldn't have told him we were coming?"

"She understood exactly what I was saying. I can't imagine she would've told him." Zoe took a step toward Jude. "Just how dangerous *is* this guy?"

"Until we question him, we can't be sure."

Zoe folded her arms tightly across her chest, her eyes turned to slits. "Stop trying to spare my feelings, and just tell me straight-out. You know Adele is like a mother to me!"

Jude's phone rang. He glanced at the screen. "Hang on a minute." He put the phone to his ear. "Yeah, Aimee. What's up?"

"We found a backpack Hamelin had in his locker at Haven House. He's got stacks of one-hundred-dollar bills and some note cards that match the notes we have in evidence. We also discovered a bottle of ketamine and several unused needles. Size ten shoes. We also have a bag of dirty clothes. We should have his DNA in short order. Want to bet it's a match?"

"Great work!" Jude said.

"Sheriff, we also found a pair of amethyst earrings. We're sending a picture to Barry Stein's iPhone to see if they belonged to Jeanette. She had a February birthday, and amethyst was her birthstone. If these belong to her, we've got our Bathtub Killer."

"Excellent work, Aimee! We came up empty at Adele Woodmore's. But I'll put out an APB on Hamelin's truck and get a warrant for his arrest. They can't have gone far." Jude disconnected the call and put the phone back on his belt clip.

"You didn't answer my question," Zoe said. "How dangerous is Murray Hamelin? Do you think he killed Flynn Gillis?"

Jude searched her eyes. No point in trying to be low key about the situation. "Zoe, the evidence suggests worse … he could be the Bathtub Killer."

Zoe's knees gave out, and Kyle caught her. "Come over here and sit. I'm Kyle. I'm with the FBI. Let me explain what's happening."

⚜

Zoe stood in the kitchen at the eatery and rested in Pierce's embrace. "Go ahead and say 'I told you so.' I have it coming."

"I'm not going to rub it in," Pierce said. "I wanted to be wrong."

"If anything happens to Adele …" Zoe's voice cracked. "I should have tried harder to get her to stay away from Murray."

"Ultimately, it was her choice, babe. Isabel tried more than once. You told me what she said to the sheriff. Adele was willing to let her quit rather than give up whatever it was she thought she had with this Murray character."

"I don't want to lose her." Zoe began to sob. "You know what she means to me. She's only lived here six months. It's not enough time. I can't lose her."

Pierce held her tighter. "Don't look for the worst-case scenario. Maybe he won't hurt her. She's the sweetest thing on the planet. Maybe she's won him over."

"And maybe all he wanted was her money, like Isabel said."

Pierce sighed. "I'm *so* sorry this is happening."

There was a loud knock, and then Vanessa Langley burst into the kitchen. "I heard about Adele. I can't believe this!"

She came over and hugged the two of them. "Ethan offered to watch after the guests so I could come keep vigil with you. I called Pastor Auger and got the prayer chain going."

"The prayer chain at Saint Catherine's is on their knees too," Pierce said.

"Do you need me to watch Grace for you?"

"Maddie came over to watch her and offered to stay all night if we need her to. It would really help me, though, if you'd stay with Zoe until I get off." Pierce kissed the top of Zoe's head. "Babe, I need to prepare these orders before our customers walk out. Are you all right hanging with Vanessa while we're waiting for news?"

Zoe nodded. "I called Father Sam. He was going to call Hebert and Tex. They'll be here any minute. We can sit with them."

"Good." Pierce tilted her chin. "You want something to eat? I can fix you a seafood salad that's to die for."

"I can't. Not now." Zoe stroked his cheek. "I'll be fine. I need to get out of here and let you fill orders. Maybe Vanessa would like something."

"No, thanks. I've already had dinner. I just came to help any way I can."

"Just take care of Zoe," Pierce said. "And come get me the minute you hear something."

"We will."

❧

Adele sat in the passenger seat of Murray's truck, fanning herself with the memorial folder from Jeanette Stein's funeral and swatting mosquitoes. How far had Murray driven around the rookery? It seemed as if he had gone considerably farther than he had earlier in the evening. All she could tell for sure was that they were on a gravel road and parked in close proximity to the big pond.

Lord, no matter what he's done, I don't believe this boy is all bad. Help me to help him.

Murray reached in the open passenger-side window, took a can out of the glove box, and shook it. "Here, use this. I can't do anything about the heat, but we don't have to get eaten alive by these monster mosquitoes."

Adele took the can of insect repellent and covered herself in the fine mist. "The little devils have always liked me. They never took a bite out of Alfred. Funny how that is." She handed the can back to Murray. "Thank you, hon."

He walked away without commenting and leaned on the

front fender, his profile to her, and sprayed himself with insect repellent.

Adele moved her gaze around the thick, hazy blackness and couldn't make out much of anything. Where was the full moon when she needed it? She could hear the chirping of egrets, herons, and ibis in the rookery, though they were considerably less noisy than they had been earlier.

"So what are you planning to do with me, Murray?"

He didn't answer.

"Maybe it would help to talk. Zoe said you were a murder suspect. Is it Flynn Gillis? Is that why you wanted me to think Noah did it? I won't be angry if you lied. Talk to me."

Murray said nothing.

"You're either guilty or you aren't," Adele said. "I'd just like to know which it is. It's not going to change the things I like about you."

He charged over to her open window and tossed the can of insect repellent on the seat. "Let's get something straight, Adele. I couldn't care less whether you like me or not! I'm not the person you think I am. The sooner you accept that, the easier this will be."

"I'm trying to figure out what *this* is."

"Please … just shut up and let me think!"

"Are you going to kill me?"

Murray pushed away from the sill and walked away. She heard him swear as he disappeared into the trees.

She picked up the memorial folder and began to fan herself again. No one would find them out here—at least not tonight. Was there any way to escape? Even if she knew which direction to go, how far could she make it in the dark on this uneven terrain, trying to balance with a cane?

Fear seized her, as much for Murray as for herself. If death were to find her this very night, she had no fear of judgment. But if death were to find Murray now, while he was an enemy of God, there would be no spiritual defense lawyer to cut a deal. There was only one sentence for the unsaved.

Lord, please don't let this end badly for either of us.

❧

Jude paced in front of the window in his office, his eyes focused on the illuminated Saint Catherine Parish Courthouse across the street.

"You're going to wear the carpet out, Sheriff," Kyle said.

"Where could he have taken her? I issued that APB within minutes."

"They might've switched vehicles."

"Then why haven't we found his truck?" Jude winced at the sharp tone of his voice. "Sorry, Kyle. I don't mean to take it out on you. I just don't want to lose him. Not now. Not when we're this close."

"I understand."

Jude stopped pacing and sat at the conference table across from Kyle. "So do you think he's going to kill Adele?"

Kyle pushed a lock of hair out of her eyes. "He'll do anything to keep from getting caught—even that. He's been totally focused on eliminating the source of his pain. He's done that. He's ready to start his life over now. He knows if he's caught, he'll get the death penalty—at the very least life without parole. He's not going to let that happen. However, from what Zoe said, I think he's actually fond of Adele. I imagine he's caught in a will struggle about now."

"Explain."

"Murray's not a sociopath. He *has* a conscience. In his mind, he did what he had to do to stop the source of his debilitating pain. He doesn't want to kill Adele. But she's the only bargaining chip he has. When we finally catch up with him, and he threatens to kill her unless we let him go, I believe he'll do it."

CHAPTER 36

Adele sat in the front seat of Murray's truck, massaging her shoulder to no avail. Did Murray have anything for muscle aches? Did he even have water? The effect of not taking her Celebrex and her pain pill at dinnertime was worse than she imagined. Being this tense didn't help matters. The pain in her shoulder was giving her a headache. How much worse would it get? Had Murray left her out here to die? What were the chances anyone would ever look for her here?

Lord, You know where I am. Please send help! Please protect Murray. Don't let him get killed. He's not ready to meet You.

She was tempted to try to feel her way back to the highway on foot. What foolishness! Even if she didn't need the cane, how could she know what lay even a few yards beyond where she was? What if she fell in water? There were plenty of hungry alligators who would make a fine meal of her.

She dabbed the perspiration off her face with the edge of her sleeve. In this darkness, the oily insect spray on her perspiring skin made her feel as if she were covered in black ink. What she wouldn't give for a package of wet wipes.

What awaited her here? Perhaps the dark night of the soul she had read about. Would her faith be tested? Would she be able to hang on to it—to trust the Lord—even if He didn't seem to answer? How she hated being imprisoned by the disability of old age.

The words from the fortieth chapter of Isaiah were almost audible to her.

But those who hope in the LORD will renew their strength. They will soar on wings like eagles; they will run and not grow weary, they will walk and not be faint.

She smiled. Spiritually, she wasn't disabled. She wasn't imprisoned. She was neither helpless nor hopeless.

Adele looked out into the night and began to sing her favorite song, the one that had sustained her anytime her troubles seemed overwhelming:

When peace like a river attendeth my way,
When sorrows like sea billows roll;
Whatever my lot, Thou has taught me to say,
It is well, it is well with my soul.

Hearing the sound of her own voice in this place of thick darkness was soothing, and the words Adele believed with all her heart gave her strength.

Though Satan should buffet, though trials should come,
Let this blest assurance control:
That Christ hath regarded my helpless estate
And hath shed His own blood for my soul.

It is well with my soul,
It is well, it is well with my soul.

Adele leaned her head back on the seat and closed her eyes. Maybe she wouldn't make it through this, but she had all of eternity to praise the God who had snatched her from the throes of despair and gave her hope. She was not going to die defeated.

My sin, oh, the bliss of this glorious thought!
My sin, not in part but the whole,
Is nailed to the cross, and I bear it no more,
Praise the Lord, praise the Lord, O my soul—

She heard rustling in the bushes, and her eyes flew open. What was *that?* Her heart nearly pounded out of chest. She could shoosh away a fox or a skunk or an opossum. But what if it was a wild pig or a bear?

A second later, a hand grabbed her wrist and squeezed.

"What do you think you're doing?" Murray's voice was loud and gruff.

"Goodness, you scared me, hon. I thought you'd gone."

He squeezed harder. "Why are you singing that song?"

"It comforts me. Why are you hurting me?"

Murray turned loose of her wrist. "How could you know that was Grandma Sophie's song?"

"I didn't. It's always been my favorite."

"She sang that song a lot."

"Then Sophie was a believer?"

"If you mean a Bible thumper, yes. I'd say she was pretty well a fanatic."

"And yet you loved her dearly." *Some of what she told you must have sunk in.* Adele rubbed her wrist where Murray had squeezed it. "I thought you had left me out here alone."

"I was leaning on a tree over there where you couldn't see me. I just needed to think without you talking."

"I see. And what are your thoughts? Are you going to kill me like you killed Flynn Gillis?"

Murray pushed away from the window, looked up at the night sky. "That jerk's not the only one I've killed. You have no idea."

In the silence that followed, Adele thought her throbbing heart must be audible.

"Are you going to tell me about it?" she finally said.

"I don't see the point."

"You might feel better."

"Who said I feel bad? I don't feel anything."

"I doubt that." Adele studied his shadow in the darkness and felt a spiritual battle raging. "I'm not giving up on you, Murray. I see the good in you, regardless of what you've done."

"There *is* no good in me."

"Nonsense. You have a spirit that was breathed into you by God Himself."

"What good is it? I'm a bad person—a killer!"

"You weren't born a killer, young man. You made choices. It's never too late to make better ones."

"I'm not interested in making *better* choices. I did exactly what I set out to do. Every one of those people had to die so things could change."

"What people had to die?"

Murray threw his hands in the air. "You still haven't figured it out, have you?"

"I'm not very good at riddles. Why don't you just tell me plainly?"

"Do I really need to spell it out, Adele? *I'm* the Bathtub Killer! Me! That's why the cops are after me. I'm not sorry I killed any of those people, so don't start in on me with the *come to Jesus* stuff. Like I told you before, God doesn't want me any more than I want Him."

Adele put her hand to her mouth and heard herself whimper. How could she have been so blind?

⚜

Zoe sat at the table by the window at Zoe B's with Vanessa, Father Sam, Tex, and Hebert. Outside, *rue Madeline* was lit up like a carnival, and tourists swarmed the street that had been closed to traffic since seven. She could faintly hear the Cajun band playing at Breaux's. She glanced at her watch. Almost ten thirty. In half an hour, everything would close. Neon lights would go off. Street entertainers would go home. Tourists would go to bed. A sweet peace would replace the bustling commerce—until the sun came up and it all started again.

Would Adele be alive when the sun came up? Had Murray already killed her? If he hadn't, was he hurting her? Was she afraid? Not knowing was almost unbearable. But would knowing be even worse?

Why hadn't she listened to Pierce when he warned her that the men from Haven House shouldn't be trusted? Why hadn't she pushed the issue with Adele?

Zoe felt someone take her hand, and she looked up.

Hebert held her gaze with his intense gray eyes. "*Lâche pas la patate.*"

"I haven't given up," Zoe said. "But I'd be lying if I told you I'm not scared to death."

"Anyting dat hurts you dis way," Hebert said, "is a *piquant* in my heart. Let me help you be strong. You don' know dat dis guy wants to harm Adele. Maybe he gonna let her go."

"Maybe." Zoe sighed. "Sometimes I hate that word."

Vanessa put her arm around Zoe and gave her a gentle squeeze. "We have to have faith. That God's with her. And that she's with Him. You and I have both had experience with coming to the end of ourselves and having to trust God. No matter what happens, Adele will be all right, Zoe. She has more faith than you and me put together."

"Adele is a charmin' lady," Tex said. "Let's hope she uses a little of it on Murray."

"He's a cold-blooded killer," Zoe said. "I'm not sure an old lady's charm will touch him one iota."

⚜

Jude sat at the conference table in his office with Kyle, Police Chief Norman, and Mayor Theroux, going over the latest developments in the bathtub killings. He heard footsteps in the hallway and looked up just as Aimee walked into his office.

"Here it is," she said. "The lab made this priority one. Skin cells found in the sweat on Murray Hamelin's clothes match the DNA we collected at the murder scenes—he's our guy."

"Excellent." Jude glanced over at Kyle and Chief Norman.

"And a bonus"—Aimee handed the report to Jude—"the earrings *were* Jeanette Stein's. Her husband identified them. Said they were a gift from her parents on her twenty-fifth birthday."

"Well, congratulations, Sheriff." The mayor leaned back in his chair, his arms folded across his chest. "At least now we know for sure."

"I believe Hamelin's still in the area," Jude said. "I issued that APB within minutes. I just don't believe he could've slipped out. That scumbag's out there somewhere. We need to look under every rock until we find him."

Chief Norman nodded. "He's probably lying low until the dust settles. This town is crawling with law enforcement."

"I'm not so sure." Kyle shook her head. "I'm more inclined to think he'll abandon his truck and leave town in another vehicle—if he hasn't already. We've got his face plastered across the airways. If he's smart, he'll dye that red hair. But he'll be a lot easier to spot if Adele's with him."

"What are the odds?" Jude said.

Kyle raised her eyebrows. "Adele's the only leverage he's got. I don't see him leaving her behind. But according to Zoe, she has some health issues that require medication. I suppose she could become more of a liability as time goes on."

"You're saying he'd kill her?"

Kyle tucked a lock of hair behind her ear. "I honestly don't know. Certainly he knows how to justify murder when he thinks it's deserved. Whether or not her frailty is enough to justify eliminating her is anybody's guess. We need to find them before it comes to that."

CHAPTER 37

Adele opened the door, slid out of Murray's truck, and stood clutching the door with both hands. She stretched her back, her arthritic shoulder throbbing. How much longer could she just sit there without moving around?

She spotted Murray sitting on a fallen log a few yards away. He hadn't said anything in over an hour. He ignored her questions, including whether or not he had anything for pain. She wanted to sing a hymn. Singing hymns always helped her on bad days. Maybe if she sang a different song that didn't remind him of his grandmother, he wouldn't get angry. She turned around, her back to Murray, and began singing softly.

I come to the garden alone,
While the dew is still on the roses,
And the voice I hear falling on my ear,
The Son of God discloses.

And He walks with me, and He talks with me,
And He tells me I am His own;

And the joy we share as we tarry there,
None other has ever known.

She stopped and listened carefully. Murray didn't say anything. He didn't stir. Adele closed her eyes and poured out her heart to the Lord:

I'd stay in the garden with Him,
Though the night around me be fall—

"Stop it!"

Adele's eyes flew open.

Murray grabbed her arm and set the footstool on the ground. "Get back in the truck. I don't want to hear any more of this garbage! Do you understand? Enough!"

Adele blinked quickly to clear the stinging from her eyes. "I … I didn't mean to upset you, hon. I'm just in a lot of pain, and singing hymns helps me forget about it."

She reached inside and got her cane, then she climbed into the truck with great difficulty. She forced herself not to cry out in pain, but there was no way to hide it.

"There's some Tylenol in my toolbox," he said.

Murray walked back to the bed of the truck and returned with a bottle of water and a packet of four Extra Strength Tylenol. "Make it last. That's all there is."

Was he talking about just the Tylenol—or the water, too? She was afraid to ask when he seemed so angry.

She tore open the packet and popped two of the pills, then took a big sip of water and handed him the bottle.

"Keep it. That's yours." He handed her the cap. "When it's gone, it's gone."

He pushed the button on his watch, and the face lit up. "The news is on."

Murray walked around to the driver's side and slid in behind the wheel. He turned the key a click and then turned on the radio and played with the dial.

She recognized the music that preceded the news on the local FM channel.

"It's eleven p.m. This is Hal Prudhomme, reporting tonight with breaking news. Authorities in Les Barbes have identified the man they believe to be the Bathtub Killer who has terrorized residents here for the past ten days. Thirty-year-old Murray Hamelin is currently at large and may be holding an elderly woman hostage.

"Sheriff Jude Prejean and FBI Special Agent Kyle Duffy followed a lead earlier this evening, which resulted in their obtaining a warrant to search Hamelin's room at Haven House, a local halfway house for the homeless. Sufficient evidence was discovered among Hamelin's personal items for an arrest warrant to be issued.

"Before Hamelin could be apprehended, he disappeared with an eighty-six-year-old woman, Adele Woodmore, a resident of Lafayette Gardens in Les Barbes. It's unknown whether Woodmore left with Hamelin voluntarily or was coerced. A source close to the story told the sheriff that Hamelin had done odd jobs for Woodmore, and that the woman had befriended him against the counsel of friends who were concerned for her safety.

"An APB was put out on Hamelin's white 2001 Ford F-150, and authorities from three branches of law enforcement are now searching for the suspect. Anyone with information on Hamelin's whereabouts or any information that might assist authorities in the case is asked to call either the Saint Catherine Parish Sheriff's Department or the Les Barbes Police Department.

"In other news tonight—"

Murray turned off the radio and seemed deep in thought.

Adele felt sick all over. Hearing it on the news made it seem more real. Murray was in so much trouble. Was there anything she could do to help him now? What was he going to do with her?

"Well, there you have it," Murray finally said. "I'm officially a fugitive. And a kidnapper. Only I killed five people, not four. They're bound to figure out I killed Flynn, even though I didn't use the same MO."

Adele cringed. Was he actually bragging? "Why did you kill Flynn? He wasn't part of your painful past."

"He was a pain in the present. The guy had no respect for Father Vince or what he was trying to do. Nobody cared if he lived or died—including him. And I figured it would keep the authorities looking at Noah and not at me—just until I finished what I'd started."

"Noah was your friend, Murray."

"They can't pin the murder on him. They don't have any proof."

Adele sighed. "Why did Noah tell the sheriff he saw you asleep in your bunk between eleven and one, when Flynn was murdered?"

"Because I stuck pillows under my covers to make it look that way. I snuck out and went to the Den, knowing that's where Flynn would end up. I grabbed him in the parking lot, strangled him, and then put him in my truck and dumped him in the Langleys' bayou. I knew the cops would suspect Noah."

Adele didn't know what to say. Could this really be the same young man she had grown so fond of?

Murray stared at his hands. "I've been trying to make it up to Noah. I gave him my painting jobs, and I bought the supplies he'll need. He'll be all right. His name will be cleared. I made sure of it."

"Made sure of it *how?"*

"Let me worry about that."

"There are others to consider," Adele said. "It's taken a terrible toll at Langley Manor. They've had multiple cancellations. I'm not even sure they can recover."

"They'll be fine. I took care of that, too."

"How?"

"I just did, all right? I don't want to talk anymore."

"Well, I do." Adele was shocked at what came out of her mouth and surprised when Murray didn't argue. "Do you realize how many people you've hurt, young man?"

"The people I killed deserved it."

"Did their spouses and children deserve it too?" Adele shook her head. "Dear, dear Murray. You've been so wounded. I can see now that you were lashing out at those you blame for your pain."

"They ruined my life."

"No one has the power to do that but you."

"Is that so?" Murray turned to her, his face contorted.

She listened as he rattled off a litany of grievances against the coldhearted CEO who fired his father, the uncaring bank president who foreclosed on his parents' home, the unsympathetic boss who fired him when the bottom was falling out of his life—and the fiancée who said she loved him and yet broke the engagement and left him when he needed her most.

"Yes, I killed them!" Murray said. "They got what they deserved!"

"And who suffered in the long run? Certainly not the victims, but their families. Can't you see what you've done? You left a whole string of *living* victims, just like you. Family members who did nothing to deserve the grief you saddled them with."

"The people I eliminated didn't care about anyone but themselves. I don't believe anyone will miss them. I did the world a favor. Les Barbes is a better place because of me. People should be thanking me!"

Adele decided not to dignify Murray's rant by commenting further.

"Don't sit over there and judge me," Murray said. "I know exactly what you're thinking."

"You have no idea what I'm thinking."

"Well, why don't you tell me?"

"You won't like it," Adele said.

"I said, *tell* me!"

Adele shuddered at Murray's tone but tried not to show any reaction. *Lord, what do I say to him? I'm frightened.*

"Come on, tell me what a loser I am. I know you're thinking it."

"That's not what I'm thinking," she said. "I'm afraid for you, Murray. I don't want to see you self-destruct."

"Too late for that."

"It's never too late to find purpose in life. But you can't do it without God."

"I don't want God."

"I know you don't, hon. But that's what I'm thinking."

"God's against me. He always has been."

"Oh, forevermore, Murray. That's a lie straight from the Devil himself!"

He looked over at her, the corners of his mouth twitching. "The Devil?"

"I see you find that amusing," she said. "It's really not a laughing matter. He's playing you."

"No one is playing me. I'm in control."

"Of what—an old woman? I'd like to know what it is you think you're in control of. You've done unspeakable acts and tried to justify them. But now you're backed into a corner, and the very freedom you hoped to gain is lost. The Devil is playing you. And he plays for keeps."

"I don't believe there's a Devil."

Adele sighed. "That's why his lies are so effective. You asked what I was thinking. And now I've told you."

Murray folded his arms across his chest, his profile taut, his lips pursed.

"I wonder what your grandma Sophie would say, if she were here."

Murray hit his palms on the steering wheel. "She's not here," he shouted. "So leave her out of this! Not another word, or so help me, I'll …"

Kill you. Adele filled in the words in the privacy of her thoughts. There was nothing she could do to save herself.

CHAPTER 38

Zoe pushed open the French doors in her bedroom, the panes of glass dripping with condensation, and walked onto the gallery that jutted out above Zoe B's. She squeezed past the wrought-iron table and stood at the railing where she had placed her red begonias into carefully spaced pots that could be seen from the street.

She looked out over *rue Madeline*. All activity had ceased. Was she the only person in Les Barbes awake at 3:00 a.m.?

She could hear the *drip drip drip* of condensation falling from the roof onto the flowers. A slight breeze had cooled the temperature to tolerable.

How was she going to accept it if something horrible happened to Adele? Why hadn't she taken Pierce's cautions more seriously and insisted that Adele reconsider her friendship—or whatever it was she had—with Murray?

Lord, I can't lose Adele. I just can't. Please protect her. Don't let him hurt her.

Zoe blinked away the image of Adele in a coffin and friends filing by her lifeless body. It wasn't fair that she should die a statistic. That she should be murdered. Was there anyone more giving? More caring? More filled with love and goodness and mercy? Anyone less deserving of dying at the hands of Murray Hamelin?

Zoe wiped a tear off her cheek. What might her life be like now, had Adele not chosen to forgive her for stealing from her? Had Adele not chosen the high road, not only by forgiving, but also by canceling the debt so she and Pierce wouldn't be saddled with paying her a thousand dollars a month for thirty months? And what if Adele hadn't told her about the King of Kings and Lord of Lords? Would she still be "playing church" and missing the personal relationship with God that had enriched her life?

Adele had touched her on so many levels. Zoe wasn't ready yet to let her go. And not in such a horrible way.

She heard the living room door slide open and close. Vanessa coughed and then came to the railing and stood next to her.

"I couldn't sleep either," Vanessa said.

"You should be home with Ethan and Carter, not babysitting me."

Vanessa linked arms with her. "You're my best friend, Zoe. I'm right where I need to be. No one loves Adele more than we do."

"I know I shouldn't be thinking of the worst possible scenarios, but I am."

"It's hard not to think about what could happen. But Adele's not alone, Zoe. We both know that. We have to trust the Lord. Look how He brought us through the ordeal when Cowen was after you. Noah showed up out of nowhere. We'd probably be dead if it weren't for him."

Zoe ran her fingers along the tacky metal railing. "Unless someone can prove it, I'll never believe he had anything to do with Flynn Gillis's death."

"Neither will I."

Zoe looked up at the summer sky, the stars indistinct in the haze. "Murray doesn't seem to care who he hurts. What's to stop him from getting rid of an eighty-six-year-old woman who's probably going to slow him down? She's defenseless against him."

"She has angels with her."

"So does he. Only his are fallen."

Vanessa sighed. "This isn't helping. Let's go inside and I'll make my special tea. It should help us fall asleep. Maybe by morning, the sheriff will have gotten Adele back and put Murray behind bars."

Adele lay across the seat in Murray's truck, wide awake and longing for her pillow-top mattress. It was kind of Murray to let her stretch out, but it was anything but comfortable, and the vinyl seat stuck to her skin. At least the insect repellent was working.

Just before she lay down, an eerie hissing sound sent chills up her spine. Murray told her that sound came from an alligator that wasn't too happy about something. How far from the water would the hungry beast go if it smelled them? Of all times not to know the first thing about alligators. She wanted to slip out of the truck and stretch her back again. But what if it was out there waiting? What if it went for her ankles? She shuddered at the thought.

Lord, I'm frightened. I don't want to die by Murray's hand or become dinner for some wild beast.

Adele curled up on the seat. She was trapped. Who would have ever thought that Murray's truck—the avenue to their adventures—would become a prison? And perhaps the place where she would die?

She remembered what Paul and Silas did in that dank, dark prison. She so wanted—needed—to sing to the Lord. And why couldn't she? How could Murray stop the music from playing in her head?

She closed her eyes and sang with all her heart, mouthing the words that resounded only in her soul:

Turn your eyes upon Jesus,
Look full in His wonderful face,
And the things of earth will grow strangely dim
In the light of His glory and grace.

O soul, are you weary and troubled?
No light in the darkness you see?
There's light for a look at the Savior,
And life more abundant and free!

Turn your eyes upon Jesus,
Look full in His wonderful face,
And the things of earth will grow strangely dim
In the light of His glory and grace.

She continued singing the verses in her mind, picturing Jesus' face and thinking about His mercy and grace to her. How blessed she was. What a glorious future awaited her.

She heard footsteps approaching the truck. Murray must be back.

The driver's-side door opened. "Adele, you need to sit up now. The news is on."

She sat up and scooted over next to the other door.

Murray got in and turned on the radio and listened to the lead story, which was almost identical to the half dozen he had listened to previously. He turned off the radio and sat back in the seat.

"You've had lots of time to think about this, Murray. What are you going to do?"

"As soon as it's light enough to see, I need to go find us a different vehicle. We need to get out of the state."

"I can't leave the state, hon. I don't have my medication."

"Don't worry. I can get you more Tylenol."

"It barely takes the edge off the pain. I didn't say anything before because I didn't want to sound ungrateful. I take two prescriptions for pain. And one for high blood pressure. And the instructions from the pharmacy said not to stop taking any of them suddenly."

Murray swatted the air. "Baloney. They put all those cautions on there to cover their tails on the off chance there's a problem. It's not going to hurt you to miss them for a couple days. Tylenol will take the edge off."

"Besides, I won't be around much longer. Right?"

Murray didn't answer.

"I think we both know that you'll have no use for an old woman," she said, "once you've made your escape."

Murray got out of the truck and shut the door, then leaned on the sill of the open window.

"When the time comes, Adele, I promise I'll make it painless. I never meant for this to happen. But I don't have another choice. You know about my dad's layoff and our house foreclosure. You know I worked for Aubry and got fired. That I was engaged to Jeanette—and I admitted to you that I'm the Bathtub Killer *and* that I killed Flynn. Your testimony could get me the death penalty."

"The authorities already have enough evidence to put out a warrant for your arrest, hon. I doubt they need me."

"Are you kidding?" Murray reached inside the truck and took the keys out of the ignition. "You know the story of my life. Add that to whatever they already know, and I'm a dead man."

"I would never reveal what you told me in confidence."

"You won't have a choice. They'll subpoena you and put you under oath. There's no way you'd lie after you swore on the Bible to tell the truth. And if you refused to answer, they'd hold you in contempt and throw *you* in jail."

Adele considered what he said and just listened.

"Look, I know you see me as this nice kid trying to get back on his feet. Don't forget I planned to murder four people and succeeded—and killed a fifth because he was a smart mouth. Believe me, the authorities will get you to tell them everything you know."

"It hurts me to think of you running from the law for the rest of your life." Adele sighed. "If you turn yourself in, accept responsibility for what you did, and cooperate with authorities, maybe the jury will have some compassion for what drove you to kill those people who hurt you."

"They won't when I show no remorse. I'll either get the death penalty or life without parole. Either is unacceptable. But I couldn't stand to be in prison."

"My young friend, you're already in prison, regardless of whether you end up in jail or manage to elude authorities."

"What are you talking about?"

Adele turned to him and met his gaze. "You already know the answer."

Murray backed away from the window. "As long as I'm not stuck behind bars, I'm free."

"You shall know the truth, and the *truth* shall set you free," she said. "Nothing else will."

"Don't quote the Bible to me! I don't believe any of it has anything to do with me."

"You knew it was from the Bible," Adele said. "I'm impressed."

"Nice try. But you're not going to rope me into talking about it."

"But we're already talking about it."

"No, *you're* talking about it. Knock yourself out. I'm going where I can find some peace and quiet." Murray turned and started walking into the shadows.

"You say you have no remorse," Adele said. "But I see a soul wrestling with guilt."

Murray threw his hands in the air and shouted, "Don't presume to know what I'm thinking—because you *don't*."

⚜

Jude sat in a vinyl lounge chair on his back patio, his hands clasped behind his head. The sleeping pill he took two hours ago seemed to have had the opposite effect. All he needed was to face the day exhausted.

The back door opened, and Colette stepped outside, carrying something in her right hand.

"I brought you some herb tea," she said. "It's supposed to help you sleep."

He smiled. "So then I'll be up using the bathroom."

"The only solution I see for your insomnia is getting out of law enforcement, which isn't going to happen."

Colette set his tea on the patio table, kissed his stubbly cheek, then sat in the chair next to him.

He reached over and laced his fingers in hers. "You don't have to sit up with me. No point in both of us being miserable in the morning."

"At least I can take a nap," she said. "I thought maybe you could use a listening ear about now. You have a lot weighing on you."

"I know in my head that it's counterproductive to dwell on what could be happening to Adele."

"But …?"

"But she means the world to Zoe. It's my job to get her back alive. I'm just not so sure it's going to go down like that."

"You think Hamelin's already killed her?"

"I can't rule it out, although Kyle doesn't think so. She thinks he's keeping Adele as a bargaining chip, in case we corner him."

"In other words, he would threaten to kill her unless you let him go?"

Jude nodded. "Exactly. And Kyle believes that he *will* kill her if he's trapped and we make any attempt to close in on him."

"The poor woman must be so scared," Colette said.

"As well she should be. Zoe said she took a liking to Hamelin and wanted to help him get back on his feet. She has to feel betrayed.

And probably a little foolish. According to Zoe, she has strong faith. That's good. Because she's going to need it."

Colette seemed lost in thought. "Jude, if they manage to get past you and actually get away, what would Hamelin do with Adele then—put her on a bus?"

Jude sighed. "Sweetheart, we have to assume that when he's through with Adele, he'll make sure she can't tell us anything."

CHAPTER 39

As the long, dark night turned gray, Adele lay wide awake on the seat of Murray's truck. It had been thirty minutes since she took the last two Extra Strength Tylenol. Why wasn't it working?

"I'm going to go find us a different vehicle," Murray said. "Do us both a favor and don't be stupid and try to leave. There are alligator dens all over the place."

Adele shuddered. She sat up in the seat, her hands over her ears. "I don't need to hear about the alligators. I'm well aware it's too far for me to walk to the highway."

"It's nine miles, Adele. You wouldn't get a hundred yards before you were ready to drop from exhaustion—and then what? You wouldn't have the strength to go on or to walk back."

"Are you walking the nine miles back to the highway?"

Murray shook his head. "I'm walking to the ranger's house. I'm going to get his van. Just stay put. I'll be back in thirty minutes."

"Please tell me you're not going to kill him." Adele suddenly felt as if she were falling. She grabbed the seat. "Oh, dear ..."

"What's wrong?"

"I'm dizzy," Adele said. "I wasn't going to say anything, but I feel quite odd."

"You just need to eat something." He walked to the bed of the truck and came back with a package and handed it to her. "All I've got is cheese crackers. That'll tide you over until I can get us out of here."

"Thank you. I'll see if that helps."

"Adele, listen to me." He paused until she met his gaze. "You can't escape. The farther off road you go, the soggier the ground is. Get lost out there, and you'll be alligator bait. It would be a horrible way to die."

"Please don't hurt the caretaker," she said. "Find another way to keep him from telling the authorities you stole his van."

"For once, can't you just worry about yourself?" Murray gripped her arm. "I'm serious. Stay put. I told you—when the time comes, I'll make it painless. Trust me, there's nothing painless about being eaten by a gator."

Zoe followed Vanessa downstairs, through the alcove, into the dining room at Zoe B's. The hum of morning customers had nearly drowned out the bluesy background music. The air was rich with the aromas of bread baking, freshly brewed coffee, and spicy breakfast meats.

They crossed the room to the table by the window, where Father Sam, Hebert, and Tex were already seated.

"Good morning, ladies." Father Sam stood and held a chair for Vanessa and then for Zoe. He pulled a chair from another table and sat on the end.

Hebert leaned forward on his elbows, his mop of mousy gray curls more tame than usual. "Is dere any news?"

Zoe shook her head. "I called Jude just a few minutes ago. They're still looking for Adele and assume she's with Murray and that he wants to lay low. Jude doesn't think they've left the area."

"Must've been a miserable night for you," Tex said.

"That about covers it." Zoe spotted Savannah coming to the table with the coffeepot, and she turned her cup over.

"Where's our little Grace?" Savannah said.

"Upstairs. Maddie offered to stay overnight and watch her for us. Which turned out to be a huge blessing. I'm really not feeling like being a mommy at the moment."

Savannah turned Vanessa's cup over and filled it with coffee, then filled Zoe's. "Any news?"

"I was just telling the guys there's nothing yet. Jude thinks they're still in the area. But the FBI agent he's working with thinks it's possible they slipped out of town, in spite of the checkpoints they set up on the main arteries in and out of Les Barbes."

"How could Hamelin get out of town if they're checking cars on the main drags?" Savannah asked.

"There are so many back roads out of here," Zoe said. "He might even know a route through the cane fields. The guy planned four murders and executed them perfectly. Surely he's got an escape route planned out."

⚜

Adele lay on her side on the floor in the back of the ranger's van, her hands tied behind her and her mouth gagged with duct tape.

Murray had thrown a tarp over her and held it down with some bags of animal feed, but at least he had rolled up a jacket and made her a pillow. The floor was miserably hard and unforgiving, and her back and shoulder ached as if she had never taken the Tylenol. She was almost in tears from the pain.

Murray had come back to the van, dressed in the ranger's khaki uniform shorts and shirt, which were only slightly big on him—and the safari hat, which almost completely hid his red hair. He also popped the lenses out of the ranger's glasses and put them on, after which he looked enough like the ranger's driver's license picture to pass for him. He also had the ranger's state credentials. Murray assured her he didn't kill the man or his wife, but that he tied them up. She prayed he wasn't saying that to appease her.

She felt the van come almost to a stop. Had they arrived at the checkpoint on Grace Creek Boulevard that Murray told her about? If he could fake his way past the authorities there, they would be headed for Lake Charles. Then what? It was unlikely that she had long to live.

Adele felt light-headed and stranger than she'd ever felt in her life. Was fear causing it? Or was something else going on?

Lord, I'm frightened. Please help me.

"We're next," Murray said. "Remember, I have the caretaker's pistol. If you try to alert anyone you're back there, I'll have no choice but to kill everyone at the checkpoint and speed away. I don't think you want that on your conscience. So just be quiet, and let's get through this."

She was aware of her whole left side tingling. Lying this way was causing her limbs to fall asleep. How much longer before he untied her and let her out of here?

The car inched forward and finally came to a stop.

"I'll needa see your driver's license, suh," said a man with a thick Cajun accent. "And proof of insurance."

"No problem," Murray said.

"Where ya headed?"

"Lake Charles. I'm meeting up with the ranger over there."

"You by yourself?"

"Except for Clifton Chenier," Murray said. "I've been listening to his greatest hits. There's just nobody like him."

"Oh, he's da king o' zydeco, hands down."

Adele noticed the tingling stopped and she couldn't feel her shoulder against the floor. Or her face on the pillow. Or her leg. Murray had stopped talking and the only sound was the purring of the car motor. What was taking so long? Had the van been reported stolen? If the officer tried to keep Murray here, would he shoot?

"All right, suh. You're good da go. Enjoy dis fine day."

"Thanks," Murray said. "It's going to be a scorcher."

"*Hot hot.*" The man laughed. "Dat's July in Looziana."

The car moved forward and then gained speed.

"We made it through the checkpoint, Adele. When I can pull off on one of these side roads, I'll untie you."

⚜

Murray pulled the van onto an unpaved road and drove a quarter mile or so until he saw a pull-off. The road was covered by a canopy of green leafy branches, and the woods on either side were dense and dark.

He had been dreading this moment for hours. He had to get rid of Adele and then switch vehicles before the authorities were on to him. If he shot her in the back of the head, wouldn't she die instantly and without pain? He would just leave her here in the woods and be done with it. He quickly dismissed the thought of predators turning her body into a banquet. This was the humane way to take her life. So why was it so hard? He'd had no reluctance or remorse when killing his other five victims.

I've grown fond of you, Murray, Adele had said to him. *You're like the grandson I never had.*

A pang of affection tore at his heart. She was the only person he had let himself care about since his parents died. Could he really point a gun at her and pull the trigger? But if he spared her life, wouldn't she be forced to tell the authorities everything she knew?

Murray sighed. He couldn't take that chance. He opened the glove box and took out the ranger's Smith and Wesson and held it in his hands. For a split second he was a little boy on Christmas morning, holding the toy gun that came with the army fatigues his grandma Sophie had bought him.

Always remember that guns should be used to protect people, Grandma Sophie had said.

Isn't that what he had tried to do—protect people from more layoffs and foreclosures and the kind of heartache that had ruined his life? The others had deserved to die. But Adele was innocent—the kindest, sweetest, most genuine person he knew. What choice did he have? One squeeze of the trigger and she would go to her God and live happily ever after. Maybe she would even see his grandma Sophie there. Heaven was for the innocent. The worthy. Not people like him.

He heard a loud motor and looked up in time to see a red diesel pickup truck pull in behind him. He quickly slid the gun under his seat and watched in the side mirror as a white-haired man wearing a John Deere cap hobbled up to his driver's-side window.

"Hey, young fella. How you doin'?"

"I got a little sleepy on the highway and pulled off to rest my eyes."

"Smart to get off da road 'fore you nod off. You're not from around here."

"Close enough. I'm from Les Barbes. Name's Seth Carrier. I'm the ranger at the state rookery."

"I've been over dere. Real nice." The man smiled and shook his hand. "Lucas Belair. I was just on my way to da south end o' my cane fields when I came up on you sittin' here. Just wanted to make sure you were all right."

"Thank you. I'm fine. Just let me rest my eyes a few minutes, and I'll be on my way to Lake Charles."

"Rest 'em all you like." Belair bent down and leaned on the sill. "Say, when you left Les Barbes, did you pass through a checkpoint? I heard on da radio da cops were stoppin' cars."

"Yes, I did—right where Grace Creek Boulevard turns into the highway. I sure hope the authorities catch the maniac that drowned all those people."

"Dey'll get him," Belair said. "He's one sick puppy, runnin' off wid dat poor old lady."

"All we can do is pray he doesn't hurt her." Murray deliberately made eye contact. "Nice meeting you, sir. Say hello next time you get over to the rookery."

The old man tipped the bill of his hat. "Will do. Have a nice day."

Murray watched in his side mirror as Belair pulled his truck around him and disappeared on the shady road. Was the old guy suspicious? Why would he be? The ranger's van and uniform were authentic enough. He had to kill Adele quickly and drag her body into the woods while he had the chance.

Murray took in a slow, deep breath and exhaled. And then did it again. He got out of the van and tucked the Smith and Wesson in his waistband, wondering if there was a special place in hell for a guy who could shoot an angel.

CHAPTER 40

Murray slid open the door of the van, stacked the bags of wild animal food over to the side, and took off the tarp that covered Adele.

"Let me get you untied so you can stretch out," he said.

He gently removed the duct tape from her mouth and then cut the rope on her wrists and ankles. Her body went limp.

Murray rolled her over on her back. What was wrong with her? Why didn't she move? Why didn't she say something?

He put his hand to her cheek and gently patted it. "Adele, it's me, Murray. Say something."

She blinked, staring at him as if she didn't know him.

"What's wrong? Come on. We need to go." Murray craned and looked down the stretch of road that led back to the highway. How long did he have before another nosy driver stopped to see what he was doing there? Or heard the shots. Maybe it was too risky. There was no silencer on the gun. Suddenly this didn't feel right. He needed a more secluded place.

Murray left Adele lying on the floor of the van and slid the door closed. He went around and climbed in behind the wheel, started the engine, and made a U-turn. He drove about a hundred yards and, in the rearview mirror, spotted what appeared to be Belair's red truck coming at a very fast clip. Could the ranger and his wife have been discovered already—and an APB issued on the van? Had the public been given that information?

Stopping wasn't an option. Belair would see Adele in the back of the van. He reached over on the seat and picked up the gun, his heart racing.

The red truck came right up on his bumper and then swerved around him, Belair waving as he drove toward the highway, leaving a cloud of dust behind him.

Murray's heart nearly beat out of his chest. He slowed the van and wiped the sweat off his upper lip. Wouldn't the smartest move be to pull over, shoot Adele, dump her body in the woods, and get out of the state as fast as he could?

His mind flashed back to their sitting together at Scoops, laughing about their Banana Mountains. She'd been wholly delighted in the moment—and in him. An unexpected wave of tenderness came over him.

How much longer could it take to do this with respect? All he had to do was find a secluded place and make sure the bullet was carefully placed so Adele died painlessly. He would wrap her in the tarp and bury her in a shallow grave—not dump her body in the woods as if she didn't matter.

He glanced in the rearview mirror and couldn't see her. She hadn't even sat up. What was wrong with her? Surely she'd had sufficient oxygen when he covered her up? What difference did it make? The less aware she was of what was coming, the better.

❧

Zoe sat with Vanessa at the table in the kitchen at Zoe B's, one hand wrapped around a cold glass of lemonade, the other tapping the table.

"I wish I could do something to help you relax," Vanessa said. "I'm praying practically nonstop."

"I can feel it. It's just so hard waiting, not knowing what's happening to Adele. I feel like my mother's been kidnapped."

"I know." Vanessa reached over and squeezed her hand. "That's why I'm here."

Zoe glanced over at her best friend. Even under stress, Vanessa was naturally beautiful. Long, shiny dark hair. Clear blue eyes and dark lashes. Classy pink sundress on her shapely size six. Zoe hadn't even put on makeup today. Why bother when she kept crying and it ended up on a tissue? But had she even remembered to brush her hair?

The ringing of Vanessa's phone startled her.

"It's probably Ethan." Vanessa glanced at the screen and nodded, then put the phone to her ear. "Hey there … So-so. We're supporting each other, but neither of us slept, and the waiting is hard. Everything okay there …? When …? That's unbelievable. What did they say …? Were they both unsigned …? Are you at the sheriff's department now …? What do the authorities think …? I can't believe this.… All right, keep me posted. I'll call if we hear anything.… Kiss Carter for me.… I love you, too. Bye."

Zoe leaned forward on her elbows. "What happened?"

"Noah found a padded envelope in his truck with two note cards inside. The one with his name on it had ten one-hundred-dollar bills in it. The note was unsigned and said, 'I'm sorry. I had to let them suspect you.' The other had our name on it, and he brought it to Ethan. It had *fifty* one-hundred-dollar bills. Our note wasn't signed either and said, 'I hope this covers the cancellations. Noah didn't kill Flynn.' Can you believe this? I'm in shock."

"I heard you say Ethan was at the sheriff's department."

"Ethan and Noah turned everything over to the sheriff. Those notes could help clear Noah. And we can't just take that kind of money without knowing where it came from. They met with Deputy Castille. He said the notes are identical to those received by other people who reported being given anonymous money. The authorities believe it came from Murray, that he's giving away the money he stole from his victims."

Zoe stopped to process what it meant. "How can Murray be such a vicious killer and then turn around and want to help people?"

"I don't know," Vanessa said, "but I wouldn't take a dime from him. It's scary, though. How could he know we were getting cancellations?"

"Only if Noah told him." Zoe lifted her gaze. "Think about it. Murray must've killed Flynn Gillis and let Noah take the heat. Then felt bad when Noah left his job and told him Langley Manor was losing business."

"Whoa." Vanessa held up her palm. "This is starting to make sense. If Murray killed Flynn, he deliberately let the suspicion fall on Noah to deflect it from himself."

"Exactly. But as time went on, he felt guilty." Zoe's mind raced with the implications. "Poor Noah. So many people misjudged him."

Vanessa sighed. "Including Ethan."

Jude sat in on the morning briefing and then walked back to his office with Kyle. He flipped the lights on.

"You want coffee?"

"No, thanks," she said. "I'm caffeined out. I think I drank a whole pot last night. But I think I'll help myself to a few of those doughnut holes."

"Those are compliments of Gil Marcel. He's a doughnut addict." Jude poured himself a cup and sat at the conference table, across from her. "We've stopped every vehicle on every thoroughfare out of Les Barbes. They haven't surfaced. I think they're still here, laying low."

"I disagree. If Hamelin intends to use Adele as a shield or a bargaining chip, he has a very short window before she can't keep up. Zoe showed us the medication she takes. Her high blood pressure could be off the charts under this kind of stress. I think Hamelin would've taken the first chance he got to get out of town with her."

"But how?" Jude said. "There's little chance they got through those checkpoints without being ID'd."

Kyle shrugged. "I don't have an answer for you. I just know Murray will be on the move. I think we should take our efforts beyond the parish. He could be in Texas by now. And if he made it that far, he's already killed Adele."

Murray drove several miles toward Lake Charles, then turned onto a gravel road with a sign pointing to Beaudette Family Cemetery. He drove a considerable distance, rocking and rolling over the poorly maintained road, and spotted the aboveground tombs several yards ahead. He pulled up alongside them and rolled down the window.

The place was eerie, almost mystical, with rays of sunlight filtering through the dense, intertwining branches of the huge magnolias that surrounded the cemetery. There were three distinct rows of tombs. Some tombs were tall brick-and-cement structures stained with mildew. Most were horizontal cement structures placed a few feet aboveground. Grass had overtaken one. A newer-looking grave closest to the road was made of polished marble, but the silk flowers in the holder were ragged and faded. It didn't look as though anyone had been here in a while.

Did he really want to do this? Did he really have a choice?

The one thing you always have is a choice, Grandma Sophie had told him.

Not this time. If he wanted to save his life, he had to take Adele's. Now. Before he got caught.

He got out and walked along the path that led to the tombs. How far above sea level was this? Would he be able to dig a shallow grave without it filling up with water? All he needed to do was make sure Adele's body was covered with enough soil that it wouldn't be discovered until he was far away.

He glanced at the thick cement crosses that graced several of the graves. This seemed a more appropriate place to leave Adele.

He trudged back to the van to get a shovel. He slid open the door, startled to see Adele sitting up, her back resting on a bag of feed. Other than her face being soaked with perspiration, she seemed alert.

"There you are, hon." Her voice was weak. "Would you mind getting my water?"

Murray reached the bottle that had rolled under the seat. He unscrewed the cap and handed it to her. "Why didn't you talk to me before?"

"When?"

"When I took the tape off your mouth and untied you. You went limp and stared at me, like you didn't know who I was. I tried to get you to talk. But you didn't say a word."

"I didn't?" Adele winced. "Goodness, I've got a splitting headache. I'm so confused. I heard voices and I tried to get up but I couldn't move. I must've been dreaming."

"Just sit here a moment and drink some water," he said.

"It's terribly hot in here."

"I'm sorry," Murray said. "I never thought to open the doors while I went to check things out."

Adele craned and looked over his shoulder. "Are we at a cemetery?"

"Yes, I pulled off the highway for a minute. There's something I need to do."

Adele paused and seemed to be thinking. "Are you going to kill me here?"

"Do you remember why we're in the van?"

"Of course I remember. You stole it from the ranger. You're running from the law, and I'm your hostage." Adele set the water down, then picked up her right hand with her left and let go. Her right hand fell in her lap.

"What's wrong with your hand?" Murray said.

"It's numb and tingly. It'll go away in a while."

"Why is it numb?"

"I've probably had a TIA. I've had several lately. But never this bad. That's probably why I didn't respond to you before. They make me sleepy."

"I've never heard of a TIA. What is it?"

"It's a mini stroke," Adele said.

"You're having a *stroke?"* Murray's pulse raced.

"Actually, it's a warning sign that I need to see the doctor and find out what's causing it—so I *don't* have a stroke. But it's a moot point if you're going to kill me. Are you? You didn't answer my question."

"We already talked about it. I said I would make it painless."

"You did. I keep hoping you'll change your mind." Adele was quiet for half a minute, then her lip quivered and a tear spilled down her cheek. "Murray, I accept that I'm going to die, though this is not the way I would have chosen to go. I've looked forward to eternity since I made peace with God. What I can't accept is what's happening to you."

"I'll be fine."

"No, you won't."

"I know how to disappear, remember? The authorities won't find me."

"It's not the authorities I'm worried about. You can't disappear from God. And someday you're going to have to face Him and answer for what you've done."

"I don't believe that."

"That's what you said. But it doesn't change the truth."

"I just don't get why you Christians are so willing to serve a God that can't wait to punish you."

"That's another lie the Devil whispered in your ear. Jesus came to earth and died in my place so I *won't* be punished."

"Oh, that's right." Murray rolled his eyes. "It's *me* He wants to punish. I'm the wicked, evil murderer."

"He took your punishment too. But until you get honest about the gravity of your actions and ask His forgiveness, you're going to have to face judgment."

"For what?" Murray pulled his gun from his waistband and held it to her head. "I wasn't wrong! I exacted justice."

"You know better than that. I see it in your eyes. I hear it in your words. God is the judge, Murray. Not you." The intensity of her gaze bore right through his defenses. "You were deeply wounded and wanted to strike back. You've made a mess of things. But you're never beyond His mercy. No one is."

"I don't want His mercy."

"Or can't believe He wants you to have it."

"I'm about to put a bullet in your brain, Adele! Trust me, He doesn't! What is it you see in me worth fussing about?"

"God didn't create a killer, Murray. Under all those bad choices there's a sweet soul that longs to be loved. If I can love and forgive you—and I do—surely the God who created you can—" Adele winced, and all the blood seemed to drain from her face.

"What's wrong?" Murray said. "What's happening?"

"There's a stabbing pain in my head. I feel dizzy. My face tingles."

"Here, take another drink of water." He set the gun down and picked up the bottle and held it to Adele's mouth.

She shook her head and looked up at him with pleading eyes. "Would you … hold … my hand?"

She held out her trembling hand, and he took it. What kind of Judas was he to comfort her just before he took her life?

Her hand was cold, her grip surprisingly strong. Her face and hair were soaked with perspiration.

"There's so much more … I want to say …"

"Don't talk. I'll go turn on the air conditioner."

"Murray, no. I … I must be having a stroke. Just let it be. I'm not afraid. It's better if I die this way.… You won't have to do something you'll regret." She brought his hand to her cheek. "I'm not sorry we became friends … just wish we'd had more time. And a happier ending. I'm never going to stop praying for you.…" Adele's voice sounded weaker. "Make sure Zoe … knows where to find me." She squeezed his hand. "Promise me."

He nodded, his vision clouded with tears. How stupid was this? Five minutes ago, he was ready to dig her grave, and now he didn't want to let her go.

CHAPTER 41

While Vanessa took a shower and Maddie took Grace to the park, Zoe stood out on the gallery above Zoe B's and watched the bustling traffic on *rue Madeline.* A black limousine pulled up in front of the Hotel Peltier. A bellman rolled a luggage cart to the rear of the vehicle and loaded bags into the back. The uniformed driver held the door while a young couple, nicely dressed, climbed in. Newlyweds, no doubt. On their way to the airport and then on to some exotic honeymoon destination.

Zoe's mind flashed back to her own wedding day and the first night she shared with Pierce in the bridal suite of the Hotel Peltier. Loving him and growing old with him was more than she deserved. Had it not been for Adele's willingness to forgive, would their marriage have weathered the lies she had so carefully guarded? So deliberately concealed?

She touched the gold cross around her neck—the cross Adele had given her the day she chose Christ as her Lord and Savior. Adele had brought her to the King—the greatest gift imaginable. And not only her, but Pierce. Was her dear friend's mission in this life over? Was the Lord going to call her home before she'd even had a chance to get to know her godchild?

Zoe closed her eyes and wrapped her fingers around the warm railing. God was in control of Adele's life. Not Murray. No matter what happened, she knew Adele would cling to the Lord with all the faith she had. And wouldn't He lift her above the circumstances, no matter how frightening they were?

Zoe wiped away the tear that trickled down her cheek. Still … if she hadn't insisted that Adele sell Woodmore and move to Les Barbes, she would never have ended up in the hands of this killer.

Lord, hold her close. In perfect peace. If it's time, receive her into Your kingdom.

⁂

Jude sat at the conference table in his office, reviewing the new evidence that Ethan Langley and Noah Washington had brought in.

"And just when I didn't think this case could get any stranger." He looked over at Kyle, whose fresh-as-a-daisy look had wilted. Her deep brown eyes were at half-mast. "You look exhausted."

"So do you. I'll sleep when we get this guy."

"Talk to me more about this Hamelin character," he said. "I'll be honest … I wasn't sure I believed you when you said he wasn't a sociopath—that he actually had a conscience. But this new evidence proves it."

"He set out to do away with those who took away his control. He did that. And now he's trying to fix what didn't go according to plan. And part of that was making sure we know that Noah Washington didn't kill Flynn Gillis."

"So if Hamelin feels guilty about Noah losing his job and the Langleys losing business, wouldn't he feel ten times guiltier for killing an innocent old woman who was nice to him?"

"No doubt. But *after* the fact. Hamelin's the type that acts first and considers the consequences later—when it's too late. In many ways, he still acts out like an angry child. If Adele represents a grandmother figure to him, and he kills her, he's going to have major regrets."

Jude got up and stood at the window. That beautiful, historic courthouse, pure white in the morning sun, represented everything righteous and good about what he did, day to day, to keep this community safe and to bring criminals to justice. How miserably he had failed this time.

"I know what you're thinking, Sheriff," Kyle said. "There's nothing you could've done differently. Hamelin executed the murders flawlessly. He didn't leave us much to go on until he killed Jeanette Stein and she didn't fit his pattern. All things considered, we ID'd him rather quickly."

"Not quickly enough if I have to tell my friend Zoe that we didn't get to Adele in time."

⁂

Murray ditched the ranger's van in the parking lot of Best Buy in Lake Charles, Louisiana. He took the license plate off a Chevy Silverado and swapped it with a white Ford Explorer that had been left unlocked in the back row. His hands were still shaking. He had done what he had to do. He couldn't second-guess his decision. If he let down his defenses now, he was going to get caught.

Murray got in the Explorer. The gas tank was three-quarters full. That should be enough. He hot-wired it, looking around for any sign that someone had seen him do it. No one had.

He drove slowly to the exit and turned onto the busy street and headed for Interstate 10. If he could get to Houston, he could disappear into the homeless culture, and his trail would be cold.

He could still see Adele's tired blue eyes as she pleaded with him, insisting that he get right with God—that he wasn't beyond God's mercy.

Adele had conviction. He respected that about her. But there was no turning back for him. What was done was done. Maybe one day he would face judgment. That was out of his control. But avoiding the death penalty wasn't. He knew how to disappear.

Why didn't he feel better, now that he had eliminated all the people who were responsible for making his life miserable? Instead he was empty—even emptier than before. All that planning. All the emotional work that went into murdering his four bathtub victims—and covering up Flynn's murder—and he still felt as if he had a mountain pressing on his heart. Why wouldn't it go away? It was supposed to go away!

The look in Adele's eyes wouldn't leave him alone. At least he didn't have to kill her. Why couldn't he have met her before he ever started down this path?

Murray heard a siren approaching from behind and began to sweat. He glanced in his rearview mirror and saw a police car speeding toward him. Should he try to outrun it? Should he jump out and try to get away on foot? Fear seized him. He'd come too far to fail now. He heard a loud horn and then spotted a fire truck a half a block behind the police car.

He pulled over, his heart hammering, and let the two vehicles pass, then blended into the traffic and headed for Interstate 10.

⚜

Zoe sat in the dining room at Zoe B's with Pierce, Vanessa, Father Sam, Hebert, and Tex. She glanced at her watch for the umpteenth time without paying attention to the time.

Hebert put his hand on hers. "*Comment ça vas?*"

"Not great," Zoe said. "The waiting is really hard. Why don't you fellas go ahead and play checkers?"

"Just doesn't seem right," Tex said. "What with Adele missin' and all."

"Well, there's no reason for you to just sit here," Pierce said. "It's not going to help the sheriff find her any faster. Actually, it would help to have something normal going on right now."

"Dere's merit to dat," Hebert said.

Zoe nodded. "Pierce is right. Let's try to maintain some semblance of normalcy. This can't go on forever."

Pierce kissed her cheek. "I'll go check on Dempsey."

"He can handle the kitchen," she said.

"I know. But it'll give *me* something to do. The waiting is driving me nuts too." Pierce got up and walked into the kitchen.

Savannah came over to the table and poured coffee refills as the guys set up for a checkers game.

"They're going to catch this monster," Savannah said. "I, for one, won't bat an eye when he gets the death penalty."

Zoe looked up at her. "I know you miss your aunt Nicole terribly."

"I keep expecting her to call. Or show up on my doorstep." Savannah sighed. "I mean, I know she's not coming back. It's just hard to accept. But I don't see why he would hurt Mrs. Woodmore. She didn't do anything to him."

"That's exactly right," Vanessa said, almost sounding protective. "We've got hundreds of people praying that he won't. For now, let's believe that God's answer, whatever it is, will be the right one."

Pierce came out of the kitchen and walked over to Zoe. He bent down next to her chair and took her hand. "Babe, Jude just got a call from the sheriff in Calcasieu Parish." His eyes brimmed with tears. "They found Adele."

CHAPTER 42

Zoe held tightly to Pierce's hand and hurried down the long, shiny corridor to the room at the end of the hall, where sheriff's deputies told them they would find Adele.

Zoe stopped outside the door, her heart racing. She had been told that Adele looked good and she needn't be alarmed about her appearance.

"I never thought her ordeal would end this way," Zoe said.

Pierce put his hands on her shoulders. "You ready?"

Zoe nodded and let him hold the door open so she could go in first.

She slowly entered the room. There was Adele. She looked like a sleeping angel. Her hair was a matted mess and she had a small cut on her face and insect bites on her arms. Zoe felt her throat tighten. What had she been through? What had that monster done to her?

Zoe stood at the side of the bed, her vision clouded by tears. She dabbed her eyes and just watched the rise and fall of Adele's chest, thinking it was the most beautiful sight in the world.

Adele's eyes opened, and she reached for Zoe's hand. "You must've been so worried."

Zoe brushed the tear off her face and brought Adele's hand to her cheek. "I wasn't sure I would ever see you again."

"God had other plans."

"Yes, He did." Pierce came over and stood next to Zoe and joined hands with them. "I'll be honest. I prayed, but I never thought we'd be hearing your voice again."

"The deputies told us what happened," Zoe said. "The doctor said you had another TIA."

"Yes, and it was doozy this time. They want to watch me overnight and make sure I'm all right." Adele opened and closed her right hand. "I can move my hand again. The feeling is back."

"We need to make you an appointment to see *your* doctor," Zoe said. "He'll probably prescribe something to help avoid this."

"Yes, I'm sure." Adele smiled. "But here's one for the record books: A TIA saved my life."

"The ER attendant told deputies that a man fitting Murray's description came in, carrying you in his arms," Zoe said. "He told them you were having a stroke. And that he was going to go park the car and would be right back. He vanished."

Adele's eyes narrowed. "The authorities won't find him unless he wants to be found."

"I wouldn't underestimate law enforcement," Pierce said. "They're determined to catch this creep. The FBI's involved now."

"Murray's just as determined not to get caught." Adele pursed her lips and seemed far away for a moment. "He'll find a big city and blend into the homeless culture."

"The authorities won't give up," Zoe said. "The man murdered *five* people."

"Yes, Murray told me everything."

"Why did he take you hostage?"

"Because I accidentally had the phone on speaker when you called the house. He knew the sheriff wouldn't shoot as long as I was with him. We were out at the rookery all night."

Pierce nodded. "That's what the deputy said."

"Murray was struggling with what to do with me. I could tell. Finally I asked him point-blank if he planned to kill me. He said when the time came, he would make it painless."

"Oh, Adele." Zoe squeezed her hand. "You must've been so scared."

Zoe listened as Adele told her about their night at the rookery and how she had sung to the Lord, both aloud and silently.

"When I praised the Lord," Adele said, "I forgot about myself. It helped me not be afraid."

"Pierce and I had the prayer chain going at Saint Catherine's. And Vanessa and Ethan did the same at their church. We prayed so hard you would have faith."

"Well, of course I *have* faith, hon. I just needed to use it. That became much more difficult when Murray got the van and had to go through the checkpoint."

Adele told them about being bound and gagged and covered on the floor of the van, and how she knew something was physically wrong.

"I remember hearing voices when we got to the checkpoint," Adele said. "The next thing I can remember is waking up in the back of the van, so hot I thought I would suffocate."

Zoe brushed the hair out of Adele's eyes. "Why don't you close your eyes and rest? You don't need to talk about this anymore."

"But I do. I want you to know everything."

Zoe cried as Adele told them about her trying to reason with Murray at the cemetery. How she told him he needed God's mercy.

"It's so like you to be more concerned about him than you were about yourself."

"He's a wounded soul, Zoe, in need of God's love and mercy and forgiveness. You understand what that's like."

Zoe did understand. But she hadn't murdered five people.

"I don't think I reached him," Adele said. "But at least I told him he needed to get right with God. There was so much more I wanted to say, but I started feeling very sick. I thought I was having a stroke and asked Murray to hold my hand."

"You're kidding," Pierce said. "The creep held your hand?"

"Yes. I told him it was better that I die of a stroke. That he wouldn't have to kill me and have that on his conscience too. I really don't know why he didn't just leave me there."

"He took a huge risk by taking you to the ER," Zoe said.

"There's a very sweet side to Murray. It's too bad he let his pain turn him into something else."

"Adele, please," Zoe said. "I don't want to hear about his good side. He murdered five people in cold blood, and the authorities will find him and bring him to justice." Zoe held her gaze. "There's something we need to talk about. Isabel told me she quit and why. She'd really like to come back. You can't live by yourself. You need someone to help you."

"I suppose I do." Adele sighed. "And Isabel's fears were certainly not unfounded."

"I hope you learned a lesson," Pierce said. "Getting close to the men from Haven House was dangerous."

"Except for Noah." Zoe poked Pierce in the ribs with her elbow. "We know he's a good guy."

"From now on," Pierce said, "let me find you a reputable handyman to do your odd jobs."

Adele looked from Pierce to Zoe and back to Pierce. "Perhaps I *was* too trusting. But don't either of you discount, for a moment, God's plan in all this. I don't pretend to know what it was. But I do believe Romans 8:28—that in all things God works for the good of those who love him, who have been called according to his purpose. Even if I overstepped, God was faithful."

"You could have died," Zoe said.

"Not unless He ordained it. I'm not saying every choice I made was the best one. But I felt from the beginning that God brought Noah and Murray into my life for a reason. And just so you know, I did order a background check on them at Isabel's insistence. There was nothing in the reports that gave me pause. So how much caution should I exercise when the God of the universe has ordered all the steps I'll ever take?"

"That's a subject for another day," Pierce said. "We need to get out of here and let you rest. We'll get a place to stay tonight. Maddie's with Grace until we can get you home."

"I love you both so much." Adele's eyes welled with tears. "Thank you for being here."

Vanessa and Ethan sat on the couch in their living quarters at Langley Manor, Carter nestled between them, Angel lying on the floor.

Noah sat in an overstuffed chair facing them, his hands folded in his lap as he seemed to stare at nothing.

The sound of the pendulum swinging on the grandfather clock was exaggerated in the silence.

"Noah," Ethan said, "we asked you here for two reasons—to ask your forgiveness and to ask you to come back to work. I'm sorry I didn't take you at your word the way Vanessa did. In hindsight, I should have. I didn't know what to think when Flynn Gillis's body was found on our property. There was so much to consider—"

"No forgiveness is necessary." Noah held up his palm. "Murray set me up—plain and simple."

"But we didn't try to talk you out of leaving," Vanessa said. "That had to hurt."

Noah's eyes glistened. "Sure it did. I love this place. I love bein' part of its history. I love keepin' the grounds beautiful. And helpin' you tell the guests the story of what great things happened here. I'm not a violent man. You can trust me with your lives. I thought I proved that."

Vanessa looked at Ethan and then at Noah. "You did."

"I trust you," Carter said. "I don't like it when you're gone."

"None of us do." Ethan got up and held out his hand. "Can we start fresh? Vanessa, Carter, and I love you. You're like family. You're as much a part of Langley Manor as we are."

Noah smiled with his eyes and gripped Ethan's hand with his own. "It's good to be home."

Vanessa got up and hugged Noah, then put his key ring in his hand. "There's an extra key on there. The caretaker house is ready.

The graffiti has been painted over. The furniture's been delivered. It's all yours."

"Well, isn't that somethin'?"

"Yaaaaaaaaaay! Noah's moving here!" Carter jumped up and down, and Angel barked and ran in circles, her tail wagging.

"What do you say we all go down and take a look?" Ethan patted Noah's back. "It really looks great. We added a little something."

"It's a cool sign in the front yard," Carter blurted out. "It says 'Noah's Place.'"

Noah threw his head back and laughed. "Well, if it's got my name on it, I guess I'd better get moved in."

CHAPTER 43

Five months later ...

On the first Monday in December, Zoe stood on a stepladder, framing the window in Zoe B's with a long garland of cypress greens she had strung with red ribbon and white lights.

"How does it look, fellas?"

"Perfect," Father Sam said. "And, I must say, this year's tree is the grandest you've ever put up."

Zoe laughed. "Wait until I tell you how we ended up with that beauty."

She climbed down from the ladder and brushed her hands together. "Pierce and I thought it would be neat to start a family tradition, so we drove over to the Christmas tree farm to cut our own. We told Grace she could choose a tree for Zoe B's and one for our apartment. We tried to steer her toward the seven footers, but she kept racing over to the taller ones. She was so excited that we didn't have the heart to say no. Pierce didn't even measure the two trees. He cut them down, confident he could make them fit. I don't know how much cutting and trimming he had to do to get this one in the stand, but he finally did. The angel on top misses the ceiling by about an inch."

"I remember when you got dat angel," Hebert said. "It was at da holiday bazaar da year you opened Zoe B's."

"There are prettier angels, and she's a little worn. But I just can't part with her."

Zoe looked up and down the almost perfect Leyland cypress that graced the center of the dining area, broad at the base and gradually tapered all the way to the ceiling.

"Lots of the decorations were handmade locally and are for sale." Zoe went over to the tree and pointed out the Langley Manor ornament Vanessa and Ethan had custom made. "I've got one of these for our tree too. Doesn't it look just like the manor house? You should see how they've decorated out there. It's magnificent."

"Maybe so," Tex said. "But you've got the prettiest tree on *rue Madeline*. Zoe B's looks mighty festive."

Hebert nodded. "Dat it does."

"Have you got the tree up in your apartment yet?" Father Sam asked.

"Are you kidding?" Zoe said. "The minute we got home, Grace pulled out all the ornaments. I let her help me put colored lights and poinsettias on the gallery railing while we waited for Pierce to trim the tree and bring it up. We had so much fun. There's just nothing like a child at Christmas."

Hebert put his hand on her shoulder. "I love dat *petite fille,* same as if I was her *papère*. I gonna have fun wid her dis Christmas. She's fuh shore old enough to enjoy da presents and not just da paper and ribbons."

"Definitely," Zoe said. "Tonight, Pierce and I are going to put up Adele's artificial silver spruce and let Grace help decorate it. We were all there when she bought it, and it looked so real I had to feel it to believe it wasn't."

"How she doin'?" Hebert said. "Isn't dis her first Christmas away from Woodmore?"

Zoe smiled. "Yes, but she's doing just great. She and Isabel get along famously. Their latest aspiration is to help Grace make a gingerbread house. They also want to take her to Lafayette to ride the Toyland Train. And out to that new Cajun Christmas Wonderland that boasts over a million lights. I did put my foot down on two things: Pierce and I want to be the first to take her to see baby Jesus in the manger on the courthouse lawn. And we want to take her to see Santa. I'm sure I'll have to have a talk with Adele about not going overboard on the gifts."

"Aw, it's Christmas," Tex said. "Doesn't hurt to spoil the little scamp."

"That's what Adele thinks too. Maybe she's right. The only thing I really want is for us all to spend time together and make some memories. We came so close to losing her."

Hebert wore a mischievous grin. "So … did she ever decide to start courtin' da fella dat keeps asking her out?"

Zoe shook her head. "Adele insists that Alfred is the only man she'll ever love. She seems content with her life. Heaven knows, she's busy enough."

"Dat's real good. But I promise you, if I could shave off ten years, I'd find a way to turn her head. She's a fine woman."

The bell on the front door tinkled, and Zoe turned just as Vanessa came into the eatery.

"What a surprise!" Zoe hurried over to Vanessa and gave her a hug.

"I am *so* enjoying having a day manager at Langley Manor," Vanessa said. "I snuck away for a couple hours to do some Christmas shopping. I thought I'd have lunch before I head back. I know I'm early, but I was hoping I could have a bowl of Pierce's seafood gumbo. No matter how hard I try, I can't make it like his."

"I'm sure there's warm corn bread, too."

"It's so cozy in here." Vanessa's gaze danced around the room. "The tree is awesome! I think it's even bigger than ours."

"Your Christmas decorations at the manor house are amazing," Zoe said. "Do you think your business will increase at Christmas too?"

"So far, it has. We have a long waiting list. But it's been that way since the fall."

"What a great problem to have," Tex said. "Sounds like y'all are better than just 'over the hump.'"

Zoe made a sweeping motion with her hand. "Sit wherever you like. I'll ask Savannah to bring us lunch, and I'll eat with you. I'm so glad you came in."

Zoe went through the swinging doors into the kitchen and told Savannah what she needed. She spotted Pierce at the long table, dressed in his chef hat and apron, laying out the ingredients he would need to fill lunch orders.

She walked over and kissed his cheek, taking a few seconds to savor the woody scent of his aftershave. "Guess what? Vanessa's here. She was Christmas shopping and decided to stop in for seafood gumbo. I'm going to eat with her, but I'm having a spinach salad. Aren't you proud of me?"

"You didn't tell her, did you?"

Zoe rolled her eyes. "Of course not. We agreed not to say anything until after the holidays. I want to be past the third month."

He patted her tummy. "Good. So what do the guys think of our humongous Christmas tree?"

"Everyone loves it. I know it takes up a lot more room than we planned, but it really does look great. And wait until you see the window. The garland I made with the greens ties everything together."

"*You* tie everything together." Pierce pulled her into his arms. "Have I told you today that I love you, Mrs. Broussard?"

"Only two or three times so far. I think you're slipping." She looked into his intense brown eyes that seemed to touch his soul. "You're a better man than I deserve, you know."

"Hardly."

"What would I be without you?"

"Or I without you?" Pierce put her hand to his lips. "But we're right here together, living our dream, soon to be a family of four—going on five."

"Five? Oh no you don't. If you want a third baby, *you* have it. I'm good for two. That was the deal."

Pierce held his arms defensively in front of him and laughed and then laughed harder. "Deal! I'm just playing with you, babe. I love the expression you get when you're adamant. You're a kick in the pants."

"I'm glad you find me amusing," she said, smiling without meaning to. "While you're wholly entertained, I'm going to go have lunch with my friend."

"Tell Vanessa I said hello." He cupped her face in his hands and tenderly pressed his lips to hers. "See you at five. I'm looking forward to getting Adele's Christmas tree up. I never thought we'd get this chance."

CHAPTER 44

Adele sat in her living room, still dressed in the red velour warm-up suit she wore when she took her morning stroll around the block.

Isabel set a cup of coffee on the side table and then sat next to Adele. "So what's the verdict? Where do you want the Christmas tree?"

"I think we have to put it in front of the window. It's going to be exquisite, and it would be a shame not to share it with passersby. But I've decided I would like some lights outside too. I wonder if it's too late to get a professional to outline the house. And maybe even my crape myrtles."

"I'm sure it isn't," Isabel said. "There are several companies that put up Christmas lights. But a lot of landscapers are getting into it now. Maybe you should ask Noah if he does it. You know the quality of his work."

Adele brought her hands together. "What a wonderful idea."

"You want all white lights?"

"I think I'd prefer to mix them. Maybe colored lights on the house and white lights on the trees. I'm open to suggestions."

Isabel smiled. "When I get back from the grocery store, we can talk about it some more. Do you want me to add anything else to dinner tonight?"

"Zoe and Pierce love your pot roast, carrots, and potatoes. Why don't you add fresh green beans and Parker House rolls? Those are Grace's favorites."

"What about dessert?"

"Pierce is bringing lemonade bread pudding."

"Wonderful. That's *my* favorite." Isabel perused her list. "I might be a while. We're out of almost everything."

"I'm going to relax with the new issue of *Better Homes and Gardens,"* Adele said. "Maybe I'll get some Christmas ideas. And I'm going to stay dressed in my warm-up suit. I'm beginning to get quite comfortable with my casual attire. Why are you smiling?"

"It's just neat to see you adjusting to a different lifestyle."

"You mean more relaxed."

Isabel nodded. "I'm really glad you let me come back here and work for you. It's so much better this time."

"It is indeed." Adele pretended not to notice the flushing of Isabel's cheeks. "Go. I'll be waiting to help put everything away when you come back."

Isabel rose to her feet. "All right then. See you in a bit."

Adele picked up the magazine and began perusing it the way she always did. She loved getting the big picture of what was in it and then going back and reading the articles that appealed to her.

She heard Isabel's car drive away.

A few moments later, there was a knock—but not at the front door. She sensed someone behind her.

"Adele, don't be scared. It's me."

She turned just as Murray walked around the couch and sat in a chair facing her. He had grown a beard. His bright red hair was neatly combed. He looked rather handsome dressed in khakis and a navy blue golf shirt.

She put her hand on her heart. "To say this is a shock would be putting it lightly."

"I know," Murray said. "I didn't know how else to do it with Isabel living here. I wanted to talk to you before I turn myself in."

"You're turning yourself in?"

Murray nodded. "I want you to know why, since you were instrumental in my decision. But first, let me say how sorry I am for the way I treated you. It was inexcusable. You'd been nothing but kind to me. I never meant for you to get pulled into my mess."

"I realize that. Have you come to terms with the wrong of what you did?"

Murray linked his fingers. "Yes. Something you said wouldn't leave me alone. You said that by killing the four people who'd hurt me, I'd left a whole string of *living* victims—just like me."

Adele nodded. "I remember."

"I realize now how right you were. All I could think about was getting even. I wanted my victims to beg for mercy, but I had no intention of giving it, just like they didn't give it to my dad or to me when we were desperate. But by doing the same thing to them, I became just like them—cold, indifferent, and heartless." Murray cracked his knuckles. "But the real victims are their loved ones. I sentenced them to a life of anger and bitterness and unanswered questions. I know what that feels like. That's the last thing in the world I wanted to do—especially to Jeanette's two little boys." Murray put his head in hands. "What have I done, Adele? I murdered five people. I've ruined so many lives. I'm sorry. I really am."

Adele's heart was moved by the genuine remorse she sensed in Murray. "You may not believe this, but I have firsthand experience with what you're saying."

"You? How? You've never killed anyone."

"I have—but with words. I told you before I haven't always been the person you see today. After I lost my baby, I lashed out at everyone. I behaved despicably. I cut people down. I stomped on self-esteem. I inflicted wounds that only God will be able to heal."

"I have trouble believing you were ever that bad."

"I was. It wasn't until I finally came to the end of myself and realized what I'd become that I turned to God and let Him fix me."

"Not even God can fix me. Not now. Not after what I've done."

"Nonsense. He did a pretty good job on Moses after he murdered the Egyptian in anger. And King David, who had an affair and then had the woman's husband killed. And Peter, who sat outside the place where Jesus was being tortured and denied he ever knew Him. And scores of others, just like us."

"Us?" Murray's eyebrows came together. "Don't put yourself in the same category as me."

"I'm a sinner, hon. We all are. The Lord's system of justice is different from ours. He's holy, and we're not. He—and only He—can fix each one of us, no matter what we've done. If we let Him."

Adele reached over and picked up the Bible on her end table. "It's all in here. God can do wonders in people who realize they need Him. Tell Him what you just told me. You have a repentant heart. What you don't have is hope and a future. That's in here too."

"You sound so much like Grandma Sophie."

"Probably because we know the same God. Here, it's yours." She held out the Bible. Her heart leapt when he took it.

"I wouldn't know where to begin," Murray said.

"My favorite is Psalm 139. If you read it as if you're the one talking, I think it might give you a whole new perspective."

"Okay. What else?"

"The gospel of John. After that you'll be so hungry for more that you won't need to ask."

"You know they'll take this away from me when I turn myself in."

"Then I'll go through proper channels and make sure you get another. Take it. Go someplace quiet and read with an open heart before you turn yourself in."

Murray thumbed through the Bible. "What if I don't get anything out of it?"

"God's Word never returns void. It's an adventure like nothing you've ever experienced. You're on the right track. Stay on it. I promise you'll find real joy. I know I did."

Murray's eyes were suddenly blue pools. "They're not going to let me post bail. Once I'm behind bars, I'll either get the death penalty or life in prison without parole. So I guess this is good-bye."

"For now. But whether I'm here or in heaven, I'll be doing what I'm sure Sophie's been doing—praying that you'll come to know the God we know."

Murray stood, the Bible tucked under his arm, and was quiet for a moment. "You haven't asked why I didn't leave you at the cemetery."

"I don't need to know. But you risked getting caught when you took me to the emergency room. You must've had a good reason. If you want to tell me, I'd like to hear it."

Murray opened his mouth to say something, then couldn't seem to find his voice. He pushed his hands deep into his pockets, a tear trickling down his cheek.

Adele pushed herself to her feet. She stood next to him, her arm around his waist, and pulled him close. "I love you, too."

"I … I don't know if I can do this by myself.…"

"You're not by yourself, Murray. Not now. Not ever."

... a little more ...

When a delightful concert comes to an end,

the orchestra might offer an encore.

When a fine meal comes to an end,

it's always nice to savor a bit of dessert.

When a great story comes to an end,

we think you may want to linger.

And so, we offer ...

AfterWords—just a little something more after you

have finished a David C Cook novel.

We invite you to stay awhile in the story.

Thanks for reading!

Turn the page for ...

- **A Note from the Author**
- **Discussion Guide**

A NOTE FROM THE AUTHOR

My sacrifice, O God, is a broken spirit; a broken and contrite heart you, God, will not despise. (Ps. 51:17 TNIV)

Dear Reader,

I loved Adele in this story! She was the kind of fearless, trusting, merciful Christian I wish I could be—that I hope to be.

When she reached out to Noah and Murray, even the raised eyebrows of her closest friends did not deter her obedience. She had never forgotten God's mercy to her, and she didn't hesitate to extend it to those who needed it most.

I loved that she didn't see herself as superior to Murray, not even when she knew his crimes, but rather came alongside him as a fellow sinner who empathized with his broken and contrite heart. Don't you know he must have been amazed and touched by that?

Few of us will ever engage in such dangerous mercy. But how often do we miss chances to minister for God because we live in fear, not of being physically harmed or financially exploited, but merely of being ridiculed or looking foolish?

If Adele had not trusted her discernment and the God who gave it to her, if she had not reached out to Murray without regard to social class or peer pressure, he might never have come to a place of repentance. Or have been open to the hope that God could free

him from the prison he had created with his obsessive desire for revenge. In the end, the spiritual good far outweighed the risks.

As Adele pointed out, mercy is always a little dangerous. It can be rejected or exploited. But mercy is for the needy—not the worthy. Our job as forgiven sinners is to receive it abundantly and extend it to others. Easier said than done, especially if our spirits are fearful or judgmental.

Adele faced the extreme. Most of us never will, and certainly we should exercise good sense in reaching out to others. But God puts opportunities in front of us where we can show mercy to those who are hurting, who've made mistakes and bad choices. Are we open to it? Adele challenged me to be a better reflection of Him. I never ever want to forget the mercy God has shown to me—or fail to offer it to others.

Whew! This was quite a ride. But we haven't heard the last of Adele Woodmore, the Broussards, the Langleys, or the characters at Zoe B's. Join me in the series finale, *Relentless Pursuit,* where we will discover more secrets of Roux River Bayou. I promise it will be an exciting and satisfying ending to this trilogy.

I would love to hear from you. Join me on Facebook at www.facebook.com/kathyherman, or drop by my website at www.kathyherman.com and leave your comments on my guest book. I read and respond to every email and greatly value your input.

In Him,

Kathy Herman

DISCUSSION GUIDE

1. What do you think Matthew 5:7—"Blessed are the merciful, for they will be shown mercy"—means? Does mercy have more than one meaning? Can you think of two different ways that Adele showed mercy in this story?

2. Do you agree with Adele that, by its very nature, mercy is risky and can be abused? Can you think of ways a believer could abuse the mercy God has extended to him or her? Why do you think Jesus told the parable of the unmerciful servant (Matt. 18:23–35)? Does that story make you uncomfortable?

3. Do you think Adele was foolish not to heed Isabel's warning about befriending Noah and Murray? Have you ever been faced with a situation where you chose to obey God and show love to someone in spite of the cautions of friends or family? Did you see positive results? Do you think it's possible to obey God and not see favorable results? Do you think God "has your back" when you step out in faith with the intention of obeying Him?

4. Do you think the Good Samaritan (Luke 10:25–37) practiced dangerous mercy? Could he have been robbed or killed in his attempt to take the wounded man to shelter? Could the innkeeper have exploited his generosity and charged him more than was actually spent? Why do you think Jesus told His disciples to go and do likewise? What do you think the lesson is here?

5. Have you, like the priest and the Levite in the story of the Good Samaritan, ever passed by someone who needed help because you were afraid to stop, or were too busy, or just didn't want to get involved? Are we always called to stop when we see someone in need? Does the need always have to be material? Are there incidences when the need is for emotional support? Or spiritual guidance? Or a listening ear? What needs did Murray have? Did it go beyond the material? Who might we come across day-to-day that needs a touch of mercy?

6. Did you understand why Adele didn't see herself as superior to Murray, not even when she knew his crimes? Have you ever been able to show mercy to someone whose sin, by man's standards, was much worse than yours? Do you think God rates sin by bad, worse, worst? Is mercy something that is deserved? Or is receiving what we don't deserve the very nature of mercy?

7. Had Adele been murdered, would that have been proof that she was wrong to reach out to Murray? Did you understand why Isabel chose to quit? Why Pierce didn't want Grace around the men from Haven House? How might you have reacted, if you were Isabel? If you were Pierce? How might Murray's life have been different if Adele had chosen to play it safe?

8. There was no excuse for Murray's violent response to the people who hurt him, but if they had treated him with kindness and mercy, do you think he would have been a different person? Do you think we should be careful how we treat others and teach